About the Authors

Born and raised just outside of Toronto, Ontario, **Amy Ruttan** fled the big city to settle down with the country boy of her dreams. After the birth of her second child, Amy was lucky enough to realise her life-long dream of becoming a romance author. When she's not furiously typing away at her computer, she's a mum to three wonderful children who use her as a personal taxi and chef.

Married to the man she met at eighteen, **Susanne Hampton** is the mother of two adult daughters, Orianthi and Tina. Her varied career titles have included dental nurse, personal assistant, contract manager and now Medical Romance author. The family also extends to a Maltese Shih-Tzu, a poodle, three ducks and four hens. Susanne has always read romance novels and says, 'I love a happy-ever-after so writing for Mills & Boon is a dream come true.'

USA Today and *Wall Street Journal* bestselling author **Janice Lynn** has a Master's in Nursing from Vanderbilt University and works as a nurse practitioner in a family practice. She lives in the southern United States with her Prince Charming, their children, their Maltese named Halo; and a lot of unnamed dust bunnies that have moved in after she started her writing career. Readers can visit Janice via her website at: janicelynn.net

The Surgeon Collection

The Surgeon's Touch

AMY RUTTAN

SUSANNE HAMPTON

JANICE LYNN

MILLS & BOON

First Published in Great Britain 2023
by Mills & Boon, an imprint of HarperCollins*Publishers* Ltd,
1 London Bridge Street, London, SE1 9GF

www.harpercollins.co.uk

HarperCollins*Publishers*
Macken House, 39/40 Mayor Street Upper,
Dublin 1, D01 C9W8, Ireland

ISBN: 978-0-263-31968-2

MIX
Paper | Supporting
responsible forestry
FSC
www.fsc.org FSC™ C007454

SAFE IN HIS HANDS

AMY RUTTAN

This book is dedicated firstly to my husband, Chris. I couldn't do this without you.

A big thanks to my critique partner, Ann R, who read this book in its many incarnations and never once complained about reading it yet again, and my editor Suzanne Clarke who whipped my hero into shape!

Also a big thanks to a certain group of ladies, in particular Kimber, for cheering me up every day!

And lastly a big thanks to all the physicians and healthcare professionals who do work in remote places because of their passion to provide healthcare to everyone.

CHAPTER ONE

DAMN. WHAT'VE I done?

Dr. Charlotte James had been watching the arrivals board in the Iqaluit airport for some time. She was so focused on arrivals she didn't even notice the people coming and going around her. A watched pot never boiled, or so the old saying went, but she couldn't help it. This was probably the longest she'd ever stood still. In her job there was no time to stand still. In fact, she hated it. She could be doing so many other things. Filing, for instance.

Not that she particularly *liked* filing. She preferred her organized chaos. However, there were a ton of files on her desk, and Rosie had been pestering her for a week to put them away. Instead, she was waiting here for *his* flight to arrive.

"Flight 207 from Ottawa now arriving at gate three."

The past, when it came to Dr. Quinn Devlyn, was where it needed to be: firmly locked away. She'd moved on and she had no doubt his life had, too. He was, after all, at the top in his chosen specialty, and she was right where she'd always wanted to be.

This time Quinn Devlyn wouldn't blindside her or suck her into some crazy off-kilter distracting, albeit passionate, love affair.

No, siree.

Her life was good. Not perfect but, then, whose was? Charlotte was happy.

Courage.

She spun around and saw the plane taxi in on the small airstrip, blending in with the stark, white landscape of Canada's High Arctic. The only color out there was the brightly painted houses that dotted the landscape. Her pulse thundered between her ears.

He's here.

The pit of Charlotte's stomach dropped to her knees. No. Scratch that. Make it the soles of her feet. Not since her MCATs had she felt this way, as though she was perpetually on the verge of hurling.

She was seriously beginning to doubt her sanity in bringing her ex-fiancé up to Cape Recluse. It wasn't a place where she could avoid him easily. He'd be constantly underfoot and she was dreading every moment of it. Would she be able to resist him? The only time she had resisted him had been when he'd left. When their relationship had ended, she'd never wanted to see him again, but his presence here now was a price she was willing to pay to help out her friend.

Get a grip on yourself.

A blast of cold air shook her from her reverie. Her gaze focused on the tinted windows, watching the passengers head across the tarmac to the warmth of the bright yellow airport building. Immediately she picked Quinn's form out of the group of passengers.

Tall and broad, even though he was huddled down under his collar against the cold. Just the sight of him made her heart beat a little bit faster, her cheeks heat and the butterflies in her stomach go crazy. Her pulse thundered between her ears like a marching band. She hadn't seen him in five years—not since he'd walked out on her—but he was making her feel like a giddy teenager again.

Don't let him affect you like this, Charlotte chastised herself. She'd moved on with her life. The wound he'd left in her heart had finally healed.

The double doors opened and he stepped into the airport, moving to the side to let more people in from the frigid cold. He set down his luggage and unwound his scarf.

Damn, he still looks as good as ever. Charlotte had been kind of hoping Quinn's fast, career-driven lifestyle would've caught up with and aged him, but he looked as sexy and charming as ever.

Even from a few feet away she could see there was a bit of gray around his sandy-brown temples, but it suited him. Made him look more dashing and debonair. Some stubble shadowed his chin, but it didn't hide the faint line of the scar that crossed his lips. A tingle of heat shot through her body as she suddenly recalled the way his lips had brushed across hers. A flush of goose bumps spread across her skin just at the thought of the way he would kiss a path down her body, his strong hands caressing her, holding her.

What're you doing? She was not some lovestruck goofy med student anymore. She was a physician with a thriving practice. There was no way she was going to let him in again.

Hell would have to freeze over, not that it would take much, given the current temperature outside was minus thirty.

Charlotte shut those memories away firmly, refusing to think about them any further.

Instead, she remembered how he'd brushed off the miscarriage of their child as being for the best.

As a chance to move to New York and pursue their careers.

Only New York had not been what she'd wanted. She was where she wanted to be. Not to follow him had been her decision, her right to go after her dreams.

I can do this for Mentlana.

This was all for her best friend. The only thing close to a family she'd had since her father had died when she was ten. Charlotte never knew her mother, who'd died when she was two. Mentlana and her family had been there with open arms when Charlotte had returned to Cape Recluse after Quinn had left and she'd lost her baby.

Correction: *their* baby.

Now Mentlana needed help and Quinn was the best when it came to neonatal medicine. For her best friend, Charlotte would face death itself. Even though, as far as she was concerned, Dr. Quinn Devlyn was far more dangerous than the Grim Reaper. She'd take him on, anyway.

Quinn would save Mentlana's baby.

Mustering her courage and holding her head high, Charlotte strode over to him. All the while her heart was racing and her knees shook like they were about to give out on her. He looked up, his chocolate gaze reeling her in as she moved toward him. His eyes were twinkling and she suddenly remembered how easy it was to get lost in those eyes.

They were hypnotizing.

The thought frightened her and she stopped a foot away from him, frozen in fear. Distance from him would be the safest.

Remember, he left you. You can't get hurt again. You're over him.

She couldn't let her guard down when it came to Quinn Devlyn.

Not now that she was finally whole again.

"Well, well. If it isn't the great wilderness physician," he teased, as his eyes roved over her from head to toe, a haughty smile on his lips and that damn dimple in his cheek popping up.

His mocking tone made her grind her teeth just a bit. She pressed her lips together, forcing a smile. "Dr. Devlyn. I'm glad you could come."

"It's Dr. Devlyn, now? When did we become so formal? I know we didn't part on good terms, but can we drop the formalities?" The spicy scent of his cologne—a clean scent of masculine soap and something else—teased her senses.

"Fine, but first names are as far as we go, do you understand? You're here in a professional capacity. Nothing more."

"Agreed. I would expect nothing less, Charlotte."

It was the way he said her name that triggered the memory. The two of them together for the first time, locked in a small hotel room in Niagara Falls, and the way he'd whispered her name against her neck.

"God, Charlotte. I need you."

I need you. Never, I love you. She should've taken that as a sign when she'd said yes to his proposal in the first place, but she'd been so blinded by love.

Charlotte nodded, but blooming warmth in her stomach spread to her cheeks. "Did you have a good flight?" she asked, trying to make small talk.

"As good as can be expected. The man next to me seemed to invade my space a lot, but overall it was as enjoyable as any other flight." He pulled up the handle to his rolling suitcase with a snap. The tone was a bit arrogant and that attitude was why she'd never brought him to Cape Recluse when they had first got engaged. Quinn had champagne tastes and was a city slicker through and through. Of course, if she'd brought him home when they had first got engaged it might've saved her some heartache.

Then she wouldn't have lost the baby, except she didn't regret carrying his baby, even for such a short time. She had known from the get-go that Quinn was not a family man. In her youthful naivety she'd thought she could change him.

How wrong she'd been.

Let it go.

It was no longer her job to care what Quinn Devlyn thought. "Well, we'd better get up to Cape Recluse. It's a two-hour flight there and there's talk of a storm coming in from Labrador. Also, I'd like to get up there before it's dark."

"It's two o'clock in the afternoon," he said, puzzled.

"The sun sets early up here."

"I thought this was the land of the midnight sun?"

"In summer… This is winter. We have long periods of night."

"Yikes." Quinn shook his head. "So how are we getting there?"

"I fly." Charlotte turned on her heel and strode off toward the other section of the airport where her plane was kept in a private rented hangar. Quinn kept in step beside her.

"What do you mean, you fly? As in a plane?" His tone was one of surprise and perhaps awe.

"Yes, I don't have wings." To prove her point she flapped her arms. Quinn rolled his eyes; he had never been one for foolishness in public places.

"You know what I mean. When did you learn how to fly?"

"About four years ago, after a man died in my arms from a very *mild* myocardial infarction. His death could've been prevented if we'd had regular flights from Iqaluit to Cape Recluse. By the time the air ambulance landed, Mr. Tikivik was dead. It was then I decided to learn how to fly, so I could fly my patients to Iqaluit if need be."

"So you're a physician and a paramedic, as well?" The tone was sarcastic, making her bristle with annoyance. His attitude on job specifications certainly hadn't changed one bit.

"What else are they supposed to do? Plan their medical emergencies to fit around a pilot's schedule?"

"I didn't mean to upset you. I think it's a lot to ask for limited pay."

Charlotte turned to face him. "Money doesn't mean that much to me. Lives mean more."

Quinn didn't respond but looked a bit taken aback. Guilt assailed her. She didn't want to pick a fight with him, not after he'd come all this way and on his own dime.

"Sorry," she apologized.

"For what?" he asked.

"If I insulted you."

"You didn't. You have nothing to be sorry about."

"Of course." Charlotte shook her head. Quinn never had hidden the fact that success and to be the best in his field drove him. In his eyes you were nothing without those attributes.

"I'm interested in meeting Mentlana Tikivik and examining her and the baby. Still, I don't quite understand why you don't just fly her down to Toronto."

"She has a pulmonary embolus."

Quinn whistled. "Does she know about the diagnosis of the fetus?"

"Yes, I told her." Charlotte sighed. "I told her I was bringing a specialist up to determine the severity of the CCAM. She's aware of what may have to happen, and she's fine with it. She wants to do whatever it takes to save her baby."

Just like I would've done to save mine.

A lump formed in her throat as her mind wandered back to that horrible day when she'd spotted the mass on the baby's lungs. She'd recognized the congenital cystic adenomatoid malformation, or CCAM, for what it was, and there had been no way she could fix it. She was only a general practitioner. She wasn't qualified.

"Of course." He nodded. "Did you explain the procedure to her?"

"Oh, yes." Charlotte couldn't help but smile as she remembered having to go through each step of the procedure, like she was talking to a first-year surgical resident.

"Did she understand?" Quinn asked, confused.

"Eventually," Charlotte replied.

"Eventually?"

Charlotte laughed. "She understands, but Mentlana is very…inquisitive. I'll warn you now, she'll bombard you with questions."

"No need to warn me. I've dealt with worse, I'm sure. I've

consulted on many patients before and I've a way of explaining complex medical procedures so patients understand me."

Charlotte rolled her eyes. "Your pride is healthy, I see."

Quinn smiled. "I have an excellent bedside manner."

In your dreams, perhaps.

"Right, I forgot about your charming persona with patients." She snapped her fingers. "You're something of a McSteamy."

"A...what?"

"Never mind, it's a *Grey's Anatomy* joke."

"Didn't that character die?"

Charlotte smirked. "I didn't know you were a *Grey's Anatomy* fan."

He sighed. "What I meant was that I have a way of getting people to open up to me. I have a winning personality."

Charlotte cocked an eyebrow. "Is that so?"

Quinn chuckled. "Okay. Look, what I meant was I'll be able to explain it to her and gain her trust. I've done this surgery before."

Trust was important, especially in the Inuk culture. Trust was important to her, too. She'd trusted Quinn. She'd never forget how deeply in love with him she'd been. Quinn had claimed her heart, body and soul. He'd taken her innocence and had then crushed all her hopes and dreams when he'd walked out on her after she'd lost their baby.

"It's for the best, Charlotte. We're not ready. We have our careers ahead of us."

The day he'd walked out had been the day he'd lost her trust. She'd never let him in again.

Never is a long time.

"Hey, are you okay? You zoned out, there, for a moment," Quinn said, waving a hand in front of her face.

Charlotte shook the painful memory away. "If you're sure you can handle Mentlana, I'll leave you to it."

"Charlotte, your friend will be totally at ease and informed during the entire procedure."

"Trust is not easily given by people in a small, close-knit and isolated community."

"Trust me." He grinned, a dimple puckering.

"I did that once before," she muttered.

"What?" he asked. He hadn't heard her, but when had he ever? When they'd been together, everything had been about him and she'd been so in love she'd been content to follow.

It had taken her a long time realize she'd been so desperate to have her own family she'd been blinded to the fact she had been engaged to a man who was already married—to his work.

"Don't worry about it." Though Charlotte wasn't entirely sure he could fit in with the residents of Cape Recluse. A man like Quinn would stick out like a sore thumb.

"Should I worry?" he asked.

"So, I was surprised to learn you're in Toronto," Charlotte said, changing the subject but also feeding her nosy side. New York had been Quinn's dream destination, his Mecca, his reason for leaving her, but when she'd called he'd been in Toronto.

"My father's health deteriorated two years ago. He offered me a position at the hospital. He wanted to groom me to become Chief of Surgery." Quinn frowned and quickened his pace. Charlotte had an inkling it was a touchy subject. At least that explained why he'd given up his practice in Manhattan and moved to Toronto. It impressed her that he'd returned home to help his father, despite his history with his parents.

"Did he retire?"

"No." His voice was stiff. "No, he died."

Good going, dingbat.

"I'm so sorry. I didn't know."

Quinn shrugged. "It was his fault. He didn't practice what he preached. Excessive smoker and drinker. Cancer caught up with him."

"Still. I'm sorry." Charlotte didn't know what else to say.

She knew Quinn hadn't had the best relationship with his parents, but it was still hard to lose one. She was practically a pro in that department.

She led him into a warm hangar where her little Citation jet was waiting. Quinn whistled in appreciation.

"Where did you get this?" he asked.

"I bought it at an auction. It's a '93 and was in bad shape interior-wise, but I didn't care about that. I kitted it out to transport patients."

"It's a beaut."

Charlotte grinned. She was proud of her jet and it made her preen that Quinn looked up at it in admiration. When they had been choosing their specialties, he hadn't been overly impressed with her choice of general practitioner.

You don't need his approval.

"Well, then, we'd better get going. I'll be back in a moment. I just have to clear something with the hangar's manager."

Charlotte jogged away. Quinn's personality was the same: overconfident, arrogant and cocky. But none of that mattered right now. His self-assuredness would probably be just the thing needed to save Mentlana and her baby.

And that was all that mattered.

What am I doing here again? Quinn asked himself, as another round of turbulence rocked the plane. Yet he knew exactly why he'd come. Because of Charlotte.

He'd had to see for himself that she was okay. Honestly, had he expected a broken, sad woman stuck in a dead-end job in the wilds of nowhere?

Yeah, in fact, he had.

When she'd refused to come to Manhattan after her miscarriage, he'd known she was done with him. Though it had smarted, he hadn't been a stranger to rejection from someone he loved. He'd dealt with it and had thrown himself completely into his work, but some perverse part of him had needed, *wanted* to see her again. When he'd left her she'd been so ill, so fragile.

Now she was whole and healthy.

It was like the miscarriage had never happened. She was confident, happy in her job. Hell, she'd even learned how to fly a plane. When he'd seen that jet, he'd been impressed. She wasn't the same girl he'd left behind. It seemed she was stronger for their parting.

Whereas he was not.

He glanced down at his hand and flexed it. The leather of his glove creaked, his hand inside, stiff.

A year ago, he'd been in a car accident during a bad bout of fog on the highway. His hand had been crushed. Quinn flexed his hand again, curling and then releasing it. Yes, it'd been broken and he'd undergone countless surgeries to repair it, but he could still use it. His hand had mended with time. Perhaps Charlotte's heart had, too, in the five years they'd been apart.

He doubted it. When Charlotte had greeted him it'd been so formal. So forced.

"Whoa, that was a bit rough," he remarked, as they hit more disturbance. He was no stranger to flying, but that was the most jarring bit of turbulence he'd ever experienced. Of course, he was used to first-class seats instead of being crammed into a small cockpit beside the pilot, especially an alluring pilot like Charlotte.

His shoulders almost touched hers in the tight space, just a near brush of her body against his sending his blood pumping. Just being in her presence again aroused him. Charlotte was a strong aphrodisiac, like ambrosia, and she had tasted just as sweet, too.

Blast. Get ahold of yourself. You're not some randy med student. You're going to be Chief of Surgery when you return to Toronto.

Only he couldn't get ahold of himself. She looked exactly as she had when he'd first laid eyes on her. The slender figure and bright red curls were exactly the same. Her face, with only the barest hint of makeup, still looked as fresh and innocent. It was like time hadn't touched her.

Perhaps the cold preserves people up here.

Quinn shook his head. He'd never understood her desire to live on top of the world. He hated winter at the best of times. The frigid air seemed to reach down his throat and scald his lungs with ice.

"Is something wrong?" Charlotte asked casually, not looking at him.

"What makes you think something's wrong?"

The plane lurched and she adjusted her controls. "You're muttering to yourself. Not used to a small plane, eh? Prefer first class?"

"Well, at least I can get a drink in first class." He rubbed his hand. "That, and I'm not used to turbulence that seems more like bull-riding at the Calgary Stampede."

Charlotte grinned. "This is mild."

"Good God. Mild? Are you certain?"

She chuckled. He'd always liked her laughter. "Positive. There's a storm coming."

"Did we hit it?"

She shook her head. "Nope. The storm is chasing us. We'll beat it."

Quinn shuddered. *Snow. Ice.* "I don't know how you live up here."

"I like the rugged wilderness."

"I thought you were afraid of bears. Isn't this bear country?"

She laughed, her green eyes twinkling. "This is true."

"You never did tell me why you're afraid of bears."

"It's silly, really."

"Come on, humor me. There's no in-flight movie, either."

"No. I'm not telling you." She grinned and adjusted some more knobs.

"Come on. I promise I won't say anything." He waggled his eyebrows, teasing her.

She shot him a look of disbelief. "No way. And stop that eyebrow-waggling."

"What, this?" He did it again for effect. Quinn had forgotten it drove her batty and he'd forgotten what fun it was to tease her.

"Lord, you look like a demented Groucho Marx or something."

"I'll keep pestering. You know I have a bit of an annoying streak."

"A bit?" A smile quirked her lips. "Fine. It's because I'm afraid of being eaten alive."

He cocked an eyebrow. "Is that so?"

Charlotte's creamy white cheeks stained with crimson and fire flooded his veins as an image of her, naked, flashed through his mind. He could still taste her kisses on his lips, recall her silky hair and her smooth skin under his hands. Their bodies had fit so well together. It had been so right. His body reacted to her presence. So pure and so not the kind of girl his parents would want for him.

They'd never approved of Charlotte but he hadn't cared. He'd pursued her at first because she was good looking, bright and he'd known it would irk his parents to no end. She had not been like the boring girls they'd kept throwing in his path. Charlotte had not been suitable.

No, Charlotte had been exciting and taboo. Somewhere along the way he'd fallen in love with her. Only they'd wanted different things. She'd wanted a family. He hadn't. With his loveless childhood, Quinn knew he wasn't father material.

When his relationship with Charlotte had ended, his mother had reminded him frequently that Charlotte hadn't been the woman for him. His mother did like to rub salt into a wound.

And they'd been right. Charlotte hadn't been the woman for him.

They were so different, but her difference was what had excited him most.

Quinn pushed aside all those thoughts. They would do nothing but get him into trouble. He was a professional.

A surgeon.

The plane jolted and she was thrown against the dash. Quinn unbuckled and reached out, steadying her. The scent of her coconut shampoo wrapped around him, reminding him of the summer they'd spent in Yellowknife, in a cabin on the shores of Great Slave Lake. Endless nights of blistering passion under the midnight sun.

"Are you okay?" he asked, closing the small gap between them. He could see her pulse racing at the base of her throat.

"I'm fine. Fine." She cleared her throat and shrugged her shoulders. Only he didn't move his hands from her shoulders. He enjoyed holding her again and she didn't shrug out of his arms or move from his touch.

"Are you certain?" he asked again. The blush still stained her skin, her gaze locked with his and her breathing quickened. She parted her lips and he fought the urge to steal a kiss from her. But he wanted to.

So badly.

CHAPTER TWO

LET GO OF HER. She didn't want you.

"Charlotte?" His voice cracked, he cleared his throat. "Are you okay?"

She broke the connection and turned away. "I'm fine. You'd better buckle up in case we hit some more turbulence." She didn't look at him but she appeared perturbed.

"Sure." He could take a hint. Quinn cursed himself inwardly for letting his guard down. When he'd decided to come up here he'd told himself to keep emotionally detached from her, but two hours in her presence and he was being swayed by her again. Just being around her and he forgot what had passed between them—for him it was like they'd never been apart.

She was like a drug that intoxicated him quickly.

Charlotte's cold brush-off brought him out of the past into the present, and keenly reminded him of how lonely his life had been without her. He didn't like to be reminded of that.

He buckled back up and looked out the window as the clouds dissipated. In the distance the white landscape became dotted with brightly colored buildings, which appeared to be raised on stilts above the snow, smoke rising steadily from the chimneys.

So this is Cape Recluse.

The cape was at the mercy of the elements and the Northwest Passage surrounded it on three sides. The town itself was nestled against a panorama of majestic mountains. Squinting, he faintly made out what looked like a tiny airstrip on a sheet of ice.

The whole town looked barren and very, very rustic. It was like something out of the old frontier towns of the Wild West, only snow covered. Quinn knew he was on the edge of civilization, here.

This was what Charlotte preferred over New York?

She flicked on the radio and gave out her call number. "Preparing to land."

"Roger that," came the crackling acknowledgment over the line.

Charlotte brought her plane in to land. Quinn was impressed with her piloting abilities as she brought the aircraft to a smooth landing on the slick airstrip. When the wheels of the plane touched the ice, the jet skittered slightly, but Charlotte kept control and then visibly relaxed.

As she swung the plane round towards the small hangar, Quinn saw a group of villagers milling about.

"That's quite a homecoming."

"Yes, well, there's not much winter entertainment up here," Charlotte said.

"I'll bet there isn't." Quinn regretted his muttered comment the moment it had slipped past his lips.

Smooth move.

Charlotte's eyes narrowed and flashed in annoyance, but all she said was, "Well, we'll get you settled."

She taxied the plane into the hangar.

"Sounds good." He could do with a long, hot shower and some sleep, but judging from the size of the town he didn't see any four-star accommodation nearby. The sooner he dealt with Mentlana Tikivik's case, the sooner he could get back to Toronto, and sanity.

* * *

Charlotte's pulse rate felt like a jackhammer at the moment and she hoped Quinn hadn't noticed how much he had affected her.

Damn.

One stupid little embrace during turbulence had set off all sorts of crazy hormones zinging through her body.

His stay in Cape Recluse was going to be more trying than she'd originally thought and had tried to tell herself it would be. To make matters worse, there were no hotels in town and Quinn would be staying with her. He *had* to stay with her.

When his arms had wrapped around her in the cockpit, her blood had ignited and her common sense had wrestled with the side of her that had wanted to toss aside the plane's controls and throw herself into his arms.

Totally irrational.

She was the fly to his spider, apparently.

It wasn't like she was desperate. She'd gone on other dates with good-looking, exciting men, but she hadn't lost her head around them.

And that was the point. Quinn always made her feel giddy, like a lovestruck fool. He was exciting, sexy and handsome, and made her body burn with a pleasure she hadn't felt since he'd left.

Every day she'd be forced to face Quinn, the man who had broken her heart, but she had to do this for Mentlana. She knew she'd be putting her heart at risk, and it had only recently mended since he'd left her for the greener pastures of New York. She'd rarely thought of him for the last couple years.

Liar.

Of course she'd thought about him, even though for the last couple years it hadn't been as constant as it had been before that. Except for one day. Every year on the anniversary of the day she'd miscarried the baby and had nearly bled out, she'd thought of him and what could've been had he not walked away.

Only, what could've been was just a fantasy. Quinn wouldn't have settled down. She realized that now.

Her throat constricted as she tried to swallow down those emotions. When she thought of what could have been, when she thought about the family she'd always dreamed of, she fought the urge to break down in tears.

Don't think about it.

Charlotte took a deep, calming breath, removed her headpiece and climbed out of the cockpit.

"Doc Charley!"

Charlotte glanced up to see George, her paramedic, approaching the plane. She embraced George, who was like a brother to her.

"Good to see you, Doc. Good flight?" he asked, though Charlotte knew he wasn't really *that* concerned about her flight. He was a pilot, too, and the Citation was like his baby. George moved away and stroked the side of the jet for good measure. "Any problems?"

"None. Your baby is fine and the flight was good." She glanced back to see if Quinn was disembarking okay. He appeared to be, as he climbed stiffly out of the cockpit.

"Dr. Devlyn." Charlotte waved him over, and Quinn strode over, his gaze intently focused on George. He didn't respond. Charlotte gritted her teeth. "Quinn, this is George Atavik. He's my paramedic and copilot. George, this is Dr. Devlyn, the specialist from Toronto."

George grinned, flashing brilliant white teeth. His dark eyes lit with sincerity. "Good to meet you, Dr. Devlyn. Thanks for coming up this far north to help out."

"The pleasure is all mine and, please, just call me Quinn," he replied, shaking George's hand. He glanced at her, his dark eyes twinkling mischievously, a look that spoke volumes, like he was undressing her right there on the spot, as he whispered, "Just Quinn."

"George is Mentlana Tikivik's brother," Charlotte said, clearing her throat. Why she'd blurted that information out she didn't know. It was like she wanted Quinn to know there was nothing between George and her. She watched for any sign of reaction from Quinn, but there was none. All he did was nod politely.

"I'll take care of the plane, Doc Charley. I checked the weather satellite earlier and I was worried you were going to be delayed by that storm coming in from Labrador." George chatted away, totally unaware of the tension Charlotte keenly felt hovering over them.

"I was, too, for a moment," she answered absently.

"I'll go and collect my bag," Quinn said, walking back toward the plane, where people in the hangar were unloading his suitcase and some supplies Charlotte had brought up. So like him to be haughty.

It's Quinn.

Even though she knew she shouldn't follow him, Charlotte hurried after him.

"Are you still tired from the trip?" she asked.

"A bit," Quinn answered. "Don't you and George have to deal with the plane?"

"George can handle it. He'll yell if I'm needed."

"He seems like a nice fellow, I hope he makes you happy."

Charlotte did a double take. Quinn thought she was with George and, despite the fact they'd once been intimate, was wishing her happiness. So unlike the selfish man he'd been when he was younger.

"Quinn, George is like a brother to me." Again, why was she telling him that? She should've let him think George was her lover, and then she shuddered at the thought. She'd babysat George at one time and he'd been a terror. "Besides, George is too weird, too into his Westerns. I think that if given the chance, he'd trade in his paramedic bag for a saddle and six-shooter." She said the last part loudly.

"Yeah, yeah, laugh it up. Clint Eastwood is da man!" George called back.

A look of pleasure flashed momentarily across his face. "Well, that makes for a good partnership between physician and paramedic."

"Doc Charley!" The frantic call made both Charlotte and Quinn spin around. Charlotte saw Lorna, the village midwife, come running into the hangar.

Charlotte didn't need to be told. Her instinct kicked in and she grabbed her medical bag from the top of the pile of supplies. "What's happened? Is it Mentlana?"

Lorna nodded. "She started bleeding, and I don't know if it's from the fetus, the placenta or something else."

Oh, God, no.

Charlotte remembered the way she herself had almost bled to death when she'd lost her baby. Sweat broke out across her brow. Charlotte glanced at Quinn, who was standing close to her. His lips were pressed together in a firm line and he looked a little pale as he nodded his understanding, obviously ready to follow her lead.

"Where is she?" Charlotte asked.

"The clinic." Lorna was wringing her hands nervously.

"Thanks, Lorna." Charlotte started running, praying she wasn't too late.

"Is everything okay, Charley?" Mentlana's voice was anxious as Charlotte peeled off the rubber gloves and placed them in the toxic medical waste receptacle.

"Your cervix is irritated, that's all." Charlotte had been relieved on her arrival to see the blood loss was minimal, but enough to worry Lorna. Given all the things wrong with Mentlana and her high-risk pregnancy, Lorna had reacted quickly and done the right thing.

"Well, yours would be irritated, too, if you were carrying around an elephant."

Charlotte chuckled. "I'm going to have Dr. Devlyn, the specialist from Toronto, perform an ultrasound to make sure there's nothing wrong with the placenta or the baby. But the heartbeat is strong, and from the internal, the placenta is still in place. If it had been an abruption there would've been a lot more blood."

And death. Charlotte kept that thought to herself. There was no sense in worrying the pregnant woman over nothing.

Mentlana visibly relaxed as she took her feet out of the stirrups and rearranged the sheet over her lower half. Charlotte ran her hands under the tap and scrubbed them thoroughly.

"Do you want me to get Genen? He's probably climbing the walls."

"Let him wait for a moment. I want to talk to you."

Confused, Charlotte pulled her wheeled stool over to her friend's side nonetheless. Mentlana was leaning up on one elbow, a serious look on her face.

Charlotte knew that look all too well. It meant business.

"What's your question?"

"This doctor from Toronto, he's the one, isn't he?" Mentlana asked.

Charlotte's heart skipped a beat. "What do you mean?"

Mentlana's eyes narrowed, glinting as black as coal as she fixed Charlotte with the serious gaze that made Genen and George almost wet their pants. "Don't lie to me, Charley. This is the guy, right? He's the guy who broke your heart and left after you lost the baby. The one you wouldn't bring home to meet us. The one who, if I wasn't pregnant and in need of him, I'd give a stern kick to the crotch."

Charlotte stood. Letting out an exasperated sigh, she scrubbed her hand over her face. "Yes. Dr. Devlyn is the one."

Mentlana reached out and grabbed her hand. "I know how

hard it is for you to trust him, to bring him here, and I know you're doing it for me and the baby. Thank you."

A sob caught in Charlotte's throat but she controlled it. She forced a wobbly smile and smoothed Mentlana's jet-black hair from her forehead. "I would do anything for you, even face the devil himself—or Devlyn, in this case."

"Witty." Lana chuckled. "Now I'm *really* interested in meeting him."

Charlotte rolled her eyes and padded towards the door. "Well, he does have the bedside manner of a bull in a china shop, most days. Stay tight. I'll bring him in to see you in a moment."

"Tight, right." Mentlana snorted as Charlotte shut the door to the exam room. Just as she'd thought, Genen was pacing, and the rest of the family was crowded into the small reception area of her clinic. Genen almost rushed her as she approached.

Charlotte held up her hands. "It's nothing, just an irritated cervix. Mother and baby are fine, but I'll have the specialist do an ultrasound to be absolutely certain."

Relief washed over Genen's face. "Can I see her now, Charley?"

"Sure. But just Genen," she said, as the entire Atavik and Tikivik clan seemed to rise. Scanning the clinic area, she couldn't see Quinn anywhere. Biting her bottom lip, she headed over to George.

"Where's Dr. Devlyn?"

"In your office. I thought he'd be most comfortable there."

The blood drained from Charlotte's face. "My office?" *Oh, God.* She hadn't had a chance to clear away her personal items, including the cherished, faded old sonogram. The ultrasound he hadn't even bothered to attend. The same sonogram he'd just grunted at when she'd shown it to him.

"Don't you want to see? It's amazing!"

"It's not like you haven't seen a sonogram before."

"I know. But, Quinn, it's our baby."

He shrugged. "I have to go, Charlotte. I'm late for my rounds already."

He hadn't wanted to see it then and even though it was childish, she didn't want to share it with him now. Not after five years. He didn't deserve to see it or share in any part of her grief.

CHAPTER THREE

TRYING NOT TO panic, she thanked George and headed towards her office. She raised her hand to knock and then thought better of it. Why should she knock? It was her office and he was the visitor. She walked in. Quinn wasn't behind her desk, but was staring out the window at the snow swirling over the inlet. He turned when she entered, his face unreadable.

"Is Ms. Tikivik stable?" he asked.

"Yes. It was an irritation of the cervix, but I'd like you to do an ultrasound and check the status of the fetus yourself."

"I will." He glanced back out the window. "I have to say I've never seen so many houses tied down to cables and supported on metal beams. It's like they're a bunch of beach houses or something."

Charlotte couldn't help but smile. "The houses are raised because of permafrost. There are no basements in Cape Recluse. The village also has a lot of high winds. We may seem sheltered, with mountains surrounding us, but it's really very windy. We have to tie everything down."

Quinn's eyebrows arched. "I guess. With no trees to form a windbreak."

"Yeah, you could say that."

"It's quite interesting—the landscape, that is."

Now it was Charlotte's turn to be impressed. He'd never been overly interested in anything else before, beyond the next surgery.

Well, he'd been interested in her until she'd got pregnant and decided to become a family physician.

"Yes. It is an interesting vista," she agreed.

Quinn shivered and then nodded. "This is some community. They all seem to care for one another, like family." He shook his head. "It's like the Brady Bunch up here or something."

"That's because they genuinely do care. It's a small place and everyone knows everybody. There are no secrets."

That caught his attention and he shot her a questioning look. "Really? No secrets?"

"Nope. Not a single one." Suddenly she had a bad case of butterflies. She was nervous. Perhaps it was the fact they were in an enclosed room, alone. After her reaction to him earlier, the last place she wanted to be was in a private office with him.

He strode over to her, his eyes soft, with a twinkle of devilment still dancing there. As he reached out and brushed an errant curl from her face, a zip of delight traveled down her spine. His knuckles brushed her cheek, causing her body to waken. One simple touch from him and her body responded as if it had been in a slumber for the last five years.

Maybe it had. No other man had been able to arouse her by a simple touch before. It angered her that Quinn was the only one who could.

"Don't," she whispered, her voice catching in her throat.

"What?"

"Touch me with familiarity."

Quinn moved his hand. "I'm sorry, Charlotte. It's force of habit, even after all this time."

Tears stung her eyes and she cleared her throat before taking a step back. "You shouldn't keep the Tikiviks waiting."

"Do you have some scrubs for me?"

"Of course. See Rosie at Reception and she'll get you fitted." Charlotte tucked her hair behind her ear as he stared at her, the tension in the room almost palpable. Why wasn't he leaving? "Is there anything else?"

Quinn glanced away. "No. I'll go and see Rosie now."

Quinn walked past her and Charlotte watched him go, unease and apprehension twisting her stomach. When he left the room she snatched the picture frame off her desk and stared at the sonogram, thinking about the baby she'd lost. He or she would've been five years old, now, and she couldn't help but wonder if the baby would've had the same sandy-brown hair and deep brown eyes as Quinn. Perhaps their baby would've favored her, with red curls and emerald eyes, or been a mixture of them both.

Closing her eyes, she pictured a rambunctious boy, like she always did when she thought about her lost baby. He'd have had rosy cheeks, sandy-brown hair and green eyes. She felt the sting of tears and brushed them away quickly.

Why was she letting herself feel this way again?

Why was she letting Quinn Devlyn in again?

Because I never let him go.

Sighing, she opened her filing cabinet and pushed the picture to the back before locking the drawer. She slipped the key into her pocket. It was really a moot point, now. There *was* no baby of theirs, not now and not ever.

Quinn peeled off the clothes he'd been wearing for the last several hours. He was bone weary and absolutely freezing, but this was the moment where he shone, being a surgical god.

His hand trembled slightly and he gripped it.

Just tired, that was all.

Besides, this was nothing big. Just an ultrasound and a consult. If this tremor continued he'd remove himself from the case. The patient's life and that of the baby were more important than proving to the world he was still a viable surgeon.

You can do this.

Quinn pulled on the scrubs. As he splashed some water on his face, his mind wandered to the sonogram he'd spied on Charlotte's desk.

Their baby.

The one they'd lost. It had been the scariest moment of his life. Not even the accident that had damaged his hand had been as terrifying as the moment when they'd lost their baby. Charlotte had bled badly after she'd miscarried. He'd found her collapsed on the floor of their apartment.

"Hold on, honey. Hold on, Charlotte." He reached down and stroked her pale face.

Quinn shuddered, sending the horrific nightmare back to where it had come from. That moment had been far worse than the accident he'd endured alone.

Seeing the sonogram on her desk, in a frame, had only reminded him of the pain when they'd parted. At the time, he hadn't been too keen on the idea of a baby in their lives. How could he be a good, loving father when he had such a role model as his own cold, detached father? A baby was not part of his plans. However, it had hurt him when she'd lost it, to see her in pain. To watch her grieve and know there was nothing he could do about it. It had made him feel powerless.

And he didn't like feeling powerless. Not in the least.

There were times in the neonatal unit, when dealing with babies born prematurely, that his mind wandered to what might've been.

But that was in the past. Their baby hadn't survived. So he'd told himself it wasn't meant to be, and had instead focused on becoming one of the best surgeons in his field, burying his sadness over the loss in his work.

Now he was at the top of his game.

And lonely as hell.

Another reason why he hated these godforsaken outposts of the North. He didn't get Charlotte's fascination with staying up here.

Even though her life had been spared, the North had still cost him Charlotte.

She had refused to leave and go with him to New York.

Had refused to talk to him or even look at him. All she'd done was hand back the ring, along with everything else he'd given her, because in her note she'd stated she wanted no reminders of him.

Why did she still keep the sonogram?

Of course, he had no right to pry. The baby was gone.

He jammed the clothes he'd taken off into a suitcase, stuffing the unwanted emotions to the dark recesses of his mind, as well. He didn't have time to let his personal feelings get in the way. There was a patient waiting, counting on him. He exited the bathroom, pulling his luggage behind him. The hairs on the back of his neck stood on end and he knew instinctively all eyes were glued to him. Turning, he smiled and waved awkwardly. No one returned his greeting.

Good Lord.

He approached Charlotte's nurse, the one who had given him the scrubs. Lavender scrubs, no less. Quinn made a mental note to see if there were any blue or green in stock. He wasn't partial to any shade of purple. Perhaps he was a bit of a pig for thinking this, but he felt a bit emasculated in such a feminine color.

"Sorry, I don't remember your name," he apologized.

"No worries. I'm Rosie, and I can take your luggage for you, Dr. Devlyn."

"Thanks. And the patient?"

"In exam room one."

"Thanks again."

The eyes, he was pretty sure, followed him all the way to the exam-room door. The tension was so thick you could slice it with a knife. Perhaps they were shocked to see a man in lavender.

Quinn knocked on the door and Charlotte answered. A smug smile tugged at the corner of her lips as she looked him up and down.

"I think that's your color," she teased.

"Think again," he snarled.

Charlotte stifled a giggle and stepped to one side. "Come in."

Quinn entered the large exam room, his gaze resting on the Inuk couple in the corner. The woman was exceptionally pretty, with black hair and eyes to match. There was a dimple in her cheek as she grinned up at her husband.

"Mentlana, Genen, this is Dr. Devlyn. He's the specialist I told you both about."

Genen stood and came over to grasp Quinn's bad hand, shaking it firmly. Quinn didn't wince, even though the man had a strong grip.

Quinn approached Mentlana and was surprised by her measured gaze. This woman was picking him apart with her eyes and he felt like a slab of meat.

"A pleasure to meet you, Mrs. Tikivik."

"And you, Dr. Devlyn. Charley wasn't wrong. You *are* cute."

He arched his brows and held back the grin threatening to erupt.

"Ahem." Charlotte cleared her throat from behind him and now it was his turn to stifle a laugh. Craning his neck, he looked back at her. She was conveniently staring at the ceiling, but her blush was evidence of her embarrassment. He liked the way the pink bloomed in her creamy white cheeks.

Focus.

"Well, thank you for the compliment. I'd like to do an ultrasound, now, if that's okay?" he asked, steering the subject back to the examination. But he planned to use Mentlana's little disclosure of information to get him a manlier color of scrubs. Right now he had a job to do. Now was not the time for frivolity or personal feelings. "Do you have a full bladder?"

"When don't I?" Mentlana replied. "Please, before I burst."

"I'll get the ultrasound machine," Charlotte said.

Charlotte wheeled the machine over and then dimmed the lights, refusing to meet his gaze.

So, I still make her uncomfortable.

That thought secretly pleased him.

Getting to work, he uncovered Mentlana's belly. "Sorry. This is a bit cold."

"That's not cold, Dr. Devlyn. Outside is cold."

He grinned, but didn't engage in any further pleasantries. He had a consult to complete. Quinn placed the probe against her abdomen and began to adjust the dials to get a clearer picture. Genen leaned forward, his eyes transfixed on the image on the monitor.

"Well, from what I can see, your placenta, though previa, is fully attached and not bleeding."

"That's a relief." Genen kissed his wife's hand. "And the baby?"

"The bleeding is not being caused by the baby. I have to run some more tests to determine the severity of the CCAM, but other than that, his heart is beating and he's moving well. His other organs are forming satisfactorily for a gestational age of twenty-one weeks."

"Thank you, Dr. Devlyn. I appreciate it," Mentlana said.

"I want you on bed rest, though." He turned to look at Charlotte. "I'm sure Dr. James will agree with my assessment."

"Yes," Charlotte said. "I think we've had this discussion before."

"For how long?" Mentlana's gaze traveled nervously between him and Charlotte.

"For the remainder of your pregnancy. With your pulmonary embolism and placenta previa alone, it's for the best," Charlotte said, brushing back Mentlana's hair.

Mentlana nodded. "Okay."

"We'll call you when I'm through analyzing your labs and diagnostic images." Quinn wiped the sonogram gel from her abdomen and then turned back to the machine. "Until then, take it easy."

"Sounds good, Doctors."

Quinn saved various shots of the baby's heart and other organs to determine whether or not he would have to do the surgery in utero. It would be better if he could wait until the baby was full term to deliver it via Caesarean and do the operation on the newborn.

He'd done *that* surgery several times since his hand had been damaged.

If the baby could wait until its birth, by then he might be able to figure out a way to get Mentlana to Mount Hope, where his surgical team could assist him. Even Iqaluit would be better than here.

Charlotte may be a competent physician, but she was no surgeon.

She could've been great if she'd only come to New York with me.

Quinn stood up and left. He knew Charlotte followed him, and so did the collective gaze of the mob huddled in the waiting room as they passed to get to Charlotte's office.

Once they were behind the closed doors he wandered over to the window and wrinkled his nose in dissatisfaction at the swirling snowstorm, which had caught up with them.

Then again, it would make a nice photograph and he was glad he'd brought his camera. Since his father's death, he had been indulging in his secret passion for photography. Something his father had always stated was a waste of time.

He was on sabbatical, as his father had just died when Charlotte had called, and he'd planned on taking a trip to India to photograph scenery. Instead, he was up in the High Arctic and not getting paid much to be there.

The money didn't matter to him.

His father would roll over in his grave if he knew, and he already knew how his mother felt about this excursion.

"You don't have time for a charity case, Quinn. You have to prepare to take your father's place!"

God. He hated winter. It probably stemmed from the fact he'd been forced into endless hours of hockey practice by his father, when all Quinn had wanted to do was take photography lessons. Photography hadn't been manly enough for his father, whereas hockey was the sport of champions.

"Don't they have winters in Toronto?" Charlotte asked, breaking the silence.

Quinn glanced back at her. "Pardon?"

"The way you're scowling at the snow."

Quinn shrugged. "You know I hate winter."

"How could I forget?"

"I'm not the only Canadian who does. Think about all the snowbirds that go to warmer climes every winter."

Charlotte's eyes widened. "You want me to picture you as an old man in a RV?" Her eyes twinkled with mischief.

"Ha, ha. Very funny."

"I'm sorry about the scrubs." A devilish smile played across her lips.

"You're not in the least. You enjoyed watching me give the locals a fright."

Charlotte laughed and he couldn't help but join in. "I'll see if George has any spares."

"Much appreciated."

"What do you think of Mentlana's condition?" she asked, mercifully changing the subject.

"Your assessment is correct, though I don't know the severity of the CCAM yet."

"How long will it take you to determine that?" she asked, her voice tight and her lips pursed together in a thin line. He could see she was stressed about Mentlana.

Charlotte always got over-attached to people.

"A few days. I want to be absolutely certain. I sent the scans to your computer and I'll email them to my laptop later. I have an internet stick, because I figured there's no Wi-Fi up here."

Charlotte nodded. "Wise move."

Quinn moved away from the window and took a seat on the opposite side of the desk. As soon as he sat down he noticed the little frame with the sonogram picture was gone. He didn't search the room for it as he didn't want Charlotte to know he'd seen it. Apparently she'd hidden it. It irked him that she was hiding it from him.

Like it had never existed.

Like *they* had never existed. And that saddened him.

He shook that thought away.

"I'm glad it was just an irritated cervix." Charlotte sat across from him, her back ramrod straight, her fingers laced in front of her.

"There are no pools of blood darkening on the scans. The fetus is thriving, despite the CCAM. I take it they knew the gender beforehand. I hope I didn't make a blunder with that."

"They knew."

Quinn nodded. "I'm hoping we can get Mentlana to twenty-five weeks before I even think of doing in utero surgery to repair the lungs—that way, if we have to deliver, the baby has a better chance of survival."

Unlike ours, who miscarried at a mere sixteen weeks.

"In utero surgery is needed?"

"It may not be. We'll monitor her. She may go to term and then the baby's lungs can be repaired after delivery, but if there's much more fluid collection we risk hydrops. If that's the case we'll have to place a shunt in the fetus's lungs so the fluid can drain into the amniotic fluid and take the pressure off the lungs. Then, when the baby is full term, we can resect the lesion on him. Really, that would be the ideal situation."

Quinn rubbed his hand, which had begun to bother him again. He needed to do his strengthening exercises. "There has to be a way to get to Iqaluit, though. You don't have the facilities here to deliver a baby by Caesarean, let alone operate on a fetus in utero."

"She has a pulmonary embolism. I can't fly her."

"What about low altitude?"

"I've thought of it, but with the sudden storms and mountains...it's risky. It would double the flight time."

"It's risky leaving her up here. When the time comes we need to get her to Iqaluit. If she makes it to twenty-four weeks, we need to consider flying her down there."

Charlotte scrubbed her hand over her face. "You're right. I know it. All right, when the time comes we'll fly her at low altitude to Iqaluit, but if her water breaks or a storm hits, we'll have to do it here. I've been stockpiling supplies."

"Supplies won't cut it. I need a *proper* surgical team to assist me. I'm sorry. You alone won't be of any use in this situation."

Charlotte's eyes flashed in annoyance. "I'm more than capable of assisting you, Dr. Devlyn."

"Have you done surgeries here before?" he asked, intrigued.

"Yes, but never this kind. It's why I need you here, Quinn." She reached across the desk and took his hand. Her small, delicate hand fit so snugly in his. Warmth spread across his chest. He wanted to pull her closer to him.

He hadn't realized how much he'd missed her.

Don't. She didn't want you.

Quinn pushed her hand away.

It was too little, too late. There was no going back.

She cleared her throat and her expression was serious. "Will you let me assist, Dr. Devlyn, or do I have to hire help?"

As much as he was tempted to tell her to bring up a surgical team, he knew the money would be coming out of her own pocket and he couldn't do that to her.

"If it comes down to it, I would like you to assist."

CHAPTER FOUR

CHARLOTTE WAS TAKEN aback. She wanted to believe that Quinn trusted her abilities as a surgeon and was willing to let her help save her best friend's baby, but a niggle of self-doubt gnawed at the back of her mind.

She knew what his thoughts about general physicians and surgeons had been in medical school. Quinn had believed in the discipline, drive and focus of training for years in a specialty, which of course had been very egotistical of him. He had been obsessive when it came to his training. In med school he'd do anything to scrub in on any surgery and she knew he never gave up on a challenge. That's why he was at the top of his field so young.

Charlotte hoped he had changed, though she seriously doubted it. As her father had always said, a leopard didn't change its spots.

Why am I worrying about this?

Quinn was no longer her concern. She didn't care what he thought about her chosen career path and, frankly, if he was going to let her assist in a once-in-a-lifetime surgery, she was going to take it.

Even if it was because Quinn had no other option.

"I think I'm going to have a shower and peel myself out of these oh so charming scrubs." Quinn rubbed his hand, wincing momentarily, and then stood up. "Where am I staying and where can I call a cab?"

Guilt assuaged her. She wasn't heartless. He was exhausted and here she was thrusting him straight into the exam room the moment the plane had touched down. Although it hadn't been intentional, it had just happened that way.

"There are no cabs and there's no hotel." Charlotte stood and walked over to the door. She needed an escape route for what she was about to tell him. Even though she hated having to share a clinic space with him for the next twenty-and-some-odd weeks while they monitored Mentlana, it was even worse having to share accommodations with him.

Already it was proving hard to keep her attraction for him under wraps, but there was nothing to be done. Cape Recluse had no hotels, motels or anything of the kind. The people in this town opened up their homes to strangers. Quinn would be more comfortable at her home, which was connected to the clinic, than at the home of someone he didn't know.

"No hotel?" Quinn's eyes widened. "Am I supposed to crash here?" He glanced down at the old brown sofa that had once adorned their college apartment. "I think I'm too old to curl up on the 'Couch of Gibraltar,' here."

"I have a guest bedroom at my place." Heat began to crawl up her neck and she prayed the blush wouldn't reach her face.

"Are you asking me to spend the night?"

"N-no," she stammered.

Quinn grinned and crossed his arms. Even though he thought the lavender emasculated him, that was far from the truth. He was still as sexy as ever and she wanted to tear those scrubs from his body to get to what was underneath.

Whoa, slow down.

Where had that thought come from? True, it'd been a long time since she'd been with a man...the last time having been with Quinn. Her heart skipped a beat just thinking about it. Maybe that was the cure. To have one last night and get him out of her system. Warmth spread through her at the thought of that foolish notion.

Get a grip on yourself.

Sleeping with Quinn Devlyn was the last thing she needed to do.

"So let me get this straight. You're inviting me over to your place to spend the night?" He was teasing. He wasn't going to let it go. Quinn was annoying that way. He moved closer and Charlotte raised her hands and took a step back.

"It's not like it's in my bed. You'll be in the guest bedroom with its *own* bed. Same general house, two separate beds."

Quinn's brown eyes gleamed with devilment. "You're mentioning the word bed quite a lot, whereas I haven't even once."

Charlotte snapped her fingers. "Ha, you just did."

"Someone has bed on the brain," Quinn teased again.

"You're welcome to find your own lodgings, but unless you want to bunk with strangers or build an igloo you're better off staying with me. Trust me, I don't like it, either."

"Igloo? You're pulling my leg."

"No, really, and, trust me, you don't want to. The bears have been bad this year."

"Bears? You mean as in polar bears?" he asked, startled.

"Yes, what other kind of bear do you think I mean? This is the North, my friend." She chuckled at the expression of horror plastered across his face as she left the room. At least it got her out of that conversation with him.

She walked out of her office to retrieve his luggage from Rosie. It was almost time for the clinic to close, but the residents knew she was only next door. She didn't even have to leave the clinic to go home as the door at the far side of the clinic led straight into her humble but comfortable abode.

"I'm here for Dr. Devlyn's luggage."

"Ah." Rosie got up and lifted the luggage, handing it to her. "He packs light."

"Always has."

"I find it strange he didn't bring his own scrubs," Rosie remarked, as she began to collect up her belongings.

Charlotte grinned, thinking about Quinn in his scrubs again. "Do you think we can get some blue or green ones?"

Rosie frowned over the bridge of her rhinestone-studded glasses. "What does he think this is, the local store?"

"I know. But please try for me, Rosie. He's used to the big city where everything is provided to physicians on a silver platter."

"In Canada?" Rosie asked in disbelief.

"Well, no. He had a private practice in New York for a while."

Rosie nodded. "That makes sense. I'll see what I can do." She zipped up her parka. "I'll see you tomorrow, Doc Charley."

"Good night, Rosie."

No sooner had Charlotte uttered the words than the doors of the clinic were flung open. George came rushing in with a stretcher. On it was Wavell Agluclark, a ten-year-old boy who was being taught the ways of his people in traditional hunting. George had his hand clamped over Wavell's thigh, which was bleeding heavily.

Rosie instantly peeled off her parka and quickly went about preparing a room while Charlotte jumped into action.

"What've we got here, George?"

"Deep laceration to the thigh, possibly a nick to the femoral artery," George answered.

"Exam room one is ready for you, Doc Charley," Rosie called out.

"Bring him in." Charlotte began to scrub while Wavell's dad, Sam, and George lifted him from the stretcher onto the exam bed. Wavell's face was pale with blood loss, pain and fear. A twinge of sympathy raced through her. She hated seeing a child in pain, but this wasn't Wavell's first accident. The boy seemed prone to mishaps.

"So what happened this time, Wavell?" she asked, pulling on a pair of rubber gloves, as Wavell was allergic to latex.

"I was cleaning fish after ice fishing, and the knife slipped," he said, through gritted teeth.

"Well, let's take a look."

George removed the gauze he'd been using to compress the wound. Gingerly inspecting the site, Charlotte could tell it was deep, but because the blood was being controlled and not gushing, the femoral artery was probably all right.

Rosie came back into the room.

Charlotte glanced over her shoulder. "I need ten ccs of lidocaine."

"Yes. Right away." Rosie skittered away to the locked medicine cabinet to prepare the local anesthesia.

"I don't like needles," Wavell murmured grumpily.

"I know, buddy, but this needle will numb your wound and I'll be able to stitch it up without you feeling a thing."

"Okay." Wavell pursed his lips. "I can handle it."

Charlotte smiled and ruffled his hair. "You're being very brave." She took the syringe from Rosie and injected around the laceration. "Tell me when you can't feel it and I'll stitch it up."

"Okay." Wavell nodded.

"He's okay, then?" Sam Agluclark asked warily.

"He'll be fine. He didn't cut the artery. Once we sew up his wound he'll need to rest for a couple of days."

"Can't feel it." Wavell slurred slightly.

"Good stuff." Sam was obviously relieved as he looked down at his son.

Rosie handed her a tray with everything she'd need for stitches. Charlotte thoroughly irrigated and cleaned out his cut with saline and Betadine, because she didn't think a knife for gutting fish was exactly clean.

Once she'd thoroughly inspected the site, she began to close the wound with sutures. Wavell didn't make a fuss but held perfectly still as she washed the suture site in more Betadine and packed it with gauze. In fact, Wavell was drifting off from the anesthesia.

"He's all done. I think it's best if you let him have a rest here. I'll get you some painkillers for later. He's to keep his leg elevated and come back in five days to get the sutures removed. No more fishing for a bit. He's lucky it didn't do more damage."

"Thanks, Doc Charley," Sam said.

Charlotte nodded and disposed of the syringes and gloves in the medical waste. Rosie and George cleaned up the rest of the stuff to send for sterilization.

"I'll help you take Wavell home in a couple of hours, Sam," George said. "Why don't you hit the hay, too, Doc Charley? You look beat."

"Thanks, George. I think I will." Charlotte washed up, and then headed back to her office. She was beat. It'd been a long, emotionally draining day. The office was dark and she gently rapped on the door, but there was no answer. Peeking inside, she spied Quinn slumped on the old worn couch. He didn't look comfortable, couldn't be comfortable. She'd crashed on that sofa many a time. And she was a lot smaller than him and even she couldn't fit quite right on it.

The name of the Couch of Gibraltar, as Quinn so lovingly called it, suited it. Although, if her memory served her correctly, she and Quinn had done more than just sleep on that couch when they had been in med school.

Charlotte smiled. He always looked so innocent like this. Too bad his acerbic wit didn't match the angelic impression he gave when he was asleep.

He had been a bit of a wild boy in college. Whereas she'd been quiet and studious, working her way through school on scholarships and odd jobs.

They were such opposites.

What did I ever see in him?

She knew exactly. He was exciting, sexy, thrilling. When he'd first walked into anatomy class with such an air of confidence, it had been like she'd been woken up from a daze. From the moment her dad had died she'd thrown herself into her work, studying, getting the best grades so she could tread in her father's footsteps. She'd ignored guys, had never gone on dates or had a hobby.

Then Quinn Devlyn had waltzed into her life and she'd found herself yearning for more. He had been talented and passionate about his work. Although animal attraction and mind-blowing sex was not what one should base a relationship on. She'd learned that the hard way. Case in point: when she'd needed him most, as she'd lain in that hospital bed after the miscarriage, he hadn't been there in the way she'd needed him to be.

He'd gone to New York to pursue a career in neonatal surgery and she had come here to take over where her father had left off, as a general practitioner in a remote community. What she'd set out to do the moment she'd had to say goodbye to her dad.

Charlotte shook her head, dispelling the painful memory, and then frowned as she looked at Quinn again. This forced cohabitation for the sake of Mentlana was going to test her to the very limits. She tiptoed over to her desk and wrote a note for him, telling him where he could find her. Then she pulled out an afghan and covered him up, but as she bent over to straighten the blanket, which had bunched up on one side, she caught sight of the scars on his right hand.

Surgical scars.

What had happened to him?

From the patterns of the scars it was as though his hand had been broken, severely. He'd had what appeared to be multiple orthopedic surgeries.

The blood drained from her face and she straightened,

backing away from him. What if he couldn't hold a scalpel? That thought was too terrifying.

He can operate. He has to be able to.

If he couldn't, Mentlana's life was at risk. Was he really that arrogant about his surgical abilities?

Yes.

She dismissed the idea. He had to be able to, or he wouldn't have a license and he wouldn't have come. He would've told her the truth.

Really?

Her throat constricted, her stomach knotted with dread. Charlotte backed out of the room and shut the door behind her. She wanted to believe Quinn was still the best fetal surgeon, but her instincts told her he was hiding something, while her heart, her traitorous heart, wanted to give him the benefit of the doubt.

Surgeons have had their hands injured before and had still been able to operate, but for the life of her she couldn't recall a single name of a surgeon who had done so. Neonatal surgeons needed steady hands for their delicate work. Were Quinn's hands still steady?

Mentlana's baby was like blood to her, and Charlotte couldn't lose another child.

Instead of closing the connecting door between her home and the clinic, she left it slightly ajar, in case Quinn woke up.

Charlotte wandered over to her bookcase, where there was a picture of her father and herself. She took it down and held it, lovingly running her fingers over the glass, as if trying to reach through and touch his face once more.

Dr. Cecil James had been a brilliant surgeon in Toronto. An innovator, a lot like Quinn. But then he'd met a nurse, Amber Lees, who'd had the drive to help others. Her father had given up his practice and headed to the North with Amber, and then they'd had her.

Her father's love of the North, even after the loss of his wife, had been instilled deep into Charlotte's being.

She set the picture back on the shelf and rubbed the ache forming in the back of her neck, trying not to think about the prospect of losing someone else she loved, because if Quinn failed it would be her fault for bringing him up here.

Dammit.

She shouldn't trust him. She couldn't. He'd deceived and hurt her before.

And she wouldn't let him do that to her again.

CHAPTER FIVE

"*Quinn.*"

He woke with a start at the faint whisper of his name. When he prized his eyes open he realized he was in a bed and he hadn't the foggiest idea how he'd ended up there. As he surveyed the room he realized he was in a king-size bed, and the walls were covered in rich cherrywood paneling. Like something found on a fine estate. How had he ended up here? The last thing he recalled was sitting down on the old brown couch in Charlotte's office, waiting for her to come back and take him to her home.

Quinn rubbed his eyes, trying to bring them into focus in the dim light of the room, but everything remained an unfocused haze.

"Quinn." Charlotte seemed to appear from the gloom like an apparition. Quinn gasped at the sight of her, not because she was in his room but because of how she looked. Her red curls tumbled down loose over her creamy shoulders. As he let his gaze rove further down, his breath caught in his throat and his blood ignited into flames. She was wearing a long white silk negligee, slit to the thigh, cut very low and exposing the creamy tops of her breasts.

"Charlotte?" he asked, stupidly because he knew it was her. Who else could it be? He'd seen her in that negligee before, when they'd gone to Niagara Falls. Just thinking of that *night of passion fired his blood, and it seemed like a lifetime ago when he'd experienced such a rush, such a hunger for her.*

Quinn shifted and realized he was wearing nothing but a sheet draped across his hips. What'd happened to his clothes?

Who cared?

Had Charlotte undressed him? The thought aroused him. God, he wanted her.

Badly.

"I hope you don't mind," she said, as if reading his mind. She moved closer to the bed but stayed just out of reach. "I took the liberty of undressing you."

Was she crazy?

"No, I don't mind in the least."

A devilish smile crept across her face as she moved to the end of the bed. "I'm so glad you came here, Quinn."

"And I'm glad you asked me."

Quinn got up and moved toward her, closing the distance between them. He took her tiny hand in his. It was so small and delicate. He entwined her slender fingers in his and could feel her pulse racing as he let his thumb stroke her wrist.

"Have you missed me, Quinn?" She bit her bottom lip and then smoothed back the hair from his forehead. "Please, tell me you have." Charlotte pressed her body against his, just a thin piece of fabric separating them.

So close.

Her lips brushed against his throat. Just a simple touch of softness against his neck caused his blood to burn with the fires of a thousand suns. A groan rumbled deep in his chest and he slipped his arms around her waist, holding her close.

"Quinn, have you missed me?" she asked again.

Had he? Or was it just in this moment of lust, his need for her that made him want to drop down on his knees and pour out his heart to her.

Yes. He'd missed her, with every fiber of his being. "Charlotte..." But even in his dreams the words wouldn't come out.

"Kiss me," she whispered, her voice husky with promise. Quinn leaned in.

A draft of cold air startled him awake. Pain traveled up his neck, resulting in a pounding headache at the back of his skull. Quinn glanced down and let out a groan of dismay when he caught sight of lavender.

"God." He scrubbed his hand over his face, stubble scratching his palm. It'd been a dream. The whole thing. Of course it had been a dream. For one thing, he doubted she had a king-size bed and cherrywood paneling in her home. Also, Charlotte wouldn't have come to him, not after what had passed between them five years ago, and this wasn't the first time he'd had this dream, either.

When he first left her he'd dreamt of her over and over again. He'd tried to banish the ghost of her with nameless women, but it hadn't worked. Instead, he'd focused on work. The dreams had faded and hadn't come back so often. In fact, he hadn't had such a vivid fantasy of Charlotte in a long time. He almost wished he hadn't woken up, that he'd been allowed to savor the moment and be with her once more, even if only in a dream, because the love they'd shared once was only that, now.

A dream.

Quinn got up, his body stiff and sore from his sojourn on the sofa. Sleeping on a stone floor would've been preferable to the couch that time had forgotten. His bad hand was numb. He flexed it and the joints cracked. It was his own fault. He'd planned to do his exercises last night but had forgotten.

He shook his hand, trying to get feeling back into it, and then headed out of the office. There was a slightly open door and he headed towards it, following the rich scent of coffee in the air. Quinn paused in the doorway of a small apartment, his breath catching in his throat.

Charlotte was puttering around the kitchen. Her red hair

wasn't loose but was pulled back with an elastic tie. The silky negligee had been replaced with a short, pink cotton nightie covered with garish red hearts. The nightie did have an advantage over the lingerie in his dream, for when she reached up into the cupboard he got a glimpse of her bare, round bottom.

Blood rushed straight from his head to his groin. Charlotte's bottom was like two round, ripe peaches ready for picking. He wanted to squeeze them and knead them with his bare hands.

Calm down.

Only, he couldn't. He remembered the first time he'd seen her, bent over her books, twirling her red curls around her finger and totally engrossed in the text. She'd seemed oblivious to the world around her. The only female who hadn't fawned over him because of his money or his looks. It had intrigued him.

It had been like a game, wooing her. He'd wanted to be the one to capture her, and he had.

As she had captured his heart.

Only he'd never let her know that because he hadn't understood love. How could he, with parents who had shown him not one iota of affection while he'd been growing up?

Charlotte had, though. He missed that.

He leaned against the door, causing it to squeak, and Charlotte whipped around, her cheeks staining with crimson as their gazes locked.

"Quinn, you're…you're up."

"Did you forget about me?"

"No." She glanced down and her face paled. She started yanking on the hem of her nightgown as if trying to make it longer, but to no avail.

Quinn didn't mind in the least.

"I think you did," he teased.

Charlotte rolled her eyes. "Did you spend the whole night on the couch?"

"Yes." He rubbed the crick in his neck. "It's been a long

time since I passed out on that thing. I remember it being a bit more comfortable."

"It was never comfortable. You're just older."

Quinn chuckled and took a seat in one of the mismatched chairs surrounding her retro vinyl kitchen table. She slid a cup of coffee in front of him. "Thanks."

"Are you hungry?"

"Starving." He took a sip of coffee, savoring the warmth spreading down his throat and chipping away at the bitter cold that crept in from outside.

"Why are you shivering?" she asked. "It's not cold in here."

"I can feel the cold seeping in."

Charlotte rolled her eyes again and shook her head. "Pansy. I'm not surprised you're hungry. You didn't eat yesterday."

"Au contraire. I had a delightful five-dollar packet of peanuts on my flight to Iqaluit." His stomach growled. "But I'll take you up on your offer of breakfast."

"Good choice. But first I think I'll change."

"Why? It makes no difference to me."

Charlotte blushed again. "All the same."

Quinn watched her head down the hall, savoring the sight of her thighs. Thighs he wished were parted for him right now. He shifted in his seat, his erection pushing against his scrubs. It was like he was some kind of hard-up adolescent again.

Charlotte returned with her nightgown covered up with a long terrycloth bathrobe. It was a shame. He'd seen her in less, but that short cotton nightie was just as appealing as the silken lingerie of his fantasies. At least the robe was much better than the scrubs he was wearing, which did nothing to hide his arousal.

"Are my bags here?" he asked.

"Just down the hall. The door to the left."

"I think I'll change." He slipped out of the seat as discreetly as he could. His room was easily found and he removed the scrubs, tossing them in the nearby hamper. There was a small basin in the bedroom and he washed his face. He'd shower later, after he'd had something to eat. The scent of bacon drifted down the hall, followed by the familiar sizzle from the stove that made his stomach growl again.

Loudly.

"Just in time." Charlotte grinned as he entered the kitchen and sat back down. She slid bacon and a fried egg onto a plate and set it down in front of him. Quinn couldn't remember the last time he'd had a good home-cooked breakfast like this.

Probably the last time I was with her.

When he'd moved to Manhattan he hadn't cooked at home. Even during the last two years in Toronto he hadn't spent his free time mastering the culinary arts. He'd spent his free time wining and dining, until the accident. After the accident he'd started doing photography, but even then he'd been out taking pictures, not lounging around at home where the hum of silence made him feel utterly alone.

The fork dropped out of his hand and clattered against the plate, his hand frozen and numb. He looked up at Charlotte but her back was turned as she continued frying eggs.

Quinn rubbed his fingers until he could feel them again, wiggling them slowly. He'd just picked up his fork as Charlotte sat down across from him with her plate. He would have to do his exercise later.

After breakfast.

"I could do with a shower," he said, just to break the silence. "That won't be a problem or interrupt your clinic or any appointments, will it?"

She shook her head. "No. Why should it? Anyway, it's Saturday and the clinic is officially closed, so no one should bother you."

Silence descended heavily on Quinn as they ate.

"And what will you do today?" he asked casually, because he had no idea what he was going to do to pass the time. Other than maybe venture out and take some pictures of snow.

"Oh, this and that. I'm always on duty." Charlotte finished eating and took her plate over to the sink.

"Don't you ever get a break?"

"Not really. I'm the only physician around these parts."

"Haven't you ever thought of hiring another doctor?"

Charlotte's brow furrowed in thought. "Yes, and I have tried, believe me. Mostly it's recent grads who come up, but they don't stay long. They stay long enough to get another job."

"Government incentive, then, eh?"

Charlotte nodded. "You've got it. They work the hours required to get med school paid for and then they're off to greener pastures."

"Smart kids."

Charlotte's eyes turned flinty and her spine straightened. "You think so?"

"I do."

"Is that why you came up to Yellowknife with me after residency?"

"Yes." There was no point in hiding the truth from her. His parents hadn't supported him through medical school. Even though he was their only child, they'd still felt he shouldn't have any handouts. When he'd followed Charlotte up to the wilds of the Canadian North it had been for purely selfish reasons and he'd told her why when they'd first got together. Charlotte must've forgotten. However, his presence here this time was because of her.

"I see," she said. Her lips were pressed together in a thin line. He'd seen that look before. She was not pleased with him.

"Look, it's the truth and I'm sorry, but I was always up front about that. Perhaps you forgot?"

"No, you're right. You were up front and you had no qualms about leaving when you were presented with an out."

"You could've come with me," he whispered.

"I didn't want to. I love the North. This was the path I wanted to take."

"I know. I make no apologies for the reasons I came to the North."

"Yes, to flesh out your curriculum vitae. I'm painfully aware of that and don't need the reminder." Charlotte snorted.

"It's a good solid plan and looks great on the résumé."

She shook her head. "Is that the only thing that matters to you?"

"My career, you mean?"

"Of course. What else would I be talking about?" Charlotte set down the dish towel she'd been holding. "I don't want to get into this with you. I already know how you feel about it."

"I'm sorry that my career was important, but it should be the top priority for any physician. Hell, for anyone who busted their ass studying in a tough industry. I'm sorry I thought of my career. Is that what you want to hear? You stayed up here and that was for your career, so why should I feel bad about going after what I wanted?"

He regretted the words the moment they tumbled past his lips. Charlotte bit her lip and shook her head, tossing the dish towel on the counter.

"You're right. You shouldn't. I'm going to go do some paperwork. I've fallen a bit behind. Make yourself at home."

Quinn watched her disappear through her bedroom door. It closed behind her with a thud.

You're an idiot, Devlyn.

He was standing stubborn on the pulpit and ideals he had preached so often. Advice he gave to fledgling surgeons in the field of obstetrics, advice that gave him nothing and no one.

He really did have the personality of a sledgehammer, most days. Pain shot up his arm and he flexed his hand.

Fleshing out his résumé wasn't the only reason he'd come to the North. Charlotte had been the reason. The true reason, and he'd blown it.

He shook the morbid memories away, suddenly craving a

drink. Only he knew Nunavut was a dry territory. Not a drop could be brought in. He'd watched the Mounties confiscate liquor from some guys who had been on their way up for some ice fishing in Iqaluit.

Quinn wandered over to the fridge and opened it. Orange juice beckoned him. He pulled it out and resisted taking a swig straight from the carton. Instead, after opening several cupboards, he found a glass. He poured himself some and drank the tangy juice down in one gulp. It burned his esophagus. Since his accident he was a little bit more sensitive to acidic things, but the burn felt good.

The burn helped him forget.

"You've already made up your mind. You don't need my approval." She was lying in the bed, so pale against the crisp white hospital bedding. The IV was still embedded in her vein, giving a transfusion. She was pallid as she stared at the far wall, not responding to his announcement about going to Manhattan to a lucrative job.

Didn't she understand? Life would be better for both of them.

"Charlotte..."

"No." She turned and looked at him, her face devoid of expression. "No."

The sound of shattering glass shook away the ghosts of his past and he stared in disbelief at the shards on her linoleum floor. His bad hand had frozen in a crab-like vise.

Quinn cursed wearily. He cleaned up the shards of glass and then headed over to the computer in the corner and wiggled the mouse. The monitor came on with a faint hum and he went directly to the folder on the desktop. Tikivik, Mentlana. He clicked on the pictures and brought up the multiple sonograms of Mentlana's baby.

Although the baby was thriving, the lesions in the paracheynma were quite visible.

Dammit.

If the lesions continued to grow then fluid would begin to collect in the lungs and he would be forced to perform in utero surgery.

Quinn rubbed his eyes, trying to shake the sleep out of them. He wasn't sure if he was up to this in these conditions, but he'd promised Charlotte. It was the least he could to do make up for the hurt he'd caused her five years ago.

Perhaps I won't have to perform the surgery.

Perhaps he could get Mentlana down to Toronto where he *could* perform the surgery, and if not him, someone just as good as him.

He'd see to it personally.

When Charlotte came out of her bedroom, Quinn was nowhere to be seen and even though she was frustrated with him, she wondered where he'd got to. She snuck off to her office, intending to spend the day doing some administrative stuff.

For an hour Charlotte stared at the paperwork. She'd been holding the same manila folder for what seemed like forever.

"This is ridiculous." She dropped the folder back onto the large amount of files teetering on her desk.

Get a grip.

She'd known when she'd called Quinn up here that it would be hard to deal with him. She'd known that, but she'd been willing to ignore her own hurt feelings, her attraction to him for the sake of Mentlana and her baby.

Why was she mad that he'd followed his dreams, just like she'd chosen to stay in the North?

Because it broke your heart that he left you.

Yet here she was, hiding away in her office instead of doing what she always did on a lazy Saturday morning, which was slumming around her house and enjoying the solitude. But she didn't want to appear like a bum in front of him.

So, what? She shouldn't give two hoots that he was in her

house. She was the reason he'd come up here, so why was she allowing Quinn Devlyn to dictate her schedule?

I'm not going to let him.

Charlotte stood up and marched purposefully, head held high, to her house. She opened the door with a "look at me, here I am" attitude and was stunned that Quinn was nowhere in the vicinity of her living area. His plate was still on the table, her carton of orange juice was sitting on the counter and her computer's tropical-fish screensaver bubbled with activity.

"Quinn?" she called out cautiously, but there was no answer.

Great. She mustered up the courage to face him, to show him that she didn't care he was here. To prove to him that he didn't affect her anymore. And he wasn't even here to see it.

Blast.

Charlotte ran her fingers through her tangle of curls and proceeded into the kitchen.

Just like him, leaving a mess behind.

His residence, before they'd roomed together, had been known as the sty for very good reason. The man was a meticulous surgeon but a veritable pig, though Rosie would say the same about her filing habits.

She picked up the orange-juice carton and shook it slightly. There was a bit of juice in it, but when she peered inside there was barely any worth keeping. Except orange juice was damn expensive up here. She'd treated herself to this carton. Charlotte chugged the remainder of the juice so she wouldn't waste a single drop.

A smile tugged the corners of her lips briefly as she recalled the numerous arguments they'd had over his propensity to leave barely a dribble in the bottom of a carton.

The last time, they'd fought over a carton of eggnog during Christmas and they'd ended up making love under the Christmas tree.

Her pulse raced as that memory replayed in her head like a

cozy movie. It'd been so long since she had thought about it. Her heart began to beat faster and butterflies began to swirl around in her stomach.

Damn.

Charlotte crumpled the carton in her hand before tossing it out under the sink. She slammed the cupboard shut, angry at herself for letting herself *feel* this way about Quinn again.

"Domestic duties prevail over paperwork?"

Charlotte startled and spun around. He was inches from her, half-naked. The scent of his body wash was masculine and spicy as she inhaled deeply.

"Uh—uh," she stuttered, and backed up to the counter. She gripped the cheap melamine as if her life depended on it.

"What?" he asked, cocking an eyebrow. "I thought I'd shower and wash off that certain smell that seems to permeate most planes."

Charlotte couldn't think straight as her gaze trailed hungrily down his body, abruptly ending at the tropical beach towel tied around his waist.

His hair curled and glistened with drops of moisture. She ran her tongue over her lips. Oh, how she wanted to run her tongue over his chest, particularly around his nipples, which she knew were particularly sensitive.

"Charlotte, you're starting to scare me."

She shook her head. "Sorry." She turned back to the sink and turned on the faucet, hoping the rushing water would drown out the erratic beat of her pulse and make him move away. "Yeah, going to do some dishes."

Only he didn't move away. He moved closer, and the heat of his body permeated her back, through the thick sweater and turtleneck she was wearing. Gooseflesh broke across her skin and she held her breath.

"Is there anything I can help you with, Charlotte?" he asked, his breath branding her flesh at the base of her neck.

Charlotte turned around again, staring deep into his deep

brown eyes. *Oh, God.* She was falling again. She had no strength when it came to him. He still made her weak at the knees.

"I…"

"What do you need, Charlotte?" He reached out and ran his knuckles against her cheek. "Tell me what you need. I'd do anything for you. You know that."

CHAPTER SIX

HE WAS SO close to her that her heart was racing. Her traitorous body was reacting to him.

"Charlotte," he whispered, and reached out to touch her.

"Hey, Doc… Whoa…sorry!"

Quinn jumped back and Charlotte saw George, a shocked look on his face, standing dumbstruck between her clinic and her home. In his hand was a plastic bag bulging with what looked like blue-and-green scrubs.

"George, come in. Dr. Devlyn and I were just talking about…" She trailed off, her brain totally blank, and Quinn just cleared his throat. He was absolutely no help.

George blushed and looked away, staring at the ceiling. "Sorry, Doc Charley. I should've knocked."

"No, it's okay, George. I was just doing dishes." She pushed past Quinn, feeling humiliated that George had walked in on them in such a compromising position. George would definitely blab about this to Mentlana and she'd never be able to live it down. Ignoring what had happened, she feigned nonchalance. "Is something wrong, George?"

"Nothing. I just brought some scrubs and came to remind you about a certain appointment today." He pointed at his watch. "You didn't forget, right?"

"Shoot," she cursed. She had. Today was her scheduled checkup on Anernerk Kamuk, Cape Recluse's oldest woman and George's grandmother. The woman who had taken in Charlotte when her father had died. Anernerk would certainly have something to say if she was late for the checkup. "I'll be ready in a few, George."

George nodded, a funny smile plastered across his face. "Okay, Doc Charley." His dark gaze landed on Quinn. "Dr. Devlyn, pleasure to see you again."

Charlotte could hear his chuckles as he closed the door to her clinic.

Dammit.

"What did you forget?" Quinn asked.

"Today is my bi-weekly check on Cape Recluse's oldest resident. She's one hundred and one, and an artist."

Quinn's eyes flew open in surprise. "One hundred and one?"

"Hard of hearing, Devlyn?" She grabbed her parka off the coat rack, but a smile tweaked at the corners of her lips.

"I'm sorry. I'm amazed, frankly. In my line of work I don't meet many people who've passed the century mark."

"It's the fresh air up here." She fished around in her pocket for the keys to her snowmobile.

"You said she's an artist. Would I know her work?" Quinn asked.

"Doubtful. Unless you're an expert in traditional Inukti-tut artwork."

"Ah, no." Quinn rubbed the back of his neck. "Don't get me wrong, though. I've seen some really intriguing native art in New York."

"Her name is Anernerk Kamuk. Does that name ring a bell in the 'it' crowd of Manhattan?"

"Not in the art scene, no, but didn't you live with her after your father died?"

Charlotte was impressed. "Oh, so you actually did listen to me when I spoke."

Quinn rolled his eyes. "Give me some credit."

Charlotte blushed. "Sorry. Yes. She's George and Mentlana's grandmother and she took me in when my dad died. Look, I have to get going or she'll raise a stink."

"Can I come?"

Charlotte paused in the middle of rummaging through her bag and stared at Quinn. "You...you want to come?"

Quinn ran a hand through his damp hair. "Yeah. If that's okay?"

She blinked in disbelief. "Sure. Can you be ready in ten minutes? I have to collect a few things from the clinic. Dress warmly and I'll meet you outside."

"Excellent. See you in ten."

Charlotte watched him pad off towards her guest bedroom. When the door shut she shook herself out of her daze and headed into her clinic to collect her bag and instruments. Actually, she was quite looking forward to seeing how Quinn dealt with Anernerk. He'd never had the best people skills when dealing with non-medical professionals, and Anernerk was a bit of a handful at the best of times.

She was going to eat Quinn alive and that thought gave Charlotte a secret thrill. It would be an entertaining appointment, that was for sure.

As she shoved Anernerk's file in her rucksack, Quinn entered her office. He was, surprisingly, kitted out in appropriate cold-weather gear and she was impressed he'd done his homework before coming up here.

"Ready?" she asked with a bit of trepidation.

"Whenever you are."

Charlotte nodded and led him outside. George was waiting on his snowmobile, ready to lead the way through the snowdrifts to the cabin on the outskirts of Cape Recluse, where Anernerk lived and still worked as an important Inuk artist.

"Hey, Dr. Devlyn. Good to see you're going with us. Grandma sure likes to get her hands on fresh meat." George chuckled again and, despite the bitter cold, Charlotte felt her face heat with a blush.

She sent a silent warning of *shut up* to George as she pulled her rucksack on. Charlotte mounted her snowmobile and glanced over her shoulder at Quinn, who was still standing by the door, shifting from foot to foot.

"Nervous?" she asked, pointedly staring at his shuffling feet.

"No. I'm freezing out here. I'm trying to keep the circulation going in my lower extremities."

Charlotte bit back her smile. "Well, let's get going. It's freaking cold out here."

Quinn chuckled and climbed on behind her. His body nestled against her back, his arms wrapped around her waist. Even though many layers of thick clothing and snowsuits separated them, she squirmed in her seat. She was suddenly very warm and it wasn't her winter clothing that was causing it.

"Are you sure you're not nervous, Devlyn?" she teased, trying to dispel her own nervousness at having him so close to her.

"Not in the least," he said. Although something in his voice told her she wasn't the only one feeling a bit edgy about being so close together again. She smiled and revved the engine. It felt so good to have his arms wrapped around her.

"Hold on to your hat."

"Wagons, ho," George shouted above the roar of the Bombardier machines, pumping his fist into the air. They took off across the snow, northeast toward the sea and Anernerk's home.

Charlotte had tried time and time again to get Anernerk to move closer to the clinic, into the main town with one of her children. Anernerk refused on the grounds that the spirits had told her that in order to paint, she needed to see where the sea met the sky without the clutter of town in the way.

A thin column of smoke rose in the air as they crested a

bank of snow. Charlotte let out an inward sigh of relief, glad to know Anernerk was still alive. Anernerk also refused most modern technologies and didn't have a phone.

Anernerk's little red house on high stilts looked warm and inviting. This was where Charlotte had lived when her father had died. This was home. Charlotte parked her snowmobile beside George's. George was humming and grinned at Quinn as he stumbled off the back of her snowmobile.

"Your first time, Dr. Devlyn?"

"On a snowmobile? Yes." Quinn chuckled. "I guess you could say I am a virgin in that respect."

George let out a large guffaw. "Well, you're a virgin no more, Dr. Devlyn. You're officially deflowered."

Charlotte rolled her eyes at the men's childish banter. The door to Anernerk's door swung open quickly to reveal a little wrinkled face peering outside. Dark eyes flashed under a mass of wrinkles.

"Are you just going to stand out there all day? I'm not going getting any younger, you know," she called down from her porch high above them.

"Oh, hush, Anernerk. We're coming, we're coming."

Quinn was stunned by the Inuk woman. Though she was a mass of wrinkles and weathered skin, he wouldn't have guessed from her fluid movements that she was over a century.

Anernerk's beetle-black gaze rested on him. There was a twinkle to them and a smile tugged at the corners of her lips. The intensity of her perusal unnerved Quinn slightly. It was as if the old woman was peering deep into his soul.

"Who've you brought to visit, Doc Charley?" Anernerk asked.

"A friend of mine from med school. He's come here to take care of Mentlana."

The woman's eyes widened. "Mentlana? Well, this is good

news indeed." Anernerk stepped aside as George and Charlotte crossed the threshold into her home.

Quinn followed up the steps, seeking the warmth that emanated from the wood stove in the center of the large room of Anernerk's clapboard shanty, which, like most of the other homes, was tethered down and on stilts. He peeled off his coat and hung it on a peg near the wood stove.

He rubbed his hands together, fast. Even though he had been wearing thick mittens, which the man at the wilderness store had assured him would keep out the cold, the bitter temperature of the top of the world still clung to his skin, sending its frosty tendrils deep into his body. His hands ached and he couldn't get the feeling back into them, no matter how hard he rubbed.

The hairs on the back of his neck stood on end and he had the sense that someone was staring at him. Quinn craned his neck and caught Anernerk's gaze. She was watching him, a strange look on her face. His face heated and he slid his hands into his pockets.

"Anernerk, how are you feeling today?" Charlotte asked.

Anernerk snorted. "How do you think I feel, Doc Charley? Cranky. I'm cranky today."

George, who Quinn had lost sight of, came in through another door on the far side of the room with a load of firewood in his arms.

"She's always cranky, Doc. You should know that by now."

Charlotte smiled patiently as she rolled up the woman's sleeve and pulled out a blood-pressure monitor. The rip of Velcro echoed in Anernerk's sparse cabin, but it was then that Quinn glanced at the walls and realized what he was actually looking at.

"Oh, my God," he whispered.

He moved closer to the nearest wall, enraptured by the thick, bold lines and swirl of primeval colors.

"Pretty cool, eh, Doc Dev?" George said.

"It's…it's like nothing I've ever seen."

Anernerk chuckled over the top of the steady pumping of the blood-pressure cuff. "I think your friend fancies my art, Charlotte."

Quinn spun round. "You've done all of this? This is your art?"

Anernerk nodded slowly, grinning, obviously pleased with his awe. "I was taught by my grandfather. A shaman. Way back when Nunavut was just a lowly outpost on the far reaches of the Northwest Territories and Iqaluit was known as Frobisher Bay."

"I've seen some of these in The Met."

Charlotte grinned. "Yes, Anernerk's art is world renowned. I told you she was an artist."

"Yes, but I had no idea she was this prolific. I can't believe I'm standing here in front of the originals."

"Of course." Anernerk rubbed her hand as Charlotte removed the cuff. "Not so hard next time, Charlotte. There's no meat left on these bones."

"Hush," Charlotte chastised gently.

Quinn found himself drawn immediately to one particular painting, one that featured a man and a woman. The man was harpooning a walrus and the woman was sewing and casting the man evil looks. He felt a bit dizzy and sick staring at it and he didn't know why.

"Hold tight, Anernerk. I have to sterilize this," Quinn heard Charlotte say, and he glanced at her briefly to see her head towards the kitchen, which was tucked off in the corner behind some swing doors.

Quinn tore his gaze away and came face-to-face with Anernerk. She was staring at him.

"I see you're particularly drawn to the depiction of the obstinate man. Do you know the story?"

"No, I don't."

"Come sit by the fire, Dr. Devlyn. I have some liniment for your hands."

"What are you talking about?"

"You may be able to fool other people with your walls, Dr. Devlyn, but you don't fool me."

"I don't?"

Anernerk shook her head. "Come, and I'll tell you all about the obstinate man."

Quinn didn't move and Anernerk rolled her eyes.

"Dr. Devlyn, I may be older than time itself but I don't bite…much." She grinned, displaying her missing teeth. She looked like those typical old witches he used to be terrified of as a child, but there was no malice about Anernerk Kamuk. He nodded and allowed her to lead him to two rockers that sat near the wood stove.

Quinn sat across from her.

"I think this tale will hit you personally, Dr. Devlyn. I think you'll find similarities between your destiny and the destiny of my dear Charlotte." Anernerk reached down in a big basket, which was overflowing with various yarns and knitting needles. She pulled out a dark innocuous bottle with no label.

"How do you know about me and Charlotte?" Quinn asked, intrigued.

Anernerk's black eyes twinkled. "There are no secrets in Cape Recluse, Dr. Devlyn."

"Are you some kind of mind-reader or shaman yourself, Anernerk?"

She raised a thick gray eyebrow. "Are you crazy? Of course not. Just because I'm Inuk doesn't mean I can converse with Nanook of the North or anything." She laughed. "Besides, I talk to Mentlana."

"Mentlana is on bed rest. She's not supposed to leave Cape Recluse. Is she coming out here, Anernerk? I need to know."

"No, of course not!" Anernerk chuckled conspiratorially and pulled out a small phone from her trouser pocket. "Shh.

Don't tell. It'll ruin the whole illusion for George and Charlotte." She hid the phone back in her pocket. "Besides, I like their visits."

Quinn couldn't help but laugh. "You have a smartphone?"

"How else do I keep in touch with my agent? The laptop is in my underwear drawer. Ain't nobody going in there. Now, where was I?"

"You were going to tell me about the obstinate man and the significance it plays in respect to me and Charlotte."

"Give me your hands," Anernerk ordered.

Quinn held them out. Her hands were rough but strong. She undid the bottle and poured the thick corn-syrupy-looking liquid into his hand. It instantly warmed as it touched him. Anernerk began to rub his shattered hand vigorously and the aches and pains began to fade as the old woman's liniment began to work some kind of magic on him. It was better than the exercise regime his physiotherapist forced on him.

"There once was a very stubborn man. Not unlike yourself, Dr. Devlyn. His wife lost their child, but instead of letting her mourn he made her work for him. As she worked, the Moon Man's dog came out and attacked this obstinate man for making his wife work before her mourning time was done.

"The man overcame the dog, killing him. The Moon Man came and fought the obstinate man, but again he was no match for such stubbornness. The obstinate man won. The Moon Man invited him to join him at his home, but told him to take the dark side of the rock and not come around the easier sunny side, or he would lose his heart."

"Lose his heart?"

Anernerk smiled and continued rubbing his hand. "The easiest path is not always the wisest, Dr. Devlyn."

"Is that so?" Quinn wanted to change the subject, but he had the feeling he wouldn't be able to.

"So the obstinate man came around the sunny side and saw an old woman sitting there, sharpening a blade. He thought he could overcome the old woman. She was weak and feeble, whereas he was strong, but he overestimated his ability and lost consciousness. When he came to, his heart had been torn from him.

"The Moon Man saved him, returning to him his broken, tattered heart. It was then that the stubborn man saw the evil, dark thoughts coming from his wife and what he had done to her, how he had hurt her by forcing her to work before her mourning time was done."

Quinn's throat constricted and he glanced towards the kitchen. He could hear water boiling and in his mind's eye he could envision Charlotte cleaning the instruments thoroughly. Did she have dark thoughts about him?

He was pretty certain she did.

"No. You're being stubborn, Quinn. Why do I have to give up my life here?"

"What kind of life is this?"

"A good life."

"We can have a good life in Manhattan."

Tears ran down her face and she turned her head away. *"No."*

"How do your hands feel now, Dr. Devlyn?"

Quinn shook himself out of his stupor and flexed his hands. They were warm, pliable.

"Ahem."

He looked up to see Charlotte leaning against a post, expressions of confusion and intrigue playing across her face.

"Thank you, Mrs. Kamuk."

He stood up and jammed his hands quickly in his pockets.

Anernerk chuckled and then whispered under her breath, "Stubborn, Dr. Devlyn. So stubborn." She looked back at Charlotte. "So, are you ready for your quart of blood, Doc Charlotte?"

Charlotte *tsked* and Quinn moved away so Charlotte could do her work. Quinn watched in admiration. She was so sure of herself now, and though he hadn't seen it at the time, this had been the right path for her.

The path away from him.

CHAPTER SEVEN

CHARLOTTE WAS CLEANING up the rest of her instruments and tucking away the specimens from Anernerk. The resident old coot was back in her rocking chair, knitting and telling stories as her needles clicked together. George was sitting beside her, listening to her and laughing.

Sometimes Charlotte wondered if it was George, the overly concerned grandson, who insisted on these visits out here. Everyone in Cape Recluse loved Anernerk.

Charlotte smiled as she watched the woman who had raised her for over a decade, warmth flooding her veins as she recalled all the good times she and Anernerk had shared. How Anernerk's entire family had welcomed her.

When her father had died she'd had no one. Her father had had no other family except distant cousins. It'd been the same on her mother's side. Charlotte often wondered if it was why her parents had been drawn to each other. Her parents had both been orphans.

As their daughter had become.

The only difference was that Charlotte had had people to love and take care of her. Her parents hadn't had someone like Anernerk to take them in.

She felt blessed.

Anernerk was as healthy as could be for someone over a century old. There was nothing to worry about in regard to the old woman's physical well-being. Charlotte was more worried about what she'd seen between Anernerk and Quinn. Anernerk had a way with people. She could win them over, charm them, and they ate up everything she said.

Even Quinn, who had never believed in all these old hokey remedies and anything even mildly spiritual in nature, especially when it came to medicine, had been mesmerized.

Charlotte had watched Anernerk rub his hands and she had also seen how quickly Quinn had hidden them and brushed off Anernerk when he'd realized she was standing there.

Why was he hiding it from her? What had happened to him?

It wasn't rocket science for Charlotte to figure out in ten seconds that he'd been injured, but he didn't seem bothered by it. Still, she needed to have a frank talk with him about the surgery.

Mentlana was not going to be used as a guinea pig to see if Quinn Devlyn's masterful surgical skills were still intact. There was a reason people donated their bodies to science.

Hell, there were dummies now that could be used to mimic surgery. He could practice on one of them, but not Mentlana.

Charlotte snapped her bag shut and wandered over to him. He was still standing in front of Anernerk's paintings. Staring at them in awe.

"I didn't think you were so interested in Inuktitut art, Quinn."

"I wasn't until I saw an auction at Christie's in Manhattan about four years ago. It was to raise money for a charity and Anernerk Kamuk's art was prominently featured. I didn't recognize the name when you said it. They raised over a million dollars that night and Anernerk's lithograph of Kagssagussuk accounted for a quarter of that million."

"Ah, so you became interested in it because of its worth."

Quinn looked at her, his gaze so intent it sent a shiver of delight down her back. He leaned in closer and she closed her eyes, reveling in the feel of his hot breath against her neck. "It was a beautiful piece. I was ignorant and had no idea."

Charlotte shrugged. "I'm impressed. But you don't know the stories related to them."

Quinn chuckled and moved away. "No, those I didn't know. That information is not readily available in Manhattan and I didn't have the time to really go searching. My practice was flourishing by then." His self-satisfied grin made her grind her teeth just a little.

She spun round. "Well, George, I think we've outstayed our welcome."

"You going?" Anernerk put down her knitting. "You just got here."

Charlotte grinned at her elderly patient. "Anernerk, we got here three hours ago."

Anernerk stood up. "I'll make you something to eat." She turned round and fixed her impenetrable gaze on Quinn. "How about muktuk, Dr. Devlyn? I can make you a nice meal of muktuk."

Quinn's eyes widened and he looked at Charlotte. Even though she was tempted to let him eat some blubber, which was what muktuk was, she wasn't that heartless. Charlotte shook her head subtly.

"Ah, thank you, Mrs. Kamuk, but I think just this time I am going to forgo your delicacy of muktuk," Quinn replied with grace.

Anernerk's eyes narrowed as she stared at Charlotte, then she crossed her arms and snorted. "All right. But at least it puts meat on your bones. Dr. Devlyn is too skinny for my liking."

"Hah!" George chuckled, jamming on his cap. "Meat on your bones, eh, Aanak? Hasn't seemed to do you any good."

Anernerk directed her wrath at George by slapping him across the back of the head.

"I thought her name was Anernerk?" Quinn whispered out of the side of his mouth.

"Aanak is the Inuk word for grandmother," Charlotte explained.

"Ah." Quinn nodded.

Charlotte stifled another laugh and Quinn looked a bit awestruck by it all. Then again, he didn't really have much interaction with others. Even when they had been together she wasn't absolutely sure if Quinn had had any *real* friends.

When they had been in medical school and interning, his whole life had been the hospital, and she'd never met his family. In fact, for a long time she hadn't thought he had any family as he rarely mentioned them. Then one day, after they had settled in Yellowknife, he'd shown up with two air tickets for Toronto. She had been going to fly out to Toronto to meet his mother and father, but two weeks before the flight she'd miscarried.

His father died. Was his mother still alive?

It made her pity him. She had lost the only parent she had known before she'd gone into med school, but she'd had the Tikiviks, she'd had Mentlana, she'd had a home.

Cape Recluse.

She had lived here for ten years before med school. It was why she'd wanted to become a physician and work in the northern communities. If her father had had access to a physician, he might not have died from the aneurysm that had claimed his life.

"Sorry, Aanak," George grumbled, rubbing the back of his head where Anernerk had cuffed him. He bent down and laid a kiss on Anernerk's cheek. Although Anernerk still looked a bit put out, Charlotte could tell she was mollified by George's apology. George snuck out the front door into the cold.

"It was a pleasure to meet you, Mrs. Kamuk."

"And you, Dr. Devlyn. I do hope I get to see you again before you leave us."

Quinn grinned and followed George outside. Anernerk turned her focused black gaze on Charlotte.

"I'll come out and see you again soon, Anernerk." Charlotte embraced the old woman.

"Find it somewhere in your heart to forgive him, Charlotte." Anernerk tucked Charlotte's red curls behind her ear. "He's a good man, just obstinate."

Charlotte's throat tightened and she fought back the tears that threatened to spill. "I'll see you in a couple of weeks."

Anernerk nodded. "You take my advice." She held out a bottle. Charlotte looked at the brown bottle in confusion. "Give it to Dr. Devlyn. He needs it. It will help him heal on the outside, anyway."

Charlotte nodded and stuffed the bottle in her pocket. "See you later."

Anernerk nodded, her eyes glistening as she hugged Charlotte tightly again.

George and Quinn were waiting for her, George on his snowmobile and Quinn shuffling back and forth in the cold, waiting for her.

She made sure her backpack was secure and climbed onto her snowmobile.

Anernerk poked her head out the door. "Next time you come I'm making Dr. Devlyn a nice big meal of muktuk, and there will be no refusal."

Quinn waved and Anernerk shut the door. "What the hell is muktuk?"

"Blubber," Charlotte replied, as she slid on her goggles. She glanced over her shoulder and saw Quinn's eyes widen.

"You're joking…right?"

Charlotte chuckled. "Nope."

"Good God!" Quinn made a choking sound, like he was going to retch.

George, sitting on the snowmobile beside them, grinned. "Aw, c'mon, Dr. Dev. It's not as bad as some of that stuff you hoity-toity physicians eat down there in Manhattan."

"Like what?" Quinn asked.

"Foie gras, caviar, tentacles." George made a wiggly motion with his hand and stuck out his tongue. "Gross."

Quinn laughed. "I'll have you know—"

"Enough!" Charlotte interrupted. "If you two have forgotten, it's below freezing out here. You can talk about strange gastronomical treats at the clinic, in the warmth. Right now, I'd really like to head back to Cape Recluse before the lab samples freeze." She turned and glared at George. "And if they do freeze, guess who's coming back to take them again?"

"Right you are, Doc Charley." George revved his snowmobile. "Let's go." He shot off west back towards town and Charlotte followed, trying to ignore Quinn's arms around her, his body pressed against her as she raced to get back to the warmth of her home and clinic.

Honestly. Men.

Quinn did take his debate about cuisine inside with George. He quite liked George, which was odd. Especially as he'd considered George competition when he'd first arrived, but Charlotte had quickly quelled any thoughts on that score. Now, George was like a buddy. Quinn knew he didn't make friends easily and didn't have many people he really considered friends. His parents hadn't encouraged any camaraderie in his childhood. Only competition.

The only real friend he'd made had been Charlotte, and look how that had turned out. He'd hurt her. Terribly.

The hum of the centrifuge echoed in the quiet clinic and he followed the noise to her little lab at the far corner of the building.

He paused in the doorway; she was hunched over the counter, her head down on her arms, watching the whirling of the machine.

He wished he had his camera on hand so he could capture this moment. She was so beautiful. Her red curls were tied back, except for one errant strand, which every so often she would blow out of her face. Quinn could remember lying in bed with her on their days off, when they'd had hours and no one to disturb them, and he would take that one curl and wrap it around his finger, as she had done that first time he'd seen her. It had been so soft and he'd felt so relaxed, so at home with her.

He'd never felt that way before meeting her.

His father had been a workaholic and the best damn cardio-thoracic surgeon in Toronto. It was ironic it had been a myo-cardial infarction that had killed him. Quinn's mother had set her son on a pedestal when he'd got into medical school at Harvard. She'd expected the same results as his father had achieved in his chosen field, not ever accepting any failure from him.

Quinn remembered how angry his mother had been when he had started dating Charlotte.

It had made him wonder, later, when he'd realized how foolish he had been to lose Charlotte, if his parents had ever truly loved each other.

Quinn hadn't realized it at the time, but Charlotte had made life worth living and he'd thrown it all away.

As if sensing his presence, she turned her head, her eyes widening when she saw him. She sat up and tucked the lock of hair behind her ear.

"Is something wrong, Quinn?"

"No... Yes."

"Is it something I can help you with?" There was a look of anticipation on her face, and she bit her lip, almost as if she was silently urging him to talk.

He clenched his fist, biting back the pain.

No.

"Just wanted to know what you wanted for dinner."

Charlotte chuckled. "Since when do you cook? Never, if I recall."

Quinn laughed and glanced down at the pristine tiled

floor. "I don't suppose there is any takeout in Cape Recluse, is there?"

Charlotte shook her head. "No takeout, but there is a diner. Would you like to go get some there?"

"As long as I'm not forced to eat that blubber stuff, sure."

Charlotte smiled, her grin lighting up the dimness of the lab. "Let me just put Anernerk's specimens away and we can grab something to eat."

Quinn tracked her movements. God, she was beautiful. Even though he knew the reasons why he had gone to Manhattan and that they'd made sense to him at the time, he now wondered why he'd left her behind.

You're an idiot.

"Come on." She took his hand and led him out of the lab. They slipped on their winter jackets and Charlotte jammed a furry toque down far on her head and wound her scarf around her face.

"It's not far, is it?" Quinn asked. "No dog sleds are needed?"

"No," Charlotte replied, despite being muffled under her thick scarf. "Just a short jog."

He hoped so. He wasn't enjoying the frigid temperatures of the Arctic. She opened the door and he was hit by a blast of icy air. He should've been used to it by now, but the low temperatures still surprised him.

They said nothing to each other as they shuffled through town to a little shack near the hangar. A steady stream of exhaust fumes floated up from the chimney—the aroma of old-fashioned cooking.

He could smell fries and his stomach growled at the thought of poutine. He was so hungry he might just take Mrs. Kamuk up on her offer to eat muktuk.

Chimes over the door jingled and they stomped their feet on the mat to shake off the snow. When he looked up, the patrons of the restaurant were all staring in wide-eyed wonder and Quinn felt like a specimen under examination at that moment.

"I should've mentioned that this diner is run by the Tikivik family," Charlotte whispered as she hung up her coat.

"Ah, so these are the hordes that were waiting in your clinic when I arrived yesterday?"

Charlotte nodded. "Yep, that would be them." She turned and waved and the group waved back then returned to their regular restaurant chatter.

"Do we wait for someone to seat us?" Quinn asked, looking around.

"It's not that kind of place, Devlyn." She took his hand again and his blood heated at her gentle touch. She led him to a corner booth and they slid into it. He sat down across from her. Charlotte handed him a vinyl-covered menu.

It was one sided and a bit smeared. She laughed as he held it with disdain. "The food is safe, Devlyn. You're hungry, I'm tired and you can't cook."

"Right. This stuff has to be better." Only his mind began to wander to the disgusting conversation with George earlier. If he continued thinking like that he wouldn't be able to eat anything.

Charlotte nodded and glanced at the menu.

"Ah, so the two doctors are gracing us with their presence tonight."

Quinn looked up at the pretty young waitress, who was the spitting image of Mentlana.

"Hey, Lucy. You haven't met Dr. Quinn Devlyn. Dr. Devlyn, this is Mentlana's twin, Lucy."

"Pleasure." He nodded.

"So, what'll it be tonight, Charley? Usual?"

"Yep."

Lucy nodded and looked expectantly at him. "What can I get for you, Dr. Devlyn?"

"What is a usual?"

Lucy chuckled. "A BLT, a salad and a diet cola."

"Sounds good, but make mine with fries. Oh, do you do poutines here?"

Lucy grinned. "Of course."

"Then that's what I'll have."

She nodded and headed back to the kitchen.

"I forgot about your affinity for poutines, Quinn. I guess you don't get many of those in Manhattan."

"Only on lunch breaks. Dinner out was more…a bit more top of the line."

"Escargots and the like?"

"Dammit." Quinn banged the table.

"What?" Charlotte asked, stunned.

"I forgot to tell George about escargots. I bet he'd be seriously squicked out."

Charlotte laughed. "He knows. He's been to Toronto many a time. He's just having some fun with you."

"That little…" Quinn laughed.

"He likes you." Charlotte smiled. "I think it's nice."

Lucy placed their drinks in front of them, grinning before leaving discreetly again.

"So, what is your obsession with food today?" Charlotte asked, playing with the straw in her glass of diet soda. "Have you suddenly miraculously learned how to cook?" There was a sparkle of devilment in her eyes.

He leaned closer to her across the table. "Do you remember the time I tried to make hamburger and cheese out of the packet and used lard instead of butter?"

Charlotte choked on her water. "Yes. It was horrific. Epically horrific, in fact." She shuddered. "I think I repressed that memory."

Quinn laughed and reached for her hand. Charlotte's eyes widened in shock at his touch, but she didn't try to pull away. Her hand was so slender and gave off the illusion it was delicate, but really it was strong. She'd had such potential to become a brilliant surgeon. Only Charlotte hadn't wanted that.

She'd wanted to be a general practitioner. Her hand felt so snug in his. So warm. So right.

"Remember the time I tried to make brownies and they only baked around the edges."

There was a twinkle in her eye. "I remember. Hard as a rock around the edges."

"But soft and gooey in the unbaked center. I must have tried to cook those brownies for three hours."

"I remember," Charlotte whispered. "I remember the smell. I was going through such bad..." She trailed off. The mirth disappeared. She straightened her spine and pulled her hand away.

He knew why she'd retreated emotionally. Quinn had known when he'd been making those brownies that she had been going through horrid morning sickness. She had been on Diclectin because she hadn't been able to keep anything down. It had killed him to see her suffer like that. So sick.

He'd tried to bake the brownies to cheer her up and butter her up to go to Manhattan. That day, the day of the miscarriage, the day Charlotte had lost the baby, had been the day he had been offered the private practice and fellowship in Manhattan. The offer had come from Dr. Robert Bryce, one of the leading neonatal surgeons on the Eastern Seaboard, and Dr. Bryce had wanted him, but Charlotte had refused to leave the godforsaken North.

That's how he'd felt about it.

Godforsaken.

Now he wasn't so sure. Charlotte was happy, and a successful physician.

And he was lonely.

"Anyway, I remember."

"Here are your meals, Doctors. By the way, Jake said they're on the house."

"No," Charlotte said, shaking her head vehemently. "We can pay, Lucy. You tell him we'll pay."

Lucy smiled, that cute dimple like her sister's appearing in her cheek. "You know Jake. He won't take no for an answer." Lucy looked at him then, her black eyes shining with warmth. "You are saving his nephew and my nephew. Jake is Genen's brother."

Charlotte sighed. "Lucy."

"It's done, Doc Charley. Deal with it." Lucy left them.

"That's awfully generous of them." Quinn turned and waved to the man behind the counter, the man he presumed was Jake.

"It's his way of saying 'thank you.' Everyone up here is family. Mentlana and Genen's baby means so much to this community."

Quinn's stomach rumbled and he looked down at his poutine. The meaty smell of the gravy made his mouth water in anticipation. The fries were fresh cut and thick and it had been a long time since he had real, home-cooked poutine.

"Lucy is actually going to be leaving us after Mentlana has her baby," Charlotte said, spearing a piece of lettuce.

"Really? Where's she going?"

"To Hamilton, Ontario. She's training to become a midwife and a registered nurse. I'm hoping she returns to Cape Recluse. I could use her."

"Doesn't Cape Recluse have a midwife? You mentioned her."

Charlotte nodded, chewing. "Lorna is getting old and ready to retire. Besides, if Lucy becomes a nurse she'll have much more training and knowledge than Lorna did. Lorna was trained by her mother…Anernerk."

"Anernerk is an impressive woman. So, midwifery is a generational thing. Well, I don't mean to interfere, but what you really need is another physician up here."

Charlotte nodded. "I know, but we've had this conversation before."

"I know." Quinn took a bite of his poutine and it was absolute heaven. God, he loved cheese curd. So bad for the arteries, but he was enjoying every bite.

"What do you think of Jake's cooking?" Charlotte asked. There was a smug smile plastered across her face.

"My compliments to the chef, for sure."

"Does it beat out all those fancy Manhattan restaurants?"

"Some. I won't lie to you, Charlotte. New York is a gourmand's paradise."

She smiled. "Really? I suppose your favorite restaurant is some crazy-ass posh spot where all the 'it' crowd goes."

"Nope. But it does serve the best fettuccine in the world."

"Mmm. I do love fettuccine."

"I know." Quinn took her hand again. "Perhaps you'll go there someday."

Charlotte put her head to one side, staring at him. "Perhaps."

Then he heard it, the distant rumble of something, something that was stirring at the back of his mind. A sound he should have recognized instantly. Charlotte heard it, too, and pulled her hand away. She stood and looked out the windows of the diner, like the rest of the patrons. Her phone started buzzing and she cursed under her breath when she pulled it out.

Far off on the horizon he could make out the flashing lights of a chopper, and the closer it got the louder the spinning of its blades became.

"What in the world...?" Quinn asked, puzzled.

"I'll wrap up the rest of your food and bring it over to the clinic, Doc Charley," Lucy called.

"Wrap up our food?" Quinn asked.

"Medical. There's an emergency. That was the text I received," Charlotte said quickly, before dashing off to get her coat. Quinn got up and tried to get his coat on before Charlotte disappeared out the door into the bitter cold towards the landing strip.

He zipped up his parka and went after her as she ran to meet the helicopter, which was making a quick landing.

Quinn's heart beat in time with each revolution of the helicopter's blade. George appeared by Charlotte's side, a gurney ready as they ducked to avoid decapitation.

Quinn hovered to the side, wanting to do something but not quite sure how trauma scenes played out up here. He watched the transfer and watched the paramedics climb into the helicopter again. Charlotte and George carried the gurney through the snow towards the clinic with a man dogging their heels.

He ran to head them off, opening the doors to the clinic and flicking on the lights.

Charlotte paid him no attention and he heard the patient's moans of pain as they came closer. His throat constricted when he got a good look at the patient on the stretcher and the obvious swelling under her thick blankets.

He could tell what was happening just by the woman's grimace and her husband's pained expression. An expression he had seen far too often, in countless men and women in waiting rooms.

The woman on the gurney was in labor and about to give birth.

He was the only qualified obstetrician currently in Cape Recluse.

Now was his time to shine.

CHAPTER EIGHT

"How far apart are the contractions?" Quinn asked.

"The medic said every fifteen minutes," Charlotte responded.

Quinn helped her wheel the gurney into exam room one. It was the largest room she had, but still a bit of a tight squeeze. Charlotte had delivered babies on her own before, but usually at the patient's home with Lorna in attendance. And there hadn't been that many births up here in recent years. This baby, for better or for worse, was on its way. The eyes of the patient, Mrs. Grise, were wide with fright, her mouth a thin line and her face white with pain.

"I tried to get her to Iqaluit," the patient's husband said nervously. "I thought we had time. It's our first and the baby is three weeks early."

Quinn shook his head and let out a *tsk* of frustration at what he saw as the man's stupidity. Charlotte could tell by the look on his face what Quinn thought of the husband's assumptions.

"You should've taken her down weeks ago." Quinn snapped as they wheeled the patient over to the far side of the exam room and transferred her to the bed.

"I wouldn't let him," Mrs. Grise panted. "I didn't want to be alone."

"It's all right, Mrs. Grise—" Charlotte started.

"Rebecca," the woman interjected through her deep breathing. "Please, just Rebecca."

"Rebecca," Charlotte said soothingly. "I'm Dr. James and I'm going to do everything I can to ease your discomfort."

"If you wanted an epidural, I'm afraid there's no time. I'm sorry," Quinn said gently to the panicked woman. The patient was terrified, and he was being very gentle with her as they continued to prep.

She was amazed. When they had been doing their residency he had never been this calm and soothing with patients before.

"It's okay. No drugs. I'm ready," Rebecca said.

"You're sure?" Charlotte asked.

Rebecca nodded. "I want a natural birth."

"Dr. James, may I speak with you?"

Charlotte was stunned by Quinn's formality. This wasn't some big city hospital. This was a small clinic, her small clinic at the top of the world.

"What?" Charlotte asked, never taking her eyes off of the patient.

"Do you have the supplies in case of an emergency C-section?" Quinn whispered.

"Do you think her case warrants it?"

Quinn shrugged. "I don't know. I'm just being prepared."

"Yes. I have everything."

Quinn gave her a half smile. "Keep her comfortable and I'll handle the rest." He turned to walk away, but Charlotte gripped his arm.

"You know you won't get paid for this. I've delivered babies before."

"And I've delivered probably ten times the amount you have. As for payment, I don't care. This is an emergency."

She should fight it, throw him out of her clinic, only he was the specialist and she knew nothing about this patient. He was right and she was stunned he was willing to do this delivery with no compensation, something the Quinn Devlyn of five years ago wouldn't have been happy about.

Still, there was his hand to consider.

"Dr. James?" Mr. Grise said, his voice panicked.

"Everything is going to be fine. Dr. Devlyn is one of the best." Charlotte turned away from Quinn, silently handing him the reins of her clinic and praying to God she had made the right decision.

"Thank you," Rebecca whispered, as her husband squeezed her hand.

Charlotte stood back with George, feeling utterly useless.

"Is Lorna on her way?" Charlotte asked.

"Her contractions are coming close together," Quinn said. "Doesn't look like Lorna's going to get here in time. Are you allergic to latex, Rebecca?"

"No," she said. "Not allergic to anything."

"Good." Quinn turned to the sink and scrubbed his hands. Charlotte helped him by drying his hands and putting on a pair of gloves. Their eyes locked for a moment as he slipped his scarred hand into the glove. Charlotte couldn't help but wonder if he'd be able to deliver the baby. She'd watched him do exercises yesterday, had watched Anernerk massage his bad hand. Would his hand be strong enough to hold such a fragile life?

Step in.

Only she didn't. Charlotte didn't want to frighten Rebecca and she didn't want George to blab to anyone that she had doubts about Quinn, the man who was going to save Mentlana's baby's life.

Quinn sat on the rolling stool and Charlotte adjusted the lamp. There was no time for modesty.

Quinn preformed the internal. "Ten centimeters and fully effaced." He looked up at Rebecca and smiled encouragingly. "Time to start pushing. Bear down. Now."

Rebecca nodded and began to push, as George counted with Mr. Grise.

Charlotte stayed by Quinn's side, watching a new life enter the world.

Please, God. Please let it be an easy birth.

She'd never seen Quinn deliver a child before. He hadn't liked her to watch him during his residency and she'd been very busy with her own. But he was gentle as he urged Rebecca on. He guided the frightened woman through the birth with so much care and concern that Charlotte's heart fluttered, and in this moment she felt very connected to him. For all his talk about power and position it was evident he was just as passionate about health care and his profession as she was.

"Good. Take a deep breath and push. Hard, Rebecca. Hard." He was easing the baby's head out. "You're doing great, Rebecca. Again."

Charlotte smiled behind her mask as the top of the head began to appear. Doctoring in a remote community was never so rewarding as at this moment. And Quinn had always questioned her about why she hadn't specialized. Here, she had a taste of it all.

Rebecca screamed, a gut-wrenching cry of agony, and Charlotte didn't blame her. This moment was known as the "ring of fire" for a good reason.

"Scalpel," Quinn said. Charlotte handed him the blade and he made a small incision to control the tearing. His hand was strong and steady as he made the cut.

"Come on, Rebecca. One more good push and your baby will be here," Charlotte urged.

Rebecca grunted as the head passed easily and the rest of the baby slipped into Quinn's waiting hands.

"A girl," Charlotte announced as she stared in awe at the tiny little life so delicately cradled in Quinn's hands. His gaze locked on her. She saw a glimmer of envy and longing mirrored there. Hope flared somewhere deep inside her. The baby took her first lusty cry of life and Quinn looked away.

"Take the baby," he said, his hands shaking a bit. Charlotte grabbed a blanket and reached down to hold the squawking infant.

As she stared down at the baby, tears stung her eyes as she thought of her own lost child. Rebecca had been so brave having a baby up here, away from what most people considered civilization. Braver than she was, even for having a baby, something Charlotte was terrified to even entertain the notion of again because she couldn't bear the thought of losing another child.

Get a grip on yourself, Charlotte.

She carefully placed the baby on Rebecca's chest, and Quinn cut the cord once it had stopped pulsating. The proud father cuddled his new daughter while Quinn delivered the afterbirth and stitched Rebecca up.

"Good job, Dr. Devlyn and Mom." George grinned at the happy parents, but Charlotte could see they were oblivious to everything. Rebecca's gaze was focused on her crying, thriving baby.

She recorded the APGAR and rubbed ointment on the baby's eyes to reduce infection. After that she gingerly placed the baby on the scale.

"She's seven pounds eight ounces."

Charlotte then took measurements of the baby. When five minutes had passed she recorded the APGAR again and gave the baby a vitamin K injection. The hospital in Iqaluit could do the heel stick tomorrow.

Charlotte swaddled the baby and took her over to the proud parents. Rebecca's arms were outstretched, tears streaming down her red cheeks. The new mother nuzzled her baby eagerly. A pang of longing rocked Charlotte to her core.

Charlotte wanted that. More than anything. More than any fear of what might happen.

"Thank you, Dr. James."

"It's Charlotte. Everyone up here calls me Charley, though."

Rebecca grinned. "Charlotte. I like that name."

"I think it's a perfect name for her," Quinn smiled. "I've always loved that name."

Charlotte blushed and smiled at Quinn. His eyes were twinkling and for a moment it was like the years had never separated them, that the hurt was forgotten. He returned her smile before turning away with the tray of instruments and medical waste.

"You can rest the night here, Mr. and Mrs. Grise. We'll take care of you, and tomorrow George or I will fly you down to Iqaluit. We'll need to notify the hospital that you've given birth here."

Rebecca nodded. "Thank you, Doctor... Thank you, Doc Charley."

"My pleasure." Charlotte peeled off her gloves and began to scrub. "George, make sure you set up a recovery room for them. I think there's a bassinet here. I always have stuff on hand. There's also some diapers and formula, if needed, in the supply room."

"I'm on it." George seemed to hesitate as he began to place instruments on a tray to be sterilized. "What happened to Dr. Devlyn?" he asked in whispered undertone.

"He's right..." Charlotte trailed off as her eyes scanned the room. He'd disappeared. "Probably went to clean up. He's done his job."

"Of course. He was fantastic. It gives me hope he'll help Mentlana." George's voice shook at the mention of his sister.

A lump formed in Charlotte's throat. "You okay to fly to Iqaluit tomorrow?" she asked, changing the subject.

"Yep. My schedule is free."

"Good."

She left the room and shut the door. Taking a deep breath, she slid down to the floor. Her knees were knocking and exhaustion hit her in waves. Emotions and adrenaline were still rushing through her. It had been watching Quinn hold the baby that had brought back a flood of emotions she'd thought long gone. He had been so tender, for a man who had always insisted he didn't want or particularly like kids, which had never made sense to her, given his chosen specialty.

The door to the clinic opened and Lorna shuffled in. Her face was haggard and she looked worn out.

"Am I too late?"

Charlotte stood, her body protesting. "Healthy baby girl. Sorry for dragging you out of bed."

Lorna shook her head. "No problem. I'll be glad when Lucy leaves soon to study midwifery. I'm getting too…"

"Tired. You're ready to retire." Charlotte offered.

Lorna smiled. "You're just too polite to say old, Charlotte."

"You're not old. Your mother, Anernerk, is old."

"I'll be sixty-eight soon, well past retirement age." Lorna slumped down in the waiting-room chair and Charlotte sat across from her.

"You can crash here for the night instead of trudging back home."

Lorna smiled weakly. "I just might take you up on that offer, help the new parents out and give you some rest."

"Thanks. Even though I was nothing more than a glorified nurse, it was an amazing experience."

"Does it make you change your mind?"

Charlotte dragged her hand through her hair. Lorna knew about her miscarriage and how Charlotte felt about becoming pregnant again. Charlotte blamed herself for losing the child. She had been an intern and had taxed her body way beyond its limits.

That's why she'd lost her baby.

"No," she answered uncertainly.

As the only doctor for kilometers around she was just as stressed, and she wouldn't lose another baby. She couldn't. It would kill her.

On the other hand, holding that baby tonight and watching

Quinn cradling that tiny little life with all the care in the world had made her rethink the decision she'd made five years ago.

If she was given the chance to carry and have another baby, she'd do so in a heartbeat.

Lorna arched an eyebrow. "There is uncertainty there."

Charlotte shook her head and stood. "I'll make you up a bed in the other recovery room."

Lorna shook her head. "Avoiding a touchy subject. Obstinate."

"You know, you sounded just like your mother, then." Charlotte chuckled and walked down the hall.

"Low, blow, Doc Charley. Really low blow. I'm old enough to be your mother."

"Keep talking…Anernerk."

Lorna let out a guffaw as Charlotte disappeared round the corner to the recovery room. She made up Lorna's room and could hear George making up the other one. Charlotte helped him settle the happy parents and the baby in the larger recovery room, the one usually used to house two patients, and got Lorna settled in the room opposite.

It was quite handy because Lorna was well versed in post-partum needs and she said she would keep watch on the new mother and baby during the night.

George collapsed on the waiting-room couch and was snoring by the time Charlotte finished sterilizing the instruments and cleaning the exam room, not wanting Rosie to have a heart attack when she came in on Monday.

As Charlotte closed down and turned off the lights, she stared at the door that connected to her home. It was slightly ajar and she could see the flicker of a television. Quinn was still awake.

She wanted to see him, to wrap her arms around him and kiss him. To finish what had almost started earlier today, but fear froze her in her tracks.

No. She couldn't deal with him tonight.

Instead, she grabbed her dinner, which had been parceled up from the diner, and wandered to her office, staring bleakly at the old couch that had adorned their apartment. Her eyes were heavy and the couch was surprisingly inviting. She locked the door to her office, peeled off her clothes and settled down on the couch, covering herself with the afghan she'd draped over Quinn only a day ago.

She was absolutely exhausted and tried to drift off to sleep, but the damn blanket smelled like him.

CHAPTER NINE

SHOUTING ROUSED CHARLOTTE from her slumber. She stumbled to her feet and the container from dinner last night fell onto the floor, scattering a few fries onto the carpet. One squished under her foot when she stepped forward and it stuck to her sock in a cold, mushy clump, making her curse under her breath.

Charlotte hopped on one foot to peer out the window. She gasped, not because it was snowing, which it was. It was the sight of Quinn outside in the snow that made her voice catch in her throat.

Quinn's outside? Voluntarily?

He was kneeling down and in his hand appeared to be a very expensive camera with a large telescopic lens. The shouting was from some of the village kids, who were rocketing past him from the slope just outside her office.

The clinic was on the far edge of town, nestled up against a slope, and because there were no houses on the one side, the village kids loved to come over and toboggan on nice days. When it was snowing big fat fluffy flakes, it was not as bitterly cold out as it would usually be.

As a kid zoomed past Quinn, the camera would follow. He was photographing the children.

I never knew he liked photography.

Or children, for that matter.

A smile quirked her lips as he moved the camera and urged a large sled of five kids down the hill. The children were laughing and he was making funny faces as the child at the back pushed off.

Quinn cheered and disappeared behind the camera, getting ready to take his picture. Charlotte was extremely attracted to this side of him, a side she'd never been privileged to see before. Watching him out there now with the village kids warmed her heart.

She left her office, changed her mushy sock, and freshened up quickly. She had her winter gear on in no time flat and was out the door to join him. There was no way she was going to miss this opportunity.

There was no wind and it wasn't bitterly cold when she stepped outside. It was just a nice winter day, with soft flakes floating down.

"Watch out, Doc!" Charlotte jumped back as a sled full of laughing kids whizzed past her. Quinn stood and grinned at her, his cheeks rosy from the cold.

"Good morning, or should I say, afternoon?"

"What time is it?" She'd been in such a rush to get outside she hadn't checked the time.

"It's one. Hey, hold up, guys. Doctor coming through." Quinn held up his hands and the eager tobogganers paused, but with a few "Awwws" as Charlotte jogged across the path of danger to stand beside Quinn. "All right, go, guys!"

With a shriek from one of the kids, the next sled set off and Quinn snapped a few shots as it whizzed by.

"I'm impressed," Charlotte said.

"By what?"

"You, out here in the *dreaded* ice and snow."

Quinn chuckled and he capped his camera lens. "I couldn't resist it."

"I didn't know you did photography."

Quinn shrugged. "It's no big deal. I dabble a bit." He

shielded the glare of the sun from the screen on the back and flicked through the images. They were beautiful photographs of the kids and other scenery. He'd also managed to take a shot of the northern lights. It was a stunning photograph that captured the green-and-purples hues of the aurora borealis dancing over the village.

"These are beautiful. When did you take that?" she asked, pointing to the image.

"Last night. You know, I've never seen the aurora borealis. I never bothered when we lived in Yellowknife, and when I was in Manhattan I kicked myself constantly for not making the time." Quinn switched off his camera. "Light pollution in the big city sucks."

"What time did you get up?" she asked, changing the subject from the city, which was a point of contention between them.

"About nine. George was taking the Grises down to Iqaluit. He was going to wake you, but you looked so darned cute huddled up on that old couch, food scattered all over the place."

Charlotte groaned, embarrassed he'd caught her flaked out and vulnerable instead of poised and sophisticated. "Thanks for doing that."

"No problem." His eyes glinted as he watched the kids haul their sleds back up the hill. "You know, I've never tried that."

"What, tobogganing?"

Quinn shook his head. "Nope, never. My parents wouldn't take me or even buy me a sled."

"I thought your dad was very much into sports. At least, that's what you told me."

"Hockey, yes, sledding, no. You can't win a gold medal for sledding."

"You can for bobsledding," she teased.

Quinn shrugged. "He wasn't much for being a team player. I just had to be the best."

A pang of sympathy hit her. Quinn may have had two parents but he hadn't had a fun childhood. Some of Charlotte's best memories of her and her father had been out on the snow, sledding and snowshoeing. Charlotte grabbed his hand and tugged him towards the hill. "We're going."

"What?" He chuckled. "You're nuts. What about my camera?"

"Jenny!" Charlotte called out to Wavell's younger sister. She came bounding up, out of breath.

"Yeah, Doc Charley?"

"Can you hold Dr. Devlyn's camera while I take him on your sled down the hill?"

Jenny's face broke into a huge smile. "Yeah, I can do that!"

"Charlotte…" Quinn started as she took the camera from him and handed it to Jenny. "I don't know."

"Come on, you big wimp!"

He raised his eyebrows. "Wimp, eh?"

She screeched as he lunged for her. She grabbed Jenny's small sled and ran up the hill, Quinn following her. When they reached the top she sat down. "Sit behind me and hold on."

"How do we push off?" he asked as he sat down, his arms wrapping around her.

"With your feet. But once we're going, tuck them up so your feet don't slow us down."

"Gotcha."

"Ready?" she asked.

"Yep. Let's get this over with."

Charlotte could hear the kids shrieking and laughing as she dug her feet in and pushed off. The sled picked up speed fast from their combined weight and they rocketed down the hill, past Jenny and the clinic. Charlotte screamed with pure joy as the wind whipped at her face and the cold air sucked the breath from her lungs.

Quinn yelled and stuck his feet out as they headed towards the only road in Cape Recluse. The sled careened to the side and they were tossed out. Charlotte did a small roll and landed on her back. Quinn rolled and landed on top of her, pinning her to the snow.

"Are you all right?" he asked breathlessly. "And my apologies for the excessive bad language."

Charlotte couldn't stop laughing. "I'm fine."

"I think I like this sledding business." He grinned down at her, his dark eyes twinkling. "You've popped my cherry twice since I've been here."

Heat spread through her like wildfire, while her body zinged with arousal. His body was heavy, pressed against hers, but it was the kind of weight she was longing for. If only all these layers of clothing weren't separating them. If only they were in her bed, naked.

She sobered instantly when she realized Quinn was still lying on top of her, in front of her clinic, in front of the village children. She could hear them laughing.

"Hey, you're too heavy. Get off me, already!"

Quinn shifted and rolled over. She scrambled to her feet and brushed the snow from her. "I'd better go change. I'm not wearing any snow pants and my jeans will be soaked in a few minutes."

She spun round and ran for the clinic, not looking back. She'd forgotten for a moment that he was not her fiancé. He wasn't anything to her anymore. Just a colleague, up here for a consult.

Quinn retrieved his camera from Jenny and bid his new fan club farewell. The sun would be setting soon and the kids had to head for home. Besides, his hand was numb from the cold, but, like he'd told Charlotte, he hadn't been able to resist the photographic opportunity.

When he was back in his bedroom he scrolled through the

pictures and saw one of him and Charlotte, racing down the hill. It seemed that Jenny was a bit of a photo aficionado, as well. He didn't mind in the least. It was something to remember that moment by.

He thought Charlotte's cold reserve was melting a bit. She was playful and laughing again, but when they had been lying in the snow, something had clicked. He'd seen it in her eyes and her barriers had gone up again. He turned off the camera and set it down.

A zing of pins and needles shot up his arm. Quinn stared down at his scarred hand and flexed it. It wasn't as stiff as it had been. His hand had been steady and sure when he'd made the episiotomy. He'd seen the look on Charlotte's face when she'd helped him put the gloves on, the moment of uncertainty. He wasn't a fool. Quinn knew she'd seen the scars. He wanted to tell her about the accident and reassure her there was nothing to be worried about, though his mother would beg to differ.

Quinn scrubbed his hand over his face and picked up his hand exerciser, clenching his hand into a tight fist and then slowly allowing it to flex again.

"You'll never regain full use of your hand. I would suggest you open up a consultation practice or move into a general practice instead of surgery, Dr. Devlyn," the orthopedic surgeon said.

"I don't accept that."

"Quinn, see sense. Even Dr. Szarsky thinks you won't be able to continue to be a surgeon. When will you listen to reason?" his mother lamented. *"You had such potential, too."*

"I still have potential. I'm still a surgeon."

"Perhaps," his father said. *"But it'll take about a year at the minimum to recuperate. By then you'll have lost your professional edge."*

"Like I lost mine having you!"

His mother's tone had been so hard and cold when she had uttered those words, *I lost mine having you.* Quinn shook those

horrible memories away. His parents had never been support-
ive except when he'd excelled.

Mediocrity had never been an option.

Except with Charlotte.

Charlotte had never judged him when he'd had a minor set-
back. She'd always cared for and loved him, no matter what
he'd done, and had cheered him on to do better next time,
without any hint of malice or remorse.

A slow-paced life in a rural clinic or a small-town hospital was what he'd secretly craved since his accident, but he'd
never admitted to it because he could've had that with Charlotte, and Quinn never admitted his mistakes.

He cursed under his breath and set the hand exerciser on
the nightstand. He got up and splashed some water on his face
at the basin. When he glanced in the mirror he saw a thick
growth of stubble and dark circles under his eyes. He hadn't
slept well. Every time he'd closed his eyes, all he'd seen had
been Charlotte.

In that moment when he'd passed the baby to her it had been
like their painful past and their separation had been washed
away. Back then, all he'd wanted had been his parents' approval. Once he'd achieved what they'd wanted from him, it
still hadn't been good enough, and when his father had died
he'd realized it never would be.

Just like he'd realized as soon as he'd left Charlotte that
there would be no going back. He'd lost her trust.

Yet that look they shared... That moment of connection
had seemed so genuine, so real, and he'd felt like he'd never
been away, that they were right back to where they'd started.
Of course, he could've just been seeing things. Charlotte had
made it pretty clear when he'd arrived that their association
was going to remain purely professional.

If he had the chance to start all over again with Charlotte,
would he?

Damn straight, he would.

His phone chimed with the familiar sound of a text message coming through. Quinn groaned and picked his phone up from the nightstand. Only two people would be texting him. It would be either the hospital or his mother, and Quinn had a gut-wrenching feeling it wasn't the hospital.

As he glanced at the screen he recognized the area code of Toronto. Two words were on the screen.

Call me.

Quinn rolled his eyes. He knew why she was doing this. She knew where he was and she didn't approve. Not one bit. His mother wasn't impressed in the least that he was giving a pro bono consult, especially for a patient of Charlotte's.

His phone vibrated in his hand.

What could possibly be so important you can't call your mother to discuss an urgent matter? I bet you would've called if it was your father.

Quinn rolled his eyes. His mother was laying on the guilt trip pretty thick—another aspect of his childhood he hadn't particularly enjoyed, being the pawn between his parents. His mother had been a master of guilt. "Had" being the operative word.

He really couldn't care less. Instead, he called his physiotherapist. He wanted reassurance.

"Ted Jones speaking."

"Hey, Ted. It's Devlyn."

There was a pause. "Devlyn! How's it up there?" Ted asked pleasantly.

"Cold."

"I bet." Ted chuckled. "How's the hand?"

"Stiff, sore. The usual." Quinn scrubbed his hand over his

face, preparing himself mentally for what he wanted to ask, dreading the answer. "My hand, do you think…? Will I regain full use of it?"

You can't avoid him for the rest of the day.

Charlotte groaned. Her conscience pricking her, she'd spent a most uncomfortable night on the couch in her office because of her conflicted emotions about Quinn. She was still wearing the same clothes as yesterday and now her jeans were soaked.

As much as she wanted to go and talk to Quinn about what had happened out in the snow, she couldn't will herself to do it. It was like her body was frozen to the spot, some sort of primeval defense mechanism to prevent her from facing Quinn and appearing like a schmuck in front of him, thus protecting her heart from further injury.

At least, that's what she kept trying to tell herself she was doing.

Really, she knew deep down she was being a coward.

"That's it." She quickly changed out of her wet clothes. She couldn't hide out in her bedroom. She was going to face Quinn and see where the chips fell.

When she opened her bedroom door she heard his raised voice filter through from the guest bedroom.

"Honestly, tell me the truth, Ted."

Quinn sounded agitated and worried.

Charlotte tiptoed down the hall. The door to his bedroom was slightly ajar. She could just catch a glimpse of Quinn sitting at the desk, holding his head in his hands and staring down at the phone, which was on speaker.

"I really can't say, Quinn. I'm only stating the facts from what I've seen in other cases."

Her heart skipped a beat. *Cases? What cases?*

"I need some kind of a ballpark idea, Ted. Just give me that. It'll put my mind at ease."

There was a loud audible sigh over the phone. "No, you

probably won't regain full function of your hand again. Your hand was crushed. You're lucky you still have it and have some range of motion."

This time her heart didn't skip a beat. It almost stopped completely. The blood was draining away from her face and the room began to spin.

Couldn't. Operate? The implications were too horrific to fathom.

She wanted to move away. Her stomach was knotting, her throat was constricted as she fought the urge to be sick. All she could think about was Mentlana and the baby. He was risking her reputation, as well. If Mentlana or the baby died because he failed to mention he was no longer fit for duty, her reputation would be on the line. The people of Cape Recluse wouldn't trust her as freely as they did now.

His ineptitude could cost her the only home she'd ever known, and that thought was too frightening.

There was no way she was going to risk her family, the people she loved, because Quinn's pride might be hurt. If he couldn't operate then there was no way he was going near Mentlana Tikivik, or anyone else, for that matter. But she also felt sorry for Quinn. His whole focus in med school had been about becoming the best, the top of his field, and now he couldn't operate. How must he feel about that?

"Can I operate?" Quinn asked.

"I don't see why not, but you'll most likely need assistance."

"I don't have access to other surgeons."

"Look, I could say you'd be fine, but without assessing your hand I can't give you a definite answer. Just keep up with the exercises.

"Thanks, Ted."

"Call me if you need some more help. Sorry I couldn't ease your mind."

Charlotte heard Quinn end the call and shut off his phone.

She tried to move away from where she was standing, but once again she was frozen to the spot.

Quinn whipped open the door and his eyes widened as he saw her, standing still in the hallway, shaking with anger and betrayal. It was her own fault. She'd allowed him into her life again. At least this time she hadn't lost a baby. At least this time her heart hadn't been blown to smithereens.

"Charlotte." His tone was weary and he rubbed the back of his neck. "I didn't know you were here."

"No," she said quickly. "No. I don't suppose you did."

CHAPTER TEN

"Charlotte…" Quinn's heart stuttered at the sight of her. She was dressed casually in a soft-looking lavender sweater and blue jeans, her red curls hanging loose over her shoulders. Her posture, however, was anything but casual, and her face was like thunder. She stood like she was on the edge of a precipice, and that one wrong move by him and she'd jump.

"Well?" she asked.

"Charlotte, I wanted to tell you. It's been something I've been trying to tell you since I arrived."

Her gaze dropped to his hand and the scars that marred the surface of his skin. He was sure she was looking past the physical ones he carried to the ones deep inside him and the haunted past that had scarred them both, and he watched as the anger in her face ebbed away.

"Tell me," she urged gently, at last.

Do not be the obstinate man.

He met Charlotte's gaze. Though her face was now unreadable and passive, her eyes were full of concern. He longed to pull her into his arms once more, to tell her everything would be okay.

Only he didn't know how to say the words, or if it would all be okay.

"Quinn, please."

"I'm still a surgeon, if that's what you're wondering. I have a medical license." It was all he could say. He was having a hard time trying to tell her that his hand had been broken. It would be like admitting his own defeat, admitting to her that he was the shadow of his former self.

"Okay," she said, confused. "I assumed so. Tell me about the scars, Quinn. What happened?"

"A car accident."

She nodded. "Go on."

"Fog caused a massive pileup on the highway. My car flipped, my hand became lodged in the door. For a while I didn't think it could be saved. Hell, when I was trapped, waiting for the paramedics, I thought I was going to die."

Charlotte's face paled and she moved into his bedroom. "Why didn't you tell me this before?"

"You brought me up here to operate on your friend. I couldn't tell you what had happened to me."

"So putting Mentlana's life at risk is not as important as saving face?"

"Of course not!" he snapped, and then took a deep breath as he sat down on the edge of his bed. "I'd never put a patient at risk. It's why I was calling my physiotherapist."

Charlotte closed the distance between them and sat next to him, taking his shattered hand in hers.

"If your physiotherapist or orthopedic surgeon cleared you for surgery and you still have your license, you can operate." It was if she was stating it because she couldn't quite believe it, and he didn't blame her one bit.

"Yes" was all he said.

"You know you can, or else you wouldn't have boarded that plane and come up here."

What if I came up here for purely selfish reasons? Which was what he wanted to say, but didn't. Instead, he pulled his hand out of hers and stood.

"I won't put your friend's life at risk. I hope you can trust me on this. Do you trust me, Charlotte?"

* * *

Charlotte didn't know what to say. The room began to spin and she was still trying to take in everything. She knew something had happened to him, but didn't know the extent. She stood and turned her back to him, unable to process what he'd just asked. Did she trust him? She didn't even know that answer herself, so how could she tell him otherwise?

"I don't...I don't know what to say."

"You don't have to say anything. You have no reason to trust me. I deceived you. I didn't tell you about my accident, but I want you to know I'd never do anything to harm a patient."

Charlotte heard his footfalls as he closed the space between them, the heat of his body against her back as he stood behind her. She moved away, stunned and not sure she could believe him. If she did and he was wrong and something happened to Mentlana... The thought was too horrifying to comprehend.

She glanced over her shoulder and her heart skipped a beat, her stomach fluttering just looking at him. Charlotte nodded slowly. "I trust you."

"Thank you." Quinn moved past her to leave, but she reached out and took his hand again. He paused and she traced the faint scars with her thumb. She could only begin to imagine the hours of pain he'd endured as they'd put the pieces of him back together.

"I'm sorry I wasn't there to help you," she whispered.

He tilted her chin so she was forced to look at him. "You have nothing to apologize for."

Charlotte's knees began to knock just a bit as she stared into his eyes, getting lost in them. His eyes were like melted chocolate and she *so* loved chocolate.

It'd been so long since his strong arms had wrapped around her. His absence in her life was akin to physical pain. A pain that had been numbed by throwing herself into her work and reminding herself of the pain he'd caused her.

Quinn's hand slipped around her neck, his fingers tangling in her hair at the nape, bringing her closer to him. His hot breath fanned her cheek. She closed her eyes, waiting for the kiss that she didn't know she longed for, but which she did, all the same.

What am I doing?

Yeah, she trusted him in his surgical abilities, but she wasn't ready to let him into her heart again. She placed a hand on his chest, keeping him at bay. "I can't. The day you left was the worst day of my life. I lost you and I lost..." She trailed off, not wanting to share the pain of losing their child. She'd borne it alone for so long.

He nodded. "I understand. I'm just grateful you trust me to do right by your friend. Thank you."

Charlotte turned on her heel and left his room. He'd gotten to her again and she'd almost let down her guard.

She hated how he affected her so.

Charlotte avoided Quinn as much as possible. She was angry at herself for momentarily allowing him to break through to her and she was angry that her hormones seemed to be over ruling her common sense.

Of course, it was hard to block Quinn out of her life when they only had two thousand square feet of combined clinic and house space. Add that to a blinding blizzard that lasted three days, keeping them housebound.

At least she had her regular work to keep her busy, when patients desperate enough were able to slog through the snow to keep their appointments. Most of her day was dealing with her job, locked in her office with only the roar of the storm outside to accompany her and her jangled thoughts.

Alone in her office, she kept reliving their doomed relationship over and over again. After it had ended, when she'd first looked back on it, she'd chastised herself for not noticing that things would never have worked out between them.

And it hadn't only been about their very different career paths. Quinn wasn't a family man. That was one thing that hadn't changed about him. Charlotte wanted a family, more than anything, and Quinn was a workaholic.

When and if she ever did meet Mr. Right, she wanted to provide two parents for her children. Charlotte wanted to give them what she'd never had.

"Doc Charley?" Charlotte looked up to see George standing in the doorway.

"Yeah, what can I do for you?"

"Closing time." A smile spread across George's face.

Charlotte glanced at the clock on her computer monitor and balked. The afternoon had flown by. She had still been working on Wavell's file, although she had pulled out the boy's sutures earlier that day.

"Have a good night," she said absently.

"It's bingo night at the community center. You up for some B.I.N.G.O?" George asked, enunciating every letter in an annoying way.

Charlotte shook her head. "I don't relish going out in that storm."

"Storm ended hours ago, Charley," George said, confused. "You must've been really engrossed in filing if you didn't even notice the silence."

Charlotte shook her head. No, she hadn't noticed the howling wind had stopped. She'd grown so accustomed to the deafening sound that she hadn't even noticed that it had ended. Apparently she truly had zoned out, because the coffee in her cup from that morning was stone cold and the cup was still full. She dropped the file and scrubbed a hand over her face.

"Are you all right, Charley?" George asked, concerned.

"Fine. Just a bit tired." She bit her lip, hoping George wouldn't see through her lie. If he did, he didn't say anything.

"Come out to the community center. Everyone is coming

tonight for bingo, a way to celebrate the storm being over. I'm even going to fetch Aanak and drag her in."

A smile tugged at the corners of her lips. "No, thanks. I think I'll keep up with my filing. Besides, I hate bingo."

George shook his head. "Suit yourself. I guess it's just me and Doc Devlyn, then."

"Quinn's going?" Charlotte was stunned. Absolutely and utterly flabbergasted. Quinn was not the community-center, bingo-card-stamping type. Except for formal mixers, Quinn had never gone out with the other students, unless it had been with her.

"Yep." There was a twinkle to George's eye. "He said he's really looking forward to it."

Now she *had* to go. She wouldn't miss seeing this for the world. "Well, I guess I can come out, seeing that Anernerk will be there and everything."

George grinned. "Ri-i-ight. You're going because Aanak will be there."

Charlotte frowned. "What exactly are you implying? And tread carefully."

"Nothing. Nothing." George held up his hands and backed out of the room. Charlotte chuckled to herself when he'd disappeared. He knew not to mess with her. He might be taller than her, but she could still give him a good noogie if she was so inclined.

She wasn't lying about wanting to see Anernerk, but the real show would be watching Quinn interacting with the townsfolk. He was not a natural people person. In fact, she knew he was only in the medical profession because it'd been forced on him by his parents, and she couldn't help but wonder what his chosen profession would've been if he'd had the choice.

He'd never had hobbies when they'd been together, other than traveling. He'd liked to see new places and had often talked about the trips he wanted to take. Perhaps he would've taken up photography.

Was that why he was taking it up now, as a fallback because of his hand injury? Charlotte groaned, annoyed with herself for expending so much thought on Quinn Devlyn. His life, his choices were not her concern anymore. Once he did his job up here she was over 100 percent positive he'd be on the next flight to Toronto.

Back to his job at the hospital in the big city and working as much as he could to stay at the top of his game.

And that was a bet she could take to the bank.

CHAPTER ELEVEN

THE COMMUNITY CENTER was packed and blaring out music. Charlotte handed her coat to the young girl behind the coat check.

"You'd better hurry up, Doc Charley. They've already started the first round," the young girl said.

"Thanks, Lizzie."

Charlotte hadn't gone over with George and Quinn as she'd had to make a house call on a sick patient, the only resident in Cape Recluse, besides Mentlana and Genen, who wasn't in attendance at bingo tonight. Besides, Charlotte was in no rush. She wanted to watch Quinn from afar to see how he interacted with the residents.

She'd been so shocked when George had told her Quinn had agreed to go. This was one bingo night she wasn't going to miss for the world. She lingered in the doorway of the main auditorium and easily picked out Quinn, near the back and by himself.

His brow was furrowed as he was bent over the cards. A smile touched her lips. They'd suckered him out of at least twenty bucks because he had about four cards sprawled out in front of him and he couldn't keep up with marking his tickets with the chips.

"He sucks. Big time."

Charlotte turned to see Anernerk at the table beside the

door. Anernerk was a pro at bingo. She could carry on any kind of conversation without missing a beat.

"What do you mean?"

Anernerk snorted. "He sucks. What more is there to say?"

"B seven."

"Boo!" Anernerk shouted. "Call something good for a change."

Charlotte stifled a laugh. Poor George was the caller and sent his dear, sweet Aanak a withering look, but only because Anernerk was engrossed in her bingo cards.

"You think I should go help him?" Charlotte asked.

"Yeah, but if you win…" Anernerk sent her a brief but silent warning.

Charlotte just grinned and made her way round to where Quinn was seated. "Having fun?"

Quinn glanced up and then laughed. "No. I think George should've been an auctioneer instead of a bingo caller."

Charlotte took the empty seat next to him and aided Quinn in catching up. "He's neither. He's a paramedic. They're trained to move quickly."

"Well, his training in this situation is not needed," Quinn grumbled.

"You wish he was slower in this case?" she teased.

"Of course," Quinn said, as he placed another chip. "I'm a novice. I was promised a night of cheap fun."

"Cheap fun? You're in the wrong town for *cheap* fun."

Quinn grinned and then chuckled. "Well, I'm used to attending soirees where plates go for at least fifty dollars and up."

"It's all relative, I guess." Charlotte placed another chip. "There, you've caught up now."

"For now." Quinn cursed under his breath as George called out three more numbers in rapid succession. "Drat. I'm literally all thumbs tonight."

"Slow it down, you!" Charlotte called out, trying not to laugh.

George raised his eyebrows in question and then spied Charlotte. He shook his head and continued in his normal tempo of firing off numbers.

"Hey, you heard the doctor. Slow it down or else." This time the demand came from Anernerk and this time George dared not ignore the request.

Quinn was stifling his laughter. "She's a bit intense about this game."

"She's competitive."

"I see where you got it from," Quinn said.

"What do you mean?"

Quinn rolled his eyes. "Oh, come on. You were out for blood at medical school. Always had to be top in the class, win every competition and every scholarship. It was damn annoying."

Charlotte glared at him, but saw the mirth in his eyes and retracted her claws a bit. "All right, I'll give you that. So, if I was *so* annoying, why did you pursue me?"

She regretted the question the moment it had left her lips when she saw the dark, hungry glint in his eyes, a look that caused warmth to spread through her body. She almost forgot where she was. Charlotte felt like that giddy med student in anatomy class, shyly watching Quinn on the other side of the classroom.

"G fifty-eight."

Quinn tore his gaze from her and set down a chip. "Damn, I think I won. Did I?"

Charlotte leaned over. "You did. You'd better call it."

"Bingo!" Quinn yelled out, standing up waving his card, letting the chips scatter everywhere. "Damn."

"Forfeit! He dropped his chips!" Anernerk said loudly, with a hint of triumph in her voice.

Charlotte couldn't control her laughter, then. She got down

on her knees and began to retrieve the bingo chips from the floor. Quinn got down and helped her.

"Anernerk is right."

"How's that?" Charlotte asked, setting a fistful of chips on the table.

"I do suck."

Quinn took a swig of his soda and leaned against the bar in the community center. He used the word "bar" loosely as it only served sodas, coffee and tea. He had excused himself from this round of bingo and had left Charlotte to hold down the fort.

In spite of Anernerk's protests, he had still won because they could track the previous numbers called.

It surprised him how much he enjoyed the game and socializing with the people in the community. That snowstorm had lasted for what had felt like an eternity. He was Canadian and used to blizzards, but nothing of this magnitude and ferocity. But then again, he'd grown up in a city, and tall buildings did serve a good use as windbreaks against whiteouts and squalls.

There was nothing here, no trees, just water on all sides and a mountain of rock, ice and snow behind the town. They were certainly at the mercy of the elements here. It was raw and powerful and for the first time he actually understood the reason why Charlotte loved it up here.

Quinn shook his head and ran his fingers through his hair. Perhaps the deafening roar of that snowstorm had addled his brain.

One thing not confusing him was how much he was enjoying his time with Charlotte. After he'd told her what had happened to him, she'd kept her distance from him. A tense silence had fallen between them and it saddened him. She ate her meals in her office and their only conversations were just cursory politenesses or talking about Mentlana's case.

He was used to silence, but he'd been alone for far too

long. When he'd arrived in Cape Recluse he hadn't realized how hungry for company he'd been, especially for Charlotte's.

He'd missed her, but he'd never really let it sink in how much. Being back in her presence reminded him of it, keenly.

Quinn didn't know what had changed and why the tense barrier that had fallen between them these last few days was gone, but he was thrilled. She seemed to be enjoying herself immensely, even though George told him she never usually came to bingo as she didn't particularly enjoy it.

Charlotte was beaming from ear to ear and she was very at ease with the people, and they with her. It was like they were family—for all intents and purposes, they were. He envied Charlotte that she really loved what she was doing.

Here she shone like the bright star she was.

Quinn had never seen her like this. Five years ago, in Yellowknife, he hadn't seen any job prospects, any chance for advancement. He'd thought of Canada's North as a dead-end career, but it wasn't.

He'd been so wrong.

He'd been too hasty when he'd left.

Watching Charlotte now, he was regretting the decisions he'd made.

"Are you going to play the next round, Devlyn?"

Quinn turned to see Anernerk beside him. She looked a bit frailer then when he'd first laid eyes on her a few days earlier. He hoped, for Charlotte's sake, that nothing was seriously wrong with her, but then, the old gal *was* over a hundred.

"Well, are you?" Anernerk winked at him.

"I may," Quinn conceded.

"I like competition. Especially, fresh meat."

"I believe your grandson remarked on that the first time I met you."

"He knows me well." Anernerk smiled and then picked up his bad hand. "Has it been troubling you much?"

"No, not too much. The blizzard caused a bit of an ache."

Anernerk nodded. "Your hand is steady enough. I wouldn't worry."

Quinn cocked an eyebrow. "I'm not. Not in the least."

Liar.

"I see," she said carefully. She released his hand and then shook her finger at him. "I'm going to get you next round. You had beginner's luck, but I think that's run out. I shall have victory."

Anernerk hobbled off and Quinn trailed after her, sitting next to Charlotte and sliding a can of ginger ale across to her.

"Milady," he said, giving a little flourish with his hand.

"Thanks." Charlotte popped the top and stuck a straw in the can.

"How are we doing?" he asked.

"Not well, I'm afraid."

"O sixty-seven."

"Boo!" Quinn called out. "This game is rigged."

Charlotte snorted and several people laughed. George was shocked, but grinned and continued with the game.

"I'm shocked, Dr. Devlyn, by such a display," Charlotte teased.

"Are you thoroughly scandalized?"

"Of course."

Quinn chuckled. "Perhaps we should call it quits. Besides, Anernerk warned me that she'd have victory, or else."

"Well, in that case, we'd better leave while the going's good." Charlotte finished her soda and Quinn collected up the game paraphernalia and handed it back to the ladies who had persuaded him in the first place to buy four cards.

They retrieved their coats and headed out into the freezing night. The moment they stepped outside, a brilliant display of vibrant green aurora borealis erupted across the sky.

"I can't believe how I missed this during my year in Yellowknife." Quinn wasn't watching where he was going and lost his footing. Charlotte reached out and steadied him.

"I think you've had a bit too much pop tonight," she teased.

"Perhaps. Or my eardrums were shattered by that raging blizzard." He gazed at Charlotte, bundled up in her parka. All he could see was the twinkle in her eyes and the tip of her nose, and he fought the urge to lean forward and press a kiss there. Charlotte let go of her hold on him, though. The light-hearted jesting they shared at the community center had vanished, replaced once more by the uneasy tension.

"It's freezing out here." Charlotte laughed nervously and stepped back, jogging the rest of the short way back to her clinic.

Quinn followed, because it was freezing, but he didn't know what had changed again and he was sad that it had.

CHAPTER TWELVE

CHARLOTTE SPENT THE night tossing and turning, just like she'd spent the last several. Quinn had changed. When he'd first arrived, she hadn't been sure that he had. He'd still seemed like the same old workaholic who'd left her.

The Quinn who had shown himself to her now was a completely different man, a man she only caught glimpses of when they were alone together away from prying eyes. A man he never allowed out in public. There were still shadows of his former self, but she was learning more about him. More than she'd ever thought possible.

Last night at bingo she'd thoroughly enjoyed herself.

Charlotte gave up any pretense of trying to sleep. She got up and dragged herself to the shower, using the last bit of hot water in her heater for the morning. She got dressed in warm layers as today she had to make a visit to Mentlana.

Quinn was nowhere in sight when she left her bedroom. She couldn't help but wonder where he was. He wasn't in the guest bedroom, because the door was wide open.

There was a pot of coffee waiting and a note from Quinn that stated he was out with George, ice fishing.

Ice fishing?

Charlotte pinched the bridge of her nose. Quinn had willingly gone out on the ice? With George?

She shook her head, filled her travel mug with some coffee and collected the items she'd need for Mentlana's checkup.

When she headed outside she could see a few brightly colored huts out on the water and she couldn't help but wonder which one Quinn was in. She could picture him bundled up, cursing at the stupidity of sitting out in the bitter cold, watching a hole for a bite on his pole.

Actually, what would be even better would be if a seal ended up popping up through Quinn and George's hole. That would certainly give him a fright. She'd be willing to endure a few hours of ice fishing just to see that.

"Quick lollygagging and get in here!" Anernerk was hanging out the doorway.

"What the heck are you doing here?" Charlotte asked. "More importantly, how the heck did you get here?"

"Genen picked me up last night from bingo. I just decided to stay here for a few days. I didn't think I was confined to my home." Anernerk pointed at her cheek.

Charlotte leaned over and gave her a kiss. "Well, since you're here, maybe I'll give you a checkup, too."

"Don't you dare!" Anernerk grinned and took Charlotte's coat. "Where's Dr. Devlyn today?"

"Ice fishing with George."

"Really? I'm impressed."

"What's going on out there?" Mentlana called out.

"You better go see her," Anernerk said. "She's going a bit squirrely, being on bed rest."

Charlotte walked down the hallway to Mentlana's bedroom. The television had been moved into the room. Actually, it looked like most of Mentlana's living room had been crammed into her small bedroom.

"How are you feeling today?" Charlotte asked.

"Don't patronize me." A smile quirked on Mentlana's lips. "Fill me in on all the gossip."

Charlotte set her bag down on the table and pulled out a blood-pressure monitor. "Gossip? There's no gossip."

Mentlana snorted. "Please."

Charlotte strapped the cuff on Mentlana's arm. "Please, what?"

"How has it been, working with Quinn?"

Charlotte groaned. Of course Mentlana had to ask that. How *had* it been, working with Quinn? Awkward at first, annoying at times and maddening as she had to constantly wrestle with her emotions, emotions she'd thought were long since buried.

"That good, huh?" Mentlana said, as Charlotte took her blood pressure.

Charlotte tapped her nose. The last thing she wanted to do was talk about it. "Your blood pressure is a little high. We'll keep an eye on it." She pulled out her portable Doppler to listen to the baby's heartbeat. She listened and didn't like the sound she heard. "Is Genen here?" she asked.

"What's wrong?"

Charlotte squeezed Mentlana's hand. "I'd like Genen to go out and get Dr. Devlyn for me. I just want him to listen to the baby's heartbeat, that's all."

"He's on the ice." Mentlana picked up her phone and texted him. "He's with George and Dr. Devlyn."

"Good." Charlotte wrote down the baby's irregular heartbeat. She'd have to get Mentlana in to the clinic for another ultrasound to check on the progress of the CCAM.

"Okay, you owe me gossip now that I'm all stressed until Dr. Devlyn gets here. Now, spill."

"There's nothing to spill."

Mentlana's gaze narrowed. "You can't fool me. You've been scarce, quiet and very unlike yourself. You've been locked away in your clinic for days."

"There was a snowstorm."

"I'm not talking just about the blizzard, Charlotte."

Charlotte sighed. "It's hard."

"Being around him?"

Charlotte nodded. "He left me."

Mentlana bit her lip. "You left him too, though."

"What do you mean? He went to New York. He picked his career over me."

"I know. His timing sucked when he left, but you didn't go with him, either. This is going to sound harsh, and I should really be careful, considering you're my doctor, but did you ever think about how he felt when you didn't go with him?"

Tears stung Charlotte's eyes. No. She never had considered his feelings, just like she'd never even considered following him to New York.

Both of them had been so stubborn, so pigheaded and set in their ways.

There had been no compromise. There never had been.

"I think you still care for him, Charlotte, even if you don't want to admit it, and I think you should give him another chance."

Charlotte wasn't sure she could. She was terrified to put her heart at risk again.

The door opened and she heard stamping by the door.

"Charlotte?" Quinn called out.

She cleared her throat, to knock the nervousness out. "In the bedroom."

Quinn opened the door, his face rosy from the cold, his hair tousled by the wind, and there was stubble on his chin. The dark green of his fisherman's sweater really brought out the dark brown of his eyes. He looked like he should be gracing the cover of some outdoor magazine. His appearance was rugged and it made the butterflies in her stomach flutter.

"Is everything okay?" he asked, a little out of breath.

"I need you to listen to the baby's heartbeat. Also, Mentlana's blood pressure is slightly elevated."

Quinn nodded. "Sure."

Charlotte stood up and let him sit down beside Mentlana. He used the Doppler, his brow furrowed in concentration as he listened to the heartbeat. After a couple of minutes he switched it off.

"Well?" Mentlana asked nervously.

"Your baby is fine. However, I'd like to do an ultrasound to check on him." Quinn stood. "Genen is on his way back. Have him bring you over to the clinic as soon as he can."

Mentlana nodded. "Okay."

Quinn gave Mentlana's shoulder a squeeze, the scars on his hand vivid against his skin because of the cold.

"It'll be all right, Mentlana. You'll see." Quinn turned and gave Charlotte a serious look, which conveyed his concern, and her heart sank.

"Walk with me back to the clinic, Charlotte." Quinn left Mentlana's bedroom.

"Of course." Charlotte packed up her things and bent down, giving Mentlana a quick kiss.

"Give him a chance, Charlotte. He didn't come up here because of me," Mentlana whispered.

Charlotte didn't answer. Instead, she left the room in silence and then slipped on her coat, following Quinn outside. The crunching of the snow under their boots was the only sound that penetrated the uneasy tension between them.

"What's your assessment?" she asked finally.

"I think it's progressed, but I won't know how much until I do an ultrasound." He opened the clinic door, holding it open for her.

"And her blood pressure… Do you think that's cause for concern?"

"We'll run a urinalysis on her when she's here." He slipped out of his coat and then helped her with hers. "Like I said to Mentlana, it'll be okay."

"How do you know that?"

"Faith?" Quinn smiled. "You said you trusted me. That meant a lot, so I hope you trust me when I say it'll be okay."

"I do," Charlotte said, and touched his arm. She did trust him, but as for everything else she wasn't sure. She moved it away from him. "I'll go get the ultrasound ready."

"Sounds good. I'll wait here to help Genen and Mentlana."

"Okay." Charlotte turned and walked down the hall away from Quinn. She was taking the coward's way out, running away from the reality that she'd played a large part in the demise in their relationship, that she may have left him long before he'd left her.

CHAPTER THIRTEEN

JUST WHEN QUINN thought he was making some headway with Charlotte she pulled away from him again. Something else had transpired at Mentlana's, but he wasn't sure what. The ultrasound had been tense, but the baby's CCAM hadn't progressed much. It wouldn't be too much longer before they'd have to fly Mentlana to Iqaluit.

Quinn helped Genen take Mentlana home and get her settled. When he returned to the clinic, Charlotte was locked away in her office, working on files, and he didn't want to disturb her, though he should. He wanted to know what was bothering her, but he also didn't want to push her away.

Instead, he pulled out his camera. First he uploaded all the pictures on his memory card to his computer and then backed up the photographs on his USB stick. Once his memory card was free of the camera, he sat down at Charlotte's kitchen table and took apart the telephoto lens to clean it out. When he'd been out ice fishing, some salt water had got into the lens so the camera's automatic zoom was not working right. The last thing he wanted was his expensive photographic equipment to get ruined.

It was the first thing he'd bought when the bandages had come off and he'd gained a bit of strength back in his hand. He loved photography, but had never able to indulge in it.

When he'd been a kid he'd wanted to be a photographer

for *National Geographic*, but when he'd announced that to his father his subscription to that magazine had ended, to be replaced by a medical journal.

Great magazine subscription for a kid of fourteen.

Quinn snorted and shook the thought of his father out of his head. There was no place for him there. Instead, he focused on the task at hand. It was delicate work, but he didn't mind it in the least. His hand hadn't been bothering him and he was able to keep a steady grip on his tools as he took apart the lens and began to clean it.

"I hope that won't void the warranty."

Quinn glanced up to see Charlotte hovering in the connecting door between her clinic and her home. She leaned against the doorjamb, watching him in fascination. The invisible wall she had put up only a couple of hours ago seemed to be down once more.

"The warranty was voided long ago." Quinn continued with his work. This time she'd have to come to him. He held his breath, waiting, and then he heard her soft footfalls as she crossed the distance between the door and the kitchen table.

"That looks like pretty intricate work. You sure you know what you're doing?"

"You doubt my mad skills?" Quinn wiped the dried salt from around the rim. "There. That should do it."

"How did you get salt into your lens?"

"I was snapping some pictures out on the ice today."

Charlotte smiled and tucked her hair behind her ear. "You weren't fishing."

"No. I hate fishing. I was there for the scenery." Quinn put his telephoto lens back together. "That was actually something my father enjoyed. He liked fishing and made me go all the time. I never caught anything, much to his chagrin."

"What do you think of the scenery up here? I mean, you weren't too interested in seeing the sights in Yellowknife."

Quinn met her gaze. "That was a different time. I was a different person."

She didn't say anything for a few moments. "I want to show you something, as you're so interested in scenery."

"I'm intrigued."

"It's outside, in the cold." Charlotte stood up.

"I'm game, but we better hurry before the sun sets."

"That's the point." She hurried into the clinic and returned with their parkas. She tossed him his and Quinn caught it.

"If it's just a sunset, I've seen many."

Charlotte grinned. "Not like this." She zipped up her parka.

"If you say so." Quinn pulled on his parka. "Lead the way."

They headed outside, towards the water. The sun was setting, and it was so low that it seemed to be touching the horizon. Being so far north, the sun looked larger in the sky. As it set behind a cloud bank, it seemed like two other small suns peeked through the clouds, giving the illusion that three suns were setting on the water.

"Wow." Quinn raised his camera and took a shot. "That *is* amazing."

Charlotte nodded. "It is. They're called sun dogs."

Quinn glanced at her. The last rays of light touched her red hair, making it seem like it was aflame. He snapped a quick picture of her, looking out over the water.

"Hey, I didn't say you could take one of me," Charlotte protested.

"I was just admiring the view."

A pink blush tinged Charlotte's skin. He slung his camera over his shoulder and moved towards her, running his hand against her cold cheek.

"Quinn, please… I'm not sure."

"You trust me, Charlotte?"

"I said I did."

"Then tell me what's wrong."

Charlotte bit her lip. "It's nothing about you. It's me this time."

Quinn was confused. "I don't understand."

"I don't, either." Charlotte sighed. The wall was up once more and he knew he couldn't press her. "It's getting dark. We need to get back to the clinic."

"Sure."

They walked in silence back to the clinic, but as they clambered over a snow bank Charlotte let out a cry of horror at what was on the other side.

Anernerk was huddled in the snow, unmoving and with no jacket.

"Oh, my God." Charlotte scrambled down quickly. "Anernerk. Oh, God. No."

Quinn was by their side in a moment. He whipped off his parka and wrapped it around the old woman. "She's breathing, but barely." He picked her up in his arms. The cold was biting at his skin, but he didn't care. This was Charlotte's family, and he cared about Anernerk, too.

Charlotte ran ahead and held open the clinic door. Quinn rushed her inside, following in the wake of Charlotte, who was preparing a nearby exam room.

Anernerk's breathing was harsh. There was a rattle in her chest.

"Set her down here," Charlotte said, placing his camera on the counter. Quinn hadn't even known he'd dropped it or that Charlotte had picked it up. The moment he'd heard Charlotte cry out, he hadn't thought about anything else except helping Anernerk.

Quinn laid the old lady down on the bed. "She can't breathe well. I'm going to have to intubate her."

"I'll get an intubation kit." Charlotte disappeared from the room.

"It'll be okay," Quinn whispered, brushing back hair from

Anernerk's forehead. Anernerk reached out and grabbed his arms, gripping him tightly with a surprising surge of strength.

"No," she said in a barely audible whisper. "No."

Quinn moved closer to her. "Anernerk, we have to."

A small smile tugged at the corner of her lips. "Don't be obstinate, Quinn Devlyn. Let me go."

Anernerk's breathing became shallower, her skin was waxy and the rattle in her chest became louder. The same sound many patients took when they were taking their final breaths.

"I have the intubation kit!" Charlotte rushed back into the room.

"She wants to go. She doesn't want intubation. It's her time."

"She can't breathe," Charlotte said, flustered and annoyed. "Goddammit, Quinn. We have to intubate her."

"No," Anernerk said. "I told him not to."

Charlotte paled. "What? Anernerk, I don't—"

"It's my time to go, Charlotte. You're a wonderful doctor, as is Dr. Devlyn, but it's my time to pass. The spirits have spoken to me."

Tears welled up in Charlotte's eyes as she leaned over Anernerk. "I can't let you go. You're all I have. You took care of me when my father died. I can't lose you."

"You have Dr. Devlyn." Anernerk reached out and stroked Charlotte's face. "I shall miss you, daughter."

"No," Charlotte cried as she gripped Anernerk's shoulders. "No, I won't let you go."

"Don't be the obstinate man's wife with dark thoughts, my child. You have to let those fears go."

Quinn held on to Charlotte's shoulders, trying to pull her away, but she shrugged him off roughly and laid out the intubation instruments.

"No," Charlotte shouted, to no one in particular. "We have to intubate."

Anernerk stretched her body and took one last breath. Her

chest stopped moving. A breeze entered the exam room and Quinn swore he could feel the old woman's soul pass through him, if he believed in that sort of thing. Which he didn't. But in this moment of Anernerk's death, he wasn't so sure.

"Time of death—sixteen-forty." Charlotte slammed the intubation tray and pushed past him, leaving the room. He heard the distant slam of her office door.

Quinn scrubbed his hand over his face and then closed Anernerk's eyes and covered her body with a sheet. He cleaned up and washed his hands, giving Charlotte her privacy as she grieved.

Twenty minutes later the door to the clinic opened and George entered the exam room. His face was broken and pale when his gaze landed on Anernerk's body.

"Charley called me. I've come to take her to the special building we have. We store the bodies out there until we can bury them."

"Of course. By all means." Quinn stepped to one side. "Do you need help?"

George shook his head. "Thanks, but no. It's Charley I'm worried about, Doc. Even though they bickered, like when you saw them, it was Grandma who reached out and healed Charlotte when she came back from Yellowknife, her and my sister. Just like when Charley's dad died, Grandma was there because Charley didn't have anyone else."

There was a bitter taste in Quinn's mouth.

He'd been the cause of her need to heal on her return from Yellowknife. He'd left her alone. It'd been his fault.

"I'll take care of Charlotte." Quinn left the exam room and headed straight for Charlotte's office, but she wasn't there.

The door to her apartment was slightly ajar and he peeked inside. She was curled up on the couch, staring blankly at the wall. She'd changed out of her heavy sweater into a T-shirt and yoga pants, her hair loose over her shoulders and a blanket lying over her hips.

When she looked at him a shudder ran down his spine. It was the same expression she'd given him when she'd been in the hospital in Yellowknife. All that was missing from the scene was the antiseptic smell of the hospital and an IV pumping blood into her veins.

Why had he walked away from her then? He'd been such a fool, but after he'd told her about New York she'd told him to go and had refused to see him. Even though they'd been engaged, they hadn't been legally family and the hospital had had to respect her wishes. He'd remained at a distance, making sure her discharge from the hospital had gone well, although she hadn't known he'd been there. And then he'd left.

It pained him that she'd shut him out of her life.

"Charlotte, I'm so sorry for your loss."

"I should've intubated her."

"She didn't want it."

Charlotte's gaze narrowed. "It doesn't matter. If I'd intubated her she'd still be alive."

Quinn moved toward her. "Be reasonable. Anernerk was a hundred and one. It was her time to go."

"No," Charlotte shouted, jumping up to face him. "They're my family. Mine. They're all I have…"

Charlotte's anger dissipated and she sat back down on the couch in defeat. She was taking out her grief on him. He didn't deserve it. He'd only been listening to the patient's wishes, whereas she had only been thinking about herself. She had let her emotions rule her. Quinn was right.

She had a tendency to be over-emotional at times. She was so used to bottling up her feelings that after a time they would erupt out of her like putting a mint in diet soda.

She was being unreasonable.

The cushion next to her dipped as Quinn sat beside her. He took her hand in his broken one. It was strong and didn't tremble.

"I'm so sorry for snapping at you, Quinn."

She leaned over and buried her face in his neck, drinking in his scent, his warmth and his strength. Strength she needed now more than ever.

Right now she needed to feel something besides pain. What she needed was physical contact with him. Even though she'd promised herself she wouldn't let him in, at this moment she wanted to drown her sorrows in him. For so long she'd been anesthetized to life and she hadn't even realized it until this moment.

Making love with Quinn would remind her she was still alive.

"Charlotte," Quinn whispered, causing goose bumps to spread across her skin. Her nipples tightened under her shirt. She pressed her body to his, trying to close off any space that remained between them.

Charlotte wanted nothing to separate them. Not at this moment.

"What can I do for you, Charlotte?" He kissed the top of her head gently as he cradled her. "I'll do anything."

"Make love to me, Quinn."

A moan escaped past his lips and his hot breath fanned her neck. "Are you sure?"

Her answer was to simply wrap her arms around his neck and run her fingers through his hair, bringing his lips to her mouth. "Yes. Make the hurt go away. Please. I need you."

No more words were needed in that moment. Her plea was silenced by a searing kiss that made her melt into him. Charlotte didn't want to let him go. As the kiss deepened he pressed her against the cushions of the couch.

"Not here," she said, reluctantly breaking off the kiss.

Quinn scooped her up in his arms, without breaking the connection of their lips as he kissed her again. He carried her the short distance down the hall to her bedroom. Her blood thundered in her ears as she thought about what was going to happen and about how much she wanted it.

He set her down and she gripped the collar of his shirt while his hands roved over her back. Quinn's pulse raced under her fingertips as she undid the buttons at the base of his throat. "I want you, Quinn."

I've never stopped wanting you.

The air seemed to crackle with almost tangible tension. It was like her first time all over again and it was only fitting. Quinn had been her first and only.

"I want you, Charlotte, but only if you're sure. You've been through so much today."

"I want this. Please."

He seemed to hesitate, but only for a moment. "I can't resist you. I've never been able to." His lips captured hers in a kiss, his tongue twining with hers. Charlotte pulled him down onto the bed, until she was kneeling in front of him. His eyes sparkled in the dim room. "I've missed you, Charlotte. God, how I've missed you."

"Me, too," she whispered. She slipped off her shoes and they clattered to the floor. Reaching for him, she dragged him into another kiss. His hands slipped down her back, the heat of his skin searing her flesh through her thin cotton shirt, making her body ache with desire. Quinn removed her shirt and then his hands moved to her back to undo the clips of her bra. He undid each one painstakingly slowly, before he slipped the straps off her shoulders.

The sharp intake of breath from Quinn when his gaze alighted on her state of half undress sent a zing of desire racing through her veins. He kissed her again, his hands moving to cup her breasts and knead them. Charlotte closed her eyes and a moan escaped at the feel of his rough caresses on her sensitized skin.

She untucked his shirt from his pants then attacked the buttons and peeled it off, tossing it over her shoulder. She ran her hands over his smooth, bare chest, before letting her fingers trail down to the waist of his trousers. He grabbed her wrists and held her there, then pushed her down roughly on the bed, pinning her as he leaned over her. He released her hands and pressed his body against hers, kissing her fervently, as though he were a condemned man, yet there was tenderness there, too.

Charlotte had missed this.

She kissed him again, snaking her arms around his neck, letting his tongue plunder her mouth, her body coming alive as if it had been in a deep sleep.

He broke the kiss and removed her yoga pants, his fingers running over her calves. Each time his fingers skimmed her flesh her body ignited, and when his thumbs slid under the side of her panties to tug them down she went up in flames. Now she was totally naked and vulnerable to him.

Quinn stood and she watched him remove his pants. Moonlight filtered through the slatted blinds. He was glorious as he bared his well-honed body to her. She remembered every exquisite inch of him. She helped him roll on a condom.

When he returned to the bed he trailed his hand over her body, lingering on her breasts. Pleasure coursed through her at his touch. He pressed his lips against one of her breasts, laving her nipple with his hot tongue. She arched her back, wanting more.

"I love making you feel this way," he said huskily.

I love it when you make me feel this way. Only she didn't say the words out loud. His hand moved down her body, between her legs. He began to stroke her, making her wet with need.

All she could think about was him replacing his hand with his mouth. The thought of where he was, what he was going to do, made her moan.

As if reading her mind, Quinn ran his tongue over her body, kissing and nipping over her stomach and hips to where he'd just been caressing. His breath against her inner thighs made her smolder and when his tongue licked between the folds of her sex, she cried out.

Instinctively she began to grind her hips upwards, her fingers slipping into his hair, holding him in place. She didn't want him to stop. Warmth spread through her body like she'd imbibed too much wine, her body taut as ecstasy enveloped her in a warm cocoon.

She was so close to the edge, but she didn't want to topple over. When she came she wanted him to be buried inside her.

Quinn shifted position and the tip of his shaft pressed against her folds. She wanted him to take her, to be his and his alone.

Even if only for this stolen time.

He thrust quickly, filling her completely. There was a small sputtering of pain, just like their first time. She clutched his shoulders as he held still, stretching her. He was buried so deep inside her.

"I'm sorry, darling," he moaned, his eyes closed. "God, you're tight. It's been far too long." He surged forward, bracing his weight on his good arm while his bad hand held her hip. She met every one of his sure thrusts.

"So tight," he murmured again.

Quinn moved harder, faster. A coil of heat unfurled deep within her. She arched her back as pleasure overtook her, the muscles of her sheath tightening around him as she came. Quinn stiffened, and spilled his seed.

He slipped out of her, falling beside her on the bed and collecting her up against him. She let him and laid her head against his damp chest, listening to his rapid breathing.

What am I doing? What have I done?

She knew exactly what she'd done. She was angry at herself for being weak and for possibly hurting them both again.

CHAPTER FOURTEEN

SHE WAS BEING watched.

Charlotte could feel Quinn's gaze boring into her back. It made her feel uneasy. Why had she slept with him again? What had she been thinking?

That was a foolish question. She knew exactly what she'd been thinking and she was now regretting it wholeheartedly in the pale light of morning. Though she had to admit she'd liked being in his arms again. Every touch, every kiss had been like a dream come true, one she hadn't woken up from when the best part had come.

Grief had pushed her carefully guarded emotions over the edge and her walls had come tumbling down.

I'm an idiot.

Charlotte glanced over her shoulder. Quinn smiled lazily at her.

"What're you looking at?" she asked.

"I just like watching you." He propped himself on his elbow. "Where are you going?"

Her stomach twisted as she thought of that little building on the edge of town and she turned her back to him again. "To see Anernerk." She stared down at her knees and tried to keep back the tears threatening to spill.

The mattress dipped and Quinn scooted towards her. "Do you think that's wise?"

"Wise or not, I thought of her as a mother. She raised me as her own and it's my duty to be there." Besides, she had to put some distance between her and Quinn. Last night had been wonderful, but it needed to end there.

"A tradition?"

"Yes." A sigh escaped. She was not relishing her duty because she didn't want to face the reality that Anernerk was gone. Someone else she loved who'd left her.

You have Quinn. All you have to do is reach out and grab him.

Did she have Quinn? He hadn't said anything to the contrary. She might trust him for his surgical abilities, but she didn't trust handing her heart over to him again. Charlotte didn't want to pin all her hope on the notion that he *might* stay. She wasn't sure if he truly understood why it meant so much for her to stay up here and devote her life of medicine to these far-flung communities.

And she couldn't ask him to stay with her, giving up the life he wanted. Neither would she hold it against him this time when he left.

"I understand. I'm just worried about your emotional state."

Charlotte stood, but wouldn't look at him. She wasn't brave enough to meet his gaze, to let him have all of her.

"My emotional state is fine." Then she met his gaze and saw tenderness, concern and perhaps something more in his eyes.

Walk away, Charlotte.

"I have to go."

"Will you be back soon?" he asked.

"Does it matter?"

"It does. I want to talk about going to Iqaluit."

Charlotte took a step back, shocked. Did he want to work in Iqaluit? She hoped she hadn't led him on. "Why?"

"Unless you have laparoscopic equipment up here, I need to get to a facility that does. We're going to do a dry run of Mentlana's procedure in a skills lab."

Her heart sank in disappointment. *What were you expecting? Really.* "Yes, well, I don't… I mean, I'll have to file a flight plan."

"Then file one. We need to get down there as soon as we can."

"You want me to come with you?"

Quinn raised an eyebrow. "How else are you going to assist me?"

"Assist you? I thought you were joking before."

"I don't joke about surgery."

"I'm flattered, but I can't go to Iqaluit with you."

Quinn frowned. "I thought you still had a surgical license."

"I do. I can still perform some surgery, but I can't leave Cape Recluse."

"Why not?"

"I'm the only physician here."

"And your only current high-risk patient is Mentlana?"

"Yes."

"Then what choice do you have? You need to go through a dry run with me in a skills lab. You fly, George flies and it's a two-hour flight, so you won't be separated from your patients up here. You can spend a few days in Iqaluit with me, practicing. This is for your best friend, Charlotte."

Damn. Quinn was right.

"I'll talk to George. We'll arrange something, but after Anernerk's funeral."

"Deal."

She turned to leave then spun back round. "You're serious? You want me to assist?"

"Positive." He lay back against the pillows. "Only you."

Only me?

It gave her pleasure to know that he did trust her, that he had faith in her abilities to assist him, a renowned neonatal surgeon.

Of course she'd be an idiot to pass up this opportunity.

She'd file the flight plan with the airfield as soon as she was able to. Right now she had to focus on Anernerk and it was going to be hard. Even thinking about Anernerk laid out, waiting until they could dig through the permafrost, made her throat constrict. They'd have a memorial in a day or so and then bury her when the ground was softer.

Charlotte slipped on her parka at the door and headed out into the cold, but winter's bite didn't have any effect on her. Her mind was whirring with several things, Anernerk, Mentlana, the baby and, of course, Quinn.

Charlotte paused in front of the little cabin and took a deep, steadying breath.

I can do this. Anernerk wanted me here. She wanted me to be a part of this moment.

The handle to the door shook in her gloved hands as she opened it and stepped inside. The local ladies, including Lucy and Lorna, had placed Anernerk's body on one of the hides Anernerk's father had cured—a caribou which had been special to the old woman.

Charlotte stepped forward without saying anything. She'd seen this ritual performed before and she'd taken part in it as well. This time, however, it was much more personal. She took the wet rag Lorna handed her and gingerly picked up Anernerk's arm. She began to wash Anernerk's paper-thin skin.

A draft rushed at her back. Charlotte turned as Mentlana lumbered into the room. Two steps and Charlotte was by her side.

"Is everything okay?"

"I'm all right," Mentlana chided.

"You shouldn't be out of bed." Charlotte gripped her shoulder. "Don't you understand what bed rest is?"

Mentlana snorted. "Please. Genen already gave me that lecture. He brought me over on the dogsled, tied to the back of his snowmobile."

"What?" Charlotte was going to have a stern talking to Genen.

"He went like five kilometers an hour. Besides, it was my idea."

"Apparently, pregnancy has rendered you into a lunatic."

Mentlana sighed. "I wanted to be here. Let me braid her hair. I'll just do that and go back home."

"Okay. But then Genen's taking you home."

Mentlana nodded. "Thanks, Charley." She moved slowly to Anernerk's head and began to brush out the snowy white hair.

They finished preparing Anernerk's body. Mentlana braided the hair beautifully and was taken back home by Genen. The elders dressed Anernerk in traditional clothing and then wrapped her body in the caribou hide on which she'd been laid out.

Charlotte stood back, tears blurring her vision, but they didn't escape. She watched the final rituals. Later there would be requiems for Anernerk and her life.

There was nothing more she could do here. It was at times like this Charlotte felt helpless, useless. She was a healer and death was a blow to her. She'd lost and death had won.

"Can I have a moment alone with her?"

The other women nodded and exited the cabin. The sound of the door shutting behind her thundered in her head like a deafening blow of finality. She was alone with Anernerk, the outside world closed out so she could say her private farewells.

Charlotte would have to be quick. It was too cold outside for the other women to be out there long. She took a step toward Anernerk, the woman who had kept her from being lost in the system as an orphan. The woman who'd encouraged and nourished her dreams. The only mother Charlotte had known. She brushed her fingers across Anernerk's cold cheek.

"Aanak," she whispered. "I love you. You saved my life. I don't know how I'll go on without you, but I know you would want me to and I will. I hope you have the peace you were looking for." Tears rolled down Charlotte's face and she brushed them away.

"May the spirits guide you home." Charlotte opened the door and the elders returned to finish the preparations. She nodded to one of the elders and slipped out of the cabin. The sun was beginning to set and the stiffness in her shoulder alerted her to the fact she'd been tending to Anernerk's body for some time.

The lights from her house flooded out on the snow and a warm sensation built in the pit of her stomach. Quinn was there, waiting for her. She didn't have to be alone tonight if she was willing to take the risk and be with him again.

That was not a risk she was willing to take. She wouldn't lead him on.

Too much water had passed under the bridge and Charlotte couldn't see a way back to reclaim what they'd had. She wouldn't lose her heart to him again.

When she entered her home the scent of garlic hung heavily in the air and her stomach rumbled in response. Her home smelled like an Italian eatery, which was odd. Nothing in town was open. Today was a day of mourning for Anernerk. When someone died, communities became ghost towns for a couple of days.

Charlotte hung her jacket on the hook by the door and peered into the kitchen. The windows were steamed up and Quinn was moving back and forth between the stove and the table.

She suppressed a chuckle when she spied the old frilly apron, which had been her mother's, wrapped around his waist. She'd kept it for purely sentimental reasons, but seeing Quinn in it, tearing around the kitchen, amused her.

On the table was a clean white lace tablecloth, and two emergency candles were alight in a couple of old pickle jars. Two glass tumblers were filled with grape juice. It was the most romantic thing he'd ever done for her.

Damn. What is he doing?

Quinn cursed as he lifted the lid on a steaming pot. He shook his hand and stuck his finger in his mouth.

"There's some aloe vera in the living room. That's best for burns."

He spun round. "You're back. I wasn't sure when you were going to come back."

"Neither was I." She took a cautious step into the kitchen. "What're you doing? I didn't think you could cook."

"I can cook one thing. Garlic bread. But I felt I needed to feed you more than that." He gestured to the bubbling pots on the stovetop. "I found some spaghetti and sauce in the cupboards. Not much fresh stuff."

"Fresh stuff is hard to come by and very expensive."

Quinn sighed. "It's pretty bad when the town's doctor can't even afford some button mushrooms."

Charlotte chuckled and picked up a spoon, stirring the clumps of spaghetti before it was too late to be saved. "There's some canned mushrooms in the cupboard."

"Sacrilegious," he teased, but he pulled out the can and opened it, draining the juice into the sink before rinsing the mushrooms off. "Oh, look at that, they're even sliced."

"Extra fancy," she teased.

"But essential for this dinner."

"Oh?" Charlotte was intrigued. "Why essential?"

"I'm trying to replicate the meal we had in Niagara Falls on our first spring break away from medical school." Quinn dumped the mushrooms in the sauce.

The first time they'd made love. She remembered. They'd stayed in a cheap motel on the Canadian side of the falls and had got two coupons for dinner at an Italian restaurant.

The last thing she needed tonight was to be reminded of that moment.

"Quinn, this isn't necessary."

"Let me do this for you, Charlotte. You're tired and grieving."

Charlotte sighed in resignation. There was no harm in letting him make dinner. They'd been sharing meals since he'd arrived and they had been innocent enough.

"Hey, bring that pasta here. The sauce is ready."

"Sure." Charlotte dumped the spaghetti back into the pot and placed it on a cool range.

"Go sit down. I'll be serving you tonight." Quinn pushed her towards the table and she didn't fight him. She sat down and waited for him to serve dinner. The garlic bread smelled heavenly and she couldn't remember the last time someone had made her a spaghetti dinner. Hell, she couldn't even recall the last time she'd eaten spaghetti. When she cooked for herself, when she allowed herself time to eat, it was fast and quick. She worried, briefly, how long the ingredients had been in her pantry.

It wouldn't matter. Quinn had tried and she was going to eat the meal, though she might regret it later. The way she was feeling now, she could eat a whole plate of muktuk if given half the chance.

"Voilà." Quinn set the plate down in front of her. A huge mound of spaghetti with Bolognese sauce and a crispy side of cheesy garlic bread made her stomach growl loudly in appreciation.

"The first taste is with the eyes."

"Is that your subtle way of telling me it won't taste good?" she asked.

He winked. "Taste is all in the mind."

"Oh, dear." She grinned.

Quinn picked up his tumbler of juice. "To Anernerk and the wonderful century she graced this earth."

"To Anernerk." The words were hard to get out and it was even harder to swallow the juice. She set down the tumbler and Quinn's hand slid across the table, his fingers twining with hers. She pulled her hand away.

"I'm sorry. I can't." She couldn't let him touch her. She was too weak.

"It's okay. You're mourning. You have every right to mourn her. You loved her."

"Thank you for understanding. I need my space."

"I went through my own situation not that long ago."

"Your father. Of course. I'm sorry."

Quinn shrugged. "Don't be. He wasn't the most loving of fathers."

"You never really told me how your parents felt about me."

"I know." Quinn didn't meet her gaze.

"That bad, huh?"

He grinned. "He wanted me to marry a socialite, or whatever Toronto's equivalent is to that. Marrying the daughter of some 'hippy'—even if she was a physician—wasn't good enough."

"My father was a doctor. He was far from being a hippy."

"You weren't my father's ideal idea of a wife for me."

"Apparently not for you, either." She regretted the words instantly.

Quinn's smiled faded and he took a bite of his spaghetti. "I could say the same in reverse."

Guilt washed over her. "You could."

They ate in silence, but it was hard to chew. The food was like sawdust in her mouth.

"My cooking is that bad, then?" Quinn asked, breaking the tension.

She glanced up and the earlier twinkle was back in Quinn's eyes. "It's great—better than those brownies."

He groaned. "Let's not bring that up again. Please tell me I'm improving."

Charlotte picked up a piece of garlic bread and took a bite. It was like pure heaven, compared to the clumpy mess that was the spaghetti. The garlic bread melted in her mouth like cheesy goodness. She could marry the garlic bread and she would if it asked her.

"I take it from your orgasmic expression that I did quite well with the bread."

"You did," she said between bites. "You're right."

"About what?"

"You can cook garlic bread. It's divine." She took another bite. "Of course, it could be because I haven't had *real* garlic bread in about three years and I'm desperate for it."

They ate the rest of the meal. She'd forgotten how delicious someone else's cooking was, even if it was Quinn's.

"What do you think?" he asked, as he poured another glass of juice.

"Could be better." She grinned and then winked.

"Better? I ought to take you over my knee and spank you for that remark."

Quinn's jest instantly sobered her up. She set down her fork and then picked up her plate, taking it to the sink.

"Did I say something wrong, Charlotte?" he asked.

"No. Nothing." It was all becoming too easy with Quinn again. He was charismatic and broke through her defenses so easily. "I'm really tired. I need to go to bed."

"Okay. I'll clean up," he said.

Charlotte nodded and without so much as a look she retreated to the safety of her bedroom, locking the door behind her. The bed was still messy and Quinn's scent still lingered in the air, causing heat to creep up her neck. The memory of last night's kisses were suddenly fresh in her brain once more.

She wanted him still, but she wouldn't give in.

Instead, she stripped her bed of the sheets and shoved them in the laundry hamper, shutting the lid firmly.

For her own sanity, she had to stick to her original plan and keep her heart on ice.

CHAPTER FIFTEEN

AFTER ANERNERK'S MEMORIAL, Quinn and Charlotte moved down to Iqaluit. Quinn's reputation as a surgeon had preceded him and the hospital was willing to bend over backwards to accommodate them. He knew the hospital was trying to woo him into staying permanently.

For a month Charlotte traveled between Cape Recluse and Iqaluit as they prepared for Mentlana's eventual surgery.

Charlotte was polite to Quinn and willing to learn, but the barriers were back up and it smarted. Although what could he expect? The night they'd made love, Charlotte had been looking for comfort, not to renew their relationship.

And he had to respect her wishes, even though he wished the reverse. Once Mentlana successfully delivered he would return to Toronto and she'd remain here.

You could stay.

Only what would be the use of staying if Charlotte didn't want him?

There were times Quinn thought she was pulling away, distancing herself from him, building those walls back up. Then at other times it was like the years hadn't passed them and their separation had never happened.

"That's it, keep the needle steady." Quinn watched the monitor as Charlotte manipulated the laparoscope in the lab. She was doing quite well. They'd done a couple of dry runs for placing a thoracoamniotic shunt, the most minimally invasive treatment for Mentlana's baby.

Quinn began to teach Charlotte everything he knew. Charlotte kept in close contact with George, who flew in once a week to take Charlotte back to check up on Mentlana and her other patients. No one else was seriously ill or needed the kind of care Mentlana did.

The residents of Cape Recluse understood what Doc Charley was doing and they didn't mind. The community was still shaken by Anernerk's death and everyone was rooting for this baby. Cape Recluse needed a happy event. This baby represented the hope of a small community.

When he'd last checked on Mentlana, her baby's CCAM was still within the safe range and wasn't pressing on the heart yet. "Yet" was the operative word. At any moment the CCAM could worsen. He was holding off operating, hoping to get her further along in her pregnancy.

The pressure to succeed was keenly felt. Mentlana was thirty weeks, now, but if he could get her to thirty-five then the baby had a better chance of survival should he have to deliver him early.

Quinn wasn't a praying man, but he was wishing for that right now with all his heart. He didn't want to have to perform an in utero procedure. The pediatric specialist in Iqaluit would be quite capable of handling Mentlana's baby and the CCAM if delivered after thirty-five weeks.

It was the surgery that had the young specialist apprehensive. Dr. Richards, the pediatrician there, hadn't done many. Indeed she spent as much time in the skills lab as Charlotte.

Plans were being put in place with the obstetrician, as well. Everything seemed to be running smoothly. However, when Charlotte had returned from her last stint in Cape Recluse three days ago, she'd seemed out of sorts.

She'd been aloof since the dinner he'd made her, but now

she looked drawn, tired and ill. He hoped she wasn't catching a cold. If she got sick, she couldn't be allowed near the O.R.

"Dr. Devlyn?" Charlotte said, disturbing his silent rumination. She'd taken to addressing him in a professional manner in front of the other surgeons.

"Good. Now place the shunt. Do you remember how?"

"I do."

Even though they weren't practicing on living tissue, there was a certain finesse about placing such a small shunt inside something so tiny and fragile.

"Then let's see."

Charlotte bit her lip, her brow furrowing as she concentrated and placed it.

"Good." Quinn let out an inward sigh of relief, his shoulders relaxing. Charlotte hadn't managed it yesterday, but each day, she was improving. His hope was that she could perform the surgery with Dr. Richards, should his hand fail. He rubbed the appendage in question. It'd been paining him after too many hours in the lab, and the thought of it not being strong enough to operate worried him.

"Excellent job, Dr. James," praised Dr. Richards, who was taking copious notes in a flipbook.

Charlotte took a deep breath and smiled. "Thank you, Dr. Richards. Now, I'd better head back to the hotel and pack. George should be here soon for my trip back to Cape Recluse."

"Of course," Quinn said. He would miss her. He always did when she returned to Cape Recluse.

"I'll call you about Mentlana's status when I examine her later today."

"Thank you, Dr. James. I look forward to your assessment."

Charlotte left the skills lab while Quinn cursed inwardly. *You're being selfish, Quinn Devlyn. Tell her you miss her.* But he couldn't. Even though he didn't want to be parted from her and wanted to heal the rift between them, he wasn't sure if he wanted to spend the rest of his life in Nunavut in the cold and ice.

The selfish side of him wondered if she'd come to Toronto to be with him, but he doubted that very much. She hadn't left the North five years ago when they'd been engaged, so why would she now?

This was where Charlotte belonged. But he wasn't sure if he did.

He turned to Dr. Richards. "I'd better be off. I have some sonograms to review." Quinn excused himself from the lab, relieved he didn't have to talk shop with Dr. Richards, who usually talked his ear off. Right now his head was pounding behind his eyes.

When he was in the locker room he pulled off his scrubs and deposited them in the laundry receptacle before washing his hands. As soon as the water hit his skin the muscles in his palm tensed, forcing his fingers to curl upwards, freezing in a clawlike position.

"Dammit," he cursed as he gripped his bad hand with his good one. He massaged the palm, willing the spasms to cease before someone walked in on him. His whole arm was tense, the muscles rigid up past the elbow. It'd been a long time since he'd had a spasm like this, where it locked his entire arm into a useless tangle of sinew and flesh.

How the hell could he even contemplate operating on Mentlana? This just proved all his fears. There was no way he could risk doing a delicate surgery such as a thoracoamniotic shunt or fetal resection when his muscle spasms were so unpredictable.

Bile rose in his throat as he thought about holding such a delicate, fragile life in his hands and having a spasm like this. He would crush the fetus.

His muscles began to relax under his ministrations. Once his arm ceased tensing up he was able to relax his fingers.

Quinn's other hand ached from massaging his damaged one so long and so hard.

Dammit.

His phone buzzed and he pulled it out of his trouser pocket. It was a text from Charlotte, who needed to speak to him before she left for Cape Recluse. He didn't want her to see him like this. He texted back that he had been held up at the hospital and then jammed his phone back in his pocket.

Quinn pulled his arm close to his side, cradling it as pins and needles coursed up and down from his elbow to the tips of his fingers. The aftermath of the spasm always felt like he'd fallen asleep on his hand. He had to leave the hospital before anyone saw his hand all clenched and tense, before anyone suspected anything. He quickly dressed in his street clothes, his hand impeding the process slightly.

How the hell was he going to tell Charlotte he couldn't do the surgery?

Right now he needed some liquid courage, but he didn't know where he was going to find it in Iqaluit and he didn't relish the idea of wandering through bitterly cold streets in an attempt to do so.

"Ah, Dr. Devlyn. Just the man I was looking for."

Quinn groaned inwardly as the chief surgeon approached him, followed by members of the board of directors. He'd nothing against Dr. Spicer or the board—in fact, he was grateful they were willing to open up their hospital and allow him to be here when their hospital was full of surgeons—but he didn't want to be stopped at the moment.

He didn't want them to see him this way.

Dr. Spicer stopped in front of Quinn and the board members closed in around him. He was trapped, his escape route cut off.

Deep breath.

"Dr. Devlyn, may I introduce you to our board—Mr. Leonard Saltzman, Mrs. Jennifer Chenery and Mr. Harry Westman."

Quinn shook each member's hand, forcing out pleasantries through gritted teeth, keeping his bad hand behind his back.

"Dr. Devlyn is a renowned neonatal surgeon. He's up here preparing for surgery on a possible congenital cystic adenomatoid malformation on an Inuk woman's fetus."

"Impressive," Jennifer Chenery said, looking him up and down with an appreciative eye. "Are you carrying out the entire procedure as well as the birth?"

"No," Quinn replied. "No. Your head of obstetrics is more than capable of assisting me. He will be delivering the infant at term."

There were a few murmurs, and Quinn knew without a doubt they were impressed. He knew Mrs. Chenery was, from the way she was eyeing him like he was piece of chocolate cake or something.

"You worked at Manhattan Mercy for a time, is that correct, Dr. Devlyn?" Leonard Saltzman asked.

"Yes, I did, and then I returned to Canada. I worked at Mount Sinai for a couple of years before taking a sabbatical after my father's death."

"Dr. Devlyn is highly praised by Manhattan Mercy's chief of surgery," Dr. Spicer told the board members.

Quinn's stomach twisted and he had a feeling about where this conversation was going, but he wasn't sure if he was in a position to listen to it. Dr. Spicer was still talking him up to the board members and Quinn supposed he was talking to him as well, but Quinn couldn't hear anything but muffled words.

"Dr. Devlyn?" Dr. Spicer said.

"Sorry, Dr. Spicer. I was thinking about… I was contemplating something about a patient's procedure. Please forgive me." Quinn tried to extricate himself from the conversation, but it didn't work.

"No problem, Dr. Devlyn. I know you're a busy man. The board members were just leaving."

Quinn nodded and shook their hands as they left, until it

was only he and Dr. Spicer standing in the surprisingly quiet corridor.

"I'd best be on my way, as well," Quinn said, but Dr. Spicer reached out and grabbed his shoulder.

"A moment of your time, Dr. Devlyn."

"Yes, of course. Lead the way." Dr. Spicer opened the door to a small consult room they'd been standing in front of.

Dr. Spicer shut the door and motioned for Quinn to sit. "I think you know why I've asked you in here."

"I have an inkling."

Dr. Spicer grinned. "We want to offer you a position here in Iqaluit. We want you to head up a world-class neonatal unit. Right now we're currently flying cases like Mrs. Tikivik to Ottawa or Toronto because se don't have the facilities or surgical capabilities, but our board of directors is planning to change that. We want to provide a service like that for our community."

Quinn scrubbed his hand over his face. "Do you think the territory will fund an endeavor like this?"

Dr. nodded. "I think so and I know the communities will rally for federal support, too. We need physicians with the know-how up here. We need to provide a more extensive neonatal facility for our patients and we want you to spearhead it."

"I don't know, Dr. Spicer." Quinn, for some unknown reason, couldn't come flat out and turn Dr. Spicer down and he couldn't think of an excuse.

So what was holding him back from accepting?

The position his father had left for him in Toronto? No. He didn't care about becoming Chief of Surgery. Not really.

Dr. Spicer looked crestfallen, but smiled nonetheless. "Understandable, but the board is willing to do whatever it takes to get you, Dr. Devlyn."

"Let me think on it."

"Of course, take all the time you need, Quinn. The offer doesn't have a termination date."

"Very generous of you."

Dr. Spicer opened the consult-room door and Quinn exited, Dr. Spicer shaking his hand as he was leaving.

Why didn't I just say no? Why didn't I say yes?

Quinn couldn't figure it out. He couldn't think straight and his mind was a bit too full at the moment. All the expectations were weighing heavily on his shoulders. And then there was Charlotte.

Beautiful, wonderful, loving Charlotte, who'd let him back inside her protective walls, or so he'd thought.

"Hey, Quinn!"

Quinn glanced over his shoulder to see Dr. Patterson, the OB/GYN on Mentlana's case, approaching. He was dressed in street clothes, with a duffel bag slung over his shoulder.

"Carlisle." Quinn greeted him, as Dr. Patterson approached. "I thought you'd gone home."

"I'm on my way." Dr. Patterson looked him over from head to toe. "You look like roadkill."

"I feel like it."

Carlisle clapped him on the back. "You need a stiff drink."

"I do, but didn't know where I'd be able to find one."

"I know just the place if you care to join me."

"I would." Quinn relaxed. "Lead the way."

CHAPTER SIXTEEN

THREE DAYS AGO, when she had last been in Cape Recluse, her life had changed because a month ago she'd lost her head and had made love with Quinn. She hadn't believed the over-the-counter pregnancy test she'd used and had Rosie draw some blood.

The blood test confirmed it as well.

She was pregnant. And shocked because they'd used protection. The condom must've failed, because there was no denying it. She was already a month gone.

It thrilled and terrified her to her very core.

She wanted a family. She wanted to be a mother, but being pregnant scared her witless. What if she lost this one? It would be too much to bear.

Charlotte stuffed some clothes in her duffel bag, trying not to think about having to leave again, especially leaving Quinn again. She tried to distance herself from Quinn, to keep her walls secure, but to no avail.

She thought about him constantly. Her heart once more belonged to him, but she wasn't sure how she could tell him that. As well as tell him that she was pregnant again. The last time she'd told him they were expecting it hadn't gone well at all.

An hour ago a text had come in and she'd picked up her phone. Quinn had got her text about needing to speak with him, but he had been held up at the hospital.

She was tempted to text him and tell him why she needed to speak to him, but a text wasn't going to cut it. She needed to tell him face-to-face, even though she was afraid to risk her heart again.

Charlotte wondered if he suspected her condition. He'd been so distracted and aloof in the skills lab today and she'd been having extreme morning sickness. She could barely keep anything down and it was beginning to show in her pallor.

No, he couldn't know. She'd only just found out herself and he hadn't noticed last time she'd been pregnant.

Perhaps he was regretting his decision to allow her to assist.

Yesterday, when she had messed up and inserted that test shunt too roughly, causing the laparoscope to go deeper, thus killing the fetus, he'd come up behind her and placed his hands over hers, guiding her through another run. His gentle, firm touch was so sure and steady.

Don't be a coward.

Charlotte had to see him, couldn't go to Cape Recluse without telling him. She left her packing and was about to go track Quinn down when there was a knock at her door. Charlotte opened it and there he was, leaning against the doorjamb.

"Quinn?" Charlotte was surprised to see him. He looked a bit disheveled and there was a strong odor of beer. "Are you drunk? Where did you find alcohol?"

"Dr. Patterson is a member of the local legion."

Charlotte stepped to the side and allowed him into the room before shutting the door. "You shouldn't be drinking. Mentlana might go into distress any time now."

Quinn shook his head. "First of all, I'm not drunk. I only had pop. Someone spilled their beer on me."

"Well, that's a relief. The last thing a surgeon of your caliber needs to be doing is drinking."

Quinn snorted. "My caliber indeed," he mumbled, as he sat down on the edge of the bed.

"What's wrong? You were acting very strangely in the lab today."

He ignored her question. "Secondly, you don't need me. You're perfectly capable of doing the surgery on your own."

Charlotte paled. "What're you talking about? I'm just a GP—you're the surgeon. You've done this countless times. You know the call to make and when to make it. I'm just here to assist."

"You're not just an assistant, Charlotte. You're going to take point on Mentlana's baby."

"You are drunk." Charlotte snorted.

"Not at all."

"Then why am I suddenly taking point?"

"My hand spasmed. I don't want to risk that happening during surgery. You have to take over. I know you can do it."

The room spun. She felt dizzy. She sat down next to him on the bed. *Take point?* She was a general surgeon, not a specialist.

"I can't take point, Quinn."

"I've already talked to Dr. Patterson. He'll vouch for your ability and be overseeing you every step of the way."

Dread coursed down her spine. "And where will you be?" she asked cautiously.

"I don't know, Charlotte. Where will I be?"

The blood drained from her face. "What do you mean?" Though she knew.

"You know what I mean." He raked his fingers through his hair. "Damn it, Charlotte, I can't stay here."

Charlotte's heart skipped a beat and it felt like a great weight was pressing on her chest, stopping her from breathing. He was doing it again. He was finding some excuse and running away.

"What about Mentlana?"

Quinn cursed under his breath. "I just told you, you and Carlisle Patterson can handle it. I can't."

"I think you can."

He looked up at her, angry. "Dammit, Charlotte, my hand spasmed. If you let me near Mentlana and her baby, I might kill them."

She was opening her mouth to say something when her phone began to ring. She answered it. "Dr. James speaking."

"Doc Charley, it's George. I'm at the airport and we're transporting Mentlana to the hospital. She's gone into preterm labor."

"I'll be right there." Charlotte snapped her phone shut. Her stomach lurched and she came precariously close to losing her lunch. There was so much more she wanted to say to Quinn, but she didn't have time to deal with him and his brooding.

Mentlana needed her.

"What's wrong?" he asked.

"What does it matter to you? You're heading back to Toronto to wallow." She tried to push past him but he grabbed her arm and spun her round.

"Charlotte, I won't risk her baby. If I do the surgery on Mentlana and she or her baby dies, you'll loathe me."

"You care how I would feel about you?"

Quinn's face relaxed. "Of course, I do. I don't want to kill the baby. I'm afraid. My hand…it clenched so hard today."

Charlotte touched his face. "You won't. I'll be with you every step of the way."

"If I'm handling the fetus… Oh, God, I don't even want to think about it." He tried to move away, but she gripped him by the shoulders.

"You can do this. I'll help you."

She held her breath, waiting for his response. Quinn nodded. "All right. And you're right. I can."

"Good. Now, we have to head to the hospital. That was George on the phone and Mentlana has gone into preterm labor."

Quinn nodded again. "I'll grab a coffee in the cafeteria.

Hopefully the on-call obstetrician is smart enough to try and stop the contractions. Let's go."

Charlotte grabbed her purse, ready to face whatever fate had to throw at them.

Charlotte was reading Mentlana's chart while Mentlana was napping. The obstetrician on call had been able to stop the contractions, so they had that going for them: the less stress on the baby the better, and a contracting uterus wasn't particularly helpful to a fetus with a CCAM.

Genen had been absolutely frantic until they'd got everything under control, then he'd crashed and was sleeping on a nearby cot while Lorna knitted in the corner. The clicking of Lorna's knitting needles mixing with the beeps and hums of the monitors in the dim room was oddly soothing to Charlotte.

She'd been on her feet for almost twenty-four hours since Mentlana had arrived. George had gone back up to Cape Recluse as they needed someone with some medical experience there.

"How's it looking, Doc?" Lorna whispered.

"She's stable. Dr. Devlyn is going to do a portable sonogram soon. He's just gone to get the machine. And then we'll assess what needs to be done."

Lorna nodded slowly. "How about you take a rest? You're in your first trimester and with your history of the previous miscarriage you need to take it easy."

Charlotte's mouth dropped open. "How did you know?"

Lorna shrugged but didn't look up from her knitting. "I've been a midwife longer than you've been alive, Charlotte James. I know when a woman is expecting." Lorna glanced up at her. "I'm thrilled for you, by the way."

"Thank you. I have to admit I'm nervous."

"You have every right to be, but I'm sure everything will be okay."

"No one can be certain of that." Charlotte sighed. "I mean,

there are so many variables, so many things that could go wrong."

Like car accidents. Look at Quinn—he'd had a terrible one that had damaged his surgical hand and only his hand. What were the odds on that?

"Yes, that's true," Lorna admitted. "But if you worry about the what-ifs, you'll make yourself sick. You're a physician. You're looking at statistics of what can go wrong all the time. But look at the number of births that go right. What happened to you was a tragedy, Charlotte, but it wasn't anything you did that caused you to lose your baby."

Charlotte nodded. "You're right."

"I know it." Lorna went back to knitting, a smug smile plastered across her face. "Your baby will be healthy, as will you, Doc Charley."

"What?" Mentlana asked groggily. "Who's pregnant?"

Charlotte pulled a rolling stool up beside Mentlana. "How are you feeling?"

"Like a beached whale, of course." Mentlana winced. "Now, who's pregnant? Dish the dirt. I may be drugged up with who knows what, but I know I heard Lorna and you talking about a pregnancy." Mentlana's eyes widened and Charlotte didn't need to tell her anything. Her friend had figured it out. "You're pregnant."

"Yes. It's me."

"Oh, my God, that's wonderful, Charley." Mentlana paused. "It's Devlyn's, right?"

Charlotte rolled her eyes. "Who else's would it be?"

"Does he know?"

"No." Charlotte's cheeks flushed. "I want to tell him but…"

"You're afraid," Mentlana offered.

Charlotte nodded. "Terrified. The last time didn't end well. He wasn't thrilled about the prospect, either."

"You need to tell him. He has the right to know." Mentlana reached out and took her hand, giving it a squeeze. "And if he wants no part of it, you'll have a baby. You'd make an excellent mother."

Charlotte smiled. "Thank you."

Mentlana grinned. "I'm so happy for you." She rubbed her belly. "You know, I always wonder about that phrase about God only giving you what you can handle. I wondered about the purpose of making me and my child so sick and putting us through this torment, but I think I know why, now."

"Mentlana, I wouldn't wish that kind of fate on anyone."

Her friend smiled. "'Oh, ye of little faith.'"

"How are we this morning?" Quinn asked as he pushed a portable sonogram into the room. Genen roused from his slumber with a groan. "Sorry, Genen," Quinn apologized, realizing he'd woken him up.

"It's okay, Doc," Genen yawned.

Quinn set up the machine but he squeezed Charlotte's shoulder as he passed. "You okay? You need your rest. You look beat."

"I'll rest after I know how Mentlana's baby is doing." Charlotte saw Mentlana's pointed look, but Charlotte kept her mouth shut as Dr. Richards walked into the room, followed by Dr. Patterson.

"Genen, Mentlana, this is Dr. Richards, a pediatric specialist, and Dr. Patterson, the head of obstetrics. They'll be helping us with your baby."

"Nice to meet you," Genen said quietly, taking a seat beside his wife.

"I'll just do a quick sonogram to see how the baby's CCAM is progressing."

"Sure thing," Mentlana agreed, but Charlotte could tell by the waver in her voice that she was nervous. It was the first sign of apprehension Mentlana had expressed in a long time. Even when they'd wheeled her into the hospital yesterday she had been pretty upbeat. Nothing seemed to faze Mentlana Tikivik.

Charlotte admired Mentlana's bravery. She reached out and brushed Mentlana's hair back from her forehead, but when she looked up she saw a strange expression—a cold, calculating look—pass over Dr. Richards's face, like she was trying to find some fault with her.

The sound of the baby's heartbeat filled the darkened room and Charlotte forgot about Dr. Richards and watched the baby on the screen. The lesion was growing and soon hydrops would start. Mentlana could develop mirror syndrome. If that happened, the baby's chance of survival greatly diminished.

Charlotte's stomach twisted and she resisted the urge to give in to the morning sickness. *Please, don't let me throw up now.* The last thing she needed was Dr. Richards poking her nose into why she was vomiting during a routine sonogram.

"There we go," Quinn announced. "All done." He wiped off Mentlana's swollen belly and then sent Charlotte a quick look which conveyed his concern, one she understood all too well.

"Well, Doc Devlyn?" Genen asked, his voice tight with barely contained worry.

"We're going to discuss the next steps, but I'm pleased your contractions have stopped now, Mentlana. That's very good."

Mentlana nodded and gripped Genen's hand. "Thank you, Doctors."

Quinn escorted Dr. Patterson and Dr. Richards out of the room. Charlotte kissed Mentlana's forehead. "I'll be back as soon as I can with some news. Just relax, take it easy, bug the nurses for anything you want...."

Mentlana chuckled. "Okay."

Charlotte left the room and pulled a cracker out of her pocket. She had a sleeve of them in her lab coat. Her morning sickness was turning into all-day sickness. She had to get a consult with Dr. Patterson soon and get some Diclectin to keep her vomiting at bay.

When she approached the meeting room she could hear

raised voices. It was never a good sign when surgeons disagreed.

"Dr. James shouldn't be allowed to do the surgery."

Charlotte paused, hearing Dr. Richards's voice over the din. Her heart skipped a beat and then sank to the soles of her feet. Her first instinct was to back away, but Mentlana was her patient and Quinn needed her. She wasn't going to be bullied by the other surgeons. With a deep breath she pushed open the door. The arguing stopped immediately

Dr. Richards's lips were pursed in a tight thin line as their gazes locked.

"Dr. Richards." Charlotte nodded curtly. "I understand you have some problem about my involvement in this case."

"Dr. James, it's nothing," Quinn said, trying to soothe the tension in the room.

"I would love to hear everyone's opinions, Dr. Devlyn." Charlotte took a seat across from Dr. Richards. "Every surgeon's input is invaluable, especially when it involves Mentlana Tikivik."

It was a good move to pump up a young surgeon's ego. Surgeons could be silly and petty creatures that way. It was like her mother's old saying about catching more flies with honey than vinegar. Or Anernerk's saying of always treating your children with respect because they'll replace you one day, and from the way it sounded, Dr. Richards was trying to replace her in the surgical suite.

Dr. Richards was shocked. A small smile even cracked her usually serious facade. "It's not that I question your skill and value as a physician, Dr. James. I have spent a lot of time with you in the lab and am vastly impressed with your handling of instruments. You have the skills of a surgeon, but I'm concerned about your familiarity with the patient."

"What do you mean?" Charlotte asked.

"There's a reason physicians don't operate on family members, whether blood or a close bond."

"And your point?"

Dr. Richards's eyes narrowed. "I don't think you will act rationally in there. With myself, Dr. Devlyn and Dr. Patterson, I think Mrs. Tikivik will do just fine."

Charlotte gripped the edge of the conference table, her stomach lurching with a wave of nausea. "I understand your concern, Dr. Richards. Yes, I will admit I have a close relationship with my patient, but I can assure you I will not be irrational. Are you from Nunavut originally, Dr. Richards?"

"I don't understand the point of the question. What does that have to do with this situation?"

"A lot, in fact," Dr. Patterson interjected. He sent Charlotte an encouraging look. "I think I understand what Dr. James is getting at."

"Well, I don't."

"Just answer it," Quinn said.

"No. I'm not from here. I'm from Vancouver."

"People in remote communities can be very untrusting of strangers. This territory is very close-knit, given its vastness. I've know the Tikiviks for a long time and they trust me. If you try to remove me from the O.R., it will only upset Mrs. Tikivik, possibly putting her into distress."

"Dr. James is correct. And Mrs. Tikivik is very...strong-willed," Quinn said delicately, though a hint of a smile played on his lips. "I need Dr. James to assist me. I've known her for a long time, too, and I value her skills. Dr. Richards, you are needed to monitor the fetus and take care of the child if an EXIT procedure is required. Dr. Patterson's main concern is the health of the mother."

Dr. Richards assessed Charlotte. "Your points are valid. You've swayed me and I concur."

Quinn sent a glance that conveyed his relief. Charlotte nodded and pulled out another cracker, shoving it into her mouth as Dr. Richards flipped open her notebook.

"Now, can we discuss the real reason we're here?" Quinn

clicked on his slide show and the large screen in the board-room lit up with sonograms of the fetus. "The fetus is at a gestational age of thirty weeks and, as you can tell, the lesion has grown." Quinn used a pointer to indicate the lesion. "The fetus will develop hydrops soon."

"And given Mrs. Tikivik is already a high-risk candidate, I have no doubt she'll develop mirror syndrome, which will quickly escalate into fatal pre-eclampsia," Dr. Patterson added.

"What're you suggesting, Dr. Devlyn?" Dr. Richards asked.

"We need to perform a fetal resection today."

"And that is the best course of action?" Charlotte asked. "It won't tax Mentlana, having two C-sections so close together?"

"It's the best option, Dr. James," Quinn said seriously. "The fetus will feel nothing and will have the benefit of his mother's blood supply from the placenta, a chance to heal in the womb and to let the lungs develop more. Mentlana will have to remain in Iqaluit and be monitored for preterm labor."

Charlotte nodded. "I'll inform my patient."

Quinn turned to Dr. Patterson. "We need an O.R. prepped."

"We'll have one ready within the hour. The longer we wait, the greater the risk her blood pressure will climb." Dr. Patterson stood.

Charlotte got up and left the boardroom. Her heart was pounding and it felt like it was going to burst out of her chest.

You can do this. I know you can.

She could, and she would for Mentlana. She paused at the door to Mentlana's room and saw she was alone, staring at the wall. The room was still dark, but Genen and Lorna were no longer there.

When Charlotte entered the room, Mentlana looked at her, her face drawn and all the apprehension her friend had been trying to hide finally bubbling to the surface.

"Hey, Charley." Mentlana's voice wavered. "What's the verdict?"

"Where's Genen?" Charlotte asked, sitting on the edge of the bed.

"I sent him to get breakfast. Someone had to eat something around here."

Charlotte nodded. "You'll be able to eat soon."

Mentlana inhaled, her hand shaking in Charlotte's. "Tell me."

"Do you want to wait for Genen?"

"No. Tell me."

"The lesion has grown quite a bit since the last sonogram. The baby is at risk of developing heart failure and you are at risk of developing pre-eclampsia, which is fatal."

Two big fat tears rolled down Mentlana's cheeks. "Oh, God."

"We're going to do a fetal resection of the CCAM."

"What does that mean?"

"We're going to do something similar to a C-section but not deliver the baby. We'll partially delivery him, repair the lesion and place him back in your womb."

"Why don't you deliver him?"

"The idea is to try and keep him in there for as long as possible, until he's full term and we deliver him via C-section."

Mentlana's face paled. "That's the best course?"

Charlotte nodded. "Yes."

"Will the baby feel pain?"

"No." Charlotte squeezed Mentlana's hand. "This is the best course of action. Trust me."

"I do. You'll be there, right?"

"Yes. I will." Charlotte stood. "I know this is a lot to take in. Two C-sections are not ideal close together, but your baby has a better chance of survival this way."

Mentlana sighed and closed her eyes. "I'll face whatever I have to, to have my child."

"I know. I admire you for that."

Mentlana opened her eyes. "You will, too, when the time comes."

Charlotte nodded. She was beginning to believe it, but Mentlana was still something amazing and special to her. "I know physicians aren't supposed to say this to their patients, but I love you."

Mentlana grinned. "I love you, too. I'm glad you're here."

Charlotte hugged her, tears flowing. "Oh, dammit, stupid pregnancy hormones."

Mentlana laughed and brushed away her own tears. "I like seeing this side of you, Charley."

"What side?"

"The non-obstinate one."

Charlotte just shook her head. "I'll find Genen for you."

"Thanks, Charley."

Charlotte nodded and left the room. She didn't care who saw her tears, even Dr. Richards. She was done hiding her emotions.

She was done being obstinate.

CHAPTER SEVENTEEN

CHARLOTTE WATCHED QUINN scrubbing up. They were alone for the first time since she'd decided to tell him she was pregnant. She prayed she was doing the right thing, telling him before the surgery, but she couldn't keep it in any longer. She had to tell him.

"How are you feeling?" she asked, cautiously.

"Nervous, but I'm confident."

"The only fear is fear itself." She was quoting something her father had always said to her when she'd been hesitant to try new things as a child.

"Easy for you to say." He gave her a half smile, teasing her.

"I'm afraid of other things, but I'm willing to face the thing that terrifies me the most."

"What?"

"I'm afraid of carrying another child, Quinn." Tears stung her eyes. "I'd never thought of becoming a mother again, but I watched Mentlana and her trials and tribulations to have one. She was so brave, but for me the idea hurt too much. I'm still terrified, but I'll face the fear of losing it again because it's what I want."

Quinn's eyes widened, and he paused in scrubbing. "You're pregnant?"

Charlotte nodded and her knees began to knock. "I'm not

telling you this to force something from you. I can do this on my own. I want this. I just… You have the right to know."

Quinn remained frozen. "I don't know what to say."

"There's nothing to say, Quinn. You don't have to be a part of it."

"Thank you for letting me know. It's a lot to process."

"I know you're not thrilled—"

"Who says I'm not?" Quinn interrupted.

Charlotte sighed. "You weren't exactly over the moon last time. You were relieved when I lost it."

Quinn shook his head. "No, not at all. I was just as hurt as you were. I was trying to ease your pain my stupid foot-in-mouth way by hiding it. I thought by telling you about a great medical opportunity you would follow me, but I thought you were blaming me for the loss of our baby and that you hated me."

Charlotte felt the blood drain from her face. "I…I don't know what to say."

"Charlotte, you want to know my fear?"

"Of course."

"I was afraid of being a father. I didn't have the best role model to base any experience on. I was afraid of screwing up our child's life."

"Excuse me, Dr. Devlyn?" A nurse from the O.R. appeared. "We're ready for you to go over the instruments with the scrub nurse."

Quinn nodded. "Thank you."

The nurse disappeared and Quinn shook the water off his hands. "We'll talk about this later, Charlotte."

Charlotte nodded. "Of course."

He disappeared into the O.R. and she felt like she was going to faint. She felt relieved and over-the-moon happy. He'd mourned the loss of their first child just as keenly as she had.

Yes, she'd carry this child, no matter what the outcome. She wanted this baby.

Badly.

* * *

Quinn stood by the surgical table in the operating room. He was scrubbed in and ready to go. Mentlana hadn't been brought in yet, but he knew they were prepping her.

It'd been a long time since he'd been in this position. He stared at the surgical tools on the tray in front of him. Tools he was all too familiar with. He knew every nuance of them, how they functioned and at what step in the procedure he would need them, but still replayed it over and over again in his mind.

It was a way to calm and reassure himself he was capable of doing the surgery.

Steady. Just count.

He focused on the instruments—the scalpel, the sutures, the small, delicate tools he'd need to operate on such a fragile being. He flexed his fingers in the glove. There was no pain, just a bit of numbness.

Steady.

He took a deep breath. The room was chilly and the antiseptic smell calmed him. The nurses were shuffling around the room, doing their own counting as they set up the instruments, and that was reassuring.

Everything is going to be okay. I can do this.

Quinn closed his eyes and replayed in his mind the last fetal resection he'd done. The one he'd done before his accident. The baby was a healthy, thriving toddler now. Just like Mentlana's would be in a year's time.

When he thought of babies, though, his mind went to the one Charlotte was carrying. He smiled, though no one could see it behind the surgical mask. What if Charlotte was going to be on this table and it was their child's life in another surgeon's hands or his own? How would he deal with it? He had to be at the top of his game. He wouldn't let Genen down.

This baby was going to survive. His hand wasn't going to spasm.

I will succeed.

"Are you all right, Dr. Devlyn?" the scrub nurse asked cautiously, as she began to lay out the instruments in order.

"I am, thank you…"

"Bernice."

"Bernice. Good. I do like to know the name of my scrub nurse. Have you attended a surgery like this before?"

The nurse nodded. "At SickKids in Toronto."

Quinn's eyes widened. "This isn't where you work?"

Bernice shook her head. "No. I'm from Toronto and came as a favor to Dr. James. She said you needed a scrub nurse who'd assisted surgeons in this procedure before."

Quinn exhaled, relief oozing out of his very pores as the tension in his shoulders dissipated and he loosened up. Charlotte had done this for him? Any lingering concern he had vanished in that moment. With a good scrub nurse he'd be able to focus on the task at hand and not worry about instructing some other nurse on what he needed and when. Bernice would instinctively know what to hand him at each stage.

"I could kiss Dr. James right about now. I'd kiss you, too."

"You can't tamper with the sterilized field, Dr. Devlyn." Bernice chuckled, her eyes twinkling above her surgical mask. "I really don't fancy scrubbing in again, but I do appreciate your enthusiasm for my presence." Bernice moved off to continue her preparations.

I can do this.

The doors to the operating room slid open and Dr. Patterson entered the room. The nurses slipped on his gloves and Quinn nodded in greeting to the obstetrician.

Ready to do this again.

"It's time." Charlotte stepped aside as the orderlies wheeled the gurney in the room. Genen looked nauseous and worried. It broke Charlotte's heart, but she couldn't let her emotions take hold of her right now. At least her own nausea had subsided, thanks to some Diclectin that Dr. Patterson had given her a few hours ago when she'd approached him about morning sickness. Each pregnancy was *supposed* to be different, but again she was being plagued with horrible morning sickness. You'd think the odds would be in her favor.

Of course, she didn't want to think about the odds right now. If she did she'd only dwell on the statistics, which weren't in Mentlana's favor right now. Charlotte took a deep breath, trying to take Lorna's advice to heart. She was trying not to worry about a bad outcome, and to think on a good one. Though it was hard to break a habit of a lifetime when you kept getting dealt a rotten hand most of the time, and had to work for every little thing.

Mentlana and her baby would survive.

She had to believe it. For the first time in her life she had to believe in more than medical science. She had to put her trust and her hope in faith.

Mentlana and Genen kissed, which tugged at her heartstrings. The orderlies lifted Mentlana onto the gurney while her nurses began to hang the IV bags and catheter.

"Genen, you can walk us down the hall," Charlotte offered. "But because she's going under general anaesthesia, you can't come into the theater."

"I want to be with her," Genen protested.

"I know you do, but you can't. When we deliver the baby at the end of her pregnancy, you can. She'll have a spinal then and be wide awake. Trust me. It's for the best you wait out here, Genen."

Genen nodded and held tightly to Mentlana's hand as the orderlies wheeled the gurney out of the room. Charlotte followed beside them as they whisked Mentlana off to the operating suites. They stopped at the double doors and Charlotte moved away, pulling Genen to the side as Mentlana disappeared.

"You can't go any farther, Genen. I'm sorry."

Genen was visibly shaking, his dark eyes moist with tears. "Please, take care of her, Doc."

"Of course I will...I promise." Although she never promised any patient, the words just slipped past her lips and she prayed that she'd be able to honor that promise.

Genen nodded and Charlotte went through the double doors into the surgical suites. Her stomach twisted in a knot as she tied back her hair and scrubbed her hands. Through the window she could see Mentlana was already laid out on the table, the lights dimmed save for the bright surgical light.

Mentlana's face was pale as she stared at the ceiling, terrified. Charlotte glanced at Quinn, who appeared calm as he chatted to the scrub nurse from SickKids.

Bernice was an old friend and a bit of a present from Dr. Harriet Preston, who'd suggested Charlotte call Quinn when she'd first discovered the lesions on Mentlana's fetus.

"You know who the best in that field is, Charley. I don't have to tell you."

She hadn't wanted to call Quinn, but Harriet had been right. He *was* the best and now she was so glad she'd screwed up her courage and called him.

Once she'd finished scrubbing, she entered the O.R. and was gloved. She headed over to Mentlana's side.

"It's going to be okay, Lana."

"Charley?" There was relief in her voice. "Is Genen okay?"

"He's fine."

"Good." Dr. Patterson began to wash Mentlana's swollen abdomen with Betadine. "Ugh, what's he doing down there, painting a fence or something?"

Dr. Patterson chuckled. "I'm quite adept at fence-painting, too, Mrs. Tikivik, though don't tell my wife."

"I like you, Dr. Patterson." Mentlana grinned, but her lips quivered. "I'm scared, Charley, so scared."

"It'll be okay, Lana. I promise."

"What if...?" Mentlana trailed off and then shook her head.

"No what-ifs. It'll be okay. Trust me."

Mentlana nodded. "I do. I trust you with every fiber of my

being and I trust Dr. Devlyn because you do. You do trust him, don't you, Charley?"

"I do. He's the best."

Mentlana sighed. "I'm ready."

"Are you ready, Dr. Devlyn, Dr. Patterson?" the anesthesiologist asked.

"Yes," Quinn replied, his voice steady and calm, which reassured Charlotte. "Ready when you are, Dr. Horne."

Dr. Horne stepped forward. "We're going to put you under now, Mrs. Tikivik." A nurse placed an oxygen mask over Mentlana's face while Dr. Horne injected something into her IV line. "Just breathe deeply, Mrs. Tikivik. Good. Now start to count back from one hundred, please."

Charlotte left Mentlana's side as she counted, each number sounding more and more slurred. She stood beside Quinn.

"How are you feeling?" Quinn whispered.

"Fine. Dr. Patterson gave me something for nausea, but I'm ready to assist. How are you?"

"Excellent. This will be a success, Charlotte."

"Do you promise?"

"I never promise."

Charlotte bit her lip. "I know you can't."

He leaned over and whispered, "Off the record, I do. I promise."

"The patient is sedated," Dr. Horne said.

"All right, ladies and gentleman, let's proceed." Dr. Patterson stepped forward to perform the incision. "Ten blade."

Charlotte watched in wonder and amazement as Dr. Patterson skillfully operated on Mentlana, exposing her uterus and cutting into it. It'd been a long time since she'd assisted in surgery and she'd forgotten what a thrill it was, but she wouldn't trade this thrill for the high she got by dealing with her patients every day.

Often she wondered if she'd done the right thing by turning down a residency as a surgeon and entering general practice, but standing here and knowing every aspect of Mentlana's medical history, whereas these specialized surgeons only knew snippets, made Charlotte realize she'd made the right choice. Charlotte knew everything about her patients. She knew and understood the whole picture, and for that she was thankful.

"We're ready now, Dr. Devlyn." Dr. Patterson stepped back.

Charlotte looked at Quinn and nodded. *You can do this, Quinn.* She hoped she conveyed everything she wanted to say to him in a single look as he moved into position and began the fetal resection.

She stood by his side, waiting to see if she'd be needed, but he didn't ask her for help. His hands were fluid and gentle as he carefully lifted the baby out of Mentlana's abdomen and began the surgery to remove the lesion.

"Amazing," Dr. Richards whispered behind Charlotte. She glanced over her shoulder to see the pediatric specialist watching Quinn with total hero-worship.

Charlotte grinned in admiration at the man she loved, handling the baby so gently. The procedure flew by. He'd been so terrified that he'd need her, that he'd hurt or kill the baby, but he'd had nothing to worry about. All Charlotte did was hold the retractor and Bernice handed him the instruments he required.

"Damn," Quinn cursed.

The blood drained out of Charlotte's face as he paused, the baby resting in his hand.

"Dr. Devlyn?" Bernice questioned.

Quinn shot Charlotte a look.

"Cramp?" she asked.

"Yes." There was tension in his voice.

"Are you okay, Dr. Devlyn?" Patterson asked.

"Perfectly. My stamina is the worse for wear, but if Dr. James assists me, I should be fine. I'm almost finished."

Charlotte nodded. "Dr. Richards, please hold the retractor for me."

Dr. Richards stepped forward and she slipped her hand over

Charlotte's, taking the retractor without moving it and applying the same pressure Charlotte had been using.

Charlotte gently gripped Quinn's hand. The muscles were taut, and she began to palpate the palm, easing the muscles.

"You can do it," she said under her breath, encouraging him.

Quinn nodded and finished the resection. Charlotte stared down at the almost-full-term baby. Though he had ten weeks to go, he was beautiful, with the start of a full crop of thick black hair and some baby fat was beginning to flesh out his limbs. The baby's body was still covered in protective lanugo. Tears stung her eyes as she looked into that tiny, precious face. Mentlana and Genen's whole world, being held in Quinn's healing hands.

Live.

"There," Quinn announced, relief and joy in his voice. "Help me place the fetus back in the womb, Dr. James."

"Of course." She cupped her hands underneath Quinn's and they gently placed the baby back in his mother's uterus.

"Amazing," Dr. Richards whispered again in awe.

"It is." Quinn's gaze locked with Charlotte's just for a brief moment. As they placed the baby back in utero the baby's arm shot out of the incision and latched onto Quinn's finger, squeezing it.

A sob caught in Charlotte's throat as she watched the baby in amazement. The tiny infant was reaching out for human contact and comfort.

"Will you…?" Quinn's voice shook. "Help me, Charlotte."

She brushed the little hand off Quinn's finger, despite its firm grip, and set it back in place.

"She's all yours, Dr. Patterson," Quinn said, stepping back.

"Thank you, Dr. Devlyn. Okay, let's get Mrs. Tikivik closed. Zero Vicryl, please, Bernice."

Quinn walked away from Mentlana towards the scrub room. His job was done. Charlotte didn't follow but remained by Mentlana's side. She was confident Dr. Patterson and Dr. Richards would be able to handle the rest of the surgery expertly, but she'd promised her friend that she wouldn't leave.

Charlotte glanced over towards the scrub room. She wanted to follow Quinn, wanted to hold him in her arms and thank him for saving her friend's life, but that would come later. She moved around to Mentlana's head. The anesthesiologist was monitoring the machines and Charlotte pulled over a rolling stool and sat by her friend. Ignoring the tube that helped Mentlana breathe and her taped eyes, she stroked her friend's hair, hoping Mentlana could sense her presence.

"Everything's all right, Lana," she whispered. "The baby is fine."

And I'll be fine, too.

CHAPTER EIGHTEEN

QUINN KNEW CHARLOTTE couldn't follow him out. He knew she'd be faithful and remain by Mentlana's side, but right now he could use her. He needed to see her friendly face and share in the joy that was surging through him.

I did it.

His hands shook as he leaned against the cold tiled wall of the scrub room. He peeled the rubber gloves from his hands, disposed of them and then removed the surgical gown and stuffed it into the laundry bin, followed by his scrub cap.

His knees were wobbly as he pressed his foot against the bar, allowing the water in the scrub sink to rush over his skin without having to touch anything. Quinn glanced down at his hands, his broken one and the scars that crisscrossed his skin, scars he'd been ashamed of. They no longer bothered him.

They represented a point in his life he'd rather forget and wished had never happened. The memory of the accident that had almost cost him his life would remain with him, but the crash would no longer haunt him. Anything life could throw at him was not insurmountable, not with Charlotte by his side.

In that moment when the baby had reached out and curled his hand around his finger, squeezing him to let him know he was there and alive, had been a miracle.

Never in his years as a fetal surgeon had he ever experienced such a moment, such an affirmation of life.

A life he'd saved.

He'd survived the accident that had damaged his hand, when so many hadn't. He was lucky he had been given a second chance, at surgery and at a future with Charlotte.

Quinn scrubbed his hands. He'd been terrified at the prospect of this moment, but had kept it to himself.

Now there was one more life he had to save.

His own.

There was no way he was going to allow Charlotte to walk out of his life again because they couldn't agree to practice medicine in the same place. Quinn was not going to make the same mistake twice.

He was lucky she hadn't moved on, that she was still single and wanted him. He wasn't going to tempt fate. This time the odds were in his favor. The fates were smiling on him and he was going to make everything right.

Quinn left the O.R. suites. First he'd find Genen and update him on his wife and child and then he was going to make some changes.

It was time to stop being so selfish.

It was time to live.

"Where am I?"

Charlotte straightened and leaned over Mentlana's bed in the recovery room. She took her friend's hand and rubbed it gently. Mentlana was still groggy. They'd woken her in the O.R. after the surgery was complete, but she hadn't been quite awake after several general nudges.

Charlotte remained by her bedside in Recovery, wanting to tell Mentlana herself that her son would be fine.

"Where am I?" Mentlana asked again.

"Recovery."

"Charley?"

"I'm here." Charlotte smiled as Mentlana's eyes fluttered open.

"Thank you for staying with me." Mentlana's eyes closed again.

"Don't fall asleep again. You need to stay awake." Charlotte stood and gestured to one of the nurses. "They're going to check on you, okay?"

"Don't go, Charley. Please."

"I promise I won't."

Charlotte stepped back so the recovery-room nurses could check Mentlana's vitals, the baby's vitals and the incision, but she stayed where Mentlana could see her. The effects of the anesthesia were wearing off. Charlotte watched as Mentlana came out of her haze of medication.

"I'll be back again in ten minutes, Dr. James," the nurse said as she drew the curtain around Mentlana. Charlotte sat back down.

"How's the pain?" she asked, rubbing Mentlana's leg.

She winced, her face pale. "Not pleasant, but the nurse shot some morphine into my butt."

Charlotte grinned. "You should be feeling good in a few minutes."

Mentlana nodded. "So tell me. I'm ready to hear whatever you have to say, good or bad."

"All good," Charlotte whispered, barely containing her glee.

Mentlana perked up, more alert. "What?"

"Dr. Devlyn corrected the baby's CCAM. If we can keep him inside you for a bit longer and get him closer to term, everything should be okay."

Tears began to roll down Mentlana's face, and her shoulders shook as she reached out and grasped Charlotte's arm. "It hurts to cry."

Charlotte tried to swallow the lump in her throat but couldn't, and soon she was weeping in joy along with her friend.

"Thank you," Mentlana said, wiping away the tears with the back of her hand.

"You're welcome."

"You thank Quinn, too." Mentlana closed her eyes, tears still streaming. "I don't even know how to begin to thank him."

"You'll find a way." Charlotte's voice was still wobbly and she cleared her throat to regain her composure. "Why don't you make him a great big honking plate of muktuk?"

Mentlana grinned. "Perhaps I should, but I think he'd rather receive my thanks through you. He didn't come up here because he's a humanitarian, Charley. If you were just any old physician he wouldn't have come. He would've found another one or I would've had to fly to Toronto and break the bank to do it. The reason he came up here, at his own expense, was you."

Warmth crept up Charlotte's neck. Mentlana spoke the truth. Quinn loved her and she loved him. "Still, I think he has a certain fondness for you, Mentlana."

"Good. Or I'd have to kick him in that soft spot I spoke of before." Mentlana winked. "Don't let him get away, Charley. Don't let him walk away from you and that precious bundle you carry. Even if it means you have to leave us in Cape Recluse and head to the bright lights of the city."

"I won't." Charlotte stood. "I know I'll have to leave here to live in Toronto. I'll miss you."

"And I you, but you can always visit. You do know how to fly."

Charlotte laughed and stroked Mentlana's face affectionately. "The nurses are going to give me heck for getting you all emotionally riled up."

A devilish grin spread across Mentlana's face. "I'll tell them where to go. You helped save my baby. You and Dr. Devlyn have given me everything I've ever wanted."

Charlotte kissed her forehead. "Rest. I'll see you later."

"Tell him, Charley. Tell him and don't let him go."

Charlotte nodded and left the recovery room. Her heart

was singing with joy as she walked down the corridor of the hospital with a spring in her step.

Tell him, Charley. Tell him and don't let him go. Mentlana's words were weighing on her. Her friend had never been so right. For five years she'd waited and mourned the loss of their baby and the loss of Quinn.

Now he was back in her life and she was pregnant again. She'd do anything to keep Quinn in her life, even if it meant leaving the North and moving to the city, be it Toronto, Manhattan or Abu Dhabi. Charlotte didn't care. She just wanted Quinn.

She had to be flexible and not so stubborn.

Charlotte's hand drifted down over her abdomen and she thought about the little life just starting out in her womb. She meant to go and find Quinn, tell him how she felt and how she was willing to go anywhere, risk everything to be with him.

This was for the best. Her baby needed a father. She'd finally have the family she'd always dreamed of since she'd lost her parents.

She also needed Quinn. Charlotte was aware of that now. She couldn't live without him.

Her phone buzzed and she pulled it out. Quinn had texted her, asking her to meet him in the on-call room on the fourth floor.

A heavy weight had been lifted from her shoulders and right now she was going to make everything right. She wasn't going to let Quinn Devlyn get away. She was going to show him exactly what he meant to her and she hoped he'd feel the same.

The on-call door was open and she slipped inside the room. When she entered, Quinn was seated on a cot, his elbows resting on his knees as he stared at a small box in his hands. He looked down at it, seeming sad and puzzled. What did he have to be sad about? He should be rejoicing. Two lives had been saved. A miracle had been performed, thanks to him.

Charlotte crossed the room and sat down next to him, placing her hand on his knee.

"Quinn, are you all right?"

He gazed at her and smiled. "Of course."

Charlotte let out a sigh of relief. "I thought you were upset."

He shook his head. "Fine. I'm fine. How's Mentlana?"

"Sore, but very grateful." Charlotte kissed his cheek. "You did it. You kept your promise to me."

"My hands cramped, but I did it. With your help."

"They're healed. I hope this outcome gives you more confidence."

"It gives me a bit." He grinned.

"It should give you more than a bit, Quinn. You're a surgeon, a surgical god again. Unfortunately, our outcomes are not always what we want or expect, but if we don't try...if we don't try to save a life, that's the real crime."

Quinn leaned over and kissed her, a tender kiss that brought tears to her eyes. He stroked her face. "I'm ready to come back from my sabbatical."

Charlotte's heart skipped a beat, her stomach churned. He was going to return to surgery, but *where* was the big question. Wherever it was, she'd follow him. She was ready, as much as she hated living in the city.

"What's wrong?" he asked, confused. "Look, I know you don't want to live in the city..."

"No. I'm certain of what I want, too."

"Certain of what?"

"That I can leave here to follow you." She ran her fingers along his jaw, the stubble tickling her fingertips. "I'll go wherever you need to. Wherever you want to."

"You don't have to leave. You belong up here. This is your home."

"Quinn, you're my life now. Wherever you are, I'm home. I won't lose you."

"You won't. I was made an offer by this hospital to be the

head of the neonatal unit. They want a state-of-the-art facility here and I'm the surgeon they want to lead that project. I accepted, Charlotte."

Charlotte was floored. Her mouth dropped open. She knew she must look like a gaping fish by the way Quinn started to laugh. "You…you what?"

"I'm head of the up-and-coming new neonatal unit. Honestly, Charlotte, how hard can that be to understand?" He was teasing her.

"What about your chief of surgery position in Toronto? The one your father groomed you for?"

He shrugged his shoulders. "My life is with you and your life is here. You wouldn't be happy in Toronto, in close proximity to my mother."

"I thought you hated the North. The cold? The ice?"

"I did, but that was the old me. I'll grow used to the cold, and there are other aspects I love, but the most important draw is you, Charlotte. Besides, there are always vacations." Quinn stood and pulled her into his arms. "I love you, Charlotte. If it wasn't for you, I wouldn't be so damn happy again."

"And I love you."

"I do have one condition, though, and it does involve a city."

Charlotte cocked an eyebrow. "Oh?"

"You need to find another physician for Cape Recluse. I need my wife in Iqaluit with me."

"Deal." Charlotte kissed him, lightly brushing her lips against his.

Charlotte knew there was no way she was going to be able to hold back her tears. She was getting everything she wanted. Cape Recluse wasn't too far away that she couldn't keep an eye on it from Iqaluit—she could easily open a practice in the city. All she wanted was Quinn. She wouldn't be obstinate. He was sacrificing big money and the metropolitan way of life for her.

"If it wasn't for you, Dr. Devlyn, I wouldn't have a chance at motherhood again. I love you."

Quinn stepped back and held out the box. "I know I couldn't afford one before, being in med school and all."

Charlotte took the box and opened it. The sparkle of a diamond took her breath away. "Oh, my God."

"It's a diamond from a mine up here. I was assured of that. I wanted you to have a stone that came from the land you love."

"Quinn, it's beautiful."

He took her hand and slipped the ring on her finger. "Marry me, right away. Tomorrow even. We've waited long enough and I can't wait even a second longer. I don't want to waste any more time."

Charlotte wrapped her arms around him. "Yes, I'll marry you as soon as possible. I've waited a long time for this moment."

Quinn grinned and slipped his hand into her hair, dragging her into another toe-curling kiss.

"Shall we go visit Mentlana and Genen and bask in their happiness?" he asked breathlessly a few moments later.

"I'd like that."

They kissed one more time and walked out of the on-call suite hand in hand, with the future ahead of them.

There was no place in their world for obstinate people. Charlotte knew beyond a shadow of a doubt she'd always fight for Quinn, their family and the love they'd been given again.

Always.

* * * * *

BACK IN HER HUSBAND'S ARMS

SUSANNE HAMPTON

To the very special women in my life who have helped me through life's challenging times and made me stronger.

Your friendship is more precious than diamonds and a treasure greater than gold.

And to Charlotte for being the most amazing editor... thank you for your unlimited patience and encouragement.

CHAPTER ONE

SARA FIELDING MADE her way along the wet footpath, dodging the small potholes that had filled with water from the overnight rain, her feet tucked inside flat knee-high boots. It was eight in the morning and bitterly cold. She tugged her collar up against the breeze that was cutting through her heavy overcoat, wishing she had worn her woollen tights.

Winter mornings in Melbourne were brutal, she remembered, and today was no exception. It had been thundering down when her plane had landed only an hour before and she had caught a cab straight into the city. The rain had paused momentarily but the overcast sky promised another downpour at any moment. Her favourite pair of brown leather gloves were only just preventing her fingers from freezing around the handle of her briefcase, so she quickly picked up her pace. She didn't want to arrive at the hospital soaked to the bone.

Sara had been living in Adelaide for the last three years and this was only her second trip back to Melbourne in all that time. The first had been four weeks ago when she'd travelled over to finalise her visa at the American embassy. Sara had had serious reservations about returning to Melbourne at all. She would have preferred any other city, but it was the United States embassy that processed South Australian visa applications. She'd had no choice.

Melbourne held wonderful memories but also a sadness that she really didn't want to face. She had told herself it was only an overnight stay. A quick trip. Nothing to worry about. But now, looking back, she realised she should have listened to her intuition and stayed far away from the town where Tom Fielding still lived. She was already planning a new life in Texas. So much further from Melbourne. So much further from the temptation of Tom Fielding.

She now knew that she couldn't trust her heart, or her body for that matter, around the man. He wasn't a bad man, quite the opposite, in fact, but he was definitely the wrong man for her. Against her will, Sara's thoughts were dragged back to that brief trip and how terribly wrong it had all gone.

Day one had been fine. The visa application had been processed without any hiccups. It had been day two when Sara had found herself sitting alone at Vue de Monde on the fifty-fifth floor of the historic Rialto building. She had ordered her meal and had been in high spirits, sipping her white wine and thinking about her impending trip to Texas.

She had been offered a position at a large teaching hospital in San Antonio. It was going to be a fresh start, a chance to move on and find a life that might just fulfil her dreams. Sara had finally grown tired of her life revolving around what everyone else wanted. Sacrificing her dreams, her hopes, for the needs of everyone else had become a pattern until three years ago. That fateful day when she'd decided she couldn't give up on one particular dream. She hoped this move would give her the chance to realise that dream. The dream of becoming a mother. She knew she had the packing, the shipping and all that a move of that distance entailed, but it would be worth every bit of effort. She would be free to live her life on her terms.

Suddenly her thoughts were stolen. As was her breath. Both taken by the vision of a man she'd thought she would never see again.

Sara did a double take. *Could it be?* She shook her head a little. *Could it really be him?*

He walked into the restaurant and took a seat at a table by the window. It had been three years since she had last seen him. They hadn't contacted each other since she'd left. No telephone calls. No letters. Nothing.

Perhaps it was her imagination. Perhaps it was someone who looked just like him.

Then she reminded herself there was really no other man who came close to his looks, his stature, his charisma. It was definitely Tom Fielding. All six foot two inches of him had crossed the room and had turned every woman's head as he'd done so.

Sara's heart raced a little as she watched him take the wine list from the waitress. She saw the waitress attempt to flirt, it was subtle, but enough for another woman to notice. Tom was unmoved. He didn't appear to notice or, if he did, he didn't respond. The flustered waitress placed the napkin in his lap and hovered, a little longer than necessary.

Sara felt a tightening in her chest and butterflies awakening in the pit of her stomach as the reality of being this close to Tom hit home. She had forgotten the effect he had on her. And apparently still did. Her emotions began playing havoc, sending her mind into a tailspin. She looked away. Swallowing hard, she began to play with her cutlery absent-mindedly.

She hadn't expected so many mixed emotions to come in to play. Attraction, regret, melancholy, guilt, even a hint of lust. This was not supposed to happen. This was a bad dream playing out. Sharing the same restaurant as Tom was not in the plan, and her options to escape the uncomfortable situation were limited. She could hardly leave the restaurant after ordering her dinner. Most likely it would draw even more attention to her. She didn't want to look back in Tom's direction but she was drawn to him. Drawn to him just like the conflicting desire to gaze at an open wound.

Tom chose a wine and handed the waitress back the wine list. He looked out the window across the sweeping views of the Melbourne skyline. The panorama of lights all twinkling against the black sky. Then he turned in his seat, just a little, but enough to see Sara.

He didn't move. He froze in his chair, staring in silence. Sara did the same. She had no idea what he was thinking. She barely knew what she was thinking as she looked at the handsome curves of his face and the generous sweep of his broad shoulders in his tailored black jacket. The ultra-modern restaurant was dimly lit and combined with the dark charcoal and earthy brown tones of the sleek decor it was difficult to make out very much. Except that he was still handsome. So very handsome.

It wasn't cocky good looks he possessed. It was as if he just didn't know how appealing he was to women. He had always been that way. He obviously knew on some level that he was attractive but he never took advantage of it or seemed impressed by the gift nature had bestowed on him. Tom Fielding was a lot deeper than skin alone.

He stood up then hesitated for a moment, as if to

seek some sort of approval to approach. But he did anyway. Her stomach was a tangled mess of nerves as she watched him drop his napkin on the table and cross over to her. His eyes didn't leave her face for an instant.

'Sara,' he began, as he bent down to kiss her cheek. The scent of his cologne filled her senses. It wasn't overpowering, it was subtle and sensual. It was Tom.

'It's so good to see you,' he continued.

Sara was momentarily speechless. She knew she was in Melbourne, it wasn't as if they had bumped into each other in an isolated town on the other side of the world. Perhaps she shouldn't have even been surprised, but it was still overwhelming.

'Lovely to see you too, Tom,' she finally breathed in reply. It was a struggle as she felt her heart cramp.

'May I?' he asked, as his hand rested on the empty chair.

Sara nodded and he pulled out the chair and sat down at her table. Out of habit, he reached across and touched her hand.

Looking back in the harsh light of day, Sara realised that had been her first mistake. She should have kept Tom Fielding at arm's length. It had begun to rain, and Sara regretted not asking her cab from the airport to drop her at the nearest coffee shop to the hospital. She needed a short black to wake herself up after the early flight and couldn't bear the thought of cafeteria coffee. She was in search of the strength only a barista could provide. Picking up her steps even more, her mind raced back to that night. That silly, stupid night four weeks ago.

Dinner alone had turned into dinner for two, then a stroll, and then drinks at a bar in the city. Scars had a way of fading a little in the soft lights of the evening, particularly when wine was involved. Old times, old feelings, old reasons for falling in love replaced the wounds and hurt. Her defences became shaky and, against her will, they finally fell.

Reason didn't have a chance. Just before midnight, they were alone in her hotel room. Tom looked more appealing than any man she had ever seen. Sitting on the edge of her bed in his long black jeans, his suede boots a little dusty, his dark blond hair pushed back in waves that brushed the collar of his white linen shirt. His jacket was flung over the small sofa by the window.

He looked like a cowboy. *Her cowboy for tonight.*

And it could only be for tonight. For old times' sake, she reasoned silently. There was no chance of anything more. They had tried that and it didn't work. She wasn't going there again. She wasn't giving up her dreams for this man. But she knew her heart was finally out of harm's way. It was safely protected inside the walls that she had carefully erected when she had walked out and left him, so she gave in to her desires. It's only one night, she reassured herself.

He was staring straight at her with his bedroom eyes. Despite wondering if she was about to make one of life's bad decisions and one she might just regret, she seemed too powerless to stop herself. Was it lust or was it love? She wasn't sure but it was going to happen.

'Don't tell me to stop, I know what I'm about to do…' she started.

Suddenly her words were cut short by his lips pressing against hers. His hands gently cupped her face as his mouth captured her sigh. She didn't fight him. She didn't want to talk any more. Her hands instinctively reached up and pulled him closer. Her body arched with desire. She was aflame with the heat in his fingers as his hands slid under her clothing to stroke her bare skin. His kisses became more urgent and she opened her mouth to him. She wanted to feel him, to have him, just once more. To feel his body next to hers and to taste him. He unbuttoned her blouse and slid it from her warm skin, tossing it on the floor as he trailed moist kisses down her neck.

'I want you, Sara, and I'm going to have you tonight,' he breathed low and heavy with desire as his fingers traced gentle lines along the bare skin of her thigh.

His hands moved to the curve of her spine and he pulled her even closer to his hard body. She felt her pulse racing as her fingers threaded through his hair and she kissed him more deeply than before. They fell back onto the bed, discarding the last remnants of clothing before their bodies became one.

Sara Fielding had woken in her hotel room the next morning more confused than she thought possible. It had all seemed so clear the night before. Just two people sharing a night of pleasure. Two consenting adults needing each other. Nothing more. But now it was anything but clear. She realised just how vulnerable she still was with Tom. She pulled the sheets up to her chin like a flimsy shield. A feeling of dread hit the pit of her stomach.

As daylight slipped through the gap in the heavy curtains she could see the fine stubble on his chin. The satin sheet was barely covering him, and his tanned chest was sculpted like a statue. They had made love all night and he was still the caring, amazing lover she remembered. But she should never have done it. She looked up at the ceiling of the room, wondering what possessed her to be so stupid and impulsive. It was not like her.

She had spent the last three years trying to push past the hurt and disappointment and then, in a few passionate hours, she had ignored her own logic and risked opening up old wounds. She couldn't blame it on the wine, she hadn't even finished her drink at the restaurant and had hardly touched the martini at the bar.

Hormones, memories, melancholy, maybe even the remnants of the love they had once shared, had over-ridden the voice of reason and they had returned to her room together.

Now, in the light of morning, she wanted to scream at herself. *Why?*

In a few short weeks he would officially become her ex-husband. The divorce would be finalised. She had managed to stay away for all those years, finally finding the resolve to ask for a divorce, and then, just before it became official, she'd slept with him.

She rolled her eyes in disappointment and confusion. Her lawyer had told her that Tom wasn't contesting the divorce. He had signed the papers. It was just a matter of legal processes being completed.

Perhaps it was knowing that the divorce would be finalised that made her feel safe. That was crazy, she knew, but it was the only explanation she could muster. The divorce was a piece of paper. It wasn't a shield. It couldn't protect her heart.

Tom began to stir. She closed her eyes and feigned sleep. She wasn't sure what to say. Was it *Thank you for a lovely evening* or *I know we slept together but just so you know, I'm not in love with you any more?*

She needed time. Perhaps he would wake up and leave. She felt her stomach knot, not unlike the night before when he'd walked towards her at the restaurant. All those old feelings, the good and the bad, were sitting heavily in her chest.

She wasn't sure if she had imagined it, but as she'd been falling asleep in Tom's arms the night before, she thought she had heard him whisper, *I love you*. She didn't want to go there. She wasn't about to get involved with Tom again. It would be too easy to fall back into his arms. She had taken so long to not need him in her life. To finally realise that she had a right to live her life the way she wanted, whatever it might cost her.

She lay as still as she could. Her breathing was light but laboured as her nerves played with her anxiety level. Last night they had given in to the chemistry they had always shared. But their differences were still there. That hadn't changed and they would never be able to move past what had torn them apart. Sara watched Tom slip from the bed and collect his clothes from all over the room. She wondered if he felt the same. A little part wished he had tried to wake her, to hold her and to talk through their differences. To solve the issues they had and to make love again.

Reason reminded her that it would never happen, so leaving without a word would be best. She hoped he'd leave a note on the hotel stationery. That's all she should expect. All she wanted, she tried to convince herself.

She had loved every minute of his hands and his body on hers. The tenderness and sense of belonging had been undeniable but now, hearing him dressing in the other room, she knew it had been wrong. It had been a lapse in judgement for both of them.

The door of the bathroom opened and Tom emerged fully dressed. Sara closed her eyes again. She didn't want him to catch her awake, thinking about what might have been. He fumbled for his boots then slipped on his jacket. She watched through half-open eyes as he made his way to the desk and scribbled something on the hotel notepad. Quietly, he crossed to the door of her room, opened it and left quietly. He was gone.

As the door shut, Sara sat bolt upright. She was so grateful he was gone. *Or was she?* She felt horribly confused. There was nothing sweeter than falling asleep wrapped in Tom's arms, the heat of his naked body pressed against hers.

But she had to move on. He wouldn't change. He couldn't change. And she was tired of changing for everyone else. She almost had the divorce. She would be free. They would be free of each other. They were two very different people with very different priorities.

She wanted children.

He didn't.

And this time she was walking away to live her life, her way.

She remembered climbing from the warm bed and heading to the shower. Trying to make sense of the night was pointless, she decided as the warm water ran over her back and shoulders. Images of Tom making love to her came rushing back. She closed her eyes and turned to face the water head-on. The water soaked her hair and ran down her face. She was leaving for Texas in eight short weeks. And she would never see Tom Fielding again.

She turned off the water and wrapped herself in a fluffy white bath towel and returned to the scene of the crime. There was a wrapper or two that she didn't want the hotel staff to find, so she picked them up and put them in the bin. Tom was so very good at being bad but he was always very careful.

She crossed to the desk and picked up the note.

Dear Sara,
Lovely to spend time with you. All the very best
for Texas.
Always,
Tom x

She smiled, a bittersweet smile at the sadness of the situation. Two people who loved each other but who both had to accept it could never be.

Sara hadn't really pushed for divorce at first but now, with a new life in America awaiting her, she no longer wanted to be Dr Sara Fielding, wife of Dr Tom Fielding. She needed to be single. To have a chance at happiness and a family.

She had only filed for the divorce six months before. She had held onto the idea he would change his mind for too long and she knew it. But Tom had finally agreed to sign the papers. He too had accepted they were over. The way he'd left this morning showed that. Last night had been like two friends who had given in to their emotions for just one night. But her rationale was fragile in the early morning light.

The sudden sound of an ambulance siren brought Sara back from her reverie. She was beside the tall red-brick hospital walls of Augustine General Hospital and quite close to the front doors and the hospital office of her good friend Stu Anderson. Just after she'd returned from her first trip to Melbourne, Stu had mentioned he was in need of a locum oral surgeon to oversee his private practice while he was away. Sara had had the time and had wanted to help out so she had agreed to work the four weeks before she left for the US.

She was aware returning to Melbourne could hold some difficulties but she also knew she had to push past the hurt and accept the shortfalls of the city. The shortfalls being her failed marriage and the sadness that weighed down her memories of the time she had spent there. She'd studied, she'd fallen in love and she'd left. Now, all these years later she thought she needed to accept that life wasn't perfect here but she didn't need to stay away any longer. She just needed to keep her emotions in check.

With this new resolve, it hadn't seemed such a bad idea when she had agreed to help out but now, being back in the city, memories of the night she had spent with Tom came charging back, and she was a little more anxious about her stay.

She tried to remind herself that Melbourne was a big city. She could avoid the Vue de Monde, and the martini bar. That wouldn't be too difficult as there were many more restaurants and she wasn't that fond of vermouth anyway. And luckily Tom consulted at a hospital the other side of the city.

Mindful of the hospital traffic, Sara kept to the pedestrian pathway as she made her way to the entrance. The ambulance had pulled up in the emergency parking bay and the paramedics, now joined by two hospital staff, were already removing the gurney from the back of the vehicle.

She walked around to the automatic sliding doors of the visitors' entrance. At least she was finally under shelter. Removing her heavy overcoat, she shook the excess water out over the large grey rubber mat before she placed the coat over her arm and stepped inside. Thankfully, inside the hospital was much warmer than outside. She slipped off her gloves and placed them into the pocket of her coat. Crossing to the information counter, she ran her fingers through her damp hair and wiped the moisture from her face.

'Hello, I'm here to see Dr Anderson. Oral maxillo-facial surgery.'

The receptionist smiled, although the second glances Sara was receiving from the other administration staff made her think her appearance was a little battered by the weather. She quickly realised her hair was more than just damp when she felt trickles run down her temples and into her left ear.

The young woman picked up a box of tissues from behind the high grey and white panelled counter and offered them to Sara. 'It's really coming down out there, isn't it?'

With an embarrassed smile she took a few tissues and mopped her wet forehead, cheeks and ear.

'You need to take the elevator at the end of this corridor up to the fourth floor and you'll find the oral surgery consulting rooms on the left as you step out.'

'Thanks,' Sara replied, trying to stifle a yawn. The effect of a long night of surgery, combined with an early morning flight, was starting to show. Sara had tried to keep busy since her last trip to Melbourne; she hadn't wanted any time to think about what she had done. Unfortunately, returning to Melbourne was rapidly bringing it all back.

Tom Fielding sat in his office on the fourth floor of Augustine General Hospital, thinking back to the night he'd spent with Sara, the way he had thought about it every day for the last four weeks. Each day since that fateful night vivid, unwanted memories had reminded him of how much he still loved his soon-to-be-ex-wife. Still wanted her but couldn't have her. He had decided to give her the divorce, hand her back her life and return to his alone. But that one night together had destroyed the solace he had finally found; it ate away at his core that there was no future for them. They had different goals, different plans for their lives, and there was no common ground any more.

Except in a hotel room at midnight.

Tom remembered his surprise and elation when he'd spied his beautiful ex-wife sitting alone across from him in the restaurant. In his eyes she was still the most gorgeous, captivating woman in the world. She was intelligent, kind, caring, strong willed and the most giving lover a man could want. A shared dinner had led to drinks and then to her hotel.

Once he had been inside her room, Tom hadn't been able to control himself any longer. Sara had made it very clear that she wanted him just as much. He had been risking everything, including his sanity, but he'd wanted this woman more than life itself. Even if it was for just one last time.

In the morning Tom had opened his eyes to see his wife lying beside him. Ex-wife, reasoning reminded him. She was sleeping so soundly. She was so beautiful. Her short blonde hair had been a mess, a beautiful mess. A mess he had created when he'd been making love to her all night. The curves of her naked body had been softly lit by the rays that had peeped through the curtain break.

He'd resisted the urge to stroke her soft, tempting skin. She was such a sound sleeper, he knew that from the time they'd spent as husband and wife, but he hadn't wanted to risk waking her. He'd known he had to slip from the bed and leave. It would be best for both of them. Trying to make sense of what they'd done would be impossible. Sara had made it very clear that she was heading overseas. She was starting a new life and he had to do the same. He had to give her the divorce. He had to give her the freedom she needed and return to his life without her.

He loved her, and maybe she still loved him a little at least, but in a few weeks they would be divorced. She had reminded him of that fact last night in the restaurant. She was moving on, she had told him at the bar where they'd enjoyed a martini together. Leaving for the US in a few weeks to start afresh in a new country, she had told him at the door of her hotel room at midnight.

They hadn't talked about their past, they hadn't talked about their work. And they hadn't spoken about their differences. They'd spoken about the present, about light-hearted subjects. It was as if they had been two strangers who hadn't wanted to know anything too deep about each other.

It was an unspoken agreement; each knowing they would only share one last night. Tom didn't want to hold up his end of that unspoken agreement. He wanted his wife back. He wanted to wake up every morning with her in his arms. But he was a logical man and he accepted that could never be.

Before he'd left the room he had paused to take one last look at Sara still asleep in the rumpled bed sheets. She'd looked like an angel. *His angel for one last night.*

CHAPTER TWO

'SLOW DOWN...AND tell me how exactly you came to misplace a patient?'

'I'm not sure, Dr Fielding. His name was...oh, what was his name again? That's right...Kowalski...Joseph Kowalski. I can't believe he's gone. I messed up big time. I'm so sorry, Dr Fielding. I'm really sorry. I'm such an idiot.'

'Johnson, take a breath. I examined Mr Kowalski in my ward a little over an hour ago. He had multiple mandibular fractures and if I'm not mistaken a blood alcohol close to point two. He was in a hospital gown and hooked up to an IV. I can't see him travelling very far without being noticed.'

Sara Fielding stepped back from the open doorway to where she couldn't be seen. *Dr Fielding?* What was he doing here? He didn't consult at this hospital. He was the oral and maxillofacial consultant at Lower North Eastern on the other side of the city. It was where she had done her training. It was where they met. Why was he here? He must be visiting Stu to say goodbye, as they were friends. They had all been friends once, she reminded herself.

'I know, right, how far could he get?' the young voice returned in varying pitch, trying to convince himself of a good outcome. But his struggle showed when his voice gave in to a nervous stutter. 'I—I spoke with Security at the b-back and front gates and he hasn't left the grounds.'

'Well, that's comforting, I'd hate to see footage of our escapee on television tonight. We don't want to see our director's face on the six p.m. news if they splash shots of the bare backside of an inebriated elderly man, still attached to an IV stand, walking down Swan Street. I can only imagine the paperwork involved with that Ministerial inquiry.'

Stunned, Sara collapsed back against the wall out of the view of Tom and the young man she assumed was either a final year undergraduate or an intern. *Our director?* Her heart was racing and her stomach had tied itself in a knot. She didn't hear any of what he was telling the young man after those two words, she just heard the thumping of the blood in her temples. Tom Fielding must now be consulting at this hospital. *Her hospital.*

'Security, please.' Tom spoke into the phone then, while waiting for the connection, he began skimming through the unread emails on his computer screen. After a moment, he continued. 'It's Tom Fielding, I'm just checking on the status of a missing patient. Joseph Kowalski. Admitted to the oral surgery ward about two hours ago, apparently did a runner out of the ward... Oh, okay. The cafeteria—poor man's probably hungry. So where is he now? Right, that's unfortunate. I'll send the intern to collect him promptly. Thanks.' With that he hung up the phone.

'Well, Johnson, I suggest you head to the florist on the ground floor. Kowalski's in there, trying to purchase a bouquet, and apparently while searching for his imaginary wallet underneath his hospital gown he has

managed to show the family jewels to the volunteers.
They're a little disturbed, so you need to calmly head
down and collect him. But remember, you're no good
to anyone, and particularly not Mr Kowalski, if you
beat yourself up about it. You followed hospital procedure. You notified Security, and me, and they have
him. Good outcome, so just head off and take him back
to the ward pronto.'

Sara clenched her eyes closed. Her mind was struggling to process what was happening. It made no sense
to her. Stu had set up the appointment at the hospital to
discuss his caseload and show her around the operating
theatres. Then he was going to take her to his practice,
which was apparently only a few blocks away. There
had definitely been no mention of Tom in the conversation. If there had been she wouldn't have agreed to
come. Nervously, she smoothed her skirt and tugged
her jacket back into position.

More than anything, she wanted to run. To disappear and not face Tom again. But she couldn't. She had
made a promise to Stu to locum for him for the month.
A promise she couldn't break.

The heat began rising in her cheeks. Her heart began
beating a little faster. Elevating anxiety was threatening
her composure but she was fighting back. She tried to
put the situation into perspective quickly. She had limited time to find a solution, a tidy way to process this.

The practice would occupy most of her time. There
would be Theatre two days a week or perhaps only one
and a half. She would be consulting at the private practice at least three days, maybe even three and a half.
Thoughts of their recent night together, their romantic
whirlwind engagement and their year as husband and
wife had to be replaced hurriedly with a professional

demeanour. She needed to rebuild those walls that had protected her for the last three years and which would once again be her saviour when she walked into the office to face Tom.

Clearly his presence at the hospital would complicate things but she wouldn't run and hide. She needed to face this head-on. She was thirty-two years old now with a respected medical career. The fact that they had spent one crazy night together couldn't affect their work, they had to put it behind them.

Perhaps he already had done that, she told herself. He had left the hotel room without a word and he hadn't contacted her since, so he must be feeling the same way. She desperately needed to freeze her heart before she saw his face.

Reaching down for her briefcase, she waited a moment for the young man to leave. With her head held high, she would walk into Tom's office and behave as if nothing had ever happened.

Unfortunately, she assumed the young man would be walking, not running, and not straight into her.

His full weight met with her tiny frame, sending her crashing back into the wall and her briefcase tumbling down to the ground.

'Oh, no, I'm so sorry. I didn't see you there,' he gasped, as he reached out to steady Sara. 'Are you okay?'

Sara was stunned into silence for a moment. Finally she managed to mutter, 'I'm fine, really.' She was a little shaken but didn't want to make a fuss. Bending down to gather her belongings, she didn't think the day could get any worse.

'No, you're not. You're bleeding. You've cut your leg!'

Sara spied the gash on her knee. The open lock on her briefcase must have cut her before it hit the ground.

'Come with me. You'll have to sit down while I get some antiseptic and gauze.' The young man directed Sara into the office he had just left. Tom's office. This was not the entrance she had hoped to make, which had been walking in confidently and meeting Tom on an equal footing. Now, limping in, she wasn't going to meet him on any footing.

Tom didn't lift his eyes from the papers he was reading on his desk. Sara noticed his white exam coat was still thrown over the chair. He had always hated wearing it, and apparently he still did. The top button of his blue striped shirt was undone and there was no sign of a tie.

'They're waiting downstairs, Johnson…you need to get there stat.' His voice was stern but not abrasive.

Sara stood in the doorway supported by her apologetic assailant. Across the room she watched the man who had captured her heart all those years ago and who had made love to her only a few short weeks ago. For the briefest moment time seemed to stand still. Her resolve to forget their history vanished and she found herself wondering how it would be if things had been different between them.

She hated feeling this way. It wasn't fair and she couldn't allow her feelings to cloud her future. The chemistry they shared had allowed the anger and frustration to dissipate over dinner and drinks. But here in the hospital she would fight it. Her biological clock was ticking louder than her heart and she was determined that Tom Fielding would not rob her of the chance to have a family. She would not make that sacrifice. Letting him leave the hotel room had proved to Sara that she had the reserves to do it. To walk away a second time, and to let him do the same.

Tom's eyes were shadowed by a slight frown before he lifted his head and met her gaze. Abruptly the frown vanished and he stood to his feet.

'Sara, I thought you were in San Antonio. What are you doing here?' Suddenly Tom's eyes dropped to the injury on her leg. 'Are you hurt? What on earth happened?' Concern etched his voice as he crossed the room with long purposeful strides. He drew her into his arms and pulled her close to his firm body as Johnson released his support.

Sara resisted Tom's hold. She tried to pull away but his strong arms held her still.

'I crashed into her, Dr Fielding. I didn't see her. I'm sorry. She was waiting outside but I was in a hurry and *boof*—I hit her.' The young man re-enacted the collision with his hands.

'Grab that chair,' Tom said, motioning towards the large armchair that sat by the window. 'Bring it here quickly.'

The young man dragged the chair across the room and Tom gently lowered Sara onto the cushioned leather.

'There's a first-aid kit in the cupboard to the right of the bookcase.'

Sara heard the instructions Tom gave to Johnson but her eyes were transfixed on Tom as he crossed the room to retrieve a small footstool by the bookcase.

He looked every bit as gorgeous in the daylight as he had that night just a month ago. His lean, angular face was slightly tanned and his grey eyes were luminous beneath his sandy brows.

He smiled at her as he carried the footstool back, his

wide sensual mouth slowly curving upwards. But she would not reciprocate.

Tom had no place in her life any more. In fact, he should never have been there. They were two very different people with completely different priorities in life.

Sara swallowed hard. 'It's just a little scratch, honestly. It's nothing…' Her words were cut short when she felt the warmth of his hands on her bare skin. He looked into her eyes as he knelt on the floor beside her, gently lifting her leg and placing it on the stool. He moved the hem of her skirt slightly to assess the damage to her knee. She swallowed hard. She hated that the feel of his fingers lightly touching her skin sent shivers down her spine. Again she wished she had worn heavy woollen tights, but this time it wasn't because of the cold.

Johnson handed him an antiseptic wipe and some gauze.

'It's just a superficial wound. I'll clean it up but I think a plaster will suffice.'

'I'm so glad and I'm so sorry, I mean it. I can't believe what a day I've had and now this—'

'We'll be fine here, Johnson,' Tom interrupted. 'Go and collect your patient but this time just take it a little slower.'

'Are you sure? You don't need anything?'

'Positive,' Tom replied, not taking his eyes off Sara.

Sara watched from the corner of her eye as the young man put the first-aid kit back on Tom's desk, picked up her briefcase and overcoat from the doorway, put them by her chair and left the room.

And left them alone.

Tom's hands were still cradling her leg. The plaster was securely attached to the clean wound but he didn't want to release her. He had forgotten how good it felt to have Sara this close. He had no idea why she was in his office but for the briefest moment he didn't care. She was with him again. Near him again. And he could touch her soft, warm skin. Her perfume was invading his senses. It was the same fragrance she had always worn. So little had changed and yet so much had changed for ever.

Finally he came to his senses and reluctantly released his hold, standing up and moving back to his desk. He looked at the woman before him. She was as beautiful as the day they'd met, the day they'd married and the day she'd left him. But she *had* left him.

'What brings you back to Melbourne and my office?' he asked, as he rested back against the wooden frame and folded his arms across his chest. 'I thought you'd be in Texas by now.' He suddenly felt the need to protect himself. Then the realisation of why she had come to the hospital hit him. She must have grown tired of waiting for the divorce papers to make the return trip to her, so she had made the visit to collect them herself.

'The documents are with my lawyer. No doubt they'll be with yours tomorrow.'

Sara suddenly realised that Tom had no idea either. He was obviously equally clueless that they would be working at the same hospital.

'I'm not here for the papers, Tom. Although I'm glad to hear that's progressing,' she announced. 'No, actually, I'm here to work for a month, filling in for Stu.'

'You're filling in for Stu?' Tom was gobsmacked.

'You never said anything that night when we...' He hesitated for a minute. He didn't want to allude to what he knew they were both thinking. He cleared his throat. 'When we bumped into each other. I'm surprised you didn't say anything.'

Sara just stared at him for a moment, trying desperately to push the vivid snapshots of the evening from her mind.

'I didn't know back then, when we...' She paused. It was becoming more awkward and uncomfortable by the minute. 'That night, well, I hadn't spoken with Stu and I had no idea you consulted here. But even if I had known, if you remember, we didn't talk work at all.'

Tom nodded in silence.

Sara knew she would never have accepted Stu's proposal to fill in for him if she had known Tom worked at the hospital where she would be operating. She had assumed he was safely ensconced at the other side of town. But she had to deal with the situation. There was no other choice. Stu would never find another oral surgeon on short notice and she would never leave him high and dry like that. She just had to deal with Tom.

'So, what are you doing at this hospital?'

'I'm the associate professor of oral surgery.'

Sara was taken aback. Tom hadn't said a word that night. With a title like that, and the extraordinary workload and dedication to achieve such a position, he had certainly earned some bragging rights. But he had said nothing about it. She wanted to say how proud she was of him, but of course pride carried ownership or at the very least attachment, and she couldn't afford either.

'Congratulations, Tom,' she finally decided, keeping it simple. 'That must have been a lot of work. You must be the youngest associate professor on staff.'

'So they say. But I'd completed my PhD, and had a year post-doctoral experience so I met the selection criteria. The board approved my appointment for three years and I'm only six months into it,' he responded. The PhD had kept his mind from missing Sara after she left. It had provided him with a focus and purpose in getting up each day.

'I still operate on private patients but I'm more involved with the teaching and rotation programme in the undergraduate, graduate and professional curricula and the development of post-qualifying modules. But enough about me. I'm still in shock that you are Stu's mysterious replacement.'

'What do you mean, mysterious?' Sara replied, giving him a puzzled look.

'I mean he hadn't told me who was filling in at the practice. Stu told me that he had it covered but not that you were his replacement.'

Sara was even more confused. Stu's private practice was not his concern. 'Why do you discuss his practice? Don't you still have your own?'

Tom gave her a wry look. 'Because we're partners, Stu's a partner now in my old practice—he bought in a few months ago. I only consult there one day a week now. The hospital consumes most of my time, but I still wanted to maintain some patient contact.'

Sara was completely flustered for a moment. Not only was Tom consulting at the hospital where she would be operating but he was also a partner at the practice where she would be consulting for the next month. She would be working at Tom's old practice. This was quickly spiralling into a disaster.

'Oh, well, at least this will be uncomfortable for both of us,' she said honestly.

Tom stood watching her carefully, looking for clues as to what she was thinking and, more importantly, feeling. He wanted some signs that would let him into her head. There was nothing. She really had shut him out. That night had been nothing but a moment of passion between two lonely people in a big city. Nothing more.

He knew then and there what he had to do. He had to keep his ex-wife away from his heart. Or he'd go mad. It was crazy and he knew it but he still loved the woman sitting there, so close but emotionally so distant. The woman who had captured his heart all those years ago still held it quite firmly in her hands. He had to push her away. Or, more to the point, he had to push her out of his reach.

He didn't need a reminder of why she'd left. Or why she'd had to leave. They had shared that discussion too many times to recall.

Any feelings she'd once had for him were clearly gone. He had to accept it. And so he adopted the same detached demeanour. A demeanour very far from his true feelings.

'There really shouldn't be any problems. That night…' He paused. 'Let's just say old habits, reminiscing, we crossed the line, both of us. It won't happen again. But, hey, we got it out of our systems. Like an itch that needed a good scratch, and now it's done we can both move on.'

Sara was thrown by his response. It was cold. He really was over them. An *itch*? That sounded so unlike the Tom she had known. Still, three years had passed and he had obviously changed. Or, just like her, was he putting on a façade to make the arrangement they found themselves in a little less awkward? It didn't matter. They both knew and understood the rules.

Without answering, Tom crossed back to her and reached for her leg. Sara jumped as his hand gently lifted her leg down from the stool and placed her foot back on the floor.

'We're good, Sara…we're good.'

* * *

Sara wasn't so sure. She was going to be operating at the hospital for a month. That meant bumping into each other, on ward rounds, near the OR. There were too many opportunities where they would see each other.

The way her body had reacted to Tom made her realise only too quickly that the chemistry she shared with him wasn't just a memory. She suddenly worried if her love for him would ever truly be over. But they had no future. She would not give up on the idea of bringing children into the world. Being a mother was a dream she wanted to hold onto but Tom never wanted to be a father. That was written in stone.

She had spent too long getting him out of her head and her heart.

Sara looked at him, and even through her tired eyes she could see the man who won her love was still as handsome and charismatic as ever. *It's four short weeks. It can't be that difficult.*

'I'm a little tired—can we discuss the work schedule later? We can sort out the personal arrangements too over the next few days. I'm happy with the financial separation the way it is. It won't change after we divorce. You won't need to support me, so it should be done very quickly.'

There was an uncomfortable silence between them. She had no idea what was going on in Tom's mind but he clearly wasn't about to share anything. She had said her piece and cleared the air.

'Quick and painless, like an extraction of an upper molar,' he said matter-of-factly.

Sara knew when Tom became uncomfortable he always used dark humour. It was how he masked his emotions.

'Not quite,' she replied, then chose to change the subject. 'After the four weeks here, I'm off. I don't know a lot about Texas but the position sounded exciting and I jumped at it,' she told him as she crossed to one of the floor-to-ceiling bookcases that lined the room. Part of her didn't want to go to the US. Part of her still wanted Tom. But she also wanted more.

Sara lightly ran her fingers over a row of leather-bound medical books standing next to one another on the shelf and thought back to all of the nights she had spent poring over books just like them as a postgraduate student at the university library, hoping to come close to Tom's knowledge and skill. But it wasn't just his ability and compassion as a doctor that had her in awe, it was his commanding presence as a man that had drawn her to him. He had been her lecturer and her mentor but more than that, she had wished he was her lover.

She had felt on some level there was chemistry that ran between them. She would watch him standing at the lectern, speaking to all the medical students, and she had hoped, as his eyes had scanned the lecture hall, that he had seen her as more than just his student. She had wanted him to see her as a woman. A woman who respected his knowledge, admired his skills but wanted to know more about him as a man.

Sara would daydream in the tram on the way home, a bag full of handwritten notes at her feet and a laptop in her backpack, about the two of them driving home together. She had pictured them talking about their days, comparing notes on cases and discussing surgical procedures. Sara remembered back to the long nights when she would lie in twisted sheets staring at the ceiling in the darkness of her university bedroom. She would picture the curves of his handsome face, the skin wrinkling softly around his grey eyes when he laughed, and the warm, masculine scent of his body.

Not being able to say how she felt during those many months of study was at times almost impossible. But she knew better than to say anything to her incredibly handsome tutor. It was more than likely that her romantic musings were one-sided. She didn't want her imagination to steer her into attracting more of his attention. He was almost seven years older, infinitely wiser and often intimidating. And she was his student. Capable and willing to learn, passing with distinctions, but still his student.

She thought he would be more interested in dating one of his peers, yet there were moments when she felt there was something more. She would ask a question, or answer one that he had posed, and he would appear genuinely impressed.

There were times when his eyes seemed to linger on her a little longer. His mouth would curve ever so slightly and his eyes seemed to be smiling. Her heart would skip a beat, and she hoped she didn't blush. Sometimes he would ask her to stay late with a small number of postgraduates to discuss a topic or alternate prognosis in greater depths. On more than one occasion he bumped into her in the university cafeteria and they shared a table and talked of things other than work.

She wanted more than anything for his interest to be more than just academic, and these chats led her to believe it was, but he was a complicated man. She decided that until her training was over and he made his feelings clear she would keep her own locked safely inside her heart.

Sara never regretted that decision. Soon after she graduated and found a role in a private practice based in Brighton, Tom invited her to a celebratory dinner. She was so surprised and happy. It was a dinner for two. Standing at the door of the restaurant as they waited for their table, his soft hands cupped her face and gently turned her towards him. Tenderly, he reached down and kissed her.

It took Sara's breath away. Her intuition about his feelings had been right all along. The man of her dreams, of all her late-night fantasies, was kissing her. And not caring who saw them.

She remembered every wonderful warm feeling that rushed through her body when, with love in his eyes and a wicked grin, he whispered huskily that given the chance he would never let her out of his sight again. He told her he wanted to keep her in his arms for ever.

It was a whirlwind romance. Every second weekend they spent away at different cosy bed and breakfasts all over Victoria and then, three months after their first date, Tom surprised Sara with a trip to Paris. Winter had set in and they had planned on heading to the ski slopes of Mount Hotham. The night before they were due to leave for the snow, sitting by the heater in Sara's apartment eating raisin toast and sipping on hot chocolate, Tom told Sara there was a slight change in plans but one he hoped she would like. He suggested that she should pack some summer clothes and her passport instead of thermal underwear. As Sara frantically emptied her suitcase of her sweaters, ski pants and thick socks, hurriedly replacing them with cotton dresses, shorts and T-shirts, she told him that he was crazy.

And he told her that he loved her.

Tom managed to keep the new holiday destination a secret until the cab arrived at Tullamarine airport and he carried their luggage to the Air France check-in. Sara was so excited that she felt her eyes brimming with tears as she took her boarding pass, destination Paris.

Together, they spent a blissful week at Hotel Mansart on Paris's Right Bank. They strolled hand in hand around the Tuileries Garden and along the pathways lined with tulips. Tom was the most romantic, wonderful lover and Sara knew without doubt that she was totally and completely in love. She couldn't help but smile with happiness as they sat together by the sparkling pools in the warmth of a perfect summer day. A perfect day with her perfect man and Sara thought life couldn't be any more wonderful.

But it could. And a short time later it did. As they stood admiring the Maillol sculptures in the soft light of sunset, Tom fell to one knee and slipped a diamond solitaire ring on Sara's finger. She gasped and nodded before she kissed the man of her dreams and fell into his arms. She knew with all of her heart it was where she belonged.

After years of study to qualify as an oral and maxillofacial surgeon, Sara was twenty-eight years of age and Tom was about to turn thirty-five so they decided to have a very short engagement and that night as they lay in each other's arms they set a wedding date only three months away.

Sara was going to spend her life with a man she completely and utterly adored and she had never been so happy in her life…

'Sara. Yoo-hoo, I asked you when exactly you're leaving for cattle country?'

CHAPTER THREE

SARA RAISED HER chin and turned around to face Tom. She looked across the room to see him sitting back down in his high-backed leather chair. She thanked the heavens that, no matter how extraordinarily talented her estranged husband was, at least he wasn't a mind-reader.

She was angry with herself for the way she was reacting to him again. She was so distracted. Closing her eyes for a moment, she took a deep, calming breath. She had to get her emotions under control. Tom was bringing back feelings that she couldn't afford to entertain. She had other plans.

But now, seeing Tom again, her heart began questioning her head.

Would she ever find a man she loved as much as Tom?

She had dated a few men over the past three years but not one of them had ever matched up. She always compared her dates to Tom. She hated that she did it. And she hated that they never came close.

She cursed silently as she studied him. He wasn't going to ruin her life. She could be happy one day and have the big messy family that she'd always wanted. She deserved a man in her life who was willing to give her that family.

'Listen, Tom, I think that it's best I head to the hotel and put my feet up for a while.'

There was a knock on the door, forcing Sara to step back. A tall, well-dressed woman entered, a clipboard in hand. She was very attractive and Sara guessed her to be in her late twenties. Her hair was short and dark in a Cleopatra cut, which suited her almond shaped eyes and Mediterranean features.

'Tom, I'm sorry to interrupt but I thought you should know that tomorrow afternoon's list has an alteration. The mandibular advancement, Troy Reeves, has cancelled. Influenza. I've rescheduled him for the twentieth of the month. With any luck you'll finish surgery by six tomorrow night.'

'Christina, this is Sara,' Tom said, as he reached for the amended list. 'Sara, this is Christina, my secretary.'

Both women smiled courteously.

'Christina, if you've done your bit, go on home,' Tom told her. 'I really appreciate you coming in on a weekend. I'll make it up to you.'

'Don't be silly, Tom. I'm happy to help out under the circumstances and I'll see you around seven.' With that she headed back to the open door. 'Nice to meet you, Sara.'

Sara smiled and with equal grace said goodbye before the door closed.

'Don't know what I'd do without her,' Tom remarked casually. 'She's a remarkable woman.'

Sara felt an unexpected ache in her heart when she heard him talk that way about another woman. And they had plans at seven. They had a date. It was ridiculous to be feeling anything other than elation. But she didn't. She felt jealous. It was insane. Why should she care what he thought of or, for that matter, did with other women? Tom could date other women. And now he'd signed the divorce papers he could marry another woman. *As long as she didn't want children.* It wasn't her concern what he did.

You wanted a divorce and now you have it within your reach. And don't forget it, she reminded herself as she tried to pull her thoughts back to the situation at hand.

Before Sara had a chance to open her mouth, the door burst open again. She spun around and found herself being hauled into the arms of a tall, rather robust man with a bushy beard. She felt dwarfed by his stature. He hugged her ferociously and then stepped back.

Sara had to steady herself. It took a moment for her to register just who was on the giving end of the exuberant embrace.

'Sara,' he said. 'You're looking great. How long has it been?'

'Stuart!' she managed to return, realising it was her old friend hiding beneath the thick facial hair. His trademark mop of russet curls hadn't changed at all, now she took stock of him, neither had his twinkling brown eyes in rimless glasses. 'Gosh, it must be three years or more. Last time I saw you would've been…at…um…your…' She stumbled over her words.

A cough echoed from across the room. 'I think Sara's trying to say it was at your anniversary party just before we went our different ways,' Tom interjected. 'And by the way, Stu, it would've been nice of you to let me in on the fact Sara was filling in for you. I had no idea.'

Stuart just shrugged his shoulders. 'Should've read the memo I left on your desk in the office.'

'Maybe you should have just told me.'

'I'm not your secretary, Dr Fielding. We're partners!'

Sara smiled at the banter. They were like bickering children.

'It's lovely to see you again, Stu,' she cut in, to change the subject before it escalated further.

'Just wonderful to see you, gorgeous. You haven't changed a bit. Stunning as always,' he said, stepping back. 'I'm sorry I was delayed in ICU. I wanted to be here when you arrived and talk through everything but since Tom is here I'm sure he can run you through my caseload and his as well. He's going to take over my day at the hospital and you will cover his day there. It's easier than trying to have you cover at the hospital for me. Way too much paperwork in this place,' he said, rolling his eyes.

'Okay, I'm happy to fit in where I can,' Sara said after hearing the update. She'd had no idea she would be covering for anyone else, let alone Tom, but it did make sense.

'I'm glad I got to thank you in person before I leave. You're a trouper. Dana and I can't tell you how much it means to us.'

'It's my pleasure. Are you looking forward to your time off?'

'It's not exactly time off for the sake of it. I'm taking time out to be with Bonny. She was hurt in an accident up on the farm. The tractor lost its grip on an embankment. It rolled into a ditch where Bonny was playing.'

'Oh, my...' Sara's hand instinctively covered her mouth. 'When did that happen?'

'A few weeks back. She's okay. She's out of hospital now. I mean, all things considered, she's doing really well. It was a dirty great tractor and she's so tiny and it could have been much worse. Thankfully there were huge great boulders that took the full weight of the tractor. It fell sideways and Bonny got injured when the metal toolbox lost its moorings and landed on her. She was knocked unconscious and her leg was pinned underneath the exhaust pipe.' The pain in his eyes couldn't mask the distress he was feeling at retelling the story.

Sara was horrified at the thought of Bonny pinned beneath the tractor. She felt her own spine rush with cold and then tears begin to build. She blinked them away.

'I didn't want to guilt you into coming so I didn't mention Bonny when you offered to fill in. It would've been unfair to put that sort of pressure on you.'

'It wouldn't have been pressure. You know I would do anything for you and Dana. I'm just so incredibly sorry to hear about all of this,' Sara told him truthfully. 'I'm glad I'm here, and I hope you can just focus on Bonny and get her better even sooner.'

'She's up and walking but still in a frame,' Stuart told her. 'But she's determined to get back on those little feet of hers. I know she can do it and I think she's going to get better that much sooner with me home full time to help her through the physio. I'm usually home three days a week then here in Melbourne, consulting, the other four.'

Sara watched as Stuart looked pensively down toward his hands and nervously twisted his wedding band back and forth. She felt helpless to ease the almost tangible pain he was suffering.

'She hasn't regained her speech yet,' he began, in little more than a dying whisper.

Sara reached for his hands and encircled them in her own.

'If she's anything like you, little Bonny will be back on her feet and telling you off before you know it.'

He coughed to clear his throat and slowly pulled his hands free of hers and stepped away from her. Sara suspected it was some sort of male strategy he was using to keep his emotions in check.

'I know she will. It's Dana that needs convincing. The specialists have told us with family around her full time she'll be racing ahead. I originally organised a nurse to help out with the twins so Dana could spend time with Bonny, but now, thanks to you taking over for the next month, we can keep it just the family and I know it will make all the difference to her recovery.'

Stuart wrapped one arm around her shoulder and pulled her close again in a bear hug. 'Dana sends her love and hopes you can visit us at the farm soon. We've had it for two years now. Dana really wants you to meet the twins. They're nearly one and, of course, Bonny's almost seven now.'

Sara felt a twinge of guilt for not returning to Melbourne to visit Stuart and Dana. The four of them had shared some wonderful times together, but after the separation Sara had felt the need to stay away from risk of seeing Tom. She'd emailed often and called occasionally. She'd sent them a basket filled with toys and baby gifts when the twins were born. But for the last few months she had been too focused on planning the trip and hadn't spoken to them. Obviously because of the accident and their priority being Bonny, they hadn't reached out to her either.

'It has been far too long since I saw you,' she began. 'I really would love to visit you and Dana on the farm when Bonny is up to it.'

'Of course, Dana would love it,' he responded. 'Sars, some things never change, you know, like you and Tom. Good friends you can always rely on in times of need.'

Sara was having trouble concentrating. Her mind was spinning with images of helpless little Bonny lying in the ditch beneath the tractor. She could only imagine how devastating it had been for the family.

She was deep in terrible, vivid thoughts she didn't want to have filling her head, when Stuart's prickly beard brushed against her neck as he kissed her cheek to thank her yet again.

'I won't forget this, kiddo,' Stuart told her. 'If there's ever anything I can ever do for you, just ask.'

'Don't you think twice about it,' she returned. 'Just get Bonny well—that's enough for me.'

'Well, I expect to see you up on the farm the first break you get.' He smiled and was gone, leaving her alone in the office with Tom.

The atmosphere in the office changed within moments.

With calm composure Sara walked to the door and softly closed it. Her hand quietly released the handle before she turned on her heel and marched over to his desk. 'Why didn't you tell me about Bonny when we caught up the other night?'

'I hadn't seen you for three years, we were keeping it light and I didn't see the point. You said you were leaving to live in Texas. What could you have done? I had no idea that you were coming here to work with me...'

'Neither did I, but surely something as serious as that would rate a mention.' Sara was angry with Tom and not afraid to let him know it.

'Sara, you walked out on me. You walked out on our life together and everything we shared. You never brought up Stu or Dana that night. What right do you have to question me about my actions or what I do and don't tell you? We shared a few hours together. I don't know what's been happening in your life any more than you know what's been happening in mine. We kept it light, Sara, so don't lecture me about what I should and shouldn't have shared with you.' His lips were tight and his mouth formed a hard line.

Sara stepped back. She was acutely aware that Tom was right. She had walked away and she had no right to criticise him. She hadn't asked about Stu and Dana during the evening they'd spent together. That night she had purposely steered the conversation away from anything and anyone that linked her back to their life together.

'You're right. I'm sorry,' she said, regret tainting her voice. 'I guess it wasn't your job to bring me up to speed that night. It's just that we were so close to Stu and Dana and I wish I'd known. I wish they'd called me or I'd called them.'

Sara realised that she had only herself to blame. It wasn't Tom's fault. Her lack of sleep was finally taking its toll and she could feel that her eyes were becoming heavy.

'Tom, I've had a long night and I need to get some sleep, maybe just a short nap.' She reached for a pen and began writing on a small message pad on his desk. 'This is the name of my hotel. I'll call you in a few hours after I take a nap and perhaps we can sort out the working arrangements for the next month over a late lunch.'

Sara woke to the sound of a knock at her door.

She lifted her head from the pillow, surprised to find the room dark. She sat bolt upright and could see the bright lights of the city skyline through her window. A muted glow from the corridor was creeping under the narrow gap below her door.

Fumbling a little, she reached for the lamp beside

the bed. Her blurry eyes tried to focus on her watch. *It couldn't be. Seven o'clock, in the evening?* She must have slept for almost ten hours. She looked down to find she was still dressed in her suit and lying on top of the bed covers.

'Who is it?' she called out, as she climbed from the bed.

'Tom,' his husky voice returned. 'I thought we'd go out for a late lunch. It's nearly eight here but it has to be lunchtime somewhere in the world. Maybe in Texas they're tucking into buffalo wings.'

Sara smiled but she felt uncomfortable knowing that he was at the door of her hotel room. She remembered only too well what had happened last time.

She ran the brush through her hair once more, quickly looked in the mirror and cleared the smudges of mascara from under her eyes, then crossed the room. Her hands ran over her crinkled skirt and, as respectable as she could look under the circumstances, she opened the door.

Tom stood before her, dressed in a fine grey polo knit and black trousers. His hair was swept back from his forehead in gentle, still-damp waves. He looked as if he had just climbed from the shower. It only took seconds for his subtle cologne to penetrate her senses.

'Hello, Tom,' she managed, glad that her tone was cool, despite how nervous she felt or how handsome he looked, standing in her doorway. 'Just to let you know it's not eight, it's only seven.'

He grinned ruefully. 'No, it's nearly eight, you're on Victorian time now, you're not in Adelaide anymore. You must be tired,' he said, tilting his head to one side. 'Are you up to grabbing a bite to eat?'

She glanced down at her watch. He was right on

both counts. It was eight and she definitely wasn't in Adelaide anymore. She was in Melbourne and she was uncomfortably close to her far too handsome and soon to be ex-husband.

'I suppose I am a little peckish,' she began trying to push away how he was making her feel. She looked down and saw again how crumpled her clothes were after flying and then sleeping in them. 'Can you give me fifteen minutes to freshen up?'

'Not a problem. I'll wait downstairs.' With that he walked off down the corridor to the lift.

She watched him. The way he swayed just slightly as he walked. The way his clothes fit his masculine body. The perfect silhouette of his broad shoulders and slim waist.

'I'll be in the bar,' he called back, turning around too quickly for her to pretend she wasn't watching him.

She slammed the door shut with her foot, angry with herself once again.

The hot water over her body felt good and she wished she could stay there longer but she knew she had to get downstairs. Quickly, she applied light make-up and then searched through her suitcase for something that didn't need ironing.

She chose a salmon knitted top and cream slacks, casually draping a soft pastel scarf around her neck and slipping on her kitten heel sling-backs before she left her room.

On the trip down in the elevator Sara tried to remind herself that she was doing this for Stu and now for Bonny. There was no backing out.

The lift reached the ground floor and Sara walked across the foyer and up a few steps into the raised bar area. She spied Tom at a table but he wasn't alone. Christina, his secretary, was with him. Of course, she suddenly remembered, they had a date.

Sara unexpectedly felt a tug at her heart. It was ridiculous. Why shouldn't Tom move on? The divorce papers were on their way to the lawyer. But even so, seeing Tom with another woman made her feel unreasonably possessive.

Suddenly, as she approached the couple, a little voice inside her head demanded to be heard. *Sara Fielding, this will make it so much easier. He is taken. He's not available so keep your emotions in check.*

Sara watched the way Christina was looking at Tom. Her heart wasn't thrilled at what she saw, but her mind was elated with the couple's body language. They were at ease and relaxed with each other. So relaxed Sara felt sure they must be lovers. She swallowed hard with that thought.

'Tom, Sara's here,' Christina prompted, in little more than a whisper.

Tom turned and his eyes met Sara's. For a split second she felt as if they were the only two people in the room. It wasn't right, she knew it. Perhaps he didn't realise the effect he had on her. But she did and she had to take responsibility for her own thoughts. Right here and right now. She would never step back into Tom's life.

'Sara,' he said, as he stood and pulled out a chair for her. 'I thought you must have fallen asleep, again.'

'I wasn't that long,' she replied brightly, trying to set a light-hearted mood as she sat down. 'In fact, if I wasn't so hungry I'd probably still be in the shower.'

'Speaking of food,' Christina interrupted, 'I'd better be getting home. I want to prepare something special for tomorrow night's dinner with Robert.' She bent down and kissed Tom on the cheek. 'Thanks for the drink and thanks for listening.'

Tom patted her hand. 'Any time.'

'Sorry I can't stop, Sara,' she said, with a smile. 'Perhaps next time we'll be able to chat.'

'That would be nice,' Sara replied, with a curious frown. She watched as Christina slipped her bag over her shoulder and left.

Sara waited until Christina was out of sight before she asked the questions niggling her to distraction.

'Who's Robert? And have I just interrupted your date?'

'Date? With Christina?' he said, glancing over to see his secretary leaving the hotel. 'No, she just wanted to chat about a problem over a drink and get my take on it—some male advice, you could say. But why do you want to know about Robert?'

'No reason,' she lied. 'Just curious.' She hoped Robert was Christina's brother or friend. It meant there was still room for Tom in Christina's life.

'Well, to answer your question, he's her husband. He's been away on business for a fortnight,' Tom replied, quite happy that Sara cared.

Sara's face fell with disappointment. 'So she has a husband yet she needs you to listen to her problems...?'

Tom shot her a wry look. 'She didn't know how to break the news to her husband that she'd written off his uninsured Audi. But, come on, Sara, what's prompted the twenty questions? This isn't like you.'

'Sorry, maybe I'm a bit stressed. I've got a lot on my mind.'

'Then let's talk over dinner. What would you like? Chinese, Italian, seafood?'

What would I like? I'd like Christina to be single. I'd

like you and Christina to be having an affair. And I'd like her to want to marry you and, more importantly, you to want to marry her, giving me some perspective. I'd like to be able to say, and actually believe, that being around you for the next month will be easy. I'd like to rewind to a month ago and leave you outside my hotel room. I'd like my life to be as simple as it has been in Adelaide for the last three years.

'Italian,' Sara replied.

CHAPTER FOUR

THE WOOD OVEN baked pizza was delicious. Sara hadn't realised how hungry she was until she found herself picking up the lonely mushrooms from the empty pizza tray.

'I can order another one,' Tom said drily. 'And then maybe I'll get a look-in.'

Sara wiped the corners of her mouth with the napkin and sat back in the padded booth. She didn't bother answering him. She had seen his hands moving as fast as hers back and forth from the tray.

With a good sleep behind her and now a full stomach, Sara felt ready to sort out the working arrangements so they discussed the rosters, the patient load, the surgical amenities at the hospital and the general planning for the following month.

When they had covered everything, Tom sat back in silence and sipped his drink. His eyes were focused on a spot somewhere in the distance. A place that was taking all his attention.

Slowly he turned his face to hers. 'I know I disappointed you, Sara. As a husband, that is, but I never misled you. I was upfront about the subject of children. I'm sorry that I can't change my mind or give you the all the reasons for my decision. But I've never lied. I just needed to tell you that.'

His sudden statement took her by surprise and added to the emotional see-saw that coming to Melbourne had created.

'I'm sure you had your reasons, just as I have mine. I suppose we should have discussed it all before we married, not after.'

Sara drew breath and with it came a calmer and more resigned disposition. She had to keep emotion out of the equation. She wanted more than Tom would ever be prepared to give. And it had hurt her that he had never been prepared to consider children. She wanted all the joy a family brought, and that money and a career could never replace. The happiness of a child being given a puppy, the first artwork they brought home from school, the cuddle at the end of a day just before they fell asleep. She felt a maternal longing that with each passing year became more difficult to fight.

'I want to hear their laughter, to feel their hugs, to tuck them into bed at night. We're two people with very different priorities. You and your brother have so much in common. You both choose a career over having children. Clearly you have goals you wanted to reach. Becoming associate professor is a huge step and probably not one that would have been easy to achieve with a house full of children. I get it. Really, I do. Your career is your focus and there's no room for anything else.'

'Having a child is not the be-all and end-all...' He faltered, then dropped his gaze without finishing the sentence.

'Not to you, but to me it is,' she said with conviction. 'I couldn't give up on that dream.'

Tom lifted his eyes again to study her face. He had

always wondered what drove this need for children. He understood that the maternal instinct might kick in at a certain age. But it seemed more than this.

Finishing his drink, he decided to ask that very question.

'You know, I really do understand that most women like the idea of having babies and planning big Christmas dinners with the family and all of that,' he said. 'But with you it has always seemed like more. Am I reading too much into it, or am I right in thinking there is something else that drove you to walk away when I wouldn't see it your way?'

Sara wondered why it had taken Tom this long to ask that question. But she sensed it was that he hadn't wanted to know before now. When they had been married and the subject of children had come up, he'd changed it very quickly. Knowing the truth behind her motivations, she suspected, may have put additional pressure on him to consider her reasons and, in turn, her feelings.

'I just love children, I always have and always will,' Sara began slowly. 'And the idea of having to give that up would just mean that history was repeating itself. You already know the number of times in the past that I have had to give in to my parents' wishes. Do what they wanted. Become who they wanted me to be. I do love them, but I had to put my life on hold so many times. It wasn't always obvious, and I'm not sure if was even conscious on their behalf, but I would always end up feeling guilty if I forged ahead without their consent.

'Even as a young child, I frequently had to give up on my own dreams to live theirs. Every time I showed free will, and they thought I might make a decision for myself, they had a way of making me think I was being selfish. But I take responsibility for my feelings. I should have stood up to them and told them I was my own person. It was almost like having my spirit killed with kindness. They were so protective but it was so stifling.'

Tom listened intently. He suddenly felt guilty that he hadn't asked this question before. It had clearly formed a huge part of her childhood.

'So was medicine their dream or yours?'

'No, fortunately my career was a mutual vision. I'm not sure what I would have done if they had wanted me to walk away from that. Perhaps it might have persuaded me to take a stand much earlier.'

'This stand?' Tom cut in, interrupting the story.

'Yes, not to back down and feel guilty about wanting something for myself. I had always done what they expected, I think being an only child made me feel as if I owed them a great debt for bringing me into this world and I had to repay them. To be who they wanted me to be. At least, it always felt that way.'

'I'm sorry to hear that. I had no idea.' Tom looked at his hands absentmindedly and wondered what else he didn't know about his wife.

'In high school I was offered the opportunity to go to Germany for a six-month cultural exchange but my father told me that my mother was about to have more tests and he needed me at home to help take care of her in case the news wasn't good.'

Tom looked surprised to hear this. 'But your mother is fine. Well, she was when we visited her a few years ago. Is she okay now?'

'She's perfectly healthy now but she suffered from benign fibroids and the doctor decided on a myomectomy to remove them. They knew it wasn't a permanent solution in the sense that fibroids can grow back after the procedure. I felt an enormous pressure on me to cancel my trip. I knew they needed me, I couldn't abandon them…could I? The doctor did reassure them both that the condition and surgery wasn't life-threatening but there was more going on than that.

'I remember I wanted to head off with two girlfriends and backpack around Australia and maybe travel over to Italy and Greece after my final year at school. Well, let's just say my friends had a wonderful time but all I saw of the outback and the Mediterranean was on their postcards. My mother's hysterectomy had been scheduled during that time. Apparently my mother was one of the ten per cent that needed a second surgery. The trip had meant so much to me but I felt as if I had to give it up to keep them happy. Honestly, looking back, I don't regret what I gave up, it meant starting my medical study early, but I do wish I had drawn a line in the sand a little earlier.'

'But you all seemed to get on so well whenever I was there.'

'By the time you met them, I'd achieved everything they wanted for me, and during my training I gained back some level of independence. I had proved that I could cope without them and, of course, that they could cope without me. Plus, they loved you, so they were happy with my choice. If they hadn't liked you then I probably would have felt pressured to break up with you.'

'And would you?' he asked, looking intensely into her eyes.

Sara swallowed. 'They loved you, so that question is irrelevant.'

Tom wasn't satisfied. 'That's not an answer to my question, Sara.'

Sara could feel her heart racing. She answered him honestly. 'No, I wouldn't have. I would have told them that being with you was something I wanted more than anything in the world, that it was my dream to spend the rest of my life with you and they would have to live with it.'

Tom felt unashamedly happy with her answer but also immensely guilty. She would have fought for him. He shifted uncomfortably in his seat as he realised what he had done to her. It was her dream to be a mother and she had been fighting him for that right. He had added to the conflicts of her childhood and tried to prevent her right to choose her own path.

'So I was asking the same of you, to give up your dream of children.'

Sara nodded, her heart heavy as she thought back to the sadness of their situation.

'I suppose you thought I would soften to the idea,' he told her. 'Just as I hoped you would move on and be happy with only the two of us.'

'I guess we rushed into our marriage and we paid for the mistake later,' Sara replied.

He sipped his drink and looked thoughtfully at Sara. 'Perhaps we're both still paying.'

The early morning wake-up call had Sara up and about by six. But it wasn't a chore considering how many hours sleep she'd enjoyed. Probably more in the last twenty-four-hour period than in any other since she had chosen a career in oral surgery. And she had needed every minute of it.

Tom had dropped her back at the hotel just before

ten-thirty. They had gone by the practice and he had picked up the notes for the next day's patients. Then, downstairs in a booth near the bar, he had gone over his major surgical list and explained the treatment plans. His work was as accurate and thorough as ever. Sara appreciated the long hours he must have spent to cover the caseload at his practice for both himself and Stu, to oversee the hospital in his new role as associate professor and still have such clear and precise details recorded. She was going to be able to take over without any disruption to the patients at all.

Thankfully there were only consultations and minor surgical cases scheduled for the next two days, so she had time to familiarise herself with everything.

After Tom had left, Sara had reviewed the next day's patients, made her notes and finally given in to sleep at about twelve.

Living in the hotel was not a viable situation. Later in the day she would have to make some calls and arrange a comfortable place that was a little more affordable. She would also have to arrange for someone to pack up the last of her belongings in Adelaide and have them sent on to Texas.

As she pulled underwear from her suitcase and shuffled into the bathroom, her thoughts then wandered to Bonny. She prayed the child's recovery would be easier now her father was with her. She'd often thought that she and Tom would one day have a daughter just like Bonny, and a son...or maybe two of each. Tom was right, she had tried to convince herself that in time he would change his mind about children and realise that they did have the capacity, in terms of time and love, required to raise a family. That their careers were important but the joy they would experience bringing up a child of their own was incomparable.

But you were wrong, Sara admonished herself. He never wanted a child. He reiterated that tonight. So forget the past.

She turned the shower taps on full and enjoyed the very long shower she had wanted the night before as she tried to put outdated dreams from her mind. And know that she was doing what was right for her.

'George Andrews was due at nine. Impressions for his wafer splint. His surgery is in just under two weeks,' Marjorie, the receptionist, informed Sara. 'But his mother just called. They've had car trouble and she's called a taxi. They should be about another fifteen minutes.'

'Thanks,' Sara replied with a smile.

Marjorie was in her early sixties. Her hair was a deep auburn and cut short at the back with flattering soft curls around her forehead. She had a pretty face, with gold rimmed glasses perched on her bob nose. She was about the same height as Sara, just a little bigger in build.

The pair had introduced themselves and as far as Sara could make out, she and Marjorie would get along just fine. The woman did not appear to be the prying type and, with everything on Sara's mind, that was a huge relief.

Sara asked Marjorie not to call her Dr Fielding. Her first name was fine and made her feel more relaxed. But the reason was two-fold. She thought it might also avoid a barrage of questions from patients about her relationship to the other Dr Fielding.

Looking around the rooms, Sara couldn't help but

notice that everything had been completely revamped since she had left three years ago.

She absentmindedly ran her finger over the frame of a painting that hung nearby. A beautiful watercolour of a blue kingfisher. It was new. Everything was new. There was no sign that she had ever been there. It was as if anything she had brought into the practice had disappeared and something else now stood in its place. She wondered if their marital home had been gutted in a similar manner. Had Tom sold her favourite pieces to the highest bidder? She blinked away her unanswered questions and turned her attention back to her surroundings. It was not her business. She had left and Tom did what he wanted. She knew she had no right to judge his actions.

The decor was modern, painted in pastel tones and decorated with light-coloured wooden furniture that had a Scandinavian feel. The spacious waiting room had a large, low pine table covered in magazines, a mix of wooden and chrome chairs lined two walls and there was a wicker basket brimming with toys in the corner of the room. Something to keep little hands amused. Stu's idea, no doubt, Sara surmised. Definitely not Tom's.

Overlooking the waiting room, Marjorie's office was filled with enough computer equipment to run a small NASA project. Sara gently opened the adjoining door to find the fully equipped surgery for minor surgical procedures not needing a general anaesthetic.

She knew that the kitchen and bathroom were located at the back of the rooms. The practice was on the first floor of a quaint old two-storey building that had been totally modernised inside, whilst retaining its exterior character. It was in South Yarra, overlooking the

Yarra River. Sara had always loved the calming effect of the scenery.

Melancholy drew her back to the view and she crossed in earnest to the large picture window. Sara sighed as she took in the vista. The day was cold but the sun was shining down and it was a nice change after the gale the day before. The gentle breeze played with the last of the red-gold leaves of autumn. Weeping branches of the willows dipped in the rippling water near the riverbank. The brown-speckled ducks swam around the row of paddleboats, which were tied together and bobbing with the current at the riverbank.

She closed her eyes for a moment and recalled how a few years ago she and Tom had often stood at the same window. Sometimes they had been so immersed in each other's presence they would barely notice the view. They would hold each other tightly and discuss their days. They understood and respected each other's needs. Two tired bodies moulding as one...

'Penny for your thoughts.'

Sara jumped. She hadn't realised how far her thoughts had travelled until the deep voice broke through.

Tom's voice.

'Um, nothing, nothing at all,' she returned, nervously straightening the lapels of her short navy trench coat and brushing imaginary lint from her matching skirt. 'So, what brings you here? Don't you have a hospital to take care of?'

'Board meeting. I hate those damned things. It's always the same old bickering about increased funding cuts, meaning fewer beds and fewer staff. So I sent Johnson to take notes. That should be eye-opening for everyone, Johnson *and* the board members.' He smiled.

Sara smiled back at him in silence then he noticed the softness suddenly turn to something more professional and reserved as she adjusted her jacket and moved away to the other side of the room.

Tom looked at her, wishing things had been different. Wishing he was able to give her what she wanted and what she deserved in life. She wasn't asking for the world and to any other man it would seem fair and natural to want children. But Tom couldn't provide that. Fatherhood would never be a part of his life. He could accept it but it wouldn't be fair to keep Sara in his self-imposed childless life so he had to keep his distance.

Stirring up old feelings again would only delay the inevitable. Even if they rekindled their love, she would leave and turn his life upside down all over again for the very same reason.

Marjorie walked in from the kitchen. 'I've put the kettle on. Will you both have a cup of tea or coffee?'

'Yes, that would be lovely,' Sara answered hurriedly.

'Not for me,' Tom replied. 'I was just leaving. I'm needed back at the hospital—it was just a quick visit.' His sentence was cut short when the door opened. Tom took this cue and left. It had been a short visit, with no purpose other than to spend a few minutes with Sara. He knew he couldn't change their fate. The divorce would seal that but he had a month to enjoy her company, as a doctor he admired and a woman he desired. He was torturing himself just being near her, but he was unable to stop.

Sara watched him leave then turned her attention to a boy in his late teens and the older woman who had entered the office.

'George, Mrs Andrews,' Marjorie greeted them

cheerily. 'Please, take a seat. Dr Fielding, I mean Sara, will be right with you.'

'Where's Dr Anderson?' George asked anxiously. The metal braces on his teeth caught the light. 'Isn't he seeing me today?'

Sara stepped forward. 'No, George. Dr Anderson won't be seeing you today,' she began. 'He had to spend some time with his family. His little girl isn't very well and he asked me to step in and look after you and all of his patients. I'll be carrying out your operation.'

George had looked a little anxious when he walked in but now his worries seemed to escalate to distress. Surgery for anyone was a stressful time but Sara was aware that for an adolescent it was doubly so.

'Don't worry, George,' Sara told him. 'I won't do anything without first explaining it to you and if you have any questions, please, ask me. In a moment we'll go and take some moulds of your teeth, which will be sent off to a lab. The technician will use these moulds to make a special splint, called a wafer, and I will use this to position your jaws during surgery. I'm sure you've had impressions before.'

The boy nodded but his expression was guarded.

'I know they're a bit mucky but they don't hurt. Your orthodontist has put special pins in your braces in preparation for this. We call them high hats, and they make it easier for me to do my job.'

'Yeah, and they stick out a bit,' George complained, and pulled his lips down over the braces.

'How long will it take today?' Mrs Andrews cut in.

'Not very long at all,' Sara replied, turning her attention to the woman. 'You're most welcome to come in.'

'I'm not a child, Mum,' George growled. 'Just wait out here.'

Mrs Andrews raised her eyebrows and sat down. She clearly knew it was pointless to argue with a teenager. Sara smiled to herself. She doubted that George's bravado would hold up just prior to surgery. Then without doubt he would want his mother close by.

'Well, let's go and get started,' Sara said, and led George off towards the consulting room. Marjorie followed closely behind, leaving Mrs Andrews sifting through the magazines. The appointment didn't take much longer than twenty minutes. George didn't ask too many questions but with a mouthful of impression material that would have been difficult. After the impressions were checked by Sara, then packed and taken to Reception to be collected by the laboratory courier, Sara asked Mrs Andrews to come in.

Sara clipped the X-rays onto the wall viewer and studied them for a moment. 'Are there any questions?'

'Are there lots of guys with this problem?' George asked, rubbing his very pronounced lower jaw.

'Guys and girls,' Sara reassured him. 'You have what we call a skeletal class-three malocclusion. This means that your lower jaw is forward in relation to your upper jaw. I'm sure Dr Anderson has gone over this with you but it happened because your mandible, or lower jaw, has grown more than your upper. It's a case of one didn't grow enough and the other grew too much.'

'So you're going to pull my jaw back?'

'Not exactly.' Sara looked at the X-ray viewer, where a profile of George's skull was illuminated. 'You have a skeletal discrepancy. So Dr Anderson had planned on surgery to advance the upper jaw.' Sara pointed to the relevant facial features on the X-ray as she spoke. She moved the tiny mouth ruler she used as a pointer down to the lower jaw area as she continued. 'And set back the lower jaw. Just think of your lower jaw coming back and your upper jaw moving forward about the same amount until they sort of meet halfway and then surgery on your chin to make it a little less angular or severe.'

'I think I kind of get it,' George said. 'But I told Dr Anderson that I didn't like my nose much and he said he could fix that too.'

Sara thought it best to keep clear of decisions that were purely cosmetic. 'George, I think it's best if you and the family make that decision at home. Just call Marjorie next week if you want me to proceed with a rhinoplasty at the same time—that's the name we give to the nose operation.'

'But what do you think?' George asked, giving unexpected value to Sara's opinion on the matter.

Sara was flattered that he had asked her but she had to remain impartial. 'To be honest, George, it is a cosmetic improvement and therefore has to be a family decision. No surgeon can tell you what you should or shouldn't look like when it comes to nose shape or chin shape.'

'But if he was your son, what would you advise us to do?' George's mother asked.

Sara was taken aback by the question. *If he was my son?* She stared down at her hands clasped tightly in her lap. If I ever have a son, she thought, I would want only the best for him. I would want him to grow into a strong, perceptive individual just like Tom. Her stomach tightened a little at her reaction. Day one and Tom Fielding had safely tucked himself into her subconscious. Just where she didn't need him.

She swallowed as she looked at Mrs Andrews and George, then thoughtfully she answered, 'I wouldn't rush into any surgery on a whim. I would think it through, discuss it at home and be very sure it was something George felt very strongly about undertaking.'

She blinked away her other thoughts. It was going to be long month in Melbourne.

Sara switched off the X-ray viewer, slipped the X-rays inside the case notes and then escorted the young man and his mother back into the waiting room.

'Sara, your nine-thirty appointment, Mollie Hatcher, is here,' Marjorie said as the three approached the front desk.

Sara remembered reading Mollie's referral notes and when the child smiled nervously, Sara could see the large fleshy membrane that ran between her front teeth, giving her a gap large enough to hold a gold coin. The referring doctor had recommended a frenectomy to remove it, and even before the consultation, Sara had judged that to be the right treatment plan.

Looking over the medical history, Sara ushered in the little girl and her mother.

It was another half hour consultation, which ended with Mrs Hatcher booking a time for Mollie's minor surgery in the rooms the following week.

The day continued, with Sara seeing a steady load of Stu's patients. Most of them were new patient referrals and there were three post-operative check-ups. Tom had stepped in to cover Stu's consulting role at the hospital and Sara would be picking up Tom's private patients. It was a sensible arrangement for the weeks ahead.

She knew the next day it would be Tom's patients and a minor surgical list in the afternoon. Both men were professional and skilled surgeons and Sara hadn't disagreed with any treatment plan either had suggested for their patients. She knew the next day would be no exception. When it came to work, that was the one area that she and Tom would never come to loggerheads. He had taught her well and she would never doubt his decision. His knowledge as a consultant and his dexterity as a surgeon were second to none.

Sara was quietly honoured he had approved her stepping into the practice that he had built over many years and had then invited Stu to join. And she was pleased to be doing it without any intervention from him. He did trust her. From someone with a reputation of being one of the finest surgeons in the country, that was a huge accolade for her.

It was about six o'clock when Sara realised she had done nothing about accommodation. She would have to spend another night at the hotel and then tomorrow she had to organise something else.

Marjorie said goodnight, locked up and left for the day. Sara was tidying up the last of the case notes when she heard a key in the front door. It didn't take her long to realise who it was.

'I'm in the office, Tom. Just a few bits and pieces to tidy up.'

She heard his footsteps draw nearer and looked up to find him framed in the doorway. His face was a little drawn but still unbelievably handsome. His jaw was darkened by the first signs of fine stubble.

'I'm here to take you home.'

'That's very sweet of you,' Sara remarked. 'But I've already booked a taxi to my hotel.'

Tom crossed the room in silence. His dark eyes didn't stray from her face for a moment. 'I wasn't talking about the hotel, Sara. I'm taking you to our home.'

CHAPTER FIVE

SARA WAS STUNNED into silence.

She swallowed a lump of emotions that had converged in her throat. *Our home.* There was no 'our' anything any more. She chewed nervously on the inside of her cheek. What on earth was Tom thinking? She felt herself falling into the deep, grey eyes that were focused solely upon her. She wanted to pull away, she had to, but she couldn't pull away far enough. Her gaze dropped only to his wide, soft mouth.

A mouth that her heart could suddenly remember giving her the most tender of kisses. Sara felt so confused. Confused about her own feelings. Even more confused about Tom's. She thought they had set the parameters. She was not about to move back in with him on either a short-term or long-term basis.

Did he think by her staying in Melbourne that she would throw away her new life and come back to him? He must know after their talk the night before that she wouldn't back down. She wanted children, and it was not negotiable. Then was he looking for another few nights of passion for old times' sake? She couldn't, and she wouldn't allow him to change her plans. Her mind had to take over. Calculated logic had to kick in. She had to control her body's desire for him. If she didn't,

Sara was terrified of where it all might lead. Heart-break, no doubt, for both of them.

'There is no *our* any more, Tom.'

'You can call it my house if it makes you feel any better.'

'It does,' she returned. 'Because it's the truth. I don't belong in Melbourne. I don't have any ties here any more.' Sara closed the file of paperwork she was completing.

'I'm just trying to help,' he argued. 'Unless, of course, you'd rather pay for accommodation at the hotel for the next month.'

'So moving in with you is the best solution? I hardly think so.'

'Not with me exactly. The other half of the maison-ette, the part that belonged to Mrs Vandercroft, is now mine. She moved into a nursing home only a month after you…' Tom hesitated, not wanting to make her feel that he was blaming her for their separation.

'Well, just after we parted, so I bought it. You remember how she had one or two falls, well, they increased and finally she really injured herself on a coffee table she just didn't see. Her eyesight was failing, and she was unsteady on her feet. Her family didn't want her living alone any more and, as you know, they all lived interstate. Anyway, she had just turned ninety-eight and didn't want to haul herself up to Sydney so she moved into a nursing home not too far away. I just use the place for storage, so you can have it for the month. I was going to offer it to the locum anyway. I had no idea it would be you.'

Sara considered him suspiciously then felt a little silly for overreacting. Perhaps it was an offer with no strings. After all, he had signed the divorce papers. And he had an empty place.

She shook herself mentally. He definitely appeared to have his emotions in check.

'Well, does this silence mean you're considering my offer?' he asked, jolting her out of her thoughts.

Sara closed her eyes for a split second. She had no logical argument for refusing his offer. Only her irrational thoughts. Against her better judgement she made a decision and prayed for everyone's sake that she was doing the right thing.

'I suppose it's a sensible idea.'

But even as the words passed over her lips, weighty doubts rang alarm bells loudly in her mind. But that was her problem, not his.

Tom smiled. He knew their time together would be short-lived but apart from the great love life they had shared, he enjoyed spending time with Sara. He always had. She challenged him. She was his equal on so many levels. He just wanted a few more weeks with her and then he knew he would let her go. Let her start her new life and not make her think twice about her decision. He hoped this time when she left it might be easier. He hoped his heart wouldn't shatter this time.

As they pulled into the driveway Sara felt a tightening in her chest. They had collected her things from the hotel and made their way to his home about twenty minutes from the city. It was a corner property in a suburb filled with double-fronted cottages and bungalows.

Lit by the headlights of the car, the house looked the same as it did the day she had left. It had been one of the hardest days of her life. She had walked away from her home and her marriage, even though she had still been very much in love with her husband.

The cream stucco walls and shiny gunmetal-grey roof with green gutters hadn't changed. She and Tom had planned to have the front facade steamed-cleaned to reveal the bluestone lying beneath the thick paint but their schedules had never given them the time. It had been something they'd always put off, thinking they had plenty of time in the future.

The roses were in bloom, the way they had been that day in June three years ago. Huge open cabbage roses in deep reds and pastel pinks lined the gravel path to the front door.

Tears welled in the back of her eyes and threatened to spill over.

'Let me get that,' Tom said, as Sara reached into the boot of his late-model Lexus. Their hands touched as they tried to retrieve her luggage. His soft skin brushed against hers. Sara released her hold on the bag immediately and turned away. His touch was unsettling.

'I've got a key for you somewhere in my pocket,' he told her, as he closed the boot and followed behind her, his footsteps crunching on the gravel all the way up to the front door.

Sara's mind was anywhere but in the present and she struggled to keep on track.

'Here it is.' He handed her a key chained to a small crystal slipper. It was the one she had bought when they'd first moved into the house. She couldn't believe he had kept it all this time.

'You know, I always thought this was a little kitsch considering your good taste.'

She held the keyring in her open palm and stared at it in silence.

She remembered back to the day she had bought it. It had been the day before they'd left Prague, where they had spent three days of their four-week honeymoon. Strolling along a cobbled street, they had stumbled upon a little shop that was filled with the most beautiful crystal. Sara had spied the slipper and had known she had to have it. Tom had wanted to buy a beautifully cut crystal vase but she bought the slipper, never telling him the reason.

It was because their romance had been like a fairytale. Having the crystal keyring ensured she was never going to lose her keys, or her Prince Charming. But she knew better than to tell Tom. The logical man that he was, he never would have understood. His diagnosis would have been to tell her she was completely crazy.

Of course, he could have no idea what she was going through now. The memories, the guilt of leaving, it all came flooding back and she wanted so desperately to fall into his arms and pretend that the three years they spent apart were all a bad dream. But she couldn't. Standing there together, she knew she still did have strong feelings for him but that they weren't enough to build a life upon. She wanted more and she knew she had every right to ask for more.

'It's getting mighty cold, standing here while you admire the keyring, Sara.'

Sara looked up and him and wished she could brush aside her feelings and offer a witty retort, but she couldn't. She had agreed in the car on the way home that they would eat their takeaway dinner together, but suddenly she felt too fragile to honour her promise. The house, the keyring, they had brought too many memories to the surface and she needed time alone to sort through these feelings and put them away. Time without Tom.

'I'm sorry,' she began, rubbing her temples in a circular motion, 'but I have this splitting headache. Would you mind terribly if we didn't have dinner together? I wouldn't be very good company.'

Tom considered her for a moment in the soft light from the streetlamp. She felt that his silence hinted at disbelief but he didn't confirm it with his words.

'Of course not,' he finally uttered, and handed her the box with her dinner inside.

Sara graciously took the warm package and unlocked the front door then felt along the wall for the light switch.

'I'll call over if I need anything,' she called back, before wheeling her luggage inside and closing the door on the cold night air. And on Tom. She just wished her heart could do the same.

The maisonette was the reverse floor plan of the one that she and Tom had shared next door. Dropping her case to the floor, Sara's steps echoed down the polished hallway as she made her way into the sitting room.

The maisonette was furnished nicely but it was the antithesis of the home they had shared. It lacked the character of the home they had decorated together. With modern furniture not unlike that in the waiting room at the practice, she would be comfortable and it would be more than adequate for the month.

Tom closed the door to his maisonette, wondering what Sara was doing. Was she eating, unpacking or had she collapsed from the first day on the job? She was actually staying in his side of the maisonette. He had been living there for the last three years as he couldn't live amongst the memories of the furniture that surrounded him tonight.

This was actually the house he had intended to offer

the locum but he couldn't let Sara stay there. It was still furnished with all their belongings. For the next four weeks he would be staying in the home he used for storage. He couldn't let her know that he had kept everything. He didn't want her to know that he hadn't been able to give it away but he also couldn't live amongst it. Not yet. She had moved on...he hadn't.

He loved everything they had bought together but that was the problem—they had bought it together. When they had been happy and in love and planning their future. Tom had called his cleaning lady to move his clothes and toiletries and books from one side to the other when he'd found out Sara was working for the month.

He went to the kitchen to find a fork and then ate his dinner on his lap. He could hear Sara moving about and unpacking through the thin walls.

Even though it would only be for a few short weeks it felt like she was home. But he knew neither of them had the power to do the slightest thing about changing the paths that would eventually lead them away from one another for ever.

Half an hour later Sara threw the remains of her dinner in the bin. She was hungry and she had picked at the pasta but her churning stomach hadn't allowed her to finish it.

She worried about how she would deal with the proximity of Tom. She still loved him. She wondered if he knew it too.

'Damn you,' she cursed under her breath.

Why couldn't he talk about their differences? Tell her the reason he didn't want children in his life? Was he really that selfish or was there something that made him hate the thought of children? She had tried so hard to understand when they had been married but he'd shut the conversation down every time she'd brought it up.

She knew his brother, Heath an ENT specialist, hadn't had any children either. Sara hadn't spent much time with him as he had lived in Los Angeles with his wife until they'd divorced. It hadn't appeared to be an unhappy marriage but, like Sara, his wife had wanted children. Sara wasn't sure if that had been the precursor to her leaving or not. Shortly after the split, Heath had moved to San Francisco to practise. Although she'd seen him with Tom both times he had visited Melbourne, the subject of children had never been discussed. It was like both brothers had decided not to have children and that was final. It was a taboo subject. The elephant in the room.

Was there something in their past that stopped them from wanting a family? Sara doubted that. Whenever Tom had spoken of his parents, both of whom had passed away before Tom and Sara had begun dating, the memories he'd relayed of his childhood had been happy. He and his brother had shared a love of BMX bikes as teenagers and had then dropped that sport to both study medicine. It appeared a happy upbringing.

Sara had wanted more than a blanket refusal to discuss the idea of children. She wanted to know the truth but instead came up against his stubborn refusal to talk. She was forced to accept that his stubbornness went hand in hand with selfishness. She still wondered if there was more to it.

Despite how difficult it was to fight her feelings, Sara knew nothing could happen between them. Tom's timing was all wrong. She was leaving to start a new life. *Don't ruin it, Sara, don't put your life back on hold,* she told herself as she finished unpacking. She knew it would lead to resentment, that she would be sacrificing what she wanted and needed to keep him happy.

It won't work with Tom and you know it, she told herself. Then why did she have to feel so at home? A feeling she hadn't experienced since she had left the same house three years ago. A sense of belonging.

She put a little hot water in the sink and washed her cutlery and glass. As she dried and put them away in the drawer she decided to take a nice long soak in a bath.

There was no point in analysing her curious feelings towards Tom, she decided as she slipped into the steamy bubbles and tried to soak away her troubles. It was just reverie and lost love playing games with her emotions. It was over and they both knew it. It was an *itch*, that was all. Some time later, after almost drifting off to sleep, she stepped from the deep tub, towel-dried her warm body and slipped into her pyjamas and dressing gown.

It wouldn't take long to regain control of her feelings, she resolved. She lay back on the sofa and pulled a patterned rug over herself. It was so cold. She looked over at the heater. It was the same old gas style they had next door. And she knew she could never light it. She didn't want to call Tom and ask for his assistance but she also didn't want to wake up with chilblains in her toes.

'It's just me.'

'Hi, me.'

Sara wished for a moment that she hadn't called. Running her fingers through her short, damp hair, she worried about depending upon him for anything. She pulled the rug and her knees up under her chin, perhaps it wasn't *that* cold. She'd felt unexpectedly awkward talking to him on the phone, knowing he was next door. It was odd. She felt so at home, knowing Tom was only the other side of the wall.

Finally, she mustered her thoughts and asked him to come over and help her light the heater. It sounded like a call to a repairman. Businesslike and distant.

Her fingers and toes were quickly becoming icicles, but two minutes later she heard Tom's speedy knock.

'Hello, Sara,' he muttered, as she opened the door. He smiled wryly. 'How's the headache?'

Sara frowned at the question. The way he looked made her fumble over her words and forget momentarily that she had used the headache as an excuse to get away from him. He was standing on her porch in a dark blue dressing gown. It wrapped over low down and exposed his bare, toned chest. His hair was dishevelled and his face was shadowed with fine stubble. His legs were naked and his feet were inside leather slippers.

'Hello...Tom,' she replied, dragging her eyes back to his. She was so angry with herself. It wasn't as if she hadn't been around good-looking men over the years. In fact, she'd dated one or two handsome men. But her reaction was more than that. She suspected that it was being aware, very aware of what lay beneath Tom's loosened robe that made her feel this way.

He began shivering, pulled his robe tighter and started to rub his arms vigorously. 'Could I come inside and light the gas heater before they have to cart me away suffering from frostbite to the extremities?'

Sara nodded. 'Oh, God, I'm sorry,' she said, and stepped away from the door, allowing Tom to move past her.

'So you're feeling okay, then?'

She closed the door on the frozen night air. 'I'm fine,

truly...actually, I haven't felt better. The headache's gone. I just needed to soak in a tub for...' She paused and glanced nervously down at her watch. 'Gosh, absolutely ages. But I'm glad I did. I'll need a clear head tomorrow, I've got a full day with minor surgery. Two sets of wisdom teeth to be removed, an exposure of a canine and a few others that I can't recall off the top of my head.' She felt her heart racing and couldn't believe how she had prattled on like a nervous teenager. Why did he do this to her? It wasn't fair. She just wanted him to light the fire and leave.

Tom's mouth curved to a smile. 'They're all my patients. So make sure you do a good job, won't you?'

Sara was grateful that he had chosen to ignore her ramblings and she took his sarcastic cue. 'I'll try really hard not to lose any of them for you,' she returned drily.

He walked over to the heater, catching some creaking floorboards on the way. Standing with his back to her, he reached for the box of matches on the mantelpiece. He squatted on the ground and lit the heater. It was old but Sara remembered how quickly it heated the room. She blinked and looked away before she had time to admire his broad-shouldered physique for too long.

'Thank you, Tom,' she said, as she walked over to warm her hands by the heater. 'I'm sorry that you had to come over to do that. I never did get the hang of lighting the old heater.'

'Just what a good landlord does.'

'Of course, I forgot to ask how much you would like in rent for the place while I'm here.'

Tom looked at Sara in silence. She was trying to turn every part of their lives into a business arrangement. He knew why. And he understood she would be leaving when Stu returned. He wouldn't fight it. But he was glad to have her living close. It was almost like old times. She was all rugged up in flannelette pyjamas and fluffy slippers, her face scrubbed bare of make-up, and she was still the most desirable woman in the world.

'What figure are you looking at?' she asked. 'Three hundred, three fifty?'

Money was the furthest thing from his mind. She was a part of the house and his heart and if she had nowhere else she needed to be, she could stay for ever.

'I'm happy to pay four hundred, if that's closer to the mark…'

'Sara, I don't want anything for the place. You are doing me a favour, filling in for Stu…'

'And you are reimbursing me well,' she cut in.

'I know but that's immaterial. You can have the place…for a coffee. I need to stay awake to go over some reports so I could do with a short—'

'Short black, no sugar,' she finished his order. She smiled. It was so easy. It was like the three years had never passed. Here they were together in the house, in their pyjamas. She hated the fact that she wanted so badly to reach out and feel his arms around her. To cuddle up in front of the fire with the sound of the rain on the metal roof. To hold each other till they fell asleep, just like they'd used to.

She snapped out of it and headed for the kitchen and turned on the coffee machine. She looked back at Tom, standing by the fire. Looking so good. It wasn't fair. He was almost the perfect man. And he *was* the perfect lover.

CHAPTER SIX

MORNING CAME QUICKLY AGAIN. Sara thought she might find it difficult to sleep with Tom only on the other side of the wall but she'd fallen into a deep and restful sleep quickly. Almost the moment her head had hit the pillow.

Climbing out of bed, she showered, applied light make-up and dressed in camel-coloured trousers and a striped black and camel fine-knit sweater. She intended to throw her overcoat on top before she left. The number to call for a cab to the practice was already on her phone. Unexpectedly, there was a knock at the door.

As she opened the door, she saw Tom, dressed in dark woollen slacks, a black sweater and heavy grey overcoat, his keys in his hand.

'I trust you slept well.'

'Very,' she told him, as she took a step backwards and held the door open for him to come inside.

Tom walked in, swinging the keys around his finger playfully.

'Do you intend telling me what the keys are for?' she asked.

'Mrs Vanderbilt sold me the house and her car. At ninety-eight, she thought it was better to get off the road. I didn't argue with her—in fact, I told her it was a wise decision considering all the idiots out there now.

And that's how I came to be the owner of the 1967 Austin Healey in your driveway.'

Sara forgot about everything as she crossed the room excitedly. She knelt on the armchair and pulled back the lace drapes. With her sweater sleeve she wiped a small circle of fog from the window. There in the driveway was a mint-green Austin Healey, its duco and chrome shining in the dappled morning sun. She hadn't seen it the night before as it had been too dark when they'd arrived home. Sara adored old cars, old houses and old furniture. They had so much character and history to offer.

She turned around and beamed. 'Tom, it's so sweet of you to let me drive it. I swear I'll be so careful.'

'You can't be serious,' he said with a smirk, as he threw the keys across the room to her. 'You can drive my Lexus. I'm the only one who drives the Healey!'

A little after eight o'clock Sara pulled into the car park of the surgery in Tom's late-model Lexus. She'd had a light breakfast of cereal and toast from the contents of the fridge and pantry that she assumed Tom had stocked for her. Marjorie had just arrived and they walked into the building together.

'Not that it's any of my business, Sara, but tell me, did you decide to move in to Tom's house?'

Sara didn't try to hide her surprise. 'How on earth did you know about that?'

'Then you did?' Marjorie smiled broadly as she slipped her car keys inside her bag and patted it closed. 'Very sensible idea, Sara, very sensible. I think everything will work out quite nicely.'

Sara wasn't too sure if she should read anything in to Marjorie's comments but decided to let it go.

'It will save me a considerable amount of money over the month.'

'Lisa, his cleaning lady, dusted and polished everything, moved his things and stocked the fridge and pantry for you. Tom certainly makes our lives hectic, but we manage.'

'Moved *his* things?'

Marjorie realised that she had said too much. 'Just some boxes and bits and bobs he stored there.'

The cover-up worked and Sara didn't bother asking the woman any more questions. She picked up her pace and headed towards the door.

'I bet you were busy,' Sara said. 'Almost as busy as we'll be today.' She changed the subject as they rode up in the lift. To move further from the subject of Tom and her living arrangements, Sara asked about the fantastic network of linked computers that occupied most of the front office. Thankfully, Marjorie obliged with a lengthy discussion about her big toys and dropped the subject of her employer.

Sara had consultations with new patients all morning and was looking forward to the afternoon surgery. Being so busy kept her mind on track and most importantly off Tom.

She and Marjorie both chose something nice and light from the assorted sandwiches that the lunch delivery girl brought around. The anaesthetist, William North, arrived about one o'clock and so did the part-time nurse, Laura, whom Tom and Stu employed for the days of surgical procedures. After introductions and a friendly chat they were ready to begin the afternoon list.

'Melanie Sanders,' Marjorie called softly across the waiting room. 'The doctors are ready now if you would like to follow me.'

Melanie was seventeen years old and needed her impacted wisdom teeth removed. She had been sitting nervously with her mother.

'Hi, Melanie, I'm Sara and I'm filling in for Dr Fielding for a few weeks while he is at the hospital. So if it's all right with you, let's get started and remove those teeth that have been giving you trouble.'

While Melanie climbed into the operating chair, Sara scrubbed in, slipped on her latex gloves and a pale yellow disposable gown.

'Melanie, Dr North will give you a little shot in the hand, which will make you feel a bit drowsy. You will still be awake and able to follow instructions but you won't feel any pain, and as a bonus the amnesiac properties of the anaesthetic means you won't remember anything about this operation when you get home.'

Laura pinned a surgical bib around Melanie and then William began the sedation. It quickly took effect and Sara was able to begin the removal of the offending teeth. The X-rays were illuminated on the wall beside the chair. The procedure went well and forty-five minutes, and numerous sutures later, the four teeth had been removed and Laura escorted the patient to the recovery room.

William and Sara scrubbed and prepared for the next patient while Marjorie prepared the small surgery again.

The next patient was booked in for a similar removal of wisdom teeth. Luckily, this one was straightforward and he was soon in the recovery room.

Sara and William took a short break and were about to prepare for their third patient when Marjorie asked her to take a telephone call. It was George Andrews' mother. And it was urgent.

'It's Sara Fielding, Mrs Andrews. How can I help?'

'Sara, it's about George, he's refusing to have the operation. The other boys he mixes with have filled his head with worries. He's convinced he could die on the operating table or end up with brain damage or a jaw that has no feeling.'

Sara rubbed her forehead with the inside of her wrist. It wasn't the first time she had encountered friends throwing in their unwanted advice and worrying a patient unnecessarily.

'Don't worry, Mrs Andrews. I'm more than happy to talk to George. I'm sure between the two of us we can convince him he needs to finish his orthodontic treatment and have the operation.'

'I'm not so sure but, Sara, if he doesn't have the surgery now, I know he'll never do it. His friends have persuaded him to move up north and work as a jackaroo.'

'You leave it to me, Mrs Andrews. But it's important for George to undergo the surgery because he wants to. He'll be an adult in a few months and he should be making his own decisions. Even so, they should be informed decisions not something based on the imaginary fears of his friends.'

'I hope you can convince him because, goodness knows, we've tried everything,' Mrs Andrews confided.

Sara flipped open the appointment book. Her eyes scanned over the pages. There wasn't a time free during surgery hours for nearly three weeks and that would be too late. She would have to stay late one evening.

'Friday at seven,' Sara told her. 'Can you both be here then?'

'I'll do my best.'

Sara hung up the telephone. At that moment she wished she had the counselling skills of Tom. She knew that she was more than competent, but Tom seemed to have the edge when it came to handling patient anxieties.

With a sigh, Sara pursed her lips and returned to the surgery, where she scrubbed and prepared for the next patient. She studied the X-rays while Laura popped the young girl in the reclining chair. The patient's canine tooth had developed in the palate, so it needed to be exposed and brought into position.

'I'm Sara and I will be doing your minor operation today. Has Dr Fielding explained it to you?'

The young girl nodded and opened her mouth. She clearly wanted to get it over and done with. Sara explained what the anaesthetist would be doing and then they were ready to begin.

William started sedation while Sara checked the trays had everything ready for both the surgical procedure and then the bonding of the attachment. When she was quite sure that Josie would be free of pain, she began the procedure of exposing the tooth. Laura was an experienced nurse in oral surgery procedures and assisted Sara to attach the bracket to the exposed tooth. A fine surgical chain was attached to the bracket before being linked to the metal braces.

The bracket held well and Sara was happy that the tooth should move down into position over a few months. It wasn't long before the patient was resting comfortably in Recovery.

There were four more patients on the afternoon list and it had just passed six o'clock when the final patient left for home. Sara had enjoyed working with William and Laura and thanked them for their work.

'Any time,' William said.

'Ditto,' agreed Laura, and they both headed off.

Closing the door on the pair, Sara remembered she still had to make some calls about George Andrews.

'Marjorie,' she called aloud, trying to determine her location in the rooms.

'I'm tidying up the recovery room, Sara.'

Sara walked quickly in her direction, talking as she went.

'Do you recall any young male adolescent, class-three malocclusions who underwent surgical correction around twelve months ago?' Sara entered the small room as she finished her question.

After fluffing up the last of the generously proportioned cushions that rested on the sofa in the recovery room, Marjorie stood upright. She tilted her head to one side, thinking.

'I'd have to check. Why do you ask?'

'The phone call from Mrs Andrews. Her son George now has reservations about the surgery and I thought if he could have a word with boys around his own age who had undergone the operation, then he might feel better about it.'

'Seems like a swimming idea to me. Are you going to check with Tom before you contact them?'

'No,' Sara told her bluntly. 'I am here in place of Dr Anderson. So any decision I choose to make does not have to be seconded by Dr Fielding. He's far too busy at the hospital to ask for his opinion on something like this.'

'Whatever you think is best,' Marjorie remarked as she slipped past and made her way into the office.

Sara didn't reply. She knew it had come out a little too assertively but she needed to let Marjorie know that she was running the practice. And she needed to keep Tom as far away as humanly possible. To ensure their contact was limited to the absolute minimum. She had hoped it would be easier by now. But it wasn't. And now she doubted it ever would be.

She followed in silence and waited for Marjorie to produce the patient's records.

'I do know what you to are up to,' Marjorie said matter-of-factly.

Sara stopped in her tracks. 'I'm sorry, what did you just say?'

'That you are trying to be all independent and keep Dr Fielding at bay. But if you need to keep him at bay, that says enough for me.'

'Not dragging Dr Fielding back here doesn't explain anything other than the need to allow him to stay focused on his busy schedule at the hospital. He is associate professor after all.'

'I know how important Tom is to the hospital, Sara, but I think he's also very important to you. Perhaps you don't like being too close because you still have feelings for him,' she said, as she sat down in front of her office desk. 'Take some advice from me and don't leave it too late.'

'Too late for what?'

'To start living life again,' Marjorie began, swivelling on her chair to face Sara. 'I know for a fact that Tom hasn't been. He's been cooped up here or, according to Christina, making up any excuse to stay late at the hospital. He has no sign of a social or romantic life. It's just such a waste when a young person forgets to actually enjoy life.'

Sara was stunned. Perhaps it was his workload and, of course, the PhD would have consumed his time along, with maintaining the practice and keeping up his hours at the hospital. He had probably been doing fourteen-hour days.

She didn't want to believe that perhaps he was still hurting over the separation. Because if that was the case, surely he would have contacted her during the last three years? Reached out and said he wanted to discuss the unresolved issues in their marriage? But he hadn't. He was a stubborn man who would not change his mind and negotiate. Neither could she on something so important. Her days of backing down, of putting her needs last were over.

'Tom's social life has nothing to do with me, Marjorie. Now, if I could have those records, please. I have some calls to make.'

Marjorie's smile didn't mask her doubt at Sara's remarks as she handed over the patient's charts in silence. But something about Marjorie's disposition made Sara realise that the subject was not finished, at least not in the other woman's eyes. But a busybody receptionist was still the least of Sara's concerns.

It was around seven by the time Sara had spoken to both the boys and their families and explained the reason for her call. Thankfully they both agreed and Sara set a date for them to come in near the end of the week. She then called George's home and confirmed with his mother that he would attend one last consultation.

In allowing the boys to speak with George and for him to see their successful surgical outcomes, Sara hoped it would convince him that the results of the operation outweighed the risks.

After locking up the practice, Sara headed off to pick up dinner from a Mexican takeaway she had spied on the way to work. She vowed to get out to the supermarket the next day. The front porch light was on when Sara pulled into the driveway. It was a welcoming sight. But she could never admit it. Not to Tom. Not really even to herself.

With her takeaway in one hand and her briefcase in the other, Sara made her way up the gravel path. It was cold outside and the warm breath of her yawn made a fine steam in the crisp night air.

'Hello, there, Doc. Need some help?' Tom's familiar voice came closer with each word until he was upon her.

'No I'm fine, really I—' she started to say, before she felt him tugging at her briefcase. She struggled to retain ownership and suddenly a warm hand encircled her wrist. It was a powerful grip but tender enough to not bruise her skin. She froze. She didn't want to have these confusing feelings. His touch was unsettling. It was like a burning torch on her skin that spread a dangerous heat through her body. As much as Sara valued her imported leather briefcase, she didn't want to feel any part of Tom's body touching hers.

Her fingers purposely slipped from the handle. The briefcase fell heavily to the ground with a thud and then a crunch as it skidded across the loose gravel. Sara cringed as she imagined the scratches and tears across the fine surface but it was worth the toll to feel his hand finally release its hold on her wrist.

'What just happened?' he asked sharply. 'Do you dislike me touching you that much, Sara?'

No. I like it too much, she thought. Time had not dimmed her body's response to him and that was what she hated.

'It's nothing to do with you,' she lied. 'I'm tired and I want to eat this…' she held up the paper bag '…before it goes cold and soggy.'

'Well, why not just say so?' he demanded.

'You'd manacled me like a prisoner. You didn't give me much choice.' It wasn't true but she couldn't help her reaction.

Tom didn't reply. He just shook his head and walked away in silence. Sara wanted to run after him and apologise. She had overreacted and her behaviour had been rude. She realised what she'd done and what she'd said had been wrong. Tom certainly couldn't be held responsible for how her heart was feeling. Or for the desire he was stirring in her soul. But apologising would only bring him back and she needed to keep her distance. She needed time to sort out her feelings. Sara pulled up the collar of her coat against the cold breeze as Tom slammed his front door shut.

Sara realised she would have to work harder at controlling her feelings if she was going to get through the next month. Without doubt it was going to be the longest four weeks of her life.

CHAPTER SEVEN

MARJORIE HANDED SARA the mail. 'There's one addressed to you and it's from the country,' she said in an enthusiastic tone.

Sara was surprised. All of the correspondence that she had been dealing with was addressed to either Tom or Stu and all related to patient referrals or reports. But this large envelope was addressed to her.

Curiosity made her reach for the letter opener and open this one first. Out fell a beautiful painting of the sun in glorious shades of yellow and orange. It had a huge toothy smile and the eyes were large blue pools of paint with glitter twinkles.

Sara read the words at the bottom.

To Aunty Sara,
Thank you for giving me my daddy for a whole
month.
Love, Bonny
XXX

A few simple, heartfelt words of a child quickly brought a smile to Sara's face. Dear little Bonny with all her problems had thought to send such a beautiful painting to say thank you.

'Marjorie, isn't this the most wonderful picture you've ever seen?' Sara asked, proudly holding up the brightly coloured sheet of paper.

'Magnificent, Sara. Simply magnificent. We'll have to put it up on the pinboard in the waiting room.'

'Just be careful how you attach it to the wall,' she warned. 'I'll be taking this masterpiece with me when I go and I don't want it to tear.'

It took some time rearranging the other notices to accommodate such a big painting but finally it was done.

'Bonny's painting is like taking the sun out of the sky and having it in the room with us. It's just glorious,' Marjorie commented, stepping away to admire the decoration.

'Lucky she doesn't have her father's artistic ability.'

The voice made both women spin around in surprise. They hadn't heard the door open.

'Stu couldn't paint to save his life,' Tom added, before leaving both women and walking into his office.

There had been no 'Hello' or 'How are you?' No greeting whatsoever. Sara thought he must have decided to keep his distance after their words the previous night. She had such mixed emotions. She was upset with herself for being so rude but justified her lack of manners as a necessity to keep Tom at bay.

'What are you doing here, Tom?' she called as she followed after him.

He looked her up and down in an irritated silence. 'No food going cold? So you have time to talk today?' His eyes dropped down to the drawer of the filing cabinet that he was rummaging through.

'I was tired and cold—' she began.

'And just a little rude,' he continued for her.

Sara closed the office door and crossed to him. 'Fine,

I'm sorry. But, be fair, you've had bad days in the past and been less than gracious.'

'When?'

It was an honest question as Tom had never been rude to her in that way. They had disagreed, heaven knows how many times, but he had never been cruel or cold the way she had been to him.

'Point taken. I'm sorry for the way I behaved.' She walked to the window and stared outside in silence. She didn't want to tell him about her feelings as it wouldn't change anything. She just had to hope they would fade in time.

Suddenly she felt his warm hands kneading the soft flesh of her shoulders. She flinched and had to stifle a gasp. He stood so close behind her, his supple fingers finding the knots of tension and working them into putty. His masculine scent invaded her senses, sending red heat rushing to her cheeks and then flowing through her entire body.

'I can understand. I guess I threw you in at the deep end here, you must be exhausted.'

His hands on her body felt so good but she had no intention of letting him know that. She mustered a laugh, 'I never liked that briefcase anyway and you did ambush me somewhat.'

Tom smiled in spite of himself and gently turned her around to face him. They were so close. His soft lips, only inches from hers, were so inviting. She hated it that she wanted to taste him and hold him like she had that night a few weeks ago, and all those years before.

'I'd better be going,' he told her huskily, pulling his own feelings into check. 'You've got a full afternoon at the hospital.'

Without saying another word, Tom left.

Relieved that he had gone, Sara collapsed into the chair. She was so glad that she hadn't given in to her desire to kiss him. Just being near him and not reacting to him was so difficult, but she was determined to break through those feelings. She just wasn't sure how.

Taking a deep breath, Sara walked back into her office and gathered up her notes and X-rays for the afternoon's surgery at the hospital.

As Tom left the building he rushed to fill his lungs with the cold air. He had not realised touching Sara would stir feelings so quickly. He was doing his best to remind himself she was leaving and he needed to accept that they had no future together. There was no reason for her to stay. Nothing had changed. They both saw their lives laid out so differently. Sara saw the picket fence and a house filled with children, and he saw his life filled with work. Having children was not in his plans. He couldn't change and she shouldn't change. He loved her for being the loving, caring woman she was and it would be wrong to tie her to a life that gave her less than everything she wanted. Everything she deserved.

Sara drove to the hospital and then parked her car in the doctors' car park and made her way to the doctors' lounge on the fourth floor. It was adjacent to the oral and maxillofacial ward. She placed some groceries she had bought at the market on the way to the hospital in the refrigerator, relieved she would have a nice home-cooked meal for that evening. Fresh King George whiting and some vegetables to steam. She couldn't stomach the thought of takeaway again.

With her dinner safely tucked away, she headed up

to Theatre. She scrubbed and gowned and entered to find her drowsy patient already prepared for surgery.

'Hi, David, I'm Sara and, as Marjorie informed you over the phone, I will be carrying out today's procedure. If things go as smoothly as I envisage, you will be in Recovery in a little under two and a half hours with a brand-new-looking jaw but a bit of a sore hip for a few days.'

David smiled limply and tried to nod.

'After that you will be in ICU overnight and then off to a ward for another few days.'

'We're ready, Sara,' the theatre sister told her.

'Count slowly back from ten, David,' the anaesthetist said, and after a few moments David drifted off to sleep under the brilliant theatre lights. The nurse draped David in sterile green sheeting and prepared the surgical sites with antiseptic solution.

Sara checked the X-rays again on the viewer and then looked over towards the surgical trays nearby. 'Today we'll be undertaking a chin augmentation of this young man. We start with an intra-oral incision extending from canine to canine.' There was a first-year intern present so she briefed him on the procedure. 'I am aware of the risk to the long root apexes of the canine teeth and the associated nerve so will move cautiously.'

The operation took just over three hours. There was a short break when David was taken off to Recovery. The staff then rescrubbed and in fresh gowns and caps they returned for another three operations. The first was the release of an adult tongue-tie, followed by removal of the remaining upper and lower teeth of an elderly patient in preparation for full dentures, and the last was a complicated lower-jaw reduction and rhinoplasty. It was almost seven o'clock when they finished and the last young woman was wheeled into Recovery.

Sara thanked the staff for their skilled assistance. She then changed into her street clothes and visited the two patients in ICU, before dropping into the wards and checking the two other less serious cases. They were all progressing well. Sara reassured the concerned families that the patients all looked bruised and swollen but they were fine and then she decided to have a quick cup of coffee before heading home. She was almost dead on her feet after seven straight hours of surgery.

She had just sat down in the doctors' lounge, savouring the wonderful aroma of steaming coffee in her mug, when Tom and another doctor appeared, apparently in search of similar refreshment.

'Jake, have you met Sara? She's been kind enough to fill in for Stu while he's up on the farm.'

Sara watched as the man shook his head and walked towards her with his hand outstretched. She purposely avoided eye contact with Tom. She also noted that he hadn't referred to their relationship or history at all. She was just there to help out.

'Jake Manning, I'm in reconstructive surgery,' he told her. 'Pleased to meet you.'

'Likewise,' she told him, as she met his handshake. 'Please forgive me not standing up, but I'm done in. I've just finished a killer of an afternoon list.'

'I can appreciate how you're feeling,' he answered, and collapsed into the chair beside her, throwing his feet onto the low coffee table. 'I've had it for the day and I've only been on rounds.'

'I suppose this means I have to get the coffee,' Tom complained in jest.

Sara's eyes darted to and from Tom as he made his

way to the percolator. She tried not to stare, but the sight of his lithe body in form-fitting black linen trousers and an apricot-coloured cotton shirt was more appealing than ever.

'Sugar and white?' he enquired of his colleague.

'No, black and strong. I have a long drive home and I'll need something to keep me awake.'

'Why were the rounds so difficult today?' Sara asked as she lifted her feet up and curled them inside the chair and took another sip of her coffee. 'Heavy load or difficult patients?'

'No, that nervy intern by the name of—'

'Johnson!' Tom cut in smiling, as he crossed the room and placed the mugs heavily on the low table. 'I wondered where he'd turn up. Not that I made any enquiries, mind you.'

'That guy can talk,' Jake continued, reaching for his cup and cradling it in his hands. 'Actually, that's all he did. Talk and talk and—' Jake suddenly started slinking down in his seat. 'Don't look now, but speaking of the devil.'

The door was pushed open by a dishevelled Johnson. He looked around the room and then spied the three of them in the far corner.

'Dr Fielding, I'm sorry to bother you, I know you've finished for the day but your patient Mr Kowalski, the one who went missing and then we located him inadvertently exposing himself to the florists...'

Sara's eyes widened as she heard him recall the story. She watched him fidget nervously and then dig his hands into his white examination-coat pockets. He drew closer and sat down on the edge of the seat. 'You don't mind if I sit, do you?'

Sara leant forward and placed her mug on the table.

'Not at all. And by the way, I'm Sara, I'm filling in for Stu Anderson.'

'Oh, hi. I remember you from the other day in Dr Fielding's office. I hope your knee's okay. I'm so sorry about that. I guess I came across like a bit of a twit, I mean losing a patient and then crashing into you. I mean, it doesn't happen all that often. Actually, only twice this year, and the other one wasn't really missing, I mean, Mrs Summers died and she was taken to the morgue but no one told me. One of those admin types of problems, well, actually it was a heart problem, but then Admin didn't tell me...'

Tom dropped his cup onto the table. 'Johnson, please get to the point, it's getting late and we all want to go home. Is our patient all right?'

'Yes, Dr Fielding. It's just that Mr Kowalski doesn't have any family. He told me that his wife died about ten years ago and then the business went under. They never had any children and he lost contact with his brother, Alexander. I guess he was too embarrassed to admit that he had lost everything. He's been living in shelters on and off for the last nine years. So I would like to refer him to the social worker tomorrow, if that's okay.'

'That sounds like a good idea.'

He stood up, smiling, and backed out of the room. 'Thank you, Dr Fielding. I'll arrange it now.' And with that he was gone.

'Glad he's in your ward more often than mine,' Jake said with a smirk. 'He tries so hard I'd go mad!'

Tom leant forward and tapped his knees like a drum kit. 'He's a good kid but I think he could talk underwater. Some days it does wear thin.'

Sara stood up, smoothed her skirt and self-consciously

made her way to the sink. She wasn't sure if Tom was watching her but she felt like she was on show.

'So, Tom,' Jake began. 'I'm not giving up on the whole double-dating idea. I know you keep refusing but I have this amazing woman for you, and I can set it up on Saturday if you'd like. She's Bella's friend over from Adelaide. Pretty girl, radiologist, single....'

The sound of Sara's cup crashing onto the sink and sliding into the soapy water cut short Jake's words.

'Are you okay?' he asked.

'Tired, that's all. Like I said, it was a tough day.'

Sara wiped the suds from her clothes and concentrated on quickly washing and drying her cup. Tom lowered his voice and Sara was grateful that he did. She didn't need to hear his response but she heard Jake's answer.

'Think you're making a huge mistake, Tom. She's a great girl. Maybe next time, then.'

Sara was relieved. She wanted Tom to date, she really did, but she just wanted him to do it after she left Melbourne. When she was living in San Antonio, not now, not while she was still living next door. That would be too much to deal with.

Everything put away, she went to the fridge to collect her groceries.

'Oh, no! Where's it gone?' she exclaimed.

'Where's what?' Tom asked bluntly.

'My shopping bag, everything I bought for dinner. It's gone. Someone's walked off with it!'

Sara wasn't sure she was doing the right thing accepting Tom's dinner invitation but she was too tired to argue. He had offered to cook her a steak and she wasn't about to refuse. In fact, she was so hungry and exhausted that she would have eaten drive-through hamburgers and fries if Tom hadn't offered to cook dinner at her place.

She'd followed him home and on the way they had picked up some fresh bread from the continental deli. Tom had clinched the dinner deal with the promise of ice cream and hot chocolate sauce for dessert. He had run into his place and picked up the steaks while Sara unlocked her door and turned the lights on.

She told herself that she would simply enjoy Tom's company and, more particularly, the meal. To refuse would appear rude and also admit to both of them that she perhaps didn't trust herself to be alone with him.

'I'll throw the steaks under the grill,' he told her. 'Won't take too long. Why don't you turn the heater on and make yourself comfortable in the sitting room.'

'Because I can't turn the heater on.'

Tom gave a wry smile as he popped his head around the kitchen door. 'That's right, I forgot. I'll be right there.'

The bright light from the kitchen filtered through so she didn't bother to switch on a lamp. Tom lit the heater and they both returned to the kitchen to cook the steaks. Sara noticed how he knew where everything was, almost as if it was his kitchen. It was an odd level of familiarity, she thought, then she reminded herself that it was the reverse of their old home so it made sense that the kitchens would be the same.

Tom finished seasoning the steaks and put them on to cook. Together they prepared their meal and Sara felt so happy. She was enjoying Tom's company and trying her best to find a way to define their relationship in her mind. To find a suitable box in which to put them. Unfortunately she couldn't find a label to fit. Nothing came to mind with the feelings she still had.

The meal was wonderful and Tom had opened a nice Cabernet Sauvignon from the Hunter Valley. It was a smooth red wine that complemented the food but Sara declined, preferring a mineral water. Wine made her feel tired and she was already struggling to stay awake.

They talked about work and the cases she had seen over the last few days while they ate their ice cream, sitting together on the comfy sofa. Hours passed like minutes and they both relaxed like old times, each choosing to avoid the subject of children. They accepted in that area they would simply never agree. Then the subject of Bonny arose.

'Isn't Bonny's painting beautiful?'

Tom nodded as he took his last sip of wine and put the empty glass on the coffee table. 'Stu rang yesterday, actually, and apparently Bonny's coming along well. Better than anyone expected. She's not talking yet, she's still using a board to point to the letters of simple words, but they're confident her speech will return in a short while.'

Sara thoughtfully fingered the rim of her empty water glass. 'It must be terrible for them. I know how I would feel if she were mine. I'd be devastated—'

'Yes, I suppose you would,' he cut in. There was no bitterness in his voice, a touch of melancholy perhaps, but none of his signature hostility on the subject of children.

Tom reached across the table and affectionately brushed away the wisps of hair that were threatening to cover Sara's eyes. Her beautiful eyes. He felt sure that if they had children, they would all have those beautiful big blue eyes...

She flinched and bit the inside of her cheek. With his hand so close it was making her pulse quicken again.

Tom looked into her eyes. He needed to be honest with Sara. He knew that in order for them to find some sort of closure as their marriage ended, there should be no more unanswered questions between them. She had been honest with him about her parents and now she deserved the same. He decided it was the right time to share something with her. To let her know why he would never have children and that his decision was final. He suddenly felt safe to tell her now. To open up to her, secure in the knowledge that she would not try to change his mind. Her new life was waiting and their life together had ended a long time ago.

'Sara,' he began, 'I want to share something with you. I need you to finally understand why we are where we are. Why you're moving on and I choose to devote my life to work and not a family. You need to know. I owe it to you and I owe it to us and what we had together. I should have told you a long time ago.'

Sara was taken aback and her surprise wasn't masked. Her body shifted a little on her chair and she gently pulled her hands free from his. His desire to open up seemed so sudden. This was what she had wanted all along but he had never been prepared to do so. She was confused why he had decided to open up now. She suddenly felt the need to protect herself from what she was about to hear. She didn't know why.

'Go on,' she said, looking at Tom and his new serious expression.

'My brother Heath and I...' Tom started, then he stopped, choking on his words momentarily. 'Well, when we were young, and through until teenagers, we were mad keen on BMX bikes. It was our obsession but he was so much better than I was. He was an extremely skilled rider.'

Sara nodded. This information was nothing new. She was aware that Heath had been the under sixteen BMX state champion for Victoria at one time.

Tom cleared his throat. This was as difficult as he'd imagined. The guilt he felt was still so raw. So many years had passed and yet he could picture it all as if it were yesterday. Each time he thought about his actions it was the same regret that filled his mind and ripped at his heart. He wished he could travel back in time and change it all. Change everything. Relive his life and not be the irresponsible kid who had made a bad decision and ruined his brother's life. And consequently ruined his own chance of happiness with Sara.

'Heath was almost sixteen and I was fourteen,' he started with a sigh. 'He was at the qualifying event for the UCI BMX world championships. He just had to beat the last rider from the Gold Coast in order to win the top spot. I suggested a move that would set him apart. It was called a tail whip. It was risky but I urged him on and told him if he pulled it off he would be on his way to the next world championships. Only he didn't pull it off. He fell. And he was badly injured.'

'Oh, no.' Sara sat up. 'What happened to him?'

'Along with the broken collar bone and multiple abrasions, he suffered testicular trauma or, to be specific, testicular torsion. Long story short, no fatherhood for him.' Tom's face was contorted with guilt as he looked down at the floor. 'So how can I just go ahead and have a big happy family while he is left alone?'

Sara felt so sorry for Heath and for Tom. Both brothers' lives had been changed for ever by normal teenage behaviour that had gone wrong. It hadn't been malicious or even reckless. Sara thought adventurous was a better description. But she felt Tom was carrying a burden that wasn't his to carry.

'But accidents happen to good people every day, Tom, you know that as a doctor. Sometimes no one's to blame.'

'In this case there was. Me.'

'I know what you're saying and I feel desperately sorry for your brother but you were fourteen and you couldn't have known the repercussions.' Sara could see the pain in Tom's eyes and hear the sadness in his voice. It ripped at her heart to see his burden and to know he had been carrying this for so long. She wished he had confided in her before.

'Maybe not, but why should I walk away scot free?'

'You choosing not to have children is not going to change anything for your brother except rob him of the chance to be an uncle. And you are punishing yourself for something that happened decades ago,' she said, reaching for his hands. 'I wish you hadn't kept it from me. I wish you'd told me this years ago.'

'I couldn't because I knew you would try to make me see things your way.'

'Did you ever tell Heath about your decision?' she asked. 'I don't know him that well, we only spent a short time together, but he seemed so lovely. He's a kind, intelligent man who wouldn't expect you to give up your chance for a family. Does he even know that you made this sacrifice, and are continuing to make it years later?'

Tom looked away. 'There's no need for him to know. We're just two brothers who didn't have kids. That's it. He's never questioned me and I haven't seen the need to discuss it with him. He's still paying the price. Why should I be any different?'

'Because you're hurting more than just yourself in the process.' Sara hesitated and then decided to be more honest than she'd thought she ever would. 'You're hurting me and the children that we will never bring into this world because of your decision.'

Tom lips tightened. He knew she was right. And he didn't want to hurt her. He hated it that he couldn't give her everything in the world she wanted. But he couldn't. He knew she would be better off without him.

'This is exactly why I didn't tell you.'

'But you were a child, you were fourteen. You can't own that guilt for ever. It's not fair to you. And I don't think Heath would want you to own it for ever,' Sara argued.

'Heath's marriage ended because of the accident. They tried IVF for years unsuccessfully and it wore them down. He never told anyone but me. How can I look past that? I caused that pain. I wrecked his chance for a happy marriage and children of his own. That's not something that happened when we were kids, Sara, it happened three years ago.'

Sara looked at the man sitting opposite her and she suddenly saw a very different man. He wasn't a self-ish, career-driven man who disliked children at all. He was a man who had put his needs last. It was so sad and ironic that she finally putting her needs first and Tom's decision to place his needs last was what had driven them apart. And yet she had never suspected anything even close to that. She had thought the very opposite for more than three years.

She knew more than ever that he would always own her heart and now she needed to somehow get through to him. To make him see that he was throwing away a future with his own children and this sacrifice, however noble, wouldn't change anything. It would only seal their fate.

CHAPTER EIGHT

SARA AWOKE AND rubbed her eyes as she slowly rose from the softness of her warm pillow. She thought back to the night before. They had talked for hours. She had tried desperately to change Tom's mindset. She had pleaded with him to talk to Heath. To be honest about wanting children and apologise again for what happened but explain that they all needed to move on. Move past the hurt and the blame and find a way to be in each other's lives and accept the past.

Although Tom had seen how it was hurting Sara too, he felt in his heart he had made the right decision. It was in his eyes the only course of action. He had made a decision over twenty years ago and he wasn't going back on it. Sara had felt helpless to change his mind when he'd finally left in the early hours of the morning.

She realised she must have fallen into the deepest sleep when she turned and looked at the clock beside the bed. It was seven-thirty. She remembered talking and trying to make Tom see the situation from the outside. She remembered crying a few times too. The accident was a secret that Tom and Heath had kept from her. She had never met her brother-in-law's wife—both times she had stayed in the US while Heath had headed out to Australia to visit. Perhaps it was because she had been undergoing the IVF treatments or perhaps because they had been struggling within the marriage. Sara realised she would never know.

Tom had decided he had a cross to bear for something he'd innocently done as a child, something he felt he had to take responsibility for the rest of his life. She wished there was a way she could get through to him. Sara knew she loved Tom and even though their marriage was over she knew she would never stop caring.

She hoped, not for her sake but for Tom's, that he would one day see it differently. At fourteen, she knew only too well that boys thought they were invincible. She imagined Tom and Heath thought the same way. The idea that one adventurous BMX trick could go horribly wrong and affect the rest of their lives would have been incomprehensible to both of them.

Sara knew it was going to be almost impossible to try to sway Tom's opinion at this time. It was strange but she finally felt now, with this understanding of Tom's attitude and behaviour, that she knew him more intimately than she had ever known him before. This was the real Tom. The caring man who would not turn his back on what he perceived as the permanent scars he had inflicted on his brother. He was a hero, but unfortunately he was a misguided hero. And she had no idea how, or even if, she could change his direction.

She still felt a little tired. Her eyes had been so heavy the night before and they were no different this morning. It was out of character for her to be this exhausted and if it continued, she decided she would have some blood work done. It had been a struggle to get through the day and she'd slept so soundly when her head had hit the pillow. This level of tiredness had occurred once before and it had been anaemia. An iron supplement, spinach or red meat, she decided, might be the order of the day until her count was back up again.

Sara rolled on her back, drawing in a deep breath before she slowly exhaled. In silence, she studied the pattern of the pressed iron ceiling, not really seeing it. The night before had been as enlightening as it had been frustrating. The conversation they had shared had been the most honest they had ever been with each other. Tom had finally opened up to her, and she assumed he found it easier now they were close to finalising the divorce. It was too late for both of them and perhaps it made it less painful for him. She knew his deepest secret but was almost powerless to sway him to choose with his heart. His misguided conscience had ruled his head for far too long.

'Hello…anyone awake?'

Sara jumped at the sound of Tom's voice from the other side of the wall.

'I'm awake and just getting up,' she called back loudly.

'I made breakfast. I've just eaten mine but I have some for you if you'd like to unlock the door. The key's on the dresser.'

Sara had noticed the internal door that linked the two homes but assumed it had been locked for years. She climbed from bed and searched the dresser.

'Not here, I'm afraid,' she called back, slightly pleased there was no key and no way for Tom to be in her bedroom.

'Try the top drawer on the left, it might be in there.'

Sara sighed. He wasn't giving up. How did he know where everything was? She decided not to think too much of it. He was an organised person. She pulled the drawer open and found a neat stack of men's summer T-shirts. She assumed they were Tom's. Then she felt at the bottom of the drawer and found a set of keys.

'Got them.' She couldn't lie. She also had to let him in. With reservations, Sara unlocked the door and opened it to see Tom, still in his dressing gown, smiling at her with a breakfast tray held high. She stepped back, allowing him to enter.

'After the last fall Mrs Vanderbilt had, just before she had to be admitted to the nursing home, she wanted to know I could get through to help in an emergency. So she gave me the key,' he said. 'Made her feel more secure knowing she had someone close by to help in an emergency.'

It didn't give Sara anywhere near the same feeling as she eyed the doorway suspiciously. Her version of ground rules for their working relationship did not extend to her soon-to-be-ex-husband being able to access her bedroom day and night. It may have been a comforting thought for Mrs Vanderbilt but it was definitely was not a comforting thought for *her*.

'Anyway, I thought you might like this to start the day.' He crossed the room and placed a tray of hot coffee and a piece of toast on the bedside table. 'Don't want you feeling bad on your day off because I kept you up talking way too late last night.'

Feeling chilly, Sara climbed back into bed and pulled the covers up.

Tom was feeling anxious about the conversation they'd shared and he wanted to see firsthand that in the light of day Sara accepted his decision was not negotiable. Her newfound knowledge of the reason why he would not consider having children would never change it. His mind was made up. He took full responsibility for the accident and equally the end of his brother's marriage.

There was no other way to see it. And nothing she could say would change anything.

'You have a full day of surgery tomorrow, so rest up.' He walked over to open the curtains and thought better of it. 'Maybe we'll leave these closed and you can stay in bed for a while after breakfast. Take your time and read a book or something.'

'Tom,' Sara began, 'about last night.'

'Sara, let's not go there,' he said, turning back to face her. 'I said what I should have told you before we married. It was my fault for thinking children wouldn't be an issue. We never talked seriously about having them or not having them. I guess I assumed being just the two of us for ever would be okay with you. No doubt you, on the other hand, thought I would warm to the idea of having kids. It's my fault completely for rushing you to the altar.'

Sara's lips curved to a melancholy smile. It had been a crazy courtship. She had been excited and had never really thought too far ahead. She had been marrying the man she loved. The man she admired and respected and thought would naturally be the father of her children.

'I'm sad that now I know the truth I still can't change your mind, Tom. I think you would be the most wonderful father and I feel certain that you and Heath could work through everything if only you would speak with your brother. Tell him how you feel and see how he feels. He may have no idea that you are still carrying this guilt. He may even have moved on and assumed you've done the same. I know he would want you to be happy.'

'And I want you to be happy, Sara. It's all I've ever

wanted, but talking to my brother won't change anything. What's done is done.'

Tom swallowed hard and asked her to leave the subject alone. He was glad he had finally opened up but he
didn't want to go over the past any more. Sara just had
to accept his decision and he would accept her decision
to each travel a different path. He wanted with all of his
heart for the ending to be different but it couldn't be.
They might be heading in opposite directions but there
were another few weeks yet to spend together and that
made him happy in a bittersweet way. He leant down
and helped to plump up her pillow before he picked up
the breakfast tray and placed it on her lap.

'I'll get ready and head off to the hospital, but you
should enjoy your day off. I have lectures all day at the
university and then marking to do at the hospital tonight
so I'll be late home and probably won't see you till tomorrow. Oh, and by the way, the local grocery store
down the road is still there. You might like to stock the
fridge if you're low on anything. Still the same old family business it was when you were here and they still
make the best rock cakes ever.'

Tom smiled and left the room the way he had come
in, shutting the door behind him. He felt like a weight
had lifted from him. Although he also recognised that
when Sara did move on, marry and have a family, it
would be difficult to stay in contact. The thought of her
waking in another man's arms and sharing a life with
her new husband and children would be too much for
him to handle.

While Sara sat and ate her breakfast she tried to process
all that Tom had told her. After a night to think about
it, she felt no less frustrated. At least she now knew the

man she had married a little better. She knew now that Tom wasn't selfish. In fact, he was a man of great principles. Although principles wouldn't keep him warm at night or throw their arms around his neck when they came rushing home from school. He was certainly sacrificing a lot for his brother.

Short of a miracle and Tom seeing the light, there wasn't a lot she could do but accept Tom's decision. Thankfully the day went by smoothly. She had made a few phone calls and organised for some of the boxes of clothes she had packed for Texas to be forwarded to Melbourne. She walked down to the local grocer's and stocked the refrigerator and pantry, picking up some rock cakes as well.

Sara left one in a bag by Tom's front door.

She spent the afternoon with her feet up, reading through some notes for the next day's surgical cases. Then she watched some daytime television, cooked an omelette for dinner and soaked in a long bubble bath.

Once she was snug back in her own pyjamas, she locked the door between the adjoining houses, slipped back under the covers and drifted into a restful sleep.

On Friday she arrived early at the hospital. She had a long day's surgical list. The morning was filled with two of Tom's private patients. The afternoon with Stu's. They were all straightforward and she was keen to start. That evening she had an appointment at the practice with George and his mother, so she wanted to get away on time.

There was a break at around one, between lists, so Sara went up to the doctors' lounge to close her eyes and put her feet up for a bit.

'Hello, Sara.'

Sara opened her eyes to see Tom standing in front of her. 'Hi, there, stranger,' she managed in a cool tone. 'On your lunch break?'

He sat down. 'No, I've finished up for the day. It's the first day of the mid-year break for the students so no lectures or rotations to organise for the rest of the week. Although I'm not a great believer in the current lecture model anyway,' he announced with a frustrated sigh. 'I think we need to bring changes to medical student education, bring it up to speed by actually reducing the number of lectures.'

Sara could see he felt quite passionate about this subject. 'Go on,' she urged him, as she sipped her chocolate milk.

He turned and faced her. She couldn't help but notice his eyes light up as he spoke. He was so animated. She remembered he always was when he felt strongly about something. 'Let's face it, there have been huge changes in the world of medicine but medical education has remained the same. We're in a time warp and I don't think we're keeping up with student needs or expectations. There's been growth in information and research in all facets of medicine. Yet we keep delivering the traditional lecture style of teaching, despite class attendance falling and complaints that we're failing to produce compassionate, well-trained medicos.'

Sara nodded, agreeing with Tom's valid argument for change.

'We need to make better use of the time we're given to train doctors. I'd like to see lecture content delivered differently. Perhaps in short videos that are watched by the students in their own time, and as often as they need, to ensure they grasp the concepts and really understand the material. Class time is then freed up for focusing on patients' clinical stories as a way to apply this medical information.'

Sara was impressed as always with Tom's knowledge and passion. She knew his new role as associate professor was well deserved. He was no doubt going to make a difference at the hospital. She only wished she could be there to see the changes he made and the real outcomes for the students and the patients. She was so proud of the man she'd married and the man, she knew in her heart, she would always love.

'And now I will climb down from my soapbox,' he said with a laugh, sitting back a little and relaxing. 'I have papers to assess but other than that this week is a good one for me. I get to take a breather.'

'Some people get all the luck,' Sara sighed. 'I've got a full list for Stu and then an appointment back at the practice at about seven.'

'What if I assist?' Tom suggested, as he sat upright again and rubbed his chin thoughtfully. 'Then you can get through it even quicker.'

Sara considered Tom's suggestion for a moment. In the past, working with Tom had always been the highlight of her day. Watching the skill of the man who had inspired her and taught her so much had always been an honour, so with a nod of her head she agreed to share the operating theatre for one last time. She knew she hadn't forgotten his operating style—in fact, it was almost hers. He had been the best teacher and mentor she could have asked for as a student. If she wanted to move past their lives as husband and wife and begin again as colleagues, she needed to start now.

'I'd like that.' She smiled.

* * *

Sara was ready and waiting in Theatre when Tom appeared in the scrub room.

'Afternoon, people,' he said, as he crossed to the operating table. He looked down at the teenage boy who was at this stage already a little groggy. 'I bet you're feeling more than a bit nervous, Matt, but listen, mate, there's absolutely nothing to worry about. During the surgery we're going to bring that jaw of yours into a respectable position, and while we're at it reshape your chin a bit. You won't be able to keep the girls away after we've finished with you. But don't worry, before you leave the hospital we'll provide you with a large stick to beat them away!'

Sara smiled to herself. He was incorrigible. But that was part of his charm.

She loved the way he communicated so naturally with patients of any age. He never played the academic with his patients. He was so down to earth. She also noticed that in Theatre she was an equal. He paid her no special attention.

'Any questions before we start?' he asked. 'That's not just from you, Matt. Any questions from the crew?'

They all shook their heads as they went about their respective jobs within the operating theatre.

'Okay, Matt, you're off to sleep, mate. See you in a few hours.'

The anaesthetist took over and Matt drifted out of consciousness.

Sara and Tom worked well together. Neither had changed their approach to the operation and four skilled hands made it a relatively easy procedure.

Sara screwed the first titanium plate in place.

'Damn, I taught you well,' Tom commented lightheartedly to Sara, but all the while appreciating her level of skill. He felt a sense of pride as he watched her dexterity with the complex surgical procedure.

She smiled but didn't raise her eyes. They completed fifteen minutes ahead of time. Tom left promptly to read up on the next patient.

The entire afternoon went as smoothly. Working with Tom, Sara remembered why she had chosen oral and maxillofacial surgery as her specialty. She had watched his fingers perform magic in the operating theatre and she had been mesmerised. Not just by the tall, handsome tutor—it was his talent and love of his work that had inspired her to follow the same path.

They finished the last of the patients around five-thirty, which gave Sara plenty of time to change, pick up something to eat and be at the practice to meet with the other post-operative patients before George arrived. She crossed her fingers that George would show up and be prepared to listen to the other boys.

As she buttoned up her coat, her mobile phone began ringing.

'Hello, Sara Fielding.'

'Sara, it's Marjorie. I'm afraid I have some bad news.'

Sara frowned as she slipped her hair behind her ear to hear better. 'What is it, Marjorie?'

'Both boys who were coming along to talk to George. They've cancelled.'

'What, both of them?'

'Yes, apparently some heavy steel band, Slayer, I think she called them, has stayed on in Melbourne for a second concert and they're going. Neither were prepared to miss out.'

Sara collapsed back into the chair despondently. 'They're a heavy *metal* band, but what am I going to do now? If I don't have those boys there by seven o'clock,

George will never agree to his surgery. Stu's patient will be living on a sheep station in the middle of nowhere by this time next week.'

Sara knew there was only one other person who could convince George to go ahead with the surgery. That would be Tom. She had wanted so desperately to handle the practice on her own and to prove that she was capable and had the capacity to deal with any issues that arose. But George had already shown signs of disapproving of her. More than likely, it was the general dismissive attitude of a sixteen-year-old boy. His mother had been on the receiving end too, as Sara had witnessed firsthand.

Sara knew this was no time for pride. This was Stu's patient and she needed to exhaust all avenues before she accepted that George would cancel his surgery, a decision she knew for certain he would regret as an adult.

Sara had only an hour and a quarter now to be at the practice. There was no point turning up alone. George would not listen to her.

Sara dialled Tom's mobile. George might listen to a man. Sometimes teenage boys thought more of another male's opinion. And Tom certainly had a way with patients. It was worth trying.

She wasn't sure if Tom was still in the hospital or if he had left.

Damn, he had switched his phone to voice mail. Sara left a message and asked him to meet her at the practice. She briefly explained the situation and its urgency because of George's plans to move up north to the sheep station. She hoped he would make it in time.

She grabbed her case and rushed out to the lift. With her head down, and in a hurry, she turned the corner and almost ran straight into Johnson.

'That was close,' he said, smiling. 'Almost *déjà vu*! Seems like you're in a hurry this time.'

'You have no idea. I don't have a spare minute. I've got a surgical patient due in a little over an hour at the practice—'

'But that's only fifteen minutes from here,' he cut in, reaching down to pick up her briefcase. 'You don't have to rush, unless of course you haven't eaten, then I suppose you would need the extra time, but there's a hospital cafeteria—'

'Johnson,' Sara cut in tersely, 'I'm afraid I don't even know your first name.'

'Nigel.'

'Thank you, Nigel,' Sara said, more than a little anxious about the unfolding situation. 'But I need to find Dr Fielding.'

'He's up in the lecture theatre, tidying up, I think. If you don't know where that is, I can show you.'

'That'd be great.'

Sara followed Nigel as he led her to another floor. 'Excuse me asking,' Nigel began, through a mouthful of muesli bar, 'but are you married to Dr Fielding or are you his sister?'

'No, we're married but separated. It's all very amicable,' she added.

Nigel nodded. 'I asked, because they were all talking about it in Theatre today. With your names, they didn't know if he was on his best behaviour for his sister or his wife.'

Sara gave a wry smile, knowing she and Tom were already the topic of hospital gossip. She followed Nigel till they reached the lecture theatre, where he left her at the open double doors.

Tom lifted his head, as if he sensed her near.

'You have more patients for me?' he asked with a smile.

'Not exactly, well, not at the hospital. This is one of Stu's private patients,' she answered, as she climbed down the stairs towards Tom at the front of the large tiered room.

'My skeletal class-three malocclusion, George Andrews, has cancelled his surgery for a number of reasons. But not one of them is valid,' Sara explained, as she drew closer. 'His friends have made him worried about the possibility of death or brain damage on the operating table and on top of that Mrs Andrews informs me that they've convinced him to head up north and work as a jackeroo, where his bite won't offend the sheep!'

Tom shook his head. 'Crazy kids.'

Sara smiled as he said it.

'And what can I do?'

Sara looked thoughtfully at Tom. 'I hoped you might be able to explain to him the repercussion of not proceeding with the surgery. I honestly think he's at that age when a man-to-man talk might serve him better.'

'I'm happy to tell it like it is to George and let him weigh up his choices and let him make his decision. I think it's our best shot.'

'Sounds like a plan.'

Tom stacked the last of the papers he had been gathering, put them in a large folder and scooped it under his arm. 'Let's do it, shall we?'

There was a knock on the practice door and Sara looked up to see Mrs Andrews in the waiting room with a very surly-looking George.

'Would you like to have a subtle word with George

out there while I keep his mother busy?' she whispered
to Tom. 'I think the waiting room is less formal and intimidating.'

Tom took his cue and stood up and walked out into
the waiting room. Casually he picked a car racing magazine before flopping into a chair.

'And what am I supposed to do?' George growled.
'Sit around while you both moan about me behind my
back? I can't see why I even had to come. Complete
waste of time, if you ask me!'

'Actually, George, I have to discuss a few things
with your mother and I would like you to have a chat
with Dr Fielding.'

Mrs Andrews anxiously entered the office and
George sat down in the waiting room with an annoyed
expression upon his face.

'I almost had to drag him here kicking and screaming,' Mrs Andrews confessed. 'There was some free
concert thing on tonight—'

'And don't I know it,' Sara told her with a sigh as she
closed the door on Tom and George.

'George, I'm Dr Fielding,' Tom said, as he dropped
the magazine on the seat beside him. 'I thought we
could have a chat about the surgery. I heard you've
cancelled,' Tom went on as he moved to a chair closer
to the young man.

George just looked up with a disinterested expression. 'Do you know how long my mum is gonna be? I
wanna go already.'

'She's in there, talking to Sara, so I'm not sure. But
I'd like to chat to you about your decision—'

'I'm not having it done any more,' he cut in rudely.

Tom lifted one eyebrow and rubbed the back of his

neck. 'Absolutely your choice, mate. But I'm not sure you're cancelling for the right reasons.'

'What do you mean?'

'Well, unless you have much older and wiser friends with medical backgrounds, then they're not qualified to discuss the risks or advantages of the surgery.'

'But I could die on the table.'

'You could die bungee-jumping or doing doughnuts in your car on a dirt road up north, but you'll probably do both with your friends.'

'Probably.' George was eyeing Tom suspiciously but now seemed to be listening. Clearly the doughnuts on the dirt road had rung true.

'Listen, George, the operation is not for the faint-hearted. I won't lie to you, but without it you will have much bigger problems in the long run. It's not about appearance. Even chewing will become more difficult with a jaw discrepancy like yours.'

'So I won't be able to eat a steak?'

'George, as you get older everything will become more difficult. You have to think down the track, not just today. Your long-term health needs to be considered. Even your nutritional needs and the effect on your digestive system needs to be considered. This might not mean a lot now but later you will find it difficult. Your friends won't be there then.'

'So it's not just for looks.'

'Absolutely not, George, although that is a bonus,' Tom said with a wink. 'Never hurts to look good for the ladies.'

Tom noticed George's body language relax and become less defensive.

'Maybe I'll think about it, then,' he announced.

'Can't ask you to do more than that. But don't go to

your friends for medical advice. I'm sure they know loads about the latest apps and games, but definitely not about surgical procedures.'

'Can you tell the doctor in with my mum that I'll think about it? I'll make up my mind in a couple of days.'

CHAPTER NINE

AFTER GEORGE AND Mrs Andrews left the office, Sara thanked Tom for his successful intervention. She knew he had a way with patients, particularly teenagers, and his inroads with George proved it. As they made their way to the car park, she asked Tom about an invitation she had received in the mail a few days earlier.

'By the way, have you rung Dana and Stu with your answer yet?' she asked as she opened her car door.

He paused with her door ajar. 'Answer to what? I haven't heard from them.'

'They sent us both letters asking us to be godparents to the twins. The christening is in two weeks.'

Tom didn't mask his confusion as he hopped into the Healey and wound down the old-fashioned window. 'Honestly, Sara, I have no idea what you're talking about. I'm aware there's the christening coming up but I haven't received anything from them. Typical of Stu, he probably just left it on my desk somewhere for me to find. I'll look tomorrow and get back to you. But I have to be honest, I'm not sure how I feel about being a godparent. All things considered, I don't think it's a good idea.'

'Tom, they're not asking us to adopt them. I think it's a wonderful idea.' Sara thought it was an honour and she was sorry that they had all drifted apart over the last few years. She was determined that would not happen again and she couldn't wait to catch up with Dana again. The prospect of being the boys' godmother made her happy. It meant that she would have strong links to their family for ever. This time in Melbourne had made her realise she didn't want to leave it all behind. She loved her friends and wanted to be a part of their lives.

'I'll think about it,' he told her flatly, before starting the car to drive home. *Think long and hard about it*, he told himself. Sara's car was soon an illuminated speck in his rear-vision mirror.

The next day went along steadily. Tom told her he would be working late at Augustine's. It was about one o'clock when Sara received a telephone call from the country. She had finished with the morning's patients and was enjoying a break with a hot mug of minestrone soup when the call came through.

'Sara, hi, it's Dana. How are you?'

Sara rested the cup down on the coaster Marjorie had given her. 'Dana, I'm well, really well,' she said, leaning forward onto the desk. 'But how are things going with you? How's Bonny coming along? It was just such a beautiful painting she sent me.'

'Thanks, I'll tell her you liked it. She's coming along so well, I can't tell you how grateful we are to you for stepping in and taking over.'

'Don't worry about that. I'm just glad I could help out.'

'We'll never forget it,' Dana said softly. 'It's made all the difference. And that's why I'm ringing. We hadn't heard back from you. Sara, Stu and I really want you to be their godmother. Bonny's done so well in only a week that we've decided to have a big party for Henry and Phillip's christening. We had planned on something low key but now practically the whole town is coming.

'Sara,' Dana's voice called down the line, 'please, don't feel pressured. I understand if you're too busy. Really, I don't want you to feel that you have to. We'd love to have you up for the party just as our guest. I'm sure Stu could ask someone else.'

'I'm not feeling pressured. Not at all. I'd be thrilled to be the boys' godmother, it's just that I'm not sure if Tom will agree. He's a bit hesitant—'

'That's wonderful!' Dana cut in. 'And don't worry about Tom. Stu spoke to him today and he's on board too. Gosh it's going to be so great to see you again It's been so long and we have so much to catch up on.'

Sara nodded into the telephone. 'Yes, it will be great, really great,' she managed to reply, totally surprised at Tom's shift in attitude. What had made him change his mind? Was he coming round on some level to the idea of children after all? She realised every day just how complex Tom was and how he could still astonish her.

The afternoon was as steady as the morning. There were new patient consultations and a couple of post-operative checks.

'You certainly like to be busy, Sara,' Marjorie commented late in the day, as she placed the last of the typed reports on Sara's desk for her signature. 'You've booked a hectic surgical schedule for the next few weeks.'

'Marjorie, I'm fine. I'm not being paid to sit around and do nothing.'

'I know, but you must also look after yourself,' she said firmly. 'What about we close up and head off home? Your minor surgical list tomorrow is a long one.

Starts at eight o'clock and we won't finish much before six tomorrow evening. Laura and William North will be with us for the entire day.'

Sara agreed it was a good idea and gathered up her case notes for the next day's patients. She intended to read them briefly during the evening to refresh her memory. Locking the door, she headed downstairs.

Wistfully, Sara looked across the reflections in the river and for a moment her imagination took over and convinced her that she was heading home to spend the evening curled up with Tom instead of a pile of cold case notes. With the gas fire warming the room, she pictured Tom cuddling her as they sat together on the sofa, his arms wrapped tightly around her. But her fantasy slowly faded in the cold night air.

She came back to reality and the overwhelming loneliness of the deserted car park. Absent-mindedly, she rubbed her arms and shivered.

She knew she shouldn't allow her thoughts to wander to Tom. But thinking about him wasn't a conscious decision. No matter how hard she tried to block him from her mind, something would always remind her of him. And when she was by herself she needed no prompting to find his image creeping back in. He had unlocked the key to her heart many years ago and now, despite her protests, it appeared he had subtly crept back in.

Mollie Hatcher was on time the next morning and more than a little apprehensive about losing the gap between her front teeth.

'But my grandma says it's good luck to have a gap,' Mollie told them, her big brown eyes wide with worry.

Sara smiled understandingly. 'You know, Mollie, my grandma told me exactly the same story, and you never know—it might just be true. But it doesn't mean you have to keep the gap to keep the good luck! Especially not if it makes it hard to fit the rest of your teeth in and it stops them from meeting together properly.'

'I don't understand.'

'Well, your teeth came through with a gap. Now, if your grandma's story is true, then the good luck has already been decided for you. So there's no need to keep the gap.'

'I suppose,' she said, with a frown wrinkling the spattering of freckles on her nose. 'But will it hurt?'

'Mollie,' the anaesthetist interrupted softly, 'do you like butterflies?'

'Oh, yes, I love the big, bright coloured ones.'

William smiled. 'That's good, because I'm going to rub some special cream onto your hand and a butterfly is going to sit there and make you feel a bit sleepy. You'll still be awake and able to hear Sara and help her but you won't feel anything she does, so it won't hurt at all.'

The neuroleptanagesia quickly took effect, and Sara was able to remove the fleshy frenum that ran between Mollie's upper front teeth. She carefully sutured and then packed the site with a dressing before Laura helped the child into Recovery.

Following her appointment with Mollie, Sara's morning passed without incident—the minor surgical cases were straightforward and uneventful.

Sara's mind strayed to Tom. She hadn't seen much of him for a few days—the mid-year break was over and the hospital was monopolising his time. She had heard his car come and go at odd hours, but she had resisted the urge to pull back the drapes and peer out at him from the window. They had bumped into each other leaving for work, and Sara suggested shopping together for christening presents on the weekend. Tom seemed hesitant at first but then agreed and made a time for Saturday.

Sara had worried the day shopping would be fraught with tension but it was lovely and so far from her initial concerns. She had assumed the idea of buying presents for children would make Tom feel uncomfortable. But it didn't. Tom seemed happy enough to be looking at silver frames and other keepsakes but he had his own ideas too.

He suggested a large antique train set or racing cars as an alternative, then humoured Sara as she wandered around the delicate ornaments for about half an hour. After she asked the salesperson to reserve two stunning silver frames while she wandered a little more just to be sure of her purchase, he took Sara off to the toy department. She watched him for the first time roam around like a kid himself. He was wide-eyed and enthusiastic about what the boys would love now, and as they grew older. Which toys would be the most exciting, and how Stu could enjoy playing with the toys with his sons.

Sara felt a tug at her heart as she saw the genuine interest he had in finding something the children would love.

Finally he saw them. Two six-foot, enormous brown teddy bears.

'I'm not sure,' she said, looking up at the huge furry creatures. 'They're so big. I don't know where Dana would put them. Wouldn't it be nice to have something to keep?'

Tom nodded. 'If that's what you want, I guess you're right. We should be practical. Let's get the silver frames.'

Sara smiled. Shopping with Tom wasn't difficult at

all but it was sad seeing his reaction to the toys he would never share with his own children. She had the frames gift-wrapped and they headed off to enjoy lunch at a café before they left the city. Sara felt sure Dana would love the frames. Tom didn't say anything more but he really did love the bears.

Sara had less than two weeks left on her locum assignment for Stu.

George's surgery came around very quickly. She had called in to see him that night on the way home and gone over the procedure. He wanted the rhinoplasty as well and his mother was happy with that decision. Sara explained to George that he would be wearing anti-embolism stockings prior to his surgery and following the operation to reduce the possibility of deep vein thrombosis.

'Now, on top of everything else, I've gotta wear pantyhose?'

Sara smiled, 'No, George, not pantyhose. These are like thin white socks that compress your legs to increase the blood flow, preventing your leg veins from expanding. It stops blood pooling in your legs and forming a clot.'

He turned to his mother. 'Just make sure no one takes photos of me in the pantyhose-sock things. If that gets online I am so totally screwed.'

Sara slept well and was ready for a full day when she arrived at the hospital.

'Good morning, Rosalie.'

'Hi, Sara. Good to see you again,' the theatre nurse said, as Sara entered the scrub room. 'Long list again today.'

'Certainly is. Starts with George Andrews. He's understandably nervous. It's a long op he's looking at.' Dressed in her green theatre scrubs, with her hair secured under a surgical cap, Sara began lathering her hands and arms.

'If it goes as smoothly as last week,' Rosalie replied as she rinsed the lather from her hands and forearms, 'it'll be a dream for everyone.'

'Unfortunately we don't have Dr Fielding helping out, if that's what you mean—'

'Oh, yes, you do.' Tom's deep voice came from the other side of the small room.

Sara spun on her surgically booted heels to find him also dressed in theatre garb and scrubbing in at the opposite trough. He turned to face her at that exact moment.

'What are you doing here?' she asked. 'I have an assisting surgeon already confirmed.'

She soon found herself facing his broad back as he turned back round to rinse his hands. She watched in astonishment as he casually dried them and slipped into his latex gloves.

'Fran Burton, your assisting surgeon, just called Marjorie, who in turn called my office to say she had been held up and would be late. Great excuse to take a break from paperwork, so I'll help with the first patient and she'll be here to take over in time for number two.'

Tom had more than enough to occupy his time but he'd jumped at the opportunity to work with Sara again.

'Great,' she replied, a little surprised he hadn't just sent another resident surgeon to help. 'Let's get going.'

George was prepped and already in Theatre. The anaesthetist and two nurses were also waiting under the bright lights.

'Hi, George,' Sara greeted his anxious face. 'I won't ask you how you're feeling. I can pretty much guess the answer. But everything will be fine—'

'You don't happen to have a hip flask in your pocket now, do you? I could really do with something to take the nerves away.'

Tom laughed. 'Dr North has something even stronger planned for you. So, if you're ready, let's get started.'

George nodded and William administered the anaesthetic. The patient, groggier by the moment, began slowly counting backwards from ten. By seven he was asleep.

Tom let Sara lead the operation. He backed her up and anticipated each of her moves. She was so happy to have him working with her.

Once she had freed George's lower jaw, she removed an equal portion from the right and left sides. Tom assisted by securing the newly sized jaw with titanium plates. They worked steadily and advanced the midsection of his upper jaw. Next was the reshaping of the chin, and then they moved up to his nose. The bump was removed and after three hours the operation was complete. By all indications it was a success.

Sara had felt like she was in possession of four hands. Their chatter was minimal as each knew the other's next move, both equally skilled in the operating theatre.

Sara wished Tom would stay for the entire day. Fran was a more than capable surgeon but Tom just happened to be extraordinary. Yet professional courtesy wouldn't have her decline Fran's assistance.

'Thanks for your help,' she said to Tom as they watched George wheeled away into Intensive Care. 'It went extremely well.'

Tom considered her in silence. She felt uncomfortable as his eyes lingered on her face. She wondered what he was thinking. Was he considering her surgical skills or looking at her as a woman?

'We make an outstanding team, Sara,' he finally said. 'Texas is lucky to be getting you.' With that he bent down and tenderly kissed her cheek. He smiled sadly at her as he tugged the surgical gloves from his hands and walked away, leaving Sara standing alone in the empty theatre.

CHAPTER TEN

ICU's BUSTLING AMBIENCE of sterile efficiency was unusually sombre when Sara visited after finishing her surgical list for that day. It was around seven o'clock. All but one of her patients had been admitted to a high dependency ward after Recovery. But it was policy for the more complicated cases to spend a night in ICU.

Each of the critical care patients had an attending nurse but the faces of their carers showed little emotion as they efficiently went about their work.

The silence was broken only by mechanical sounds: the unrelenting and regular high-pitched beeps of monitors; the constant buzzers; and the deep swooshing sound of the ventilators.

Pale blue curtains separated the patients whose acute medical conditions made their lives dependent upon sophisticated monitoring equipment and round-the-clock nursing. Each curtain was drawn open at the foot of the bed and the senior nurse at the desk had a clear view of each cubicle.

'Good evening, Vanda.' Sara's voice was little more than a whisper. 'I'm here to see George Andrews.'

'Evening, Sara,' the pretty nurse replied softly, before she drew a deep sigh and checked her list. 'George is in bed nine. He's doing very well. Debbie is looking after him tonight.'

'Has his mother been in?'

'She just left. Pretty horrified, by the look on her face. But Debbie and Dr Fielding put her at ease a bit and told her it looked a lot worse than it was.'

'Dr Fielding was here?'

'Yes,' the young nurse replied. 'He's still with him now.'

Sara wasn't surprised. Tom always treated his patients like family while they were in his care. The best care for each and every one of them. That obviously had not changed. Sara made her way over to George. He was sleeping. As expected, his jaw and cheeks were a harsh blend of bruises and quite swollen. His darkened eyes looked sunken in the puffiness of his face. He had been connected to a cardiac monitor and lines from intravenous bottles providing fluid, antibiotics and pain relief fed into his veins.

'Hello, Debbie, hello, Tom,' Sara said. 'I hear our patient is doing very well.'

'Hi, Sara,' Debbie replied. 'Yes, he's fine, but, then, we never expected any problems. His chart says his op was a reasonable length but straightforward. There's no reason to think we'll have anything untoward happen.'

'Mum was in and pretty worried I hear,' Sara said quietly, as she picked up the chart and began looking over it.

'She was okay tonight. Let's face it, it's pretty scary to see a patient for the first time after oral surgery, or any surgery for that matter,' Tom replied, as he watched Sara checking the notes. 'Sometimes we just forget that we're all hard nuts after so many years. Nothing much fazes us.'

After they had checked on George and the other patients, who were settled into the wards, Sara accepted Tom's offer of a lift home. She had left the Lexus at home and walked to the hospital that morning to get some exercise but had no intention of walking home at night. He put the heater on high and Sara snuggled into the seat. She rested her face against the crinkled leather and took deep breaths. Secretly she luxuriated in the scent of his aftershave. It was all through the car. It was like old times.

Tom turned his head and smiled. He knew he had so little time with her he had decided to enjoy every minute. It was hard to be this close when he knew these were the last weeks they would ever spend together. This was it. They would part and he would never see her beautiful face again.

Sara was enjoying Tom's company. There was no tension. No animosity. It was like a truce before they parted ways for ever. The city looked extraordinarily pretty through the fogged glass. Sara knew that her relaxed mood and contentment gave her an appreciation of the normally overlooked sights. The cityscape of high-rise buildings sparkled like brightly coloured fairy-lights against the black sky.

A tram trundled along beside them, the 1920s-style red carriage lit up, and Sara watched the people inside. Businessmen in coloured suits, young women in office attire, a few teenagers and an old lady with a strange feathered hat all sat facing forward as it made its way down Collins Street, rocking a little from side to side.

In the silence of the car Sara wondered for a moment about where they were all going, and if anyone was waiting for them.

It was very cold outside and she was so grateful to be with Tom.

It was like old times. Almost. He walked her to her door and she asked him in for coffee.

'I'll take a raincheck. It's late and I've got a killer of a day tomorrow.' Tom sensed her vulnerability and didn't want to risk a repeat of that night they'd shared not too long ago. He wasn't only protecting Sara from being hurt. He knew he was vulnerable himself.

Sara felt both relief and disappointment when he turned her down. She knew it was best, because she knew she was losing her heart to Tom all over again. It was in both of their best interests that he take control before she lost hers and headed down the right path with the wrong man again.

'Mine's hectic too,' she answered with a short sigh, as she watched him cross the softly lit porch and step onto the loose gravel. 'But being so busy the week is just flying by. I can't believe the weekend's so close.'

He paused and the crunching noise beneath his feet stopped. 'Are you happy for me to drive you to our country christening this weekend?'

'That'd be lovely,' she said. 'I'm so excited to see Dana and Stu, not to mention Bonny and the boys.'

She watched as Tom crossed to his own porch and unlocked the front door. He smiled at her and they stepped inside their respective houses and closed their doors in unison.

On Saturday morning her overnight bag was packed and waiting by the front door ready for the early start, the silver frames tucked safely inside. Unfortunately it wasn't an early start. It was after eleven-thirty before they finally left for the country.

A and E was flat out from the Friday night and Tom had been called in at about six in the morning to help out with an emergency jaw reconstruction.

Tom told Sara about the operation as they drove north along the Hume highway towards Seymour. The sky above them was a clear blue, although soft grey clouds were gathering over the hills in the distance. Sara wound down the window and enjoyed the cool breeze on her face. She had wrapped a light scarf around her hair but the loose wisps were tickling her face.

'What are you smiling about?' Tom asked her. His gaze stayed on her for only a moment before he turned it back to the road.

Sara brushed away the hair, trying to tuck it behind her ears. It was no use. The wind was too strong as Tom increased the speed of the car to climb to the Victorian state limit.

'Nothing, really. I've just got hair all over the place.'

'Then wind up the window.'

She shook her head, sending more of her hair flying about. She couldn't contain her smile. 'No, I'm enjoying it. It feels so good to get away from everything. No pagers, no day lists, no…no schedules to keep!'

Her happiness was contagious and Tom's mouth broke into a broad smile as he put his foot down and took off down the highway.

An hour later they pulled into a roadhouse. It wasn't situated in a town. It was just a petrol station and restaurant on the side of the highway, in the middle of nowhere. There was flat dry scrub for as far as Sara could see. Low bushes and an occasional eucalypt dotted the pale green and brown landscape.

'How about an all-day breakfast?' he asked as he pulled up beside a petrol pump.

'Is it safe to eat here?' She made a wry face as she watched a burly truck driver jump down from his rig. The shiny red cabin door was decorated with a painting of a scantily clad woman. Suddenly the loud noise of another huge semi-trailer pulling in made her jump in her seat. The brakes squealed and then whooshed with the release of air as the huge beast came to a halt behind them.

'It wasn't that I wasn't expecting the Ritz,' Sara shouted over the noise. 'But this looks a little, well, rough around the edges.'

Tom grinned. 'You can guarantee, Sara, if the buses and trucks stop here, then the food will be the best. They can't afford to get gut problems on long interstate hauls. They'll only eat where they know the places are clean and the food is fresh.'

Hesitantly, Sara made her way inside.

Tom was right. The bacon was crisp, the scrambled eggs were deliciously fluffy and the coffee was freshly brewed.

'Dana and Stu's place is only about an hour down the road,' Tom said as he paid the bill and gave his compliments to the chef. He held the door open for Sara. 'I still don't know how he manages to drive in every week for four days and then come home for a long weekend. I like city living and country visiting…once or twice a year.'

Sara nodded in agreement. She was looking forward to spending the next two days on the farm but she couldn't stand the thought of driving that far every week, like Stu did.

'I suppose you can't take the country out of a country boy, can you?' she said as she climbed into the car and pull the door closed. 'Or the city out of us city folk.'

He didn't start the car until the last semi-trailer had pulled out onto the road. There was no point leaving first. The vintage car would only get in the way and force the semis to overtake.

They drove while chatting happily about the practice and the hospital. Soon the town sign appeared. Seymour. It was at the junction of the Hume highway and Goulburn Valley and Sara knew it would be a picturesque part of the country.

Tom turned off the highway into Seymour. The farm was outside of the main town so they headed down Station Street and stopped at the Railway Club Hotel.

'I didn't have time to get any wine for tomorrow,' Tom said, as he climbed out of the car. 'I'll just grab a bottle or two. Would you like anything?'

Sara shook her head. She was still full from their lunch. She looked around as she waited for Tom. It was a typical country town where everyone took their time and knew their neighbours. Sara watched as a group made their way to the river with their fishing gear. It wasn't long before Tom emerged with his purchases and reversed the car and continued down the street.

'How long since you were here?' Sara asked him, as she looked at the heritage buildings dotted along the main road. As they made their way through the town she admired the gorgeous gardens.

'I was only here just over six weeks ago,' Tom answered as he left the town and headed along the Goulburn Valley Highway to the farm. 'I came down with Stu when Bonny was released from hospital.'

'That must have been a dreadful time.' Sara paused for a moment and looked across the huge vineyards that surrounded the township. She was searching for the right words. 'I think seeing Bonny so badly injured and yet being unable to do anything more would have made me feel so helpless. It's so hard when only time can heal someone you care about.'

Tom said nothing but the emotion that poured into his face told Sara everything she needed to know. He still felt the pain of Bonny's injuries, that was obvious. And he still carried those of his brother.

Her heart aching with sadness at what might have been, she turned her gaze away from Tom and back to the scenery. They turned left onto a dirt road and the car bumped along the uneven surface for a half a mile before they found the entrance to the farm.

As they travelled up the last part of the potholed road to the house, Tom filled Sara in about the property. Stu and Dana had bought the house when they'd returned from Queensland. It was more of a hobby farm and a rural escape than a money-making venture.

They had bought a small number of sheep to graze over the few hectares of bush land that had been cleared and a couple of alpacas roamed around to protect the sheep from foxes. In another paddock were some grape vines but these were grown only on a small scale. Selling the grapes to local wine producers made just enough to fund the farm. There was no huge profit in this venture. Dana tended to the general running of the property and had needed to employ only one farmhand, Adrian, who also helped out with any odd jobs that Stu was too busy to deal with.

Sara stepped out in the driveway to hear a kookaburra's call from top of the lofty eucalypts.

'Did you have a good trip?' Stu asked the pair as he

approached them enthusiastically. He had heard them coming up the long driveway and was already outside, waiting for them.

'Tops,' Tom replied, as he closed the car door.

'What about you, Sara? Did you enjoy the bumpy ride in the old Austin Healey?'

'It was great, and it's even better to see you again,' she said, before she wrapped her arms around Stu and hugged his huge bear-like body.

'Dana's in the kitchen,' he told her, patting her back affectionately and walking her to the house. He opened the front door and stepped back, smiling. 'Those god-sons of yours have made one hell of a mess in their high-chairs. Food all over the place. Looks like a war zone. I was lucky to get out alive the way they were throwing stewed pears and cereal about.'

Dana was as thrilled to see Sara as she was to be there. The pair embraced affectionately.

Sara couldn't believe it had been three years—it felt like yesterday. Dana hadn't changed a bit. Her brown eyes sparkled and her long red hair was still a mass of curls tied back from her pretty face with an antique clasp. She was about Sara's height, which meant she was dwarfed by her husband. Her petite frame was dressed in jeans and a canary yellow overshirt.

The kitchen was big with a true country feel to it. Rows of saucepans and utensils hung down from the ceiling within reach of the workbench and beautiful floral curtains draped the windows. The cupboards and drawers were oak and so was the big kitchen table and chairs. The floor was tiled in aged terracotta and a pot-belly stove in the far corner warmed the large room.

Henry was the bigger twin. His brother Phillip was slightly smaller framed, though both had had a shock of red hair. Sara was thrilled to finally see them, and she could hardly wait to see Bonny.

'Where is she?' Sara finally asked, after giving both Henry and Phillip kisses on the tops of their heads. It was the only part of them not covered in food. 'Where's Bonny?'

Dana smiled so widely at the question that Sara was afraid her hostess for the weekend would burst before she told her.

'Dana, what is it? Tell me. Where is she?'

'Horseriding.'

Sara felt the colour drain from her previously flushed face. 'She's what? You can't be serious?'

Dana climbed down from the footstool after wiping the last of the pears and rice cereal from the wall. 'I'm deadly serious. Bonny's out riding her pony, Sheba, with Adrian. And she can talk again. She started speaking only two days ago.'

Sara couldn't believe what she was hearing. Bonny had still been critically ill only a month ago and now she was horseriding and her voice was back.

Dana hurriedly rinsed the checked cloth under running water and hung it over the dish drainer before she sat down at the table with Sara. But her work wasn't done and she reached over and began cleaning Phillip's face. Sara took another facecloth and busied herself with cleaning up Henry.

'It was meant to be a surprise. Bonny didn't want anyone to know she was walking or talking again until the boys' christening party. My mother and father still think she needs a frame to walk and a board to spell the words, and so do Stu's parents. Bonny thought she'd surprise both sets of grandparents by walking into church and singing the hymns.'

'That's wonderful,' Sara told her friend as she finished wiping the last of the sticky mess from Henry's chubby little fingers. He gurgled and gave a toothless grin that immediately brought a smile to Sara.

'Good,' Stu's deep voice called through the wire screen door. 'It's cleaned up. We can get something to eat.'

Dana shook her head as she looked over at Sara. 'Isn't it amazing what impeccable timing men have? It always saves them from the worst scrapes.'

Sara couldn't agree more. After Stu and Tom brought in the bags, putting Sara's in the spare room and leaving Tom's by the door to be taken out later to the guesthouse, the four of them ate lunch with the boys safely placed in a nearby playpen. Dana had prepared open sandwiches, with Sara's help.

'Savour the ones with egg filling,' Stu mumbled cheerily with a mouthful of sandwich. 'Thomasina's laying about one a week, and that's only in a good week!'

They all laughed. They cleaned up and put the boys to sleep before the four of them went out to find Bonny and Adrian. The air smelt good and fresh but the sky was almost covered with ominous-looking clouds. Although a downpour was a while off, the breeze was quite cold and the ground was still heavy from recent rainfall. Sara had worn jeans and a hand-knitted jumper on the car trip so she needed only to grab her scarf, throw her waterproof jacket over the top and slip into some knee-length rubber boots that Dana gave her.

Before they left the farmhouse, Tom took his bag to the guesthouse, not far from the main house, and changed into similar country clothing.

After a few minutes of walking they had reached the small shearing shed near the riding track.

'Uncle Tom, Uncle Tom!' came the excited cry. 'Look at me!'

Sara spun round to see Bonny, all grown up and sitting high in the saddle with her brown riding hat firmly in place, her curly auburn hair tied in long plaits and a yellow raincoat buttoned up against the breeze. Sara felt pure joy as she watched Bonny parade around them on her chestnut coloured pony.

Stu coughed to clear his throat. 'Excuse me, missy. We have another guest.'

Bonny peered down in Sara's direction and pulled Sheba's reins to a halt. 'Aunty Sara?'

'Yes, it's me, Bonny. I'm sorry I've been away so long. Too long.' Sara's throat was choked by emotion. 'It's…it's so good to see you up there. I can hardly believe it.'

Bonny's pretty face was aglow as she began a slow canter around the foursome. 'I'm walking into church tomorrow. Did Mummy tell you?'

Sara nodded. 'She certainly did, Bonny, and I know it's a secret so I won't say a word to anyone.'

'Adrian,' Stu called to the young man who followed closely behind Bonny on a glistening black mare, 'I'd like you to meet a friend of ours.'

Sara watched as he carefully turned the cantering horse and rode over to her.

'Sara, I'd like you to meet Adrian Gorden. Adrian, this is Sara Fielding.'

'Pleased to meet you, Sara,' the boy said politely, but his eyes didn't stray from Bonny for too long. Before Sara had a chance to respond, Sheba moved her head suddenly and Adrian instantly cantered back over to Bonny.

'We'd better head back as there's lots to do before tomorrow,' Dana told them. 'And that includes you, Bonny. You've got some more physio and then a hot bath. You can spend the afternoon inside with the boys.'

'What size boys are we talking about, darling?' Stu asked light-heartedly. 'Have Tom and I been grounded too?'

Dana laughed as she gently reached for Sheba's reins and turned the pony in the direction of the farmhouse. 'No. I guess you two can have the afternoon off. But don't forget you've got lots to do this evening and first thing in the morning.'

Stu saluted his wife and then bent down and kissed her. Sara looked away. The love they shared was almost palpable and it made her feel a little uncomfortable. It used not to, all those years ago, but back then circumstances had been different. That had been when she and Tom had also shared those tender moments and so much more.

'Okay, Tom, looks like we've got a few hours free. How about a trip into town and a pint with some of the locals?'

Sara spent the afternoon chatting with Bonny and helping with preparations for the next day's festivities. Dana's parents would be arriving the day of the christening but spending the night. Stu's family wouldn't stay at all because they only lived in the next town.

Sara's room was already prepared but she helped Dana ready another guest room, putting fresh sheets on the queen-sized bed. This would be for Dana's parents.

Sara offered to go out and prepare Tom's bed in the

guesthouse by herself, leaving Dana free to begin another. It was a small, self-contained unit with its own kitchen, bathroom and bedroom. Dana gave her fresh flowers to put on the table and extra blankets for the bed. It was an odd feeling and she had butterflies in her stomach as she made the bed Tom would be lying in that night. She had to push the feelings away as she tucked in the last blanket corner.

'It's lucky you have such a big place to hold us all,' she said, when she finally came back into the kitchen, where Dana was busily decorating the christening cake. It was a fruit cake in the shape of two booties and iced in the palest powder blue.

The afternoon raced by. Sara was happy to follow Dana's instructions and roll the three dozen chocolate-dipped lamingtons in coconut, blend the cream cheese and salmon for the dip and carefully fold the huge pile of blue and white serviettes. Bonny joined in and helped with the serviettes after her bath. They had decided, with all the party preparations, to leave the physiotherapy until her father returned home.

'How many guests are you expecting, Dana?'

Dana had her head in the fridge looking for the carrots to grate into the coleslaw. 'We've planned on sixty,' she said, as she stood up and crossed back to the sink with the bunch of carrots in her hand. As Sara watched Dana cut off the leafy, green tops and discard them into the bin, she couldn't help but wonder if one day she would be knee deep in preparing a family function for her own children.

The men came home around six o'clock, just in time for dinner. After the delicious meal of roast pork and vegetables, Tom chose to spend some quiet time with Bonny while the others finished their bread-and-butter pudding. He had excused himself before dessert and headed off to play a board game with the excited little girl in the family room.

Sara noticed how much he loved spending time with Bonny and how his self-imposed sentence would rob him of the opportunity to do the same with his own child. But that was his choice, she reminded herself, although it made her sad to think she could do nothing to change it. She couldn't find a way to get through to him and make him see that he was denying himself something so precious.

'It's not like Tom to refuse dessert,' Dana commented as she stacked the emptied bowls. 'He usually eats like a Mallee bull.'

'That's okay. If he doesn't come back for it, I'm happy to eat his tonight. This country air is giving me an appetite,' Sara said, helping Dana to clear the table.

The two women made quick work of cleaning up the dinner dishes, while Stu gave the boys a bottle each and Tom remained out of sight with Bonny. They could all hear the laughter coming from the other room as Tom and Bonny played card game after card game.

'I think we should all play cards tonight. What about bridge or poker?' Dana suggested, as Stu took the two drained bottles away from Henry and Phillip.

'Sounds like a great idea to me,' Stu replied. 'I'll just change my little men here, and then get the children up to bed. Give me ten minutes and then I will clean the lot of you up in a game of poker. Bridge is for sissies.'

Sara smiled. 'Poker it is.'

* * *

They were about forty minutes into poker when Stu felt a headache coming on and thought he might call it a night. Dana said she thought she might head to bed early as well, since it was going to be a big day tomorrow.

'Why don't you two head back into town and get a drink or something? I mean, you are welcome to stay here and watch television, but we are a bit boring in our old age and tend to settle down quite early.'

'We may just do that. What do you think, Sara? Up for a big night on the town?'

Sara was a little tired but thought it might be fun to head into town and see what the locals were up to.

'Sure, why not?' she replied.

'Then that's settled. You will see us later,' Tom announced, as he stood up and slipped his warm jacket on.

Stu reached into his pocket, pulled out his keys and tossed them across the room. 'Take the four-wheel drive. It's safer on the roads out here at night than that antique toy car you drive, not to mention a lot warmer.'

Tom caught the keys and nodded in agreement. Sara went quickly to her room and grabbed a warm coat and scarf.

'I'll drive,' she said with a smile, as she took the keys from Tom's hand and headed outside. The air was freezing as they climbed into the huge four-wheel drive. It took only moments to realise she wouldn't be driving anywhere.

'Change of mind, you can drive after all,' she told Tom, and then climbed out of the car. With a puzzled expression Tom stepped out of his side, walked around to the driver's door and climbed in. They both shut their doors at the same time.

'Of course,' he said, with laughter in his voice. 'You can't drive anything with a manual gearbox!'

Sara nodded sheepishly.

'You know, Sara, it has always amazed me how you can perform complex surgical procedures but can't co-ordinate your feet and hands to use a clutch and gear-stick!' He chuckled to himself and Sara rolled her eyes as they took off down the dirt road, the headlights on high beam.

It didn't take long before they pulled up outside the Royal Hotel.

'Someone told me this was the subject of a Drysdale painting. Is that right?' Sara asked as they quickly made their way to the entrance. It was so cold. There was no breeze but it was like standing inside a cold room and it was chilling them both to the bone.

'I don't know, to be honest, but I'm sure Stu would. You can ask him in the morning,' Tom said, as he held the hotel door open for Sara. He added, 'Not sure about you but I think I would prefer a hot chocolate to a wine tonight.'

Sara nodded in agreement as she blew warm air on her hands and crossed to a table near the fire.

They both enjoyed a warm drink and a light-hearted chat about Stu and Dana and their wonderful property and how amazing Bonny's progress was, considering her injuries.

Sara suddenly realised that she had forgotten to take the spare key Dana had placed in her room, and it was only when Tom looked at his watch that they saw how late it was.

As they pulled back into the driveway ten minutes later, they saw that the main house lights were turned off.

'Looks like they've locked you out,' he said.

'I don't want to wake them, that wouldn't be fair.'

'There's nothing for you to do but spend the night in the guesthouse with me.'

Sara swallowed nervously as Tom unlocked the guest-house and she followed him inside. It was lovely and warm and Sara guessed the either Dana or Stu had put on the heater for Tom before they went to bed. He turned on the lamps and she could see into the bedroom. She had made the bed earlier in the day, thinking that Tom would be lying between the sheets. That had been hard enough to think about.

She'd never dreamt that she would be lying in the same bed. Or that they would fall asleep together and she would wake in the morning to find his gorgeous face on the pillow next to hers.

Her stomach began tying itself in small knots as Tom removed his coat and slipped his heavy shoes off. When he undid his shirt and told her he was taking a shower, the knots turned to churning and her heart started to pound. She didn't know where to look as he casually dropped his shirt on the chair and slipped his belt from his jeans.

She quickly reached for a book, any book on the cof-fee table, as his trousers hit the ground and he disap-peared in to the small bathroom. She knew there was nowhere in there to place his clothes but removing them in front of her was far too unsettling. Sara put the book back down on the table, completely unaware of what was even on the cover. Her mind was spinning as she went into the bedroom and turned down the bed. She was waiting for Tom to finish his shower when she heard him call out.

'Sara, take my pyjama top to stay warm in bed tonight. I'll wear the bottoms. You'll find it in my overnight bag. And there's a spare toothbrush in there as well.'

Sara felt uncomfortable searching in his belongings but decided if she got the top while he was in the shower then she could change without him seeing her naked. She unzipped the bag and found the top and the toothbrush. Hastily, she slipped off her winter clothes and put on his warm pyjama top. Then she put the pyjama pants on the end of the bed for Tom.

'You can come in and brush your teeth, you know. There's a shower curtain.'

Sara wished she hadn't heard. 'I can wait,' she called back.

'You know I take for ever,' he called over the sound of the running water. 'You could be in bed in five minutes if you can ignore my singing while you floss.'

Sara cringed with the thought. Not at his singing but of him standing naked behind the shower curtain only inches from her. Tentatively, and with an enormous amount of trepidation, Sara opened the door and stepped inside the steam-filled room. Her bare feet crossed the tiles to the sink.

'Almost like old times,' came Tom's voice from behind the curtain.

'Almost,' she muttered, as she squeezed some toothpaste on her brush and bent forward over the basin, beginning to brush her teeth. It was the most disconcerting tooth-brushing experience she could recall.

The curtain suddenly moved back, revealing Tom's head and very naked upper torso. 'Sorry, I couldn't hear you.'

Sara instinctively closed her eyes. Tight. She didn't want to see what she knew was in front of her. The vision of her naked and extremely handsome soon-to-be-ex-husband was not something she could easily, if ever, forget.

She pointed her hand at her toothbrush already in her mouth, hoping he would understand that she couldn't talk. He did and the curtain was pulled back again.

Sara breathed a sigh of relief and finished brushing and flossing in record time. She left the bathroom, calling out goodnight before she closed the door on her way out.

Snug in her oversized nightwear, she climbed into bed. She pulled the blankets up to her chin and tried to push any thoughts of the last time she'd shared a bed with Tom from her mind. She closed her eyes and prayed she would fall asleep quickly. But that didn't happen. Tom stepped from the bathroom with his towel hung low. She didn't want to look at him but she did. In the soft light creeping from under the bathroom door she watched his perfectly sculpted body cross the room to where his overnight bag lay.

'Your pyjama pants are on the end of the bed,' she whispered softly, and again she closed her eyes very quickly and very tightly before he dropped his towel.

She heard Tom thank her before he turned off the heater and the light and slipped into bed.

'Goodnight, Sara.'

She felt his weight on the other side of the bed and the fresh scent of soap as she lay so close to the man she knew she still loved.

She was so confused that it felt so right, so good and so comforting to be sharing Tom's bed. She didn't want to feel that way. She may not have any intention of acting on it, but there was no denying she felt at home and safe in a strange bed because Tom was in it with her.

'Goodnight, Tom.'

* * *

It was about two in the morning when she woke up, feeling a little hungry. There were some cookies that she had spied earlier in the kitchen so she made her way out there quietly. Without making too much noise, she heated some milk on the stove and sat at the small kitchen table, dipping her cookies into the cup. Then she made her way back to the bedroom. The moonlight was shining though the gaps in the curtains, faintly illuminating the room. She noticed he had kicked his covers off. Without thinking too much about it, she instinctively moved to cover him.

Gently she pulled the covers up and over his bare back. He had sacrificed the warmth of his top for her. The room was now cold and she suspected his back would be icy to touch. A bittersweet smile tugged at her mouth as she remembered back to when they had been married and how she would always have to cover him during the night. His shoulders would be so cold to touch but he would be sleeping peacefully, perhaps in the knowledge that she would keep him warm.

He gave a deep throaty moan and startled her. She reeled back on tiptoe, holding her breath. His thick lashes flickered and he scratched his head.

Sara's pulse was racing. What would she say to him if he woke to find her leaning over him?

Thankfully she didn't have to find a hasty excuse. He didn't wake up. He just rolled over, tossing the blankets aside and uncovering himself again. Her breathing became steady but quite loud. For a moment she stood in silence, trying not to make a sound in case she woke him. Sara didn't dare to try covering him again. Instead, she crept back to her side of the bed.

There was a tug in her chest as she quietly slipped

under the covers, knowing she would be spending the rest of her life without him.

In ten short days she would walk away, again. Gone from Tom's life for ever. She would never be there to cover his back.

CHAPTER ELEVEN

DANA AND STU were eating breakfast with Bonny and the boys when Tom and Sara entered the kitchen.

'Morning, guys,' Tom greeted them cheerfully. 'I can tell it's going to be a great day.'

'Morning to you two,' Stu said, swallowing a mouthful of porridge and ignoring the change to sleeping arrangements. 'There's plenty of this on the stove. Unless you'd prefer cold cereal.'

'No. Porridge is lovely,' Sara said, climbing to her feet and getting two bowls from the kitchen dresser. Tom followed behind, taking two spoons from the drawer. They smiled at each other when they realised what they had done. It was like old times.

'Church is at—' Dana cut her words short when she saw the arrival of a huge delivery truck in the driveway. 'What on earth is that?'

Bonny ran to the window to look out as Stu and Dana crossed to open the door.

A uniformed man climbed down from the truck, its side emblazoned with the impressive logo of a large department store in Melbourne.

'I have a delivery for Henry, Phillip and Bonny Anderson,' the driver announced, as he neared the open door. 'I need a signature before I can get the parcel from the truck.'

'There's something for me too?' Bonny screamed excitedly, and hobbled to the door. 'But it's not my birthday or anything.'

Sara shot Tom a puzzled look and then leant over to him. 'You got the boys the bears, didn't you?' she whispered in his ear.

He nodded and smiled as he looked straight ahead. 'And one for Bonny.'

Bonny was bursting with excitement. 'Mummy, can I go out and help?'

Dana ruffled her daughter's mass of auburn curls. 'I don't think the gentleman will need too much help, sweetheart.'

The young man coughed. 'Don't believe it. I could do with some help but definitely adult size for this delivery.'

Stu and Tom followed him outside. It was only a matter of minutes before three chocolate brown, six-foot teddy bears with rotund tummies marched their way down the ramp from the truck.

Sara smiled at the sight of the first two with their checked bow-ties and then the third with a string of pale pink pearls around its enormous neck. The men were all struggling to keep their balance as they carried the trio inside.

Bonny was ecstatic and the boys' little faces lit up and they started gurgling at the sight of their huge furry presents.

'But I'm not being christened,' Bonny said, as she hugged the bear now sitting on the floor. She stood possessively beside it, running her fingers over the monstrous pearls.

'It's a get-well present from Aunty Sara and me.'
'You shouldn't have,' Stu and Dana said in unison.
'I'm glad they did!' Bonny said.

The morning went well. Dana's parents arrived at the same time as Stu's mother and father. The church service was at one o'clock and afterwards everyone came back to the house. Adrian had offered to stay behind to put out the food and see to any last-minute preparations. Dana had organised more than enough food and Stu had seen to the alcohol, so there was no shortage in that department.

'Didn't the boys behave beautifully for the minister?' Sara said, as she offered the plate of sandwiches to Dana's parents. 'Not even a whimper.'

'It was wonderful. I had tears in my eyes the moment I saw Bonny walk into the church and they stayed with me for the entire service.'

'You're too sentimental,' her husband told her. 'I knew our Bonny would pull through. She's a fighter, that's what she is.'

Sara smiled and moved on around the room with the sandwiches and then with the dips and other finger food. Finally, she carried platters of cakes and before too long it was coffee. At around five o'clock the guests started to leave.

Henry and Phillip were fast asleep, unaware of all the fuss for them. Two huge bears sat in the corner of the room, watching over them.

'I almost forgot,' Sara said, carrying a present into the room. 'Tom and I wanted the boys to have something to keep for when they are older.'

Dana unwrapped the parcel with its layers of noisy tissue paper. She gasped. 'They're absolutely beautiful.' Lying in her lap were the two ornate silver picture

frames. The family members all gathered around to admire them while Sara started to clean up.

It was about nine o'clock when the mess was under
control. They had all picked on the delicious leftovers
and were quite full.

'I hate to ruin a nice evening,' Tom said, as he
climbed to his feet from the comfortable chair by the
pot-belly stove, 'but I'm afraid Sara and I have to head
back to Melbourne.'

Tom didn't want to risk anything happening and he
was afraid one more night together might cause him to
cross the line. He knew Sara had covered him during
the night. There had been no need to open his eyes. The
warmth in her touch had radiated through his body as
she'd pulled the covers gently over him.

It had taken every ounce of his strength not to reach
up and pull her into his arms and make love to her. He
didn't trust himself. He needed to head back to Melbourne where the boundaries were more defined. Being
here with old friends made it even more difficult to remember that he and Sara would soon be divorced.

It would be unfair to both of them, he reasoned, for
anything to happen. Sara would be leaving for Texas
soon and he would once again be alone with his work.

Sara had made an appointment to see the local general
practitioner the next day after work, so she didn't mind
heading back early. The tiredness wasn't subsiding so
she thought it would be great to have some tests to confirm whether her anaemia had returned.

The next day's patients were straightforward consultations and she left on time to get through the Melbourne peak-hour traffic to the doctor's rooms. She felt

great after the two days away but still thought it was prudent to have bloodwork done to rule out anything more serious.

The doctor was a lovely older man and after Sara explained her symptoms he agreed they should do a routine blood test as well as checking her blood pressure and vitals.

'Mrs…I mean, Dr Fielding,' he began, as he undid the blood-pressure sleeve on her arm and folded it back into the pouch on his desk. 'Just run by me your symptoms again.'

'Tired, mostly, and a better appetite than usual. I was up one night recently eating at two in the morning.'

'This may seem obvious but you couldn't by any chance be pregnant could you?'

Pregnant? Sara froze. Of course not. She'd only had sex once in the last eighteen months—the night she'd spent with Tom just over six weeks ago—but they'd been careful.

'Definitely not.'

The doctor eyed her with some degree of doubt. 'So you've not had sex recently?'

'Yes, once more than six weeks ago, in fact, almost seven now, but it was safe, we took precautions. I can't be pregnant.'

'My dear, you're a medical specialist. You know as well as I do that the only one hundred per cent safe sex is no sex.'

Sara was incensed by what he'd said. But it wasn't his tone, it was the fact she knew he was speaking the truth.

Could she actually be pregnant? No, it's not possible, she told herself.

'But there's been no nausea. Nothing. I'm eating well. I think it's more likely my haemoglobin has dropped a little. I've had it happen in the past.'

'Well, I will definitely test for that,' he replied as he completed the pathology request form. 'Is your period late?'

'Maybe a couple of weeks but that's not unusual, I'm not always regular when I'm under stress. I'm moving to live in the US and it's been quite a busy time. As I said, my only complaint is being tired,' Sara said matter-of-factly, not completely sure of who she was trying to convince.

'Not everyone suffers from nausea. Some women go through the entire pregnancy without ever feeling sick, some only feel tired and have an increased appetite, so what if we go ahead and do a simple urine test to rule out pregnancy anyway?'

Sara was unimpressed with the idea. Part of her was suddenly very scared of the result. Part of her already knew the answer. But reluctantly she agreed.

He handed her a specimen jar and walked her to the door. 'The bathroom is the second on the left. Take your time.'

Sara sighed as she walked to the bathroom at the end of the corridor. It was the most nerve-racking walk she had made in her life. Her head was spinning as she thought back to that night. She knew they'd been careful, there had been wrappers on the floor to prove it. She couldn't be pregnant. *Could she?*

Sara already knew the answer. Of course she could. She and Tom made love and now she was taking a pregnancy test.

Sara returned to the consulting room with the sample. The doctor inserted the indicator strip into the jar and they both watched the strip.

It changed colour. It was very clearly blue. There was no doubting it.

Sara's head collapsed into her hands. 'How could this happen?'

The doctor turned and looked in earnest at Sara. 'A baby is not the end of the world, you know, but to make doubly sure I will request the qualitative HCG blood pregnancy test.'

Sara knew that was merely a formality. The strip result was very clear and this type of test was close to ninety-seven per cent accurate.

She was pregnant with Tom's baby.

'We have a pathology unit on hand in the practice to take your blood sample so you can have it done now and the result will come back tomorrow, but as you are already ten days late and with this positive urine analysis I think we can be quite positive that you are indeed pregnant. Although by your reaction I assume this is not something you are going to celebrate,' the doctor said with a sombre tone in his voice. 'There are options. You don't have to proceed with the pregnancy.'

Sara shook her head. 'No,' she answered. 'It's not how I had planned for it to happen but I will be having this baby.' She already loved her unborn child. It had been instantaneous. She loved the child because she loved its father. She knew that, no matter what happened, no matter how Tom reacted to this child, to his child, she would love it for ever and completely.

After the blood test was done, Sara left the consulting rooms in shock. Her heart was beating so fast she could barely breathe. *A baby?* It was a dream come true and terrifying at the same time.

How would she tell Tom? She knew he would be as shocked as her but, unlike her, he wouldn't find any joy in the news at all. Her heart began to beat a little faster and her stomach churned low with anticipation and dread. She knew she needed to tell him. She owed it to him. She paused her racing thoughts and realised it was perhaps not to him but more to the memory of what they had shared. And to finally make a stand. To stop hiding things from each other, no matter the consequences, and no matter what the state of their relationship. It might not be welcome news but he needed to be told the truth.

She also knew she needed time to adjust to the news. A few hours, a day, whatever it took to absorb the enormity of her situation. Her life would never be the same again. And Tom's life would be changed for ever when she told him. Wish as she might for Tom to be overjoyed at her news, there was really no question mark hanging over his reaction. He had made it clear he did not want a child under any circumstances, ever. He was adamant that he would never change his mind.

Sara was so confused. Her thoughts about the pregnancy, her new job in the US and, of course, Tom threatened to overwhelm her on the short trip home. There was so much to consider. Not just her feelings or Tom's, but this child had rights too. The right to know his or her father. Sara pulled into the driveway with her heart still racing.

Her mind was spinning with clashing thoughts as she climbed from the car. She suddenly felt quite faint.

'Sara, wake up,' Tom urged as he stroked her face with a damp hand towel.

Sara's eyes flickered open. She realised she was in her bed.

'What happened?' she asked.

'You tell me. I was inside and heard a thud and went outside to find you collapsed beside the car,' he told her, with his voice filled with concern. 'Are you okay now?' He carefully placed the hand towel on her forehead.

Sara stared at Tom in silence. The reason she'd fainted was not something she intended to share with Tom right now. She needed a little more time. It would only complicate his life and nothing positive would come from it, so she needed to plan how to break the news. She needed to let him know she would be okay no matter what his decision was. Sara knew he would see her pregnancy in a very different light from her.

She reached up for the hand towel, pulled it from her forehead and dropped it onto the bed as she sat up.

'I'm fine,' she replied. 'I did a lot of running around and probably didn't drink enough water. You know me, I have the world's lowest blood pressure on the best of days.'

Tom didn't know what to think but accepted her explanation. 'I'll get you a glass of water.'

'How did I get in here?' she called out. 'I thought you said I passed out by the car.'

Tom reappeared with tall glass of water. 'I carried you inside.' His face was completely serious as he handed her the water to drink. 'You should have a check-up, what with being so tired and now this. You need to get to the bottom of it. I appreciate you've always had low blood pressure, you function on a level that would have most people lying flat out in bed, but please get yourself looked at.'

Sara could see that the concern on his face and in his voice was genuine. But the real reason for her fainting would be too much for Tom to handle so abruptly. They had only just sorted through their complicated past and finally established a relationship free from blame or resentment. An announcement of her pregnancy, she suspected, would probably create both.

She would tell him about the baby. But now definitely wasn't the time.

Sara worked at the practice for the next two days, keeping busy and keeping her distance from Tom. It wasn't hard as his workload had increased steadily with the new student intake.

Sara lay in bed that night thinking about what could have been and the reality of what the pregnancy would mean in her life. She made plans in her mind. She would travel to Paris before she returned to Adelaide to live. When she returned, she would buy a small place in the eastern suburbs of Adelaide to be near to her family. She would work in the hospital or private practice and when she began to show she could say the baby was a result of a holiday romance. A fling with a handsome medico she'd met abroad.

Well, part of it was true at least. Tom was a handsome medico and they had shared a fling. It just hadn't happened in Paris this time.

It was about eight o'clock on Friday night when Sara realised she didn't have any milk. She was still exhausted and didn't want to drive to the grocery store so she thought she would ask Tom if she could borrow some. Warm milk before bed helped her to sleep through the night. She looked out into the drive but there was no sign of his car. Remembering the door between the houses, she found the key in the drawer and unlocked it from her side. She could replace the milk tomorrow.

Sara opened the door and stepped inside Tom's house, reaching for the light switch as she did so.

Immediately, she froze, her gaze falling upon all their old possessions. Everything they'd lived amongst as a married couple. Everything she'd assumed he'd discarded.

The chintz sofa and two matching armchairs. The Persian rug, another honeymoon purchase. The oval card table that was the centrepiece of his living room, an extravagant purchase that had been too lovely to leave in the antique shop in Ballarat on a weekend they'd spent in the country. Sara spun round in shock, her heart racing as she struggled to take in the whole room. Above the fireplace was the beautifully framed triptych print that Stu and Dana had given them for a wedding present, *The Pioneer* by Frederick McCubbin.

Sara roamed dumbfounded through the rest of the house and she found that nothing was missing. When her emotions got the better of her she collapsed into the soft depths of one of the armchairs. She picked up a small hand-painted vase from the tray mobile. Tears blurred her vision as she studied the delicate piece in her hand.

Never in her wildest dreams had she imagined that Tom would be so sentimental.

Being in the house was like stepping back in time.

Sara hadn't taken her belongings when she'd left. She'd thought it would have been too hard to live with pieces of furniture or ornaments that she and Tom had picked out together. Seeing it all now, she knew she had been right. The tears that had pricked at her eyes now flowed freely. It was a strange combination of sadness and regret. And unexpectedly a quiet happiness at being alone with the precious pieces that meant so very much to her and Tom. But, then, she realised, she wasn't alone. She was carrying their child.

Tom was mortified when he unlocked the door and found Sara sitting in the armchair, her head on her hand, as he walked inside.

Embarrassment fuelled his defence. 'What are you doing here?'

Sara quickly wiped her eyes on her sleeve in an attempt to hide her tears. 'I just wanted to borrow some milk.' Her voice was shaky as she felt swept back to the life they had once shared.

'I'm sorry, I didn't mean to upset you.'

After that neither said anything for a few moments.

Tom was trying not to see the sadness in Sara's eyes. He knew she would feel emotional being surrounded by all their past possessions. He had never expected her to see the house.

Sara just sat staring at Tom. There was so much she wanted to tell him, but so much she couldn't.

'Sara…' He broke off for a moment and tried to summon his thoughts. 'I haven't been living with all of this,' he said, gesturing to the furniture.

Her expression was puzzled as he spoke because she didn't understand.

He settled himself into the armchair opposite her and ran his hands nervously over the huge padded armrests. 'I don't live here. This is my spare place. This is where I store everything. For the last three years I've been living the other side, where you are now.'

Sara was even more confused. 'Then why didn't you say so earlier? Why didn't you let me move in here?'

'I felt embarrassed,' he admitted. 'I'd held onto all of this and you'd moved on. I thought you might think it peculiar of me to have kept everything, even after we were over. You didn't want anything when you left and for some strange reason I couldn't part with it.'

Sara sighed as she gently stroked the arms of the chair and then surveyed the room again.

'If you've changed your mind and want anything, please take it. It's yours to have, anything at all,' Tom said, interrupting her thoughts.

Sara bit her lip as she stopped herself from telling him that all she wanted in that room was him. Not furniture, or paintings or ornaments. Tom Fielding, the man, was all she ever wanted.

Tom wasn't sure how Sara felt. He knew she had plans he couldn't change but he hoped that for a while at least they could still keep in touch. He loved every minute he spent with her. That would never change. And until she met someone else, perhaps they could share more time together.

'I was thinking,' he began, as the awkwardness subsided. 'Maybe I could visit you in Texas over Christmas. That is, if you're not flying back to be with your family. But if you're over in a new country and wanting some company, I could check out America for a week or so. I'd have to renew my passport, but if you'd like to spend Christmas with me—'

'Stop it,' she cried out. 'Just stop.'

Sara felt her mind whirling very fast. The thought of Tom visiting and finding her six or seven months pregnant was too much to deal with. The room, Tom, the baby, it was all crashing in around her.

'You can't visit me.'

'Okay, okay,' he replied, in shock at her terse response. 'I just thought…'

Sara couldn't hold it in any longer. She hadn't wanted

to tell him but everything came rushing out, and she found herself close to tears.

'You can't come over because I won't be in Texas at Christmas or ever. I'm not going there any more. I'm going back to Adelaide to be with my family. I'm moving home to live, permanently.'

Tom looked confused and worried. 'Are they all right? Is there something I should know?'

'Yes, Tom, there is something you should know...' Sara paused for a moment. Her heart was pounding, her stomach tightening by the second. Her world was suddenly and completely out of control as the words rushed from her lips. 'I'm pregnant, Tom. I'm having your baby.'

Tom slumped back in stunned silence. He had never thought he would hear those words from Sara. He had never thought he would hear those words from any woman. He had resigned himself to never being a father. His whole world had just changed in an instant. He was shocked to the core. Sara was having a baby. His baby. She was carrying their child. And he knew it would be a beautiful child if it was anything like Sara.

He wanted to rush over and pull her into his arms and kiss her and tell her it was the most wonderful news. But he couldn't. He had to fight his natural instinct, to resist the strongest desire to be with the mother of his child and to protect and love her. He couldn't do either. It wasn't wonderful news. Not to him.

'Aren't you going to say anything?' she asked, not totally surprised by his silence.

He walked over to the window and pulled back the curtains. He was shaking inside. From the moment he'd seen Sara in the restaurant that fateful night, he'd wanted to be with her more than anything he had ever wanted. And now, knowing she was having his baby, he wanted that even more. But he couldn't.

He wouldn't allow himself to share that joy, knowing Heath would never feel the same happiness. Now it wasn't just Sara he had to turn away from, he had to turn away from two people he loved more than life itself. And he hated it that he could never know his own child. They would never meet.

The street was lit by the amber lights and it gave a strange hue to the living room. Sara could see his hand clenching the curtain but still he said nothing.

'Tom, I'm not asking anything from you,' she said honestly, and in not much more than a whisper. 'I know how you feel and I can do this alone. You asked if there was something you should know. Well, there is and this is it. We're going to be parents but I can do it alone. I will move back to Adelaide and get a place near my family. I'll be fine. You don't have to have any part in our child's life, unless you want to.' She rested her hands protectively across her stomach.

He turned to look at her in silence. She was even more beautiful. Perhaps because she was pregnant, perhaps because it was just because he knew she was carrying *his* child.

Tom fought the urge to pull her to him. To wrap his arms around her and tell her that he would protect her for ever. To tell her that he would take care of her, and their baby. But he looked across at the woman who would hold his heart for ever and he knew it would go against everything he believed in. He needed to take responsibility for what he had done to his brother. That would never go away. It was the price he had to pay. And now it was the price they all had to pay. It wasn't fair. Sara and the baby were innocent of any wrongdoing.

His silence was making her feel more uncomfortable by the minute.

Finally he opened up. His soul was being ripped apart but his answer was unwavering. He was steeling himself to push her away. 'You know how I feel about having a child. I explained everything the other night, I opened up about Heath, about the accident, about everything, and you never said a word? Why not then? Why now? Why here in this room?'

Sara was taken aback by the barrage of questions. 'Because I didn't know.'

'And you're absolutely sure you're pregnant?'

'The HCG blood pregnancy test results came back positive three days ago.'

'And you waited this long to tell me?' he asked with confusion in his eyes. 'Three days and you said nothing. There were plenty of opportunities to let me know, Sara. What's different now?'

'Nothing, absolutely nothing. In fact, I wish I hadn't told you at all!'

Sara ran from his house into her bedroom, slamming the adjoining door shut and locking it behind her.

Tom stood in stunned silence. Alone. He was angry. So very angry with himself. For what he was doing to Sara. For the accident with Heath all those years ago. And now for being careless and allowing Sara to fall pregnant. For putting her in the position of having a child that he would never raise.

He knocked on her door.

'We need to talk about this properly. I can't talk to you from the other side of a door.'

He could hear the sound of muffled crying.

'Sara, we can work it out. I will cover the costs of raising the child, I will help in whatever way I can but

I can't live with you and raise this child with you. I just can't be the child's father.'

Sara lay there, listening to the sound of Tom walking away. An overwhelming feeling of sadness engulfed her. One fateful night, when serendipity had brought them together, was now tearing them apart.

The next morning, without saying another word to Sara, Tom left for work early. He needed to keep his distance until Sara left. It was for the best.

He loved Sara with all of his heart. His feelings for her were not in question. But he also knew he wanted more than anything to be the man she needed. To be the father of her child. Not just in name, or financial assistance, but to be the one holding her hand and wiping her brow when their child came into the world. The one to get up in the night and rock their restless baby back to sleep. To take him or her to their first day at school, to sport, to music lessons and everything that Sara had talked about. But he couldn't.

He knew that Sara would be a good mother. And he would ensure the child was provided for financially. The best school, the best medical care if it was needed, the best of everything. But nothing more. He could not be the father she wanted him to be.

He knew he had to let her go. In a few days she would be on a plane and starting a new life with their child. Without him.

CHAPTER TWELVE

SARA DID NOT see or hear from Tom over the next two days. They had managed to avoid each other. She ate her dinner alone. She was leaving on an early evening flight the next day and this was the last night she would be in the house. Sara thought back to the times they had spent together, the tears and passion, the shared memories and professional admiration. The love. She had enjoyed being back in Tom's life, even though it had been only for a little while.

Tom's attitude was noble but cold. Telling her that he would take care of her financially. She didn't want any money from him. She would take care of herself and the baby very well on her own. Financial assistance wasn't what she needed.

But his skewed sense of responsibility wouldn't allow him to be a part of his child's life. The child they had created. The child she would carry for the next eight months. She was pregnant by the man she had loved for so very long and it should have been the happiest time in her life, but instead she was planning her life as a single mother.

But she didn't have time to throw a pity party for herself. She had to move on. And this time for good. No looking back. It would be months before she started to show. She could work until she was six months or even longer. She couldn't tell Marjorie about the pregnancy. She didn't want to explain any of it. She had one more day to work and then she'd be gone. One day of surgery. She had a short morning list and nothing scheduled for the afternoon. The theatre staff were clearly worried when she entered the scrub room.

'Is he operating with you?' the younger of the nurses asked, with wide eyes.

'Do you mean the other Dr Fielding?'

The girl nodded.

Sara shook her head.

The whole operating team gave a sigh of relief and started chatting happily.

'He was like a bull with a sore backside yesterday,' the senior nurse whispered into her ear, as she held the surgical gloves for Sara to slide her hands into. 'We've never seen him like this. No one wants to work with him.'

Sara looked over her shoulder but there was no sign of the man. She knew in her heart that there wouldn't be. Tom didn't want to see her again, let alone work with her.

'Hi,' came a friendly voice. 'Guess what? I get to assist you today. If that's all right with you? I mean, if you'd rather someone—'

Sara didn't have to turn round to know that Nigel was her assisting intern. 'Welcome to the team, Nigel,' she said, as they entered the theatre. For Sara it would be the last time.

The first patient on the list had impacted wisdom teeth. Confident her patient was under the effects of the anaesthetic, Sara began the routine procedure to remove the offending teeth and to suture and pack the sockets. Nigel assisted and took direction well. Sara considered him a competent young surgeon but working with Nigel couldn't come close to being in the surgery with Tom. She knew the comparison was unfair.

Tom had years of experience and Nigel was just beginning his medical career. But it was the way they knew each other's next move. The way Tom's skilled hands would work alongside hers as if their fingers were conversing. As if they shared a single thought. She pulled her gloves and cap free as she took a break following the first patient, just sitting quietly for a few moments. She felt tired but knew after the first trimester the fatigue would be more than likely to pass.

The morning went by without any problems. The cases were all straightforward and Sara was pleased with each and every result. Nigel was chirpy and eager to learn from her. They had finished the last by twelve and after changing into her street clothes and checking her patients in the high-dependency wards she said goodbye to the staff and was gone by one-thirty, heading home to collect her bags and catch her early evening flight in just over four hours' time.

With tears threatening to fall, Sara locked the front door to her home. Her eyes dropped to the crystal slipper in her trembling hand. With one foot nervously placed in front of the other, she took slow steps to his front door. Her chin quivered as she put the slipper and keys in a white envelope and laid it beside his doormat.

With knees bent, she broke down and slumped in tears at his door.

The sound of the taxi's horn brought her to her senses. She wiped her eyes and slipped on her dark sunglasses. The sky was clear blue and, although it was cold, it was bright enough to warrant this disguise.

Sara had planned one stop before she left. She thought she owed Marjorie a goodbye and a thank you.

'I'll miss you,' Marjorie told her. 'Are you sure we can't change your mind about staying?'

Sara had managed to bring her breathing to a steady pace and control her emotions. She wanted to keep it that way.

'No. I'm afraid not. You see, I've made plans to see Paris and then set up a practice back in Adelaide. I miss my family and I think it's the right time to be with them.'

'I suppose Melbourne can't compete with the sights and sounds of Paris,' the woman conceded. 'When do you leave?'

'The plane leaves in just over four hours so I must go—'

'Have a good flight.' Tom's husky voice cut in.

Sara spun round to find him standing very close to her. She wanted to reach out and hold him, to touch his face and feel his arms around her. But he kept a distance between them and she did the same.

'I went home and found you'd left so I thought I'd come in and tidy up.' He took a step back as she turned and she knew better than to close the even bigger space he had created.

With tears moistening her cheeks, she looked across at the man she loved. Marjorie left them alone and bus-ied herself in her office, closing the door behind her to give them privacy to say goodbye.

'I hope I've left everything in order.'

'I'm sure you have.' He said nothing about the tears, which he couldn't have missed.

'Take care, Tom.'

'You too, Sara, and if you need anything just call.' Tom wanted to hold her but he knew that it would break him. He would make a promise he couldn't keep, just so she would stay a little while longer. That would be selfish. 'I'll stay in touch and when the time comes I will provide you with whatever you need or want. I promise you.'

'I'll be fine,' she reassured him. But she wouldn't turn to face him. She didn't want to look into his deep grey eyes. It was over. Finally over. He clearly had no problem with her leaving.

She had no idea what she would be doing in a month. Except trying to start a life somewhere without him.

'Sara, you will never want for anything.'

Except for a husband and a father, she thought as she walked away.

Squaring her shoulders the way she had when she'd first arrived, Sara made her way to the door. She knew Tom was watching her. She willed him to chase after her and ask her to stay.

He didn't.

He let her go.

Tom stood by the window of his office, thinking about nothing but Sara. He had tried to distract himself with paperwork. It hadn't worked. So he'd walked to the window where he had been standing staring at the same static view for the best part of an hour.

It was worse, much worse, he decided, losing Sara a second time. And now he wasn't just losing Sara. He was losing much more.

Sara would be raising a child who was a part of

him. It tore at his heart that he wouldn't be there with them both.

Tom paced in front of the office window. He didn't want to think about Sara raising the child alone. He wanted to be with her. To hold her and their child every day for the rest of his life. He felt an aching regret for all he had said, and all he hadn't. How he had just let her leave. He couldn't live without her. But his brother weighed heavily on his mind too. He felt trapped.

Standing there alone in his office, Tom suddenly realised he couldn't do it. His heart was breaking. She deserved so much more. She deserved to be loved.

He had to stop her.

He couldn't and wouldn't let her go. Not this time.

He had to tell his brother. He had to face those demons from his past and apologise for the hurt he had inflicted. He had to admit his responsibility but tell Heath that now, after all these years, he had another responsibility that he would not walk away from. A far greater responsibility.

Tom finally realised that nothing he did would reverse the result of their actions as teenagers. Sara was right. He would let Heath know he was about to become an uncle and accept whatever Heath wanted to say, good or bad. He couldn't sacrifice Sara and the baby for the sake of a few brief moments that had gone terribly wrong so many years ago. Sara had told him she wouldn't make any more sacrifices, and he wouldn't let her.

He had too much to lose by letting Sara leave again. He wouldn't do it. Not today or ever. He would tell Heath how very sorry he was about what had happened but that he refused to lose the love of his life because of his own unwillingness to put the past behind him.

Tom reached for the phone. He had to do it for his child, and for his wife. He was hurting the woman he loved. And he would hurt the child she was carrying if he didn't stop it now.

With trepidation he dialled the number in San Francisco. He knew it was late at night but he couldn't wait for a better time. There would never be a better time than now.

'Hello,' came Heath's voice down the line.

'Hi, brother, it's Tom.'

'Since I don't have any other brothers I'd guessed that one, old man,' Heath responded in a light-hearted tone. 'What can I do for you? Must be urgent to be calling at this hour.'

Tom didn't know where to start. His brother's joviality unnerved him further. He knew he was going to be delivering a blow and he wasn't sure how to begin. It was the hardest call he had ever made. The culmination of years of guilt and blame. Tom felt his chest tighten. He was about to tell a man who had been robbed of the chance of ever being a father that he was going to have a child with a woman he had always loved and would love for ever. A woman he could not let go. Tom's throat went dry before he spoke.

'Sara's pregnant.'

There was silence on the phone. Tom felt a cold sweat rush over him.

'God, that's got to hurt. I know you still love her, so who's the lucky guy?' Heath said. 'Do you want me to help you take him out?'

'No, you don't need to take anyone out. It's me. I'm the father.'

There was silence again. Tom felt his stomach knot. He wasn't sure what reaction would follow.

'Awesome news. So you two are back together, then, I assume. I'm happy for you both. Congratulations!' Heath answered with elation colouring his sleepy voice. 'Sorry, Tom, I had to leave the bedroom. I'm not alone. Tory's here and I didn't want to wake her.'

Tom was surprised. Not that Heath had a woman there but that he'd never mentioned in previous calls that he was seeing anyone.

'It was one of those rare nights Tory's parents take the children so we get an uninterrupted night together and a lie-in tomorrow morning. That's a hint...don't call again unless it's an emergency.'

'Tory?'

'I'm sure I've mentioned her. We've been seeing each other for almost five months now.' Heath dropped his voice to not much more than a whisper. 'I'm going to ask her to marry me.'

Tom was stunned into silence. Happy for his brother but stunned into a mute.

'I'm the luckiest guy in the world!'

'I'm happy for you,' Tom began. 'But I never thought of you as lucky. Particularly after the accident...that I caused.'

'Tom, don't tell me you're not still harping on about that? For God's sake, man, that wasn't your fault. It was me, a bike and an asphalt BMX run.'

'I know what you're saying but I caused it.'

Heath's voice became a little louder. 'You can stop taking credit right here and now. I had, and still have, the power to exercise free will. I used it that day and I continue to use it every day. I chose a risky trick and it went wrong, but...' he paused '...that was my fault, with maybe some assistance from the universe. Just all-round bad timing.'

Tom felt the tightening in his chest loosen a little. 'But when the IVF didn't work...'

'And now you think you're to blame for my marriage breakdown?'

Tom nodded into the phone.

'You have been thinking way too much, little brother. I can't believe you've been stewing over all this. The marriage broke down because we were unhappy, unsuited and unhappy. We were trying to have a baby as a solution to a marriage with a million flaws. We stupidly thought a baby would be the glue to hold us together. That would have been the biggest mistake. I am so grateful it never happened. It would have been the child who paid the price in the end, living with two unhappy parents.'

Tom had had no idea. This was not what he'd expected to hear.

'And then I met Tory. The most wonderful woman in the world. Her husband was a marine. He was killed on a tour of duty in Iraq about three years ago. She's the best mother and just the most caring soul I could ever meet. And she doesn't want any more children. She had four. And it's a bonus that I don't have to have the vasectomy that she was going to ask me to undergo, until I broke the news about my fertility issues.'

Tom was elated beyond belief. Knowing his brother was in a great place made his decision so much simpler. They were both in love with wonderful women.

'As much as I would love to chat, it's after midnight here so I am going to say goodnight now and call you tomorrow. We rarely get a night to ourselves so I'm not about to spend it on you,' he laughed. 'Please say big congrats to Sara and can't wait for you guys to meet Tory and the girls. I did tell you I'm going to be the stepfather of four daughters, didn't I? I'm going to need a shotgun to keep the boys away if they are as gorgeous as their mum.'

With that he hung up, leaving Tom looking at the phone and wondering why he had wasted all this time.

He wasn't about to waste one minute more.

'I've been such a fool. An idiot of grand proportions,' he said to Marjorie as he rushed into the office and grabbed his car keys. 'You don't happen to know Sara's flight details, do you?'

'You're in luck. I overheard her call to the travel agent the other day and, being the busybody I am, I jotted it down,' she answered with a huge smile, as she pulled a scrap of paper from her pocket. 'It's flight three-five-two, gate seven, and hurry.'

He leant over, grabbed the paper and kissed her forehead on the way. 'Thank God you're a busybody.'

'Your ticket or booking confirmation, please, and your passport, Dr Fielding.'

Sara took a deep breath and reached for both from her carry-on luggage. Her travel agent had secured her a first-class ticket to Paris. *The city of love?* Sara knew that wouldn't be the case this time but it would fit her story perfectly. A fling that had resulted in a baby. Perhaps she would say her lover was a diplomat and he'd been forced to return to his homeland; or a politician; or...or... Sara couldn't think properly.

She would make up a story that wouldn't cause a scandal or embarrass her child. Also one that wouldn't have her child hurting for a father who didn't want to be in their lives. She never wanted her child to know that Tom had let her go. He'd let the two of them leave his life. No child deserved to think they weren't wanted and loved.

Sara rubbed her temples as she waited for her boarding pass to be issued. There was so much to plan and consider.

Tom raced through the traffic, rechecking his watch every few minutes, hoping that he would make it before Sara boarded the plane.

'Last call for passengers on Qantas flight three-five-two for Paris. Now boarding at gate seven.' The voice echoed across the international airport lounge. It was Sara's flight. This was it. For the last two hours she had sat alone in the terminal, thinking about the last six weeks. It was supposed to be a quick trip to the embassy, then a month taking care of Stu's practice. How was she supposed to know that she was already pregnant with Tom's baby when she'd arrived?

Sadness wasn't consuming her any more. The ache in her heart was lessening. She had a new life to cherish and she was in love with the baby she was carrying. She felt blessed to be having a child by the man she loved, even if he wasn't going to be a part of their lives.

Although it wasn't sadness she felt for herself—she felt sorry for Tom. He would never have any part in the life of the child she was carrying. None. He would miss out on so much joy. And love.

But she couldn't spend her life thinking about Tom Fielding. Not even another day. She had to accept what had happened and pretend that she didn't love Tom with all her heart. Until it was true. Until she had no feelings for him. She had to move on and raise their child.

There was no turning back. She knew it would be a

very long time before she returned to Melbourne. She would visit Stu and Dana one day in the future but it would take time. Time to heal the wounds. Time to build a new life…with her child.

Her head down, she made her way slowly to the departure gate. Her boarding pass was in her hand, although her heart was still nowhere to be found.

'Sara,' a familiar voice called out across the departure lounge. 'Stop, don't get on the plane!'

Sara swung her head round but there was only a sea of unfamiliar faces. No one she recognised…until he appeared. Jostling his tall frame though the throng of people. It was Tom. Desperation in his eyes, he made his way over and pulled her into his strong arms

'I'm so sorry,' he whispered. 'I love you and I was stupid for so long. But not stupid enough to let you go again.'

Sara was dazed. She had no more tears left.

'I want you and our child more than you can ever know. I've been a fool.'

He kissed her mouth and pulled her closer still.

'There's so much I need to tell you, but the most important thing is to ask you for forgiveness for the pain I have put you through. I have been so caught up in doing what I thought was right I've made even bigger mistakes. In trying to right an injustice to Heath, I committed an even greater injustice to you. I was a fool of the biggest kind.'

Suddenly Sara pulled herself free from his arms and stepped back away from him. She closed her eyes for a moment to try and gain some composure. 'Am I dreaming this? What are you doing, Tom? You chase me down and a minute before I fly away you tell me that you want me and our baby. Why? What's changed?'

'Me,' he said, with the conviction of man who knew where he wanted and needed to be. 'I've changed, Sara. I know I was stupid, putting principles before us. Before our happiness and the happiness of our child. I said that I needed to take responsibility for something that happened decades ago but I was letting you leave to bring up our child alone. That's not taking responsibility.

'What I did as a kid was reckless but to let you walk away, to never hold my child and tell him or her that they were wanted and loved would be far more irresponsible. I want you, Sara, I've always wanted you. And I want this baby, our baby, with all my heart.'

She looked at Tom and wanted so much to believe him but she didn't trust her heart. It had led her down the wrong path before.

'I've been living with a misplaced sense of guilt, and hurting you in the process. I was turning my back on the woman I love. I was driving you away. Please forgive me.'

She sat motionless for a minute, thinking about everything he had said, before she finally reached her hand across to his and nodded.

Sara looked into the eyes of the man she loved and knew he was telling her the truth. He kissed her again, and again and again, and held her in his arms for the longest time. He was happier than he had ever thought possible.

Finally he picked up her carry-on luggage and holding her hand tightly in his own, they walked away from the departure gate.

Sara stopped suddenly again. 'How did you get here, into the international terminal, without a ticket?'

Tom held up a boarding pass. 'I organised a ticket to Paris on my way here. I thought it would give me twenty-something hours to convince you to come home with me.'

Sara kissed him with tears streaming down her face.

Tom slipped her crystal keyring into her palm and closed her trembling fingers around them.

'Just promise me, Cinders, that you'll never leave me again.'

'Cinders?' she said, with eyes still bright from her tears. 'You knew about the keyring?'

'I've always known, Sara. It was another reason why I loved you. But I always felt I let my side of your crazy fairy-tale down.'

'You could never let me down,' she cried. 'Unless you let me go.' She met his kisses and melted into his arms.

'Then I promise you, Sara Fielding, you will never be let down again.'

* * * * *

HEART SURGEON
TO SINGLE DAD

JANICE LYNN

In loving memory of my papa, Floyd Green.

CHAPTER ONE

"I'M A DOCTOR, you know." No, the flight attendant didn't know, but Natalie Sterling was determined to make it on time to her presentation.

She'd heard of airlines overbooking flights, but it had never affected her. Until now.

"A pediatric heart surgeon," she added, hoping to gain empathy. Natalie couldn't recall having pulled that card before, but she wasn't one to no-show a speaking commitment if she could help it. "Bumping me to a later flight doesn't work."

The stewardess shook her head. "There's nothing I can do. It was in the agreement when you purchased your ticket that if the plane is overbooked you would have to take a later flight."

Taking a deep breath, Natalie stared at the pretty thirty-something blonde in her crisp uniform. It wasn't the woman's fault.

"It's urgent I go on this flight." She heard the almost pleading tone, but was beyond caring. She needed to get to Miami this afternoon.

"We're sorry for any inconvenience, but you're going to have to exit the plane." The forced smile on the attendant's face warned that further argument was futile and the woman was losing her patience.

If only Natalie could have kept her flight the evening

before, instead of having to delay her departure. Still, she'd been needed for an emergency surgery, and her patients came first. Always.

"What if I refuse to give up my seat?"

The attendant's obligatory smile disappeared. "I would be forced to call Security." Her tone warned Natalie would regret such a decision. "They would escort you off the plane. Are you refusing?"

Visions of herself being dragged off the plane, kicking and screaming that they had the wrong person, had Natalie cringing. Yeah, that splattered all over the news wouldn't impress Memphis Children's Hospital's board.

Feeling much like she was being punished for a crime she hadn't committed, Natalie closed her laptop, unclasped her seatbelt and pulled her case out from under the seat in front of her. "I'm not refusing, I just wondered if it was an option."

"It's not," she was assured, the stewardess's eyes still narrowed.

"Fine." Not really, but apparently she had no choice. "But you have to get me to Miami this afternoon."

She gathered her things and pulled her carry-on bag back out from the overhead compartment.

Seeing that Natalie wasn't going to give them any further trouble, the flight attendant's obligatory smile returned. "Yes, ma'am. We'll do all we can to get you to your destination as quickly as possible."

As she was passing through the first-class section, a man glanced up from his phone. He turned his head toward her about the time she registered who he was, and Natalie's gaze collided with his.

Her breath caught. Just as it had done when their gazes had met in the airport waiting area.

No matter how she'd tried, she hadn't been able to keep from glancing his way and they'd made eye contact several times. She'd felt an instant attraction, had thought that if her best friends were there they'd have pushed her to cross the room and strike up a conversation because they thought she needed a vacation fling. Natalie being Natalie, she hadn't done anything more than fight to keep her focus on her upcoming presentation rather than on the intriguingly handsome man.

She bet *he* never got bumped from his flight.

No one would dare.

There was something dark and dangerous in those ice-blue eyes. Maybe it was his inky black hair and tan skin that contrasted so dramatically with those frosty blues that gave him such a startlingly handsome look, like he belonged in some paranormal movie where he'd shape-shift into a sexy mythical being who preyed on unsuspecting women who were powerless to resist his allure.

Natalie felt his pull, felt his power, and a sexual intensity flashed through her mind. No doubt, he'd have looked into the flight attendant's eyes and told her to go pick someone else and she'd have answered, Yes, sir, and can I get you anything else with that?

Just like Jonathan.

Bleh. She wasn't going to think about her boyfriend.

Ex-boyfriend.

The lying, cheating scumbag.

Literally.

Casting one last look at Mr. Dark and Dangerous, who was watching her with the same expression with which one might watch an accident unfold, probably wondering if she was going to cause a ruckus and delay his flight, she sighed. Not a good start to her little mini-vacation wrapped up in teaching a workshop at a medical conference. As long as she got to Miami in time to give her presentation, everything would be fine.

Despite rushing through Miami Airport and hiring a taxi driver who'd taken her request to get her to her hotel as fast as possible, literally, Natalie missed the time of her presentation.

Frazzled from the delay, then the mad dash, she'd dropped her bags with the bellhop, then quietly snuck into the auditorium and slid into the back row to catch the end of what they'd filled her spot with. Settling into her seat, she glanced to the front of the auditorium and almost fell out of her chair.

No way.

Not even possible.

She was hallucinating.

Maybe she'd fallen during her jaunt through the airport, bumped her head and was in a coma, about to have a fantastic fantasy.

Must be, because the speaker at the front of the room was him.

Mr Dark and Dangerous from the plane.

He would be a fantastic fantasy.

But why was he teaching her class? And smiling and charming the crowd as if he were a natural-born motivational speaker rather than the dark, sexy overlord she'd painted him out to be on the plane? Seriously, the man was discussing heart deformities and yet you'd think he was revealing the secret of longevity by the way the attendees were on the edge of their seats.

Even as passionate as she was about surgical neonatal heart disease treatment modalities, she didn't think it was the topic that was mesmerizing the crowd.

It was him.

As he spoke, his gaze met with hers and recognition flashed in those unusual ice-blue eyes that somehow didn't fit with his pleasant expression. Probably because she'd pegged him as shadowy and menacing, not smiling and charming.

He was smiling. And charming. And had a voice that should be reading the books she downloaded to her smartphone from time to time to listen to at night. What a way to fall asleep.

Dark and dangerous or smiling and charming, the man oozed sex. She wasn't a woman who got hot and bothered from just looking at a guy. Or even hot and bothered from a whole lot of guy effort, but this man made her think S-E-X.

Hot, sweaty, body-slapping, can't-catch-your-breath sex.

Which was quite disturbing because Jonathan hadn't affected her this potently. Ever. Sex had been good, pleasurable, but just the thought of it hadn't set her nerve-endings on fire.

His presentation didn't pause, but his gaze lingered on hers, flashing with an awareness that made her nerve-endings burn. Hot, out-of-control burn.

He was gorgeous. Perhaps more so than any man she'd ever seen in real life.

Perhaps? Ha. Life had not thrown men like him into her path. Ever. As much as she'd cared for and found him attractive, Jonathan didn't have a thing on this guy. Not even on this guy's worst day and Jonathan's best. Mr. Dark and Dangerous exuded pheromones by the bucketful. His bucket ran over and was flooding the auditorium.

Natalie picked up a mini-sized notepad with the hotel's logo at the top and fanned her face. *Mercy.*

He finished his presentation, then did a question-and-answer session, fielding each question with ease, much more smoothly than she'd have done. She'd have been battling nerves at presenting to a room full of peers.

Whoever he was, he didn't look nervous. Dark, sexy overlords probably didn't get nervous. When the power of the universe was at your handsome fingertips, why sweat?

As she was doing. Her reaction had surprised her at the airport, on the plane, and even more so now that she'd seen the allure of his smile.

Applause filled the room. Natalie clapped, too. He'd done an excellent job, as if he'd been meant to give the presentation all along. She owed him for filling in when she wasn't there.

At the applause, the workshop moderator stood. "Thank you, Dr. Coleman, for volunteering to present when the vacancy opened." The moderator patted him on the back, shook his hand. "You did an excellent job, Matthew."

"No problem."

The man should really smile more because his face transformed into a work of art. Okay, so dark and dangerous had been a work of art, too, but smiling he was heart-stopping.

"I was glad to help, since I understand Dr. Sterling had travel delays," he continued, not glancing her way, but Natalie felt his awareness of her. As if he had some sixth sense that let him know exactly where she was in the room without those amazing eyes having to focus her way. That sense pervaded her entire being and scorched her insides.

Good grief, the way he affected her. Maybe because she was on the cusp of a huge career leap, maybe because she still felt the sting from Jonathan's betrayal.

Or maybe it was how pheromonally magnetic he was.

Another round of clapping and the group broke for a fifteen-minute break between sessions.

A few attendees moved forward to talk with Dr. Coleman. Natalie should thank him and introduce herself to the workshop moderator, who was also the conference chair, so she could apologize again for her delay.

Dr. Matthew Coleman. She'd never met him. No way would she have forgotten, so why did that name ring a bell?

Suddenly, her jaw dropped. Impossible. *That* Dr. Matthew Coleman had to be in his fifties at the absolute minimum. Surely. No way could this gorgeous doctor be *that* Dr. Matthew Coleman. It just wasn't feasible that he could be the renowned pediatric heart surgeon whose work she so greatly admired.

No way.

Plus, he'd been on a flight out of Memphis. *That* Dr. Matthew Coleman lived in Boston and headed up a research team making great strides with a robotic laser being developed for surgical use, including in utero. There couldn't be two pediatric heart surgeons by the same name doing innovative in-utero surgical repairs, surely?

That was when what he was saying caught her attention. He was making a comment about the robot that Dr. Matthew Coleman was one of the country's leading experts on.

Yeah, she was about to have a fan-girl moment.

Holy smokes. The gorgeous man she'd been fantasizing about on and off ever since the airport was someone she'd idolized for his brain and surgical skills for almost a decade.

What were the odds of the pretty brunette who'd caught Dr. Matthew Coleman's eye at the airport being his top competition for the hospital position he'd just interviewed for?

Not that Dr. Luiz had told him that, but he'd said there was another contender the hospital had been planning to offer the position to, prior to Matthew's interest. Dr. Natalie Sterling was who the man had repeatedly praised for her surgery skills and dedication to pediatric cardiology. She had to be who the department head had meant and, possibly, why they'd not been willing to meet the conditions Matthew had required to relocate.

Those conditions were the deal-maker—or -breaker.

Relocating to Memphis would decrease his stress by leaps and bounds in some ways, but he still wasn't sure he could give up everything he'd worked to achieve just to make the move in any case. Just because his life had been thrust into total chaos three months ago. Basically, he wanted what he had in Boston, but with less work hours and a new zip code that better fit his personal needs. Anything less and he'd stay where he was.

Which was why he'd contacted Dr. Luiz when a colleague had told him about the upcoming opening at Memphis Children's Hospital. He'd already been toying with the idea of relocating to Memphis to be closer to family—for Carrie, the little girl he now had to take care of, to be closer to family. Closer to people who actually knew how to take care of kids. But he couldn't just step away from his research and career. He wouldn't.

Maybe he should try to convince his mother to move to Boston, again. He wasn't sure what he'd have done if she hadn't been able to stay those first few weeks of Matthew's unexpected push into fatherhood. She'd been so good with Carrie. Why couldn't she have stayed longer?

Or maybe he'd resume interviews for a live-in nanny for the precious four-year-old who was now his sole responsibility. Some older woman who'd successfully raised multiple children and could get a child out of bed, have her dressed, fed, looking presentable, and to preschool on time. Something he continued to struggle with on a daily basis. None of the nannies he'd met so far had clicked, but surely there was someone out there he'd trust with Carrie?

His gaze connected with Natalie's golden one and he let out a long breath. Prior to Carrie's new role in his life, he'd have gotten her number at the airport and made plans to meet.

Instead, for the first time ever, despite his many previous flights, he'd been sweating getting onto an airplane, his mind filled with all the things that could go wrong—and recently had.

Plus, he had a four-year-old girl to think about.

Pursuing relationships with pretty brunettes wasn't on the cards. He could barely juggle his current schedule, much less adding someone else to the bedlam. He'd always excelled at everything he'd done. Who'd have thought it would be an adorable little kid who'd have him ready to pull his hair out?

He turned back to the portly gentleman from Shriner's Hospital, smiled as they exchanged business cards, then heard a voice behind him.

"Why didn't you tell me who you were?"

Knowing who it was even before their eyes made contact, Matthew turned, his gaze connecting to the brunette's. He could feel her presence as succinctly as if he had sonar outlining her shapely curves. "Excuse me?"

Her face took on a sheepish expression. "Sorry, I guess there was no reason for you to tell me, but I can't believe the coincidence that you'd be on my plane."

Not a coincidence, but there wasn't a reason to tell her about his meeting with Memphis Children's Hospital and that the job she was vying for had been offered to him. He'd turned it down when his terms couldn't be met. Natalie need never know she wasn't always the top contender.

He smiled, thinking she was even more attractive up close. Her eyes sparkled like sunshine hitting honey. Her skin was smooth and naturally tan with a few light freckles scattered across her nose. Her hair flowed silky and dark to just beneath her shoulders.

She wore a red skirt suit with a crisp white shirt that loosely hugged her curves.

"I see the airline was able to book you another flight." Perhaps it was wrong to tease, but he couldn't resist. Something about her made him want to tease, to watch her facial expressions and burn every detail into his memory.

"Too late to make it on time, though," she mused, her painted red lips curving into a smile. "Thank you for filling in."

Matthew resisted the urge to loosen his collar. "No problem. I was with the conference coordinator when he was discussing what to do with your time slot. Pediatric heart surgery of any kind is a subject I'm passionate about, so I offered to step in." He grinned. "He jumped at my offer."

"I'm sure." Another flash of those sparkly eyes and dynamic curving of her full lips. "Are you staying for the next presentation?"

At her smile, all his blood traveled south and brain operations came to a halt, making logical thought impossible. Did she have any idea of the power her eyes held to bewitch a man? Absolutely stunning.

"If so, there's an open seat next to mine," she continued. "Maybe you'd like to join me?"

Matthew stared at the biggest temptation he'd ever faced, wished the timing of meeting her had been prior to three months ago, when his life hadn't been in such upheaval. "If not?"

Uncertainty flashed across her face, but then with a determined look, she lifted her chin, stared straight in his eyes, and said, "If not, then maybe we could meet later for the conference opening dinner reception and you could tell me all about your work, because you fascinate me. Your work does, that is."

CHAPTER TWO

NATALIE WAS WAY outside her comfort zone. But her BFFs would be proud, right? She had walked up to a man she found enthralling on paper, sexy in real life, and she'd expressed her interest in him.

And in his work.

He might think her a fool. For all she knew, he had a girlfriend.

Duh. Of course a man as gorgeous as Matthew had a girlfriend. What had she been thinking? She'd practically been drooling prior to finding out who he was, and after? Well, the man mesmerized.

Not that she'd dreamed in a million years that she might act on their suggestions, but when Suzie and Monica told her to have a fling to put Jonathan out of her mind once and for all, they should have been more specific. As in, making sure who she wanted wasn't already taken. Yes, she had noted at the airport that he didn't have a wedding band, but even that didn't mean anything beyond that he wasn't wearing a ring. The star-struck look in her eyes had probably terrified the poor man.

Still, he didn't look the type to easily scare.

"I have a seat." He turned, gesturing to a spot on the front row.

Ouch. Married, dating, or whatever, she'd been shot down. Trying not to let her disappointment and embarrassment show, she glanced around and was grateful to see the next speaker at the podium. "Okay, well, it's time to restart, so…"

Awkward.

Not waiting for a response, she high-tailed it to her back row seat to shrivel up and die of humiliation. So much for going after what she wanted.

Ugh. Could this day possibly get worse?

Later that evening, Natalie stared at her reflection in the hotel room mirror.

For a few insane moments, she had let herself be guided by pure feminine interest and she'd made a fool of herself with Matthew Coleman.

Because he was a sexy beast or because of his surgical skills?

Or both?

He was brilliant. She'd read enough of his articles and research to know the man was a genius. That alone would have had her introducing herself, wanting to discuss his work, pick his brain and soak up everything he said.

That he was utterly gorgeous, well, that was a bonus.

Or could have been, had he been interested. She'd thought she'd seen interest, but she must have been wrong.

He wasn't. Had shot down her offer. End of story. Major embarrassment and utter failure at her first show of interest in the opposite sex since her and Jonathan's split, but not the end of the world. The opposite sex wasn't a priority. Her career was and she had that—so no big deal, right?

Still, the conference wasn't so big that she wouldn't bump into Matthew. She'd act as if her invitation had been casual, that she'd only been interested professionally. She was Dr. Natalie Sterling, a pediatric heart surgeon with some pretty fabulous credits to her name, thanks to having met Dr. Luiz during her residency and his having pulled her onto his research team.

No harm done in asking Matthew to dinner. It wasn't

as if she'd verbalized that looking at him made her want to take off his clothes and do wild and crazy things.

With one last look in the hotel bathroom mirror, she applied a fresh coat of lipstick, checked to make sure she didn't have any smeared on her teeth, and left the safety of her hotel room to go to dinner. Maybe she'd get lucky and she wouldn't see Matthew this evening.

Or, as her luck for the day would have it, he'd be the first person she saw when she stepped off the elevator.

Seriously, the elevator door slid open and there he was, just outside the elevator bank.

Sometimes life wasn't fair.

The man's looks weren't fair. Those eyes. So unusual. So mesmerizing. So zoned-in on her.

How was she supposed to act professional when he made her giddy as a schoolgirl? Ha. She hadn't been a giddy schoolgirl. She didn't recall ever having felt so in-ferno-hot inside.

His gaze raked over her red heels, up her bare legs to where her red skirt brushed the tops of her knees. His visual perusal continued, up and beyond to where her waist dipped in beneath her white blouse and matching red jacket. The fire burning in his icy blue eyes had her insides battling the urge to run back to the elevator versus leaping into his arms and ripping off his clothes.

He made her feel alive, hot, very female. That scared her. Probably because she wasn't one for letting her body dictate her actions and he made her body want to act. *Logic.* That was what dictated her life. Logic, and…

Those wicked blue eyes connected with hers.

Forget logic.

Her breath caught. Her skin prickled with awareness. Her thighs clenched. Any moment her heart was going to pound its way free of her chest. She might spend most of her time locked away in the sterile confines of the hospital, but she wasn't a fool or oblivious. Desire shone in his eyes and matching want burned within her.

"I was beginning to think you'd changed your mind about dinner." He smiled, his voice deep, warm, drawing her further under his spell. "I'm glad I waited."

Natalie's legs liquefied. She remained upright. Somehow. Matthew had just given her a complete once-over and now he was saying he'd been waiting on her? Had she really awakened from the light nap she'd taken, sitting on her room's balcony?

"I have a table near the front and asked a couple to save our seats," he continued. "I hope that was okay." When she nodded, he placed his hand low on her back and guided her toward the hotel ballroom, where their dinner keynote presentation would take place. "You look lovely, by the way."

His hand burned through the material of her suit, searing her skin with its warmth and making her feel a little woozy. His actions were familiar, as if he had the right to touch her. Obviously he did, because she wasn't complaining.

"I looked for you after Dr. Epsteiner's lecture, but never spotted you, not then or at any other point this afternoon."

Insides rattled at his admission, Natalie focused on each step she took and prayed she didn't stumble in her heels. Carefully, she made her way across the room. Why hadn't she slipped on her trusty flats prior to coming down?

She'd skipped the rest of the afternoon's sessions to sit on her balcony, eyes closed, listening to the surf, letting the breeze and sun compete against each other to caress her skin, to de-stress from the day's events. From life.

And to think about Matthew.

"Were you avoiding me?"

She stumbled, but recovered quickly enough that she hoped he hadn't noticed. She had been avoiding him, but she wasn't admitting that.

"Why would I avoid you?" *Because she'd acted foolish.* "I don't know you."

He shook his head. "I thought... Never mind. You're here now." His lips curved. "Let's have an enjoyable evening and remedy you not knowing me by our getting to know each other." Although he was smiling and charming, his face took on that dark and dangerous look that, no doubt, made women fall to their knees to do his bidding, as he added, "A lot better."

Willing her legs to keep her upright, Natalie gulped, accepting that she was powerless to resist his powers, and that, even if she could, she didn't want to. He was a fantasy come to life. Never would she have imagined he'd been looking for her.

She wasn't sure what had changed from his earlier decline of her offer, but now he wasn't attempting to hide his interest, his intent.

Good. Neither was she. Life was too short for silly games.

Getting to know each other better should have been easy enough during the delicious meal since their chairs were next to each other, but there were six other people at the table. Two couples who'd introduced themselves, and two male pediatricians who had gone to medical school together and met up once a year at a continuing medical education conference for old times' sake and a catch-up. All six people vied for Matthew's attention. He included her in the conversation, stopped several times to ask her opinion, but with the others at the table Natalie could barely get a word in edgewise.

Which was okay by her. She sat back, watching and listening in fascination as Matthew discussed his work. Part of her wasn't quite able to believe she sat next to *the* Dr. Matthew Coleman she'd quoted in several of her medical school papers. Another part wasn't able to believe she sat next to the sexiest man she'd ever met. All of her was dazed that both could be the same man, and that when he looked at her his eyes burned with pale blue fire.

Soon after their table had finished the meal, the moderator took the podium and called the room's attention to the front, silencing conversations around the room. Ending his discussion with the two pediatricians, Matthew turned, caught Natalie watching him—probably with a goofy *I want you* expression on her face—and grinned. Dark and dangerous had been right, because that grin threatened all her good sense.

Then again, sitting next to him made perfect sense.

Why wouldn't it? Despite her three-year relationship with Jonathan, they weren't together any more. With his devotion to his career matching hers, he'd easily fit into her life because he didn't mind the large amount of time her job ate up. Or so he'd said, right up to the moment he'd defended his sleeping with another woman by pointing out Natalie's refusal to commit more time to him and marry him.

Fine. Good riddance and thank God she hadn't been willing to marry a man who'd so readily cheat. She wanted marriage, to connect completely with another person, to someday have a family, but something had held her back from saying yes to Jonathan. Maybe it had been that she was still building her dream career.

No matter. Jonathan was history. She was free to do whatever she chose. With whomever she chose.

Her gaze connected with Matthew's.

He leaned close to her ear, giving her a waft of his spicy aftershave. "This hasn't exactly been conducive to getting to know each other."

The man smelled amazing. She wanted to breathe him in and hold her breath for ever.

"Is that what we're doing?" she whispered back, knowing her eyes revealed everything she was feeling in case he'd missed it in her husky voice.

"You want to leave?"

Yes!

"And miss the keynote?"

His lips twitched with amusement. "You want to go first and meet in the lobby in fifteen minutes or shall we leave together?"

Whether it was for her privacy or his, she liked that he was giving her the option to choose to leave together, which implied he didn't mind anyone knowing he was with her, or their leaving separately so no one would be the wiser. It was up to her to decide how they proceeded.

Still, she had a few things to clarify first.

"Are you single?"

Obviously startled at her question, he nodded.

"Then meet me by the fountain in ten." She pushed back her chair and quietly excused herself from the group at their table.

As she weaved her way through the tables to where she could make her escape, Natalie fought kicking up her high heels with joy. She felt good, light, feminine. And, even though she worried about stumbling, she was glad she had on her heels because they plumped her calves and made her legs look toned. She wanted to look good because Matthew's gaze was on her. She could feel it as surely as if his hands traced over her skin.

She made it out the door just before a happy giggle bubbled from her lips. This was crazy. She was behaving like a teenager sneaking out of the house to meet a boyfriend. She was a grown woman sneaking out of a conference keynote to meet an attractive man in the lobby.

Despite her bravado at the idea of a short-term affair with Matthew, she hadn't actually ever *had* an affair. She and Jonathan had dated for several months prior to their having sex, and she'd cared about him. She'd never had any desire for a physical relationship prior to him. She'd

been too busy focusing on her studies, her career, determined to make a difference in pediatric cardiology.

Honestly, despite Monica's and Suzie's advice to "get
laid" this weekend, she'd had no intention of doing so.
Not until she'd seen Matthew at the airport and he'd cast
a spell over her mind and body to where she craved him.

Still, what if she couldn't go through with sex for the
sake of sex and Matthew got upset?

She hesitated outside the ballroom door.

Stop it, she scolded herself. Just stop overthinking and
go with the flow. Emotional commitment was overrated.
Just look at what had happened with her last committed
relationship.

Whether it was because of the blow Jonathan's cheating had done to her ego or because she was hundreds of
miles from home, or some unknown reason, she wasn't
going to let her brain get in the way of her having a good
time. Excitement surged through every inch of her body.
Excitement that she was doing something outside her comfort zone. Excitement that a sexy man looked at her as if
he wanted to yank off her clothes and kiss her all over.

For the next three days she'd let whatever happened
between her and Matthew happen, and not dwell on the
possibility that after the conference ended it was unlikely
she'd ever see him again.

Wasn't that actually perfect? Because she needed to
focus on Memphis Children's Hospital and upping their
pediatric cardiology department to the next level. To stepping up to the new role the hospital was going to offer her.
She didn't need Matthew, or anyone else, distracting her.

But at the moment she was in Florida at a gorgeous
resort hotel and she was going to enjoy the rest of the
evening.

With Matthew.

Suzie and Monica would be proud.

Unable to drag his gaze from Natalie's retreating backside, Matthew knew he wasn't fooling a single person in the room. At the moment he didn't care.

He *should* care.

He had a child to think about, so his behavior mattered. He had to set a good example for Carrie.

But Carrie was in Memphis with his mother, as Matthew had signed up for this continuing education conference before he'd known he was going to be raising his god-daughter. He'd started to cancel, but his mother had pushed him not to, saying he needed a weekend to decompress after the past few months. Carrie was better off with his mother than she was with him anyway.

His heart pinched as he thought of Robert and Carolyn. The couple had died much too soon in a small plane crash, leaving their most precious possession to him. Four-year-old Carrie.

What had his best friends been thinking? Although serious in his professional life, he'd been a happy-go-lucky bachelor who knew how to have a good time without the burden of commitment.

Robert had been Matthew's best friend since grammar school. They'd gone through university then med school together. He'd been there when Carolyn had stolen his friend's heart, had been best man at their wedding, had been there for Carrie's birth.

Having been only children to single moms, neither Robert nor Carolyn had had any living family and had asked Matthew to be Carrie's godfather prior to her birth. Not believing he'd ever actually be raising the little girl, Matthew had agreed. Nothing was supposed to have happened to his friends.

But three months ago, it had. Something horrible that neither he nor Carrie would recover from, when the couple's small-engine plane had crashed, instantly killing them both.

If only his friends had made better arrangements for

their daughter. Surely anything would have been better than him.

Matthew paused outside the ballroom door. What was he doing? His life was in total upheaval. He should not get involved with Natalie or any other woman when his world was so topsy-turvy.

Wasn't that why he'd hesitated to accept Natalie's invitation to sit beside her?

To let her think there could be anything between them would be wrong. He had a whole new messed-up life he had to figure out. Until he did, Carrie had to be his priority. Only, so long as he made sure Natalie knew that whatever happened in Miami would end in Miami, there was no reason why they couldn't enjoy the next few days. He *needed* the next few days. He'd not had sex in months. Not since before his friends had… Hell, he didn't want to think of that anymore.

Natalie would likely tell him to kiss her lovely behind when he told her he couldn't offer more than a few days of fun in the sun. Sure, there had been a rare moment when he'd been at Robert and Carolyn's that he'd envied their relationship, the closeness they shared. But he had never actively thought about marriage or a long-term relationship for himself. He liked being single, liked being able to do what he wanted when he wanted with whomever he wanted, that if he wanted to stay at the hospital for twenty-four hours straight there was no one to complain or be disappointed that his work meant more than they did.

All that had changed with Carrie. Now, whether he wanted to or not, he had to keep a regular schedule, had to come home at night.

He raked his fingers through his hair. Yeah, he hadn't been free to do much of anything over the past three months. Instead, he'd been trying to figure out what to do with the sweetest little girl he'd ever known, who was heartbroken over the loss of her parents and who had the unfortunate luck of being in Uncle Matthew's care.

Uncle Matthew, who was now thrust into the role of *Daddy* Matthew.

For the next three days he got to just be Matthew, and to do what he wanted.

And what Matthew wanted was Natalie. Naked and beneath him.

There she was, waiting by the fountain, her gaze dancing with seduction and making his head spin. Would it be wrong if he threw her over his shoulder, carried her to his hotel room and took her every way he'd imagined over the course of the day? He couldn't recall ever wanting a woman more than he wanted Natalie. Had to be the turmoil of the past three months and his need to just… escape. That, and the fact he'd not even thought about a woman or sex since Robert and Carolyn's death. His reaction to Natalie was probably his subconscious guiding him to take what he could while he could.

He made his way to the fountain, took Natalie's hand and practically dragged her toward the elevator bank where he'd been waiting for her earlier.

CHAPTER THREE

"I want to make love to you, Natalie," Matthew told her as the elevator doors slid shut behind them.

Natalie's breath caught.

"But—" he began.

No! She didn't want there to be a "but". *Please, the one time she was willing to just let go and have a fling with a man, don't let him have a reason they couldn't.*

With his free hand he pressed the door-close button rather than a floor number, then continued. "I don't want to deceive you in any way, and, if we go further without my telling you the truth, that's what I'd feel I was doing."

Had he lied to her earlier? *Was* there someone special in his life?

Please don't be married or engaged or whatever it is that's so horrible that you have to confess before having sex.

"You're a beautiful, intelligent woman and deserve better than anything I'm able to give. Which is why I need to explain all the reasons why you should tell me no." He took a deep breath, kept those pale blue eyes locked with hers. "Beyond the next three days, I have nothing to offer to you or any woman."

Natalie's breath caught, at his words and at his hand still clenching hers.

"I don't understand," she admitted, trying to make sense of what he was saying.

"What I've wanted from the moment you stepped off this elevator before dinner was to put you right back on it, go to one of our rooms and not come out for hours."

He watched her as if he half expected her to pull her hand free and slap him.

As if.

"You're not married?"

His look of shock gave answer before his words.

"There's no other woman in my life, Natalie. It's just that my life is complicated, and letting you think there could be anything beyond the next three days would be wrong. Whatever happens between us this weekend ends when we leave Miami on Sunday. When deciding what floor this elevator stops on, keep that in mind."

So neither of them wanted anything beyond the next three days, and time was too precious to waste. She wanted him. He wanted her. They didn't need to know anything more about each other.

Well, almost nothing more.

"Are you...?" How did she ask this? She'd been a virgin with Jonathan and was screened annually at the hospital, so she hadn't had to do blood tests or anything of the sort. Trying to convince her it was time for them to take that next step, he'd gone on his own and given her a copy of his lab tests prior to their becoming physically involved. As time and their busy schedules had allowed, they'd fallen into a mutually satisfying relationship.

Or maybe it hadn't been so mutually satisfying, since he'd been having sex with another woman.

Ugh. No. She was not going to let thoughts of Jonathan's infidelity creep into this moment. All she needed to know was—how did couples usually bring up a clean bill of health? Or did they? No matter what other couples did. She would ask.

"I mean, do you have…?" She struggled to find the right words.

"I'm clean, if that's what you're asking."

Relief filled her at his answer and at how easily he'd known what she was asking.

"Me, too," Natalie assured, excitement coursing through her. Excitement and heat. White-hot heat that burned at her very core. She wanted Matthew. More than she'd ever wanted any man. Mentally and physically. She. Wanted. Him.

She reached for his hand. "We both know what we want, and it isn't a relationship." There. She'd said it. There could be no confusion. "So, truly, your comments, while gentlemanly, are a waste of valuable time when you could be impressing me in ways I'd appreciate much more." Her boldness surprised her, but good grief, he seemed intent on being a gentleman when what she wanted was a rogue lover setting her body on fire. "My room is on the eleventh floor." She reached over and pressed the button. "Are you getting off with me or not?"

Despite her brave invitation, Natalie's hands trembled as she slid her card into the key slot. Her heart pounded as the little green lights flashed and she twisted the handle, opening the door to let Matthew into her hotel room.

Even as her feet moved, carrying her inside, she asked herself how this worked. Did she go to the bathroom and freshen up? Did he? Did she just take off her clothes and get into bed, as Jonathan had always preferred?

Once they were inside the room and she heard him secure the lock, she turned to him, hoping to break the silence that had enveloped them on their ascent to her room.

Before she could get a word out, Matthew pushed her back a couple of steps to sandwich her between the wall and his hard body, his mouth covering hers. There was nothing slow, indecisive or gentlemanly in his touch.

Finally, she thought.

His mouth was ravenous. His hands roaming over her body voracious. His lean hips pressing against her belly giving proclamation of just how much he wanted her.

She kissed him, touched him with equal intensity, running her hands over his arms, his shoulders, cupping his face in her hands as his kiss deepened.

One little kiss and they'd gone straight to fast and furious.

Ha. There was nothing little about how Matthew was kissing her. Big. Huge. Gigantic. That was how his kisses felt.

That was how his body felt grinding against her.

Fireworks went off in her head, in her chest, her whole body, at his mouth moving over hers, at his hands sliding over her, tugging her blouse from her skirt and letting in a swoosh of welcome cool air across her sensitized flesh.

"I can't believe you're here, that we're doing this," she murmured as he traced kisses along her neck, her collarbone. She dug her fingers into his hair.

"You aren't changing your mind, are you?" he breathed against the indentation at her throat, his tongue darting out to dip into the sensitive flesh.

Natalie quivered.

"No. Never." She arched against his mouth. "This is what I have played over and over in my mind today."

What she needed. Crazy, but she *did* need him—this virtual stranger who was setting her body on fire. His touch, his kiss, his full attention. His body grinding against hers, hard, lean, thrilling.

"Tell me what you want, Natalie," he coaxed, pushing her blouse off her shoulders and letting the silky material pool around her red heels, revealing her lacy white camisole and matching bra beneath. Cupping her bottom, he bent, kissing the valley between her breasts. "Tell me what you've been imagining us doing."

"That," she breathed, running her fingers into his thick, inky dark hair and holding him to her breast. "I like that."

That. That. That, her body screamed.

"Me, too." Pushing aside her camisole and bra, he took a puckered nipple into his mouth and gave a gentle tug.

Natalie almost died. Or exploded. Or imploded. Or all of the above, so many sensations shot through her electrified body. His hands held urgency as he continued to caress her, his mouth claiming everything in its passionate path. Within breathless minutes he pushed her skirt up her hips to bunch at her waist so he could slide his hands inside her panties to cup her bottom once more.

Yeah, she wanted that, too.

His hands were hot on her skin, electrifying. She wanted him. Desperately. She kissed him with that desperation. Touched him with that desperation. Moved her body against his with that desperation. Her fingers found their way to his waist, to where he strained against his dress pants' zipper. After a moment's fumbling, she had his pants to where she could touch him. She explored what she craved to feel deep inside.

"Natalie," he groaned. Or maybe he'd growled.

Either way, she'd never heard her name said as Matthew had just said it. Had never felt the power filling her at how he responded to her slightest touch.

"I like this, too," she whispered close to his ear, in awe at how free she felt to touch him, at how uninhibited to give and take as she pleased. She'd never felt this freedom with Jonathan. She had always followed his lead rather than blazing a path of her own. "I like touching you and feeling your reaction and knowing I did that."

He mumbled something against her throat, where his mouth was wreaking havoc on her nervous system, but she didn't catch his words. They didn't matter. His body was telling her all she needed to know.

"I like what you're doing," she continued, barely recognizing her voice, but further emboldened by the fervor of his kisses. "I like the way you're touching me, as if you *need* to touch me." She'd never felt more desirable than in this moment, than the way his touch made her feel. He made her feel beautiful, desirable, wanton even. Unlike anything she'd ever felt or would possibly ever feel again. The knowledge promised ecstasy.

"That makes two of us," he assured her, between more ardent kisses.

"I like the way you're looking at me," she continued, her voice breathy, her fingers tightening around him. "As if you want to put every detail of me to memory."

Matthew didn't have to put every detail of Natalie to memory.

She was already there.

Every delectable inch of her.

He had no doubt he'd never forget what was happening. She was timeless, beautiful. Unforgettable.

Barely hanging on to his sanity, he took her hands into his, kissed her fingertips, then pressed against her. Eyes locked with his, her fingers moved to his shoulders, kneaded deep into his muscles as he grazed her lips with his teeth.

"More," she breathed, arching into his touch. "I want more."

Completely caught between him and the wall, she shifted her hips against him, pressing her upper body against the wall to give added pressure to the sensuous contact between their bodies.

A long leg slid up his, wrapped itself around his waist, pressing her pelvis more fully against where he throbbed.

Heaven help him.

They were barely inside her hotel room door and he was about to rip off her panties and take her like a madman.

He'd meant to take her slow, to kiss her all over, and when she was ready, take them both over the edge.

Her body was ready now.

He could feel her damp heat burning into him and that reality undid every good intention he had of *slow*. Her mouth was against his now, hard and demanding. Her hands tugged at his shirt, managing to pull the material loose. He wasn't sure if she'd unbuttoned it or popped every button. It didn't matter. All that mattered was having her.

She made him manic, illogical, driven by physical need in ways he didn't understand.

"Now," she urged, her fingernails raking over his back, then gripping his buttocks to pull him tighter against her. "I want you inside me now."

Matthew didn't need to be told twice. Supporting her weight between his body and the wall, he reached into his sagging back pocket for his wallet, pulling out a condom.

"I only have one of these," he confessed, ripping it open and making haste of putting it on. "I have the feeling I'm going to wish I had a dozen more before morning."

Her eyes molten honey, Natalie kissed his mouth, hard, full of passion, and, keeping her eyes locked with his, she guided him to his own personal heaven.

Natalie's boldness shocked her. Her boldness in how she touched Matthew, in how she wrapped both legs around his waist and took him deep inside her body with her skirt bunched at her waist and her panties pushed aside.

Her boldness in the things she said to him, in how vocal she was about what she wanted from him and to do to him.

Even more, she was shocked by how she bit down on his shoulder to keep from crying out as an orgasm rocked her body at his powerful thrusts.

Wave after wave of pleasure ripped through her.

If not for the wall, his strong body against hers, she'd

have dropped to the floor to float her way back to the land of mere mortal beings.

She thought he'd climaxed with her, but he must have somehow held back. Rather than relax against her as she'd expected, he kept moving, pounding against her as she peaked in pleasure, then started the cataclysmic climb all over again, leaving her frantically moving against him until she went places she'd never been, to heights she'd never scaled, until she went into a blissful free fall that might go on for days.

Weeks.

Just when her orgasm began to spiral out of control, his willpower broke and her body became unwound with him, every nerve cell inside her zinging to life and exploding with a heated force so amazing she couldn't believe her body remained intact.

Intact? More like turned inside out and back again.

From her biased, soaring view, this man lost in passion was a glorious thing.

A satisfied Matthew's damp forehead dropping to rest against hers as he stared into her eyes was splendid. The way her body felt was beautiful. *Everything* felt so beautiful that Natalie wondered if orgasms were mind-altering.

Her mind had definitely been altered.

"If I'd known this was how it would be, we'd have never made it off the elevator."

Looking a bit mind-altered himself, Matthew laughed. "You might be right."

"Might be?" She squeezed her thighs, loving how his eyes darkened instantly in response. He kissed her forehead, and when his gaze met hers there was a contentment in his eyes that puffed up her chest.

She smiled at him with a confidence she didn't understand, but that felt addictive. Yeah, they'd had amazing sex. This was the after part. Shouldn't she feel awkward? Embarrassed by her daring?

She didn't. She felt... She searched for a way to describe what she felt. More connected with him than with any person she'd ever known. How could she feel that way with someone she'd just met? Much freer than she'd ever been with Jonathan. She'd enjoyed their sex life, but, compared to what she had just experienced, sex with Jonathan had been boring. And not only because she'd just been pushed up against a wall still half-dressed and ravaged, rather than in bed with calm, intentional acts meant to please.

The way her body had responded was what had been different.

Matthew electrified every nerve ending, making her aware of every cell, every nuance of her body, of his body. She'd never had orgasms like those she'd just experienced. Maybe no woman had ever experienced orgasms like the ones Matthew had just given to her.

Whether it was how she'd admired his mind for years or how his sex appeal had toyed with her psyche from the moment she'd laid eyes on him, everything about this moment felt right. Perfect. For that, she hugged him.

His forehead still against hers, his breathing ragged, he searched her eyes. "What was that for?"

"A token of my appreciation." Legs feeling a little shaky, she lowered them from his waist to tentatively support her weight. She felt so languid, she might collapse on the floor.

"I'm the one who needs to be expressing my gratitude, and my apologies for not hauling your delectable body up here the moment that first workshop finished."

"No worries. I have every intention of giving you lots of opportunity to express your, um, gratitude." Her tone was flirty and it felt good. "And to let you make up for wasting time."

Had she ever flirted with a man before?

She'd always been focused on school, on her patients,

her research, her career. Focusing on a man hadn't ever been a priority. But she liked flirting with Matthew, liked the quick smile that transformed his handsome face.

Reaching for her skirt, she tugged the wrinkled material down her hips, then pressed a quick kiss to his lips. Aware that his gaze tracked her every move, she walked to the mini-fridge, took out a bottled water, twisted off the lid and took a drink.

"Thirsty?" She offered the bottle.

He took a long swig, then handed it back to her. "Not now."

His tone implied it hadn't been the water that had quenched his thirst.

Eyeing him, Natalie placed her lips over where his had been and took another drink, letting the water cool her throat.

"Thank you, Natalie."

"For?"

"You know." Winking at her, he went to the bathroom, she assumed to dispose of the used condom, then returned to the room with his pants restored.

That was when she got her first real look at his chest and abdomen. Earlier, she'd been distracted with need and sex, and had been up close to his body, but now... *Oh, my.*

Matthew without a shirt was a beautiful sight.

She'd touched that chest, kissed that chest, been pressed up against that chest, all hot and sweaty.

Feeling quite smug that she'd just had sex with the hottest man alive, she couldn't help but smile. "Now what?"

He shrugged. "Not any more of that, unless we make a protection run, I'm sad to say."

She eyed him curiously. She'd not really considered that they could have a repeat that night. Jonathan had never more than once... *Oh, forget Jonathan.* "Would you really be able to do that again?"

"Just say the word."

Surely he was exaggerating, but his answer still stroked her ego. She knew she shouldn't keep comparing what had just happened to her relationship with her ex, but he'd have rolled over and been asleep already.

Then again, she would have been, too.

Intrigued, and more than a little smug, she asked, "If I said now, you'd want to again tonight?"

He arched a brow. "You have to ask after what we just did? Of course I want to do that again."

"One box isn't enough. Buy two."

Matthew grinned at the woman tugging at his arm and grabbed another box off the shelf. "Two boxes for three nights? You trying to kill me?"

"You're the one who bragged you were able to repeat the deed anytime I said the word," she reminded with a saucy flash of her eyes.

Wondering why he'd ever hesitated in allowing himself this three-day break from reality, Matthew laughed. "You saying the word? If so, I'm sure we can find a vacant corridor."

Her eyes widened momentarily, but she quickly looked intrigued. So much for his prim and proper impression of her at the airport. Thank God he'd given himself permission to forget the real world and just play for three days. Three days to spend with this surprising woman.

Chuckling, he grabbed her hand. "Come on, Natalie. Let's go pay for our two boxes."

They'd opted to walk the beach to a neighboring hotel's gift shop rather than risk one of their colleagues seeing them stock up at the conference hotel. Matthew had enjoyed the sea air and having Natalie's hand clasped within his during the nighttime walk, but the fifteen minutes back to their hotel suddenly seemed like a long time.

"How did you get involved with the Libertine robot

project?" she asked once they were back on the beach and headed toward their hotel.

"You want to talk shop?" He just wanted to get back to the hotel and get her naked. Completely this time. He had a lot of exploring to do and was looking forward to discovering every nook and cranny.

"The Libertine fascinates me," she continued, her hand snug in his. "I've watched you perform surgery with it, you know."

He shot a look at her, the moonlight casting just enough light across her face to illuminate her beautiful features. "No, I didn't know."

"I couldn't tell much about you, since you were wearing a surgical mask, glasses and cap and the film clip pretty much only showed the surgery. I guess technically I watched a video of your hands doing miraculous things, because I don't recall anything of your face and I wouldn't have forgotten your eyes had I ever seen them." She smiled sheepishly, then went on. "From how long I've been seeing your name quoted in the cardiology world, I had thought you much older."

He got that a lot. He'd been fortunate to become involved with the Libertine from early in its inception as a surgical tool. Near the end of med school, his passion had shifted his interest to surgical advances being made in treating congenital defects in utero. Robert had followed suit.

Working for a robotics company, Carolyn had been one of the key design engineers on the Libertine. It was how they'd all met. He and Robert had been practically inseparable since grade school. Carolyn had changed that somewhat, but Matthew had felt more as if they'd added a third player to their team, rather than their friendship losing anything, when his best friend married the brilliant engineer.

He missed them so much. Three months and it didn't

seem real that he'd never see them again, never discuss the Libertine, or difficult cases. Never catch another football game while Carolyn laughed at their long-term rivalry of the Cowboys against the Steelers. Never again—

"You okay?" Natalie's voice broke into Matthew's memories.

Fighting back the hollow ache in his gut, he clenched his teeth. How had he let such depressing thoughts in tonight when he felt alive, truly alive, for the first time since before he'd gotten the call that Robert and Carolyn's plane had gone down?

"Just got lost in thought." He flashed a smile that wasn't as real as he'd like, but there wasn't enough light that she'd likely be able to tell. "How old do you think I am?"

She glanced his way a few moments, making him wonder if perhaps she saw better in the low light than he'd given her credit for, but she seemed to make the decision not to push. Maybe because she didn't want to know what he'd really been thinking about.

"Uh-uh." Her smile was wide, bright, not so over-the-top as to come across as completely fake. "I'm not guessing your age. If I go too high you might be offended. If I go too low, you'll accuse me of robbing the cradle."

Her voice was light, but her grip on his hand had tightened, offering a comfort he soaked up and was amazed at how much better her smile and touch left him feeling.

He chuckled. "No chance you robbed the cradle, Natalie. That would be me. I'm probably a good ten years older than you."

"I seriously doubt it." She told him her age.

"Eight years older," he corrected. "I'm the one who robbed the cradle, it seems."

"Eight years isn't that much," she assured. "You're barely into your forties."

A memory of his fortieth birthday, spent with Robert and Carolyn, popped into his head. They'd rented out their favorite restaurant's back room, invited a ton of mutual friends and acquaintances and surprised him with a birthday bash.

"Hey—you okay?" she asked again.

Why had his friends popped back into his head so quickly when he'd just scolded himself for letting them in on a night meant to drown them out?

His gaze cut to Natalie. Why did he find himself wanting to tell her about them?

"You quit walking," she pointed out. "And you're squeezing my hand as if you're afraid if you let go the wind might carry me out to sea."

Matthew forced his fingers to pry loose from hers, raked them through his hair. "Sorry."

"That sensitive about your age, huh? I'll keep that in mind and be sure not to make any more age references."

Pushing thoughts of his friends from his mind yet again, Matthew shook his head and gave in to Natalie's teasing. "I've no problem with being called an old man."

"Old man?" Natalie laughed, took his hand back into hers and gave him a little squeeze. "You aren't an old man. Admittedly, it's a bit kinky, but I'd be happy to oblige if that's what you want me to call you."

His smile was real. "As long as you're calling me, I won't complain."

Her gaze searched his. "For the rest of the weekend, right?"

"Right," Matthew agreed, but suddenly found it difficult to keep his smile in place. "For the next three days, I'm all yours."

Then he'd fly back to Memphis, stay at his mother's for a night, then he and Carrie would drive back to Boston because the little girl was terrified of the thought of getting on a plane, and he hadn't forced the issue.

Back to trying to figure out life without Robert and Carolyn.

Back to him struggling to raise their precious daughter in a way that wouldn't disappoint them, which seemed impossible for a sworn bachelor who still couldn't even put Carrie's hair up without missing handfuls of it from the bun.

Too bad the position in Memphis hadn't worked out so his family would be close to shower Carrie in their love and guide him in the right direction as he got this parenting thing all wrong time and again.

What did he know about raising a kid?

Nothing. His friends had been foolish leaving Carrie's upbringing to him. Robert had known Matthew had no plans to marry or have children. Truly, they couldn't have chosen a worse guardian for Carrie.

"Your hand is getting tight again," Natalie warned.

He loosened his hold. "Sorry."

"Want to talk about whatever keeps bothering you?"

He couldn't blame Natalie for asking. She'd let it go more than once, but he kept going back to places he didn't need to let his brain go.

"It's not important." Which was a lie. Everything about Robert and Carolyn was important. How he was going to handle fatherhood was important. Part of him wanted to tell Natalie, to spill everything out to her, to tell her what a screw-up step-in parent he'd been so far and that he wished he could give Carrie to a couple who knew what they were doing so the kid wouldn't turn out messed up. But losing his best friends, and his failed parenthood, weren't decent conversation for a three-day affair.

For the next three days, he was just Matthew. The dedicated heart surgeon and researcher, the fun-loving man, the devoted short-term lover.

CHAPTER FOUR

NATALIE MADE IT to breakfast just before the hotel wait staff cleared the buffet trays.

Having gone earlier to his hotel room to shower, Matthew had arrived before her and was at a table with two other men and a woman, eating breakfast. Wearing his khaki pants and blue button-up shirt with the sleeves folded to mid-forearm, a smile on his handsome face, he stole her breath.

She could hardly believe she'd had sex with him. Hot, needy, carnal sex.

Natalie lingered, overfilling her plate with sliced fruit. There was no reason she couldn't join Matthew and the others at his table, but she procrastinated, toying with toasting a slice of wheat bread.

She'd seen and touched every part of his body. With her hands, her mouth. They'd done things that just recalling was enough to make her blush and wonder who that wanton woman in bed with him had been. After all that, was she really hesitating to sit down beside him to eat breakfast?

When she'd finally gotten her plate and headed in his direction, Matthew rose from his chair.

"There's a seat at our table, Natalie. Join us."

He'd made it easy. As if he were inviting an old friend or colleague to join his table. No big deal. Only, when their gazes met, his unusual eyes held a warmth that conveyed that his smile was for her alone. Nothing had changed from the time he'd left her room. He had no morning-after regrets.

Her gaze dropped to his mouth, and she fought the urge to lean over and plant another good-morning kiss on his magic lips.

Those lips had kissed her all over. More than once. Places she'd never been so thoroughly kissed. Those hands had held her, touched her, coaxed responses she'd not known her body able to give.

Natalie gulped back the emotion looking at him filled her with. Pride, pleasure, passion. Maybe they should skip the conference and go back to her room? No, they'd decided they would both attend morning classes to earn their continuing-education credits. As much as she'd like to drag him back to her room, she'd restrain herself.

At least until morning break.

A little giddy at the thought, she smiled at the others as she joined the table.

"Natalie, this is Dr. Kim Yang, Dr. Steven Powers and Dr. Herb Fallows. They all practice pediatrics at Loma Linda in California."

She set her plate on the table and shook the outstretched hands as Matthew continued the introductions.

"And this talented lady is Dr. Natalie Sterling."

She'd swear she saw him wink at her from the corner of her eye, but she kept her focus on the others.

"Natalie is a pediatric cardiac surgeon at Memphis Children's Hospital with Dr. Ramone Luiz," he continued.

"Hi." Smiling, she sat down and turned to ask Matthew something that had been nagging at her mind and hit her again when he mentioned the hospital. "I've been meaning to ask you—why did *you* fly in from Memphis?"

For the briefest moment his face took on the dark expression he'd had on the plane, but it quickly disappeared behind a smile. "I was visiting family."

Reminding herself not to sound too personal in front of the others, she asked, "You have family in Memphis?"

Asking personal questions probably wasn't a good idea when a woman was only having a three-day affair, but she hadn't been able to curb her curiosity.

He hesitated a moment. "My mother lives just over the Hernando de Soto Bridge on the Arkansas side."

Natalie's pulse pounded at her temple. She lived on Mud Island. His mother lived just across the Mississippi River from her. That meant he probably came to Memphis from time to time to visit.

Natalie put a hold on her racing thoughts of possibly seeing him again in the future.

Three days. That was what they'd agreed to and what she'd stick to. They were only on Friday of their weekend together. They still had the rest of the day, all of Saturday and part of Sunday before she flew home. It would be enough.

Even if by some miracle Matthew wanted to continue to see her, trying to maintain a long-distance relationship would be near impossible. She already worked long hours. When she got her promotion she'd be working even longer ones, because she'd essentially continue to do her job but be taking over the parts of Dr. Luiz's job he was relinquishing with his partial retirement.

If Matthew wanted to see her during his trips to Memphis, she'd say no. Sticking to the three days would be better than trying to stretch out what couldn't last and turning a fantasy into something waiting to fall apart.

"West Memphis in Arkansas isn't that far from where I live," she said, feeling as if she should say something for the benefit of the other three at the table, who were listening in curiously.

Maybe for Matthew, too, as he'd become overly interested in his food.

If he thought he needed to worry that she would push to see him in Tennessee, he was wrong. She had her priorities, and a relationship beyond Sunday was not one of them, no matter how phenomenal a lover he was.

Fortunately, the conversation turned to the conference. A few minutes later, the two men left the table, but Dr. Yang stayed and chatted with Matthew and Natalie about everything from her vegan diet to her faith.

The room had cleared out except for the wait staff cleaning the room.

"I've kept you two from making it to the first session on time," Kim said, glancing at her fitness wristband and wincing when she realized what time it was. "Sorry."

"No problem," Natalie assured, placing her fork and napkin on her empty plate. "I was late coming downstairs anyway."

Not really late, but when she and Matthew had calculated how long they could stay in bed that morning they'd not allotted time for mealtime socializing.

"Maybe we can sneak into the back and catch the presentation highlights."

When they rose to leave the table, Kim swayed.

Natalie noted how pale she was and moved around the table. "Are you okay?"

But she was too late. Kim's eyes rolled back and her knees buckled, causing her to slump backward. Just before she hit the carpeted floor, Matthew grasped the woman, lowering her to the carpet.

"Dr Yang?" He gently shook her. "Can you hear me?"

Natalie checked the woman's pulse, normal at seventy-six beats per minute. Although unconscious, she was breathing okay, too. "Vitals are stable."

Pulling a chair to Dr. Yang, Matthew propped her feet

in the chair to cause increased blood flow to her vital organs anyway.

"Is she okay?" one of the waiters asked, stooping beside them at the commotion of Dr. Yang losing consciousness. "Do I need to call 911?"

Natalie started to say yes, but Dr. Yang's eyelids fluttered and she grabbed hold of Natalie's arm.

"No ambulance," she muttered, so low Natalie strained to know what she'd said.

Further concern filled Natalie. "You're sure? You passed out. At the minimal, you need labs."

The woman shook her head. "Not sick." Her hand lowered to her belly and she weakly smiled. "Just pregnant."

Natalie's eyes widened and she stared at the woman in surprise. "Oh."

"Congratulations," Matthew said from where he knelt next to them, but Natalie couldn't tell if he meant the word or not.

"I'll call for an ambulance if you think I need to." The waiter looked to Natalie for instruction.

She eyed the pale woman, whose color was slowly returning. "You sure you're okay?"

Kim scooted onto her elbows and paused. "I will be when this nine-month deal is up. I've heard of morning sickness, but this light-headedness is ridiculous."

"Is your obstetrician aware you're having light-headedness?" Matthew looked ready to catch the woman if she so much as wobbled.

Kim nodded and gave a heartfelt sigh. "He thinks I need to suck it up. Don't I know that other women work right up until birth, plop that baby out, then go right back to working?"

Horrified, Natalie stared at the woman, who had now maneuvered herself into a sitting position with her legs down off the chair.

"Let me guess," Matthew ventured, understanding dawning. "Your obstetrician is your husband?"

Kim smiled. "Bingo. He's a wonderful man, a wonderful obstetrician, but is struggling with empathy for his wife."

"Sounds like you need a new obstetrician," Natalie recommended, struggling with empathy for the man.

Kim shook her head. "Lee is going to deliver our baby at home. It's what we both want. I can't imagine anyone other than him delivering our child."

Kim braced her palms against the floor and pushed herself, slowly standing. She stood still a moment, testing the waters, then smiled. "I shouldn't have made him sound such a tyrant. Pregnancy hormones and these waves of dizziness have made me cranky."

Both Matthew and the waiter moved alongside Kim as she sat back at the table.

"I'm fine. I've kept you two from the conference long enough." She glanced at the waiter's name tag and smiled at him. "Jack's going to get me a glass of orange juice, and when I've finished it I'll catch the next presentation."

Natalie felt guilty leaving Dr. Yang, and advised the waiter to call for help if needed, but they did go slip into the presentation. They were twenty minutes late, and a few heads turned when they slid into their seats. Natalie didn't care. There were worse things in life than being associated with a man you had admired from afar for years, and had fallen into immediate lust with upon meeting.

Natalie and Matthew stayed through all the morning sessions and logged in their continuing education hours. Lunch was sponsored by a pharmaceutical company that manufactured immunizations.

"I'd like to attend the presentation given by Dr. Fielding on in-utero cleft palate repair this afternoon, but perhaps you'd like us to get lunch on our own?" Matthew offered as they reviewed the conference itinerary.

Natalie's gaze lifted and fires danced in the honeyed depths of her eyes. "You mean, on our own as in Room Service?"

He laughed. "I actually meant us meeting in the lobby and renting bikes to ride up the boardwalk to a place I know that has some killer seafood."

Her face was so expressive it was easy to watch her surprise that he didn't immediately take up her offer. Part of him wanted to do just as she'd suggested, but he also wanted to take her for some sunshine, rest and relaxation. He had the feeling she worked too hard.

Had the feeling?

Dr Luiz had gone on and on about her. Natalie deserved the promotion she'd soon be getting. In that regard, Matthew was glad the hospital hadn't met his terms. Natalie would probably have been devastated if had he gotten the job.

"Obviously, you learned nothing from last night." She gave an exaggerated sigh. "But, since I have to eat, I'll meet you in the lobby in twenty minutes," she promised. "But if I have to get on a bicycle for the first time in a zillion years, the food better be as good as you say, and I'm adding this to the list of things you need to make up to me later."

He chuckled. "Noted—and I'll make the wait worth your while."

Natalie had always heard the expression that doing something one had once been proficient at was like riding a bike. Once you knew how, you could just jump right back on.

She'd jumped right back on, but would be lying if she claimed proficiency. She had ridden a bicycle as a child, again when in undergrad and traveling to and from her apartment to campus. That had been several years ago, and her confidence that her bicycle wasn't going to topple over was now lacking.

Or maybe it was that she got the impression Matthew was holding back to stay close to her, that he was trying to keep up a conversation between them, and she needed to focus on what she was doing so her bicycle didn't go careening into his.

Plus, her bottom hurt on the narrow seat.

"Smile, Natalie."

As she parked her bicycle and secured a cord around the frame and locked it in place, she gritted her teeth in a semblance of a smile.

Matthew laughed. "You can do better than that."

"Ask me again when my belly is full."

"Deal." Having secured his own bicycle, he took her hand and they made their way up the wooden deck leading into the restaurant. Although it was busy, the hostess guided them to a table on one of the patios that overlooked the beach.

"Sitting outdoors okay?"

"This is fabulous." She loved the ocean, loved the feel of the breeze on her face, and the patio was covered, had an overhead fan going and offered just the right amount of shade from the hot sun. "Perfect," she added as she sat in a chair and grabbed a menu.

A waitress came by, took their drink order, and Matthew ordered an appetizer to share.

"I could have been allergic to shrimp, you know," she teased when the waitress had left.

"Are you? I can catch her and change the order."

She tried, but couldn't keep a straight face. "No."

"I didn't think so."

Curious, she asked, "Why not?"

He shrugged. "I get the impression you're a woman who has no trouble letting a man know what she wants, doesn't want," his eyes bored into hers, "or what she's allergic to."

She supposed she had given him that impression. With him, telling him, showing him what she wanted had been easy. Maybe because she knew their time was limited and there was a freedom in the knowledge that she'd never see him again afterwards.

Only, his mother was practically her neighbor, so it was possible. Why did that make her heart race?

"Right now," she began, "this woman is going to wash her hands and check to see if I sweated my mascara down my cheeks during that bicycle ride."

"No worries. You are beautiful."

He made her *feel* beautiful, and not just because he'd told her several times that day. Smiling, she winked at him. "If you get lonely before I get back, you can always sneak into the ladies' room and we could…"

He threw his head back and laughed. "You have a one-track mind."

She did. Pediatric cardiology.

Although for the past twenty-four hours she'd only thought of Matthew.

Probably because he was a renowned heart surgeon.

Or because he was gorgeously fascinating.

One or the other, but either way she was on vacation— sort of—so focusing on something besides work wasn't a crime.

A weekend with Natalie Sterling was like being at a sexual boot camp. One that tested Matthew's stamina and shocked him at how far she pushed him physically. Possibly because he knew this would be his last "free" weekend for a long, long time as he forced himself to settle into his role as Carrie's parent.

Which implied that any woman would do.

Matthew didn't buy it.

The woman lying next to him in her hotel room bed trying to catch her breath drove his body crazy, had his libido, his endurance pushed to unreal heights.

Despite his own heaving chest, he rolled onto his side, planted a kiss on her damp cheek. "That was amazing."

Smiling with that sexy, full mouth of hers, she lowered her lashes in a saucy flutter. "I thought you could do better."

He burst out laughing. "You think?"

"Life goals, Matthew," she said, and tsked, rolling to face him. "Life goals."

"Guess I better get started." He traced his finger over the curve of her bare hip.

Still a little breathless, her eyes widened. "We just... now?"

His finger made figure eights, moving closer and closer to the apex of her legs with each completion. "No time like the present. Besides, I still have to make it up to you for making you ride that bicycle instead of..."

"There is that," Natalie agreed, moving into his touch. "Guess you're right. Might take a lot to make that up to me, considering how I toppled over on the ride home."

Recalling how his insides had felt watching Natalie's front bike wheel running off the edge of the sidewalk, her losing balance and toppling over right into traffic, Matthew stilled the tracing of his hands and rolled over onto her instead. "You okay?"

"I could be better," she said, staring up at him with a challenge in her eyes and the need to be kissed on her lips.

"I'm beginning to think you're just using me for sex, Dr. Sterling," he teased.

Only, if he was just teasing, why did the truth in his words sting? Why did he want to hear Natalie deny that that was what she was doing?

"That's exactly what we're *both* doing, Dr. Coleman," she reminded, her expression guarded. "Now, didn't you mention something about making that bicycle ride up to me?"

CHAPTER FIVE

WITHOUT ANY DIFFICULTY, Matthew swapped his first-class seat for the seat next to Natalie's coach one.

Natalie had been surprised, but like her, she supposed, he was reluctant for their "three days" to end a moment before it had to.

When the plane landed, they'd go their separate ways.

"Don't."

At his single word, she opened her eyes, glanced at him in question.

"You're thinking about when the plane lands again."

"You're right. Sorry." She squeezed the hand holding hers. "It was a great conference, wasn't it?"

"Best ever."

Her gaze cut to his, knowing her eyes were full of questions, then scolded herself for caring so much at what he'd implied.

Yet, she did care.

She bit the inside of her cheek. "I agree."

"Same time next year?"

Natalie laughed a little nervously. "I wish."

"Me, too," he said.

Natalie's chest tightened. Part of her longed to ask if he was serious. Why *couldn't* they meet up again for a weekend of fun? But logic answered her question even before it could really take hold. To make plans to meet up again implied they had a relationship that would continue. They didn't.

The past three days had been perfect. To continue would be only waiting for him to leave, waiting for him to decide he didn't want any more three-day weekends together. She'd been left several times too many already in her life to set herself up that way.

Sticking to their original plan was the way it had to be.

"Thank you for this past weekend, Matthew. How does this work from here?"

His gaze narrowed. "What do you mean?"

"If we accidentally run into each other. What if at some point we are both at the same place at the same time?" After all, his mother lived in Memphis. Yes, the city was large, but stranger things had happened. "Do we pretend we don't know each other or...?" She let her words trail off.

He considered her question. "Who knows what's going to have changed between now and that time if our paths cross again?" His expression tightened. "You might have met someone and—"

"I won't have," she cut in, wanting to set the record straight. "I've learned my lesson."

His expression darkened. "You mean me? Natalie, I—"

She shook her head and hastened to assure, "No. This weekend was wonderful, and exactly what we agreed upon." She took a deep breath. "It's odd. I feel like we shared so much, that you know everything about me, but in reality you know very little."

"I know how to make you..." he continued in a whisper into her ear, winking at her when he straightened back in his seat.

Natalie blushed. "Yes, you know that." He knew her body well. She wouldn't argue with that. "But what you don't know is that two months ago I found out the man

I'd been in a relationship with for the past three years was cheating."

"Idiot."

Matthew's absolute confidence in his assessment of Jonathan made Natalie smile.

"Yes, he was. Is," she corrected. "But the truth of the matter is that he did us both a favor, because we didn't want the same things."

"You lived with him?"

Staring at the travel magazine poking out from the seat pocket in front of her, Natalie nodded. "He moved into my condo apartment just over two years ago."

"Is he still there?"

"Good heavens, no." She closed her eyes, then, realizing how he might take her having done so, she opened them. "He's gone and I'm glad."

Matthew stared at her in ways that made her want to close her eyes again.

"You deserve a life, Natalie."

Did he think she didn't know that? But deserving a life and actually getting that life didn't always mesh up. She wanted someone who wouldn't leave her, who could love her completely, but in reality her career seemed the only aspect of her life she had control over.

Fortunately she loved medicine, and her career had never let her down.

Suzie gave Natalie an "are you crazy?" look. "You didn't get his cell number or social-media account information or anything?"

After Natalie had arrived at her apartment—her practically empty apartment, thanks to Jonathan clearing out his things and quite a few of Natalie's as well—the television hadn't been able to abate the quietness. She'd called and asked her friends to meet her for a late dinner at their favorite downtown restaurant. Tonight, the partially empty rooms had made her feel claustrophobic, alone, and she'd had to get out of the apartment.

"There was no need to exchange numbers." There hadn't been. "We agreed to only three days and said our goodbyes just outside baggage claims."

They'd kept things simple. Three perfect days and nights.

She had no regrets. Other than that she wondered if she'd made a mistake in telling her best friends about Matthew. They'd obviously seen more than there was, and she needed to set the record straight.

"We're much better to have ended things today than to ruin such a perfect memory."

Both her friends shook their heads.

"At least tell me he kissed you goodbye at the airport," Monica insisted, taking a sip of her drink. "One of those long, sappy goodbye kisses that makes a girl kick her leg up and everyone else stare in envy."

"Come on," Suzie urged. "You can't not tell us if he kissed you goodbye. He didn't shake your hand or something else just as lame, did he? Tell all. Best friends want to know."

Recalling how Matthew had kissed her, Natalie smiled. "He kissed me goodbye better than any heroine has ever been kissed goodbye in any romantic movie. Way better."

He had. A kiss that had been full of so much more than just passion. There had been emotion. *Gratitude*, she assured herself. They'd both been thankful for a fun weekend. A very fun weekend. Without meaning to, Natalie added with a sigh, "A goodbye kiss for the ages."

Monica and Suzie exchanged looks, then Monica leaned across the table, wide-eyed, and gasped, "I can't believe it. You fell for this guy."

"No, I didn't," Natalie immediately denied. "He was just…" How could she describe Matthew and how he'd made her feel? "Good, that's all."

"Right. I never saw you all flush-cheeked and starry-eyed when talking about *he whose name we don't say*."

Which was how her friends referred to her ex.

"There's a reason for that. *Jonathan*," she stressed his name, "never did the things to my body that Matthew did. Not even close."

Her friends exchanged looks again, making Natalie feel defensive.

"I had a great weekend, something the two of you encouraged me to do," she reminded. "Why are you acting as if it's a big deal?"

"Why are you?" Suzie pointed out at the same time as Monica said,

"Because it is a big deal. You shouldn't have let him go."

Natalie rolled her eyes. When she'd called her friends, this wasn't what she'd had in mind.

"You both told me to have a holiday fling and I did. An amazing one with a man whose brain is pure genius and whose body should be on a pin-up calendar." She could fan her face just at the memory of his hotness. "I thought you would be proud that I'd done something so out of character."

Her friends just stared.

"Be happy for me," she ordered, getting frustrated with how they kept looking at her.

"We *are* happy for you," Suzie insisted, her big green eyes cutting to Monica for back-up. "Only…"

"Only what?"

"What if this guy was the one?"

Natalie laughed at the absurdity of her friend's question. "He wasn't. It's unlikely I'll ever see him again."

Why did that thought make her insides ache?

"Unlikely?" Suzie piped up. "Does that mean it's possible?"

"Anything is possible. His mother lives in West Memphis and he and I are both pediatric heart surgeons interested in innovative in-utero surgical techniques." Natalie shrugged. "But I don't have plans to intentionally see him again, if that's what you mean."

"Hey, Natalie," Suzie said, her expression one full of glee. "You said you don't mean to intentionally see him again, not that you didn't *want* to see him again."

Yeah, she realized that.

Life without ever setting eyes on Matthew Coleman seemed a long, hard sentence—but why pretend it could be something more?

"So, he's a pediatric heart surgeon." Monica waved a manicured hand. "It can't be that difficult to track down a number to reach him."

No, it wouldn't be. But Natalie wouldn't be tracking him down.

"I won't lie and say there isn't a part of me that would like to see Matthew again, but it's best this way."

Her friends looked doubtful. "What way?"

"With him being a wonderful memory. I've got my career to think about." It was true. With Dr. Luiz's upcoming partial retirement, she did need to focus on her career, not long for things that she'd never had and quite possibly never would. People didn't stick around in her life. Not her parents. Not her foster parents. Not Jonathan.

Not Matthew—but at least she'd known upfront he'd only be in her life for three short days.

Monica rolled her eyes.

Suzie shook her head.

"The hospital board should offer the new position within the next few weeks and I'm going to be busy, busy, busy." She sure hoped so. She needed busy. "I don't need any distractions from what really matters."

"We're not convinced that promotion's a good thing if it means you're going to be working even more."

Maybe her friends weren't, but Natalie knew better.

Heading the cardiology unit when Dr. Luiz stepped back was what she'd dreamed of long before a dark-haired, pale-blue-eyed, beautiful man had completely possessed her mind and body.

Two weeks later, Matthew pulled the phone away from his ear and stared at the device in disbelief. He couldn't have heard right.

Apparently, Carrie's fever had gotten to him and he was now hallucinating. Or maybe it was the lack of sleep over the past thirty-six hours as he'd sat up with her most of the night, afraid to sleep in case her illness worsened— in case he did something else wrong and Carrie paid the price. For the same reasons, he'd called out of work that morning. Something he'd hated to do, but Carrie's pre-school wouldn't allow her to go in with a fever and he hadn't had a sick back-up plan short of bringing her to the hospital with him. A feverish child on a neonatal cardiac unit wasn't a good idea under any circumstances, even if it had meant shuffling his entire schedule.

Glancing down at the sleeping little girl's flushed cheeks and limp body in his lap, he blamed himself for her illness. No doubt he'd messed up somehow. The pediatrician had assured him that she had a normal childhood illness that would pass, that he just needed to keep her hydrated and keep her fever down, but Matthew knew he'd been distracted, had been working long hours where Carrie had been dragged to the hospital repeatedly to make rounds with him. She'd probably picked up something in the hospital hallway.

"The hospital decided having you at Memphis Children's was worth making a few concessions," Dr. Luiz continued on the phone, sounding quite proud of the board's decision. "They're prepared to meet your conditions. All you have to do is say yes and their lawyers will draw up the contract."

Matthew's head spun. "You're serious?"

He and Carrie would be close to his mother and sister, to his family. He'd have help. Carrie would be in the care of people who knew how to care for a child.

Natalie was also there.

A wave of heat flushed his body, making him question again if Carrie's fever had overtaken him, too.

"What about Dr. Sterling? You mentioned her several times when I was in Memphis." Did Natalie know he might be taking the job she wanted? "How does she feel about this?"

"I don't foresee it as being a problem. During their reconciliation of your terms, the board plans for Dr. Sterling to directly work with you."

Matthew wasn't so confident. "She knows, then?"

"Not yet."

Which explained Dr. Luiz's comment about not seeing it as a problem. Matthew knew better, and so would Dr. Luiz soon enough.

"That's the one stipulation to your contract, by the way."

Carrie stirred in her sleep and Matthew stroked his fingers over her back in a soothing manner, waiting for Dr. Luiz's next words, already knowing what the man was going to say.

"With the lighter workload you insisted upon, Dr. Sterling is to share some of the responsibilities that were originally exclusive to your new title. Dr. Sterling is a valued member of our staff. She's excited about the upcoming projects the hospital is involved in. We see her sharing some of the leadership roles at the hospital as the perfect solution to your demands, as well as her continued role at the hospital. We don't want to lose her."

No, he imagined not. Natalie's resume was impressive.

"She will be a great asset to your work at Memphis Children's," Dr. Luiz continued. "You'll be lucky to have her on your team."

No doubt, but she wasn't going to be happy.

Nor was the hospital in Boston, his research team, his office staff.

If he accepted the position in Memphis he'd miss his life in Boston. He *already* missed his life in Boston. He'd had a great life—a booming career, loyal friends, good times and a plethora of women to fill his nights.

His gaze dropped to the child in his arms. Everything had changed, and not for the good. He didn't resent Carrie—he *loved* the kid—but he knew he wasn't cut out for raising a little girl, knew he longed for the freedom he'd known just a few months ago, knew she'd be better off elsewhere. His mother, his sister, his extended family were all in Memphis. People whom he trusted to do what was best for Carrie. As much as the thought of leaving the job he loved in Boston stung, what Dr. Luiz offered was exactly what Carrie needed.

If he said yes, he would be hurting Natalie, would be snatching away something she desperately wanted and, in many ways, deserved. She wasn't likely to forgive him.

Glancing down again at the sick child in his arms, feeling his overwhelming inadequacy in solely providing her care, Matthew admitted that being near his family would be a godsend. His parenting skills weren't up to par, and so far his live-in nanny interviews hadn't turned up a single applicant he trusted.

Had he been in Memphis he wouldn't have had to call out of work today, wouldn't have had to reschedule multiple surgeries that weren't easily rescheduled, because he would have had family willing and able to help. How many more times over Carrie's childhood would she be ill, have needs that would require an unexpected change to their normal routine?

He liked to think he'd been an awesome uncle, but what did he know about being a dad? About meeting the emotional needs of a four-year-old who had lost everyone except him?

Nothing.

Accepting the position in Memphis was a necessity.

"You're quiet," Dr. Luiz pointed out from across his desk.

Having gotten lost in his thoughts that he'd soon come face to face with a woman he'd thought about way too often over the past month, Matthew leaned back in his chair and shrugged. "It's been a long day."

It had been a long month. More like a long four months, during which his best friends had died and fatherhood had been thrust upon him, ready or not.

"But a good one. This move is good for Memphis Children's, and from what you've told me about your situation it's good for you, too. A win-win for all."

It was a win-win all the way around.

"Except for Dr. Sterling."

Despite the fact that she was technically being promoted, *she* wouldn't think she was a winner. Not when she'd thought she'd be running the whole shebang.

Would she agree to work with him?

If she didn't, if she opted to leave the hospital, perhaps it would be best. He had enough issues to deal with without adding in a sexual attraction to his new co-worker.

Dr Luiz and the board had been all too willing to go along with nothing being said, that the whole deal be kept quiet until Matthew arrived. He'd made the request due to the concerns of his Boston colleagues regarding his research, that he needed to have things settled prior to any word leaking out of his relocation. Boston's work would continue on developing the robot. Matthew had made sure of it.

Working in collaboration with the Boston team, he'd establish a smaller second team in Memphis, one that would implement use of the robot in its upcoming further expansion into in utero heart surgeries. With Memphis Children's eager to expand their pediatric cardiology department's capabilities, the timing couldn't be more perfect.

"Natalie wants what is right for her patients. You being here is for the better of all."

She'd likely hate him. He had enough personal turmoil. He could do without discord at work.

"She is an ambitious woman who has career goals. She wouldn't be human if she didn't resent my having taken what she thought was going to be entirely hers."

Dr Luiz's gaze narrowed. "She mentioned she met you in Miami, but suggested it was a brief meeting. You sound as if you got to know her better than on a casual basis."

Matthew's comment to Natalie on the plane about knowing her popped into his head and his jaw tightened. "The entire conference was three days. I know very little about Dr. Sterling."

Just that she'd smiled lazily when he woke her up at sunrise so they could watch the sun come up that last morning. That she loved the feel of wet sand between her toes. That she laughed at the corny jokes he'd told her, and that she thought strawberries were manna from heaven.

That she made love to him like a siren and slept in his arms like an angel.

That she was going to be floored by the hospital's announcement today.

A knock sounded on Dr. Luiz's office door and Matthew tensed.

Natalie.

His heart pounded in his chest, thumping wildly against his ribcage.

He was about to play a role in hurting a woman who got to him as no other ever had.

Being in Memphis was right for Carrie.

That was what mattered most.

Natalie was just…just someone he'd once spent three fantasy days with.

CHAPTER SIX

WAITING FOR DR. LUIZ to bid her to enter his office, Natalie smoothed her scrubs.

Finally, she thought.

The buzz around the hospital was that something big was about to happen. Natalie knew what that something was. She couldn't wait until the announcement was made that she'd be promoted and that they'd gotten approval for the surgical procedure they'd been working on for years. She would soon perform the first in-utero vessel transposition repair at Memphis Children's.

A dream come true. She and Dr. Luiz's research showed great promise on correcting transposition of the vessels prior to birth. She'd gone through the procedure time and again on computer models, on premature and full-term "blue" babies. She wanted those babies to be born pink, to go home with their families much sooner, to have longer, healthier lives, and believed there was no reason they couldn't. That she would get to head up the team, would get to be lead surgeon, was enough to make a girl over the moon.

"Come in."

Smiling, Natalie turned the knob and stepped into Dr. Luiz's office, only to stop short when she realized her mentor wasn't alone.

She'd recognize the back of that dark head, those shoulders, anywhere.

What was Matthew doing in Dr. Luiz's office?

All the blood in her body drained to her feet, bolting them to the floor.

He had known it was her at the door. That much was evident when he stood and turned to meet her gaze. There was no surprise in his pale blue eyes.

Natalie fought shock, though, a million emotions hitting her at once.

He looked so good, so perfect, so much better than anything her memory could conjure. Her body leapt with joy, recalling how he'd stroked such pleasure through every part of her being.

But he shouldn't be there. At her work. With her boss.

Why was he there? What possible reason could Matthew have for sitting in her boss's office?

Her brain raced. Had he told Dr. Luiz what had happened in Florida? Why would he? What did it matter if he had? The hospital had no say in whom she slept with. She doubted any of the board members cared, so long as she brought no public shame on the hospital.

Sex with Matthew was nothing any woman should be ashamed of. The man was gorgeous, brilliant, and had the ability to rock a woman's whole existence.

And how.

Nope, she was not going to let her brain go down that path.

Her gaze not wavering from his, Natalie resisted the urge to clear her throat. She would not let him know how much his being there threw her world off its axis.

"Natalie," Dr. Luiz began, "you'll, no doubt, recall having met Dr. Matthew Coleman in Miami, and I know you're a fan of his work."

Ha. She was a fan, but she doubted she and Dr. Luiz referred to the same work.

"Dr. Coleman." She reluctantly stuck out her hand. Reluctantly, because as much as she wanted to touch Matthew, for him to touch her, seeing him was wreaking havoc on her ability to think. "Nice to see you again."

Matthew's eyes searched hers, as if he was trying to determine if she believed her own words.

It *was* nice to see him. It was also making her heart pound like crazy, because he shouldn't be there. He should be a pleasant memory from her past. Nothing more.

Okay, so she hadn't been able to stop thinking about him, wanting him, but with time she would have shoved him into the recesses of her mind. At least, that had been the plan.

"Dr. Sterling," he greeted, taking her hand into his in what appeared to be a casual grasp yet was anything but. The skin-to-skin contact sent shockwaves throughout her body as surely as if he'd electrocuted her. How could he do that with just a brush of his skin against hers? "It's a pleasure to see you again."

Her cheeks heated. Mainly because Dr Luiz was observing their exchange. She tore her gaze from Matthew's and glanced at her very astute boss. Her boss who wouldn't quite meet her gaze.

Which had Natalie tugging her hand out of Matthew's scalding one.

In all the years Natalie had known Dr. Luiz, that was a first. He was the most straightforward person she'd ever met. So why was her boss avoiding making direct eye contact? She didn't understand Matthew's guilty look, and she sure didn't understand her boss's unusual behavior.

Her gaze narrowed suspiciously as she refocused on Matthew. "To what do we owe your unexpected visit?"

"Not unexpected. I invited him," Dr. Luiz informed, motioning to the vacant chair next to Matthew's. "Have a seat, Natalie."

Tension twisting in her muscles, tighter and tighter, Natalie sat.

"As you know, with my semi-retirement and the grant approval, there are a lot of upcoming changes taking place in our cardiology department."

Natalie's heart picked up pace, thundering in her chest.

"You and I have discussed that the hospital's main goal is to transform our department into one of the top facilities in the country, that we want to lead the way, rather than jumping on board with what other hospitals are doing."

This was one of those defining life moments.

Dreams were about to come true.

Only, why had he asked Matthew to be there? The only possible explanation, as crazy as it was, had her wondering if the dream was actually a nightmare.

"I'm pleased to inform you Dr. Coleman has joined our team to help us do just that, by taking my place as Head of Cardiology."

On a wave of extreme excitement and expected elation, Natalie's heart crashed down with the force of having been hit with a sledgehammer.

Nightmare it was.

Her blood drained from her face, heavily pooling in her legs, making her body feel stuck to her chair, making gravity suck at her entire being, threatening to flatten her.

Dr. Luiz was still talking but Natalie's ears roared, only letting her brain absorb part of what he was saying.

"…know you wanted the position…" *blah, blah, blah* "…know you are as ecstatic as I am about getting to work with Dr. Coleman…"

She should be, right? She'd admired Matthew's surgical work from afar for years. But she knew this department inside out, knew how to take it to the next level, and had earned the position.

Matthew had taken it from her.

"You'll be on his team, of course."

Of course. Her head spun.

"His second-in-command, with specific responsibilities…"

Second. Not in charge, but answering to Matthew.

Matthew. Oh, crap! Matthew was going to be in Memphis. All the time. Her eyes widened. Matthew was going to be working in Memphis. With her. Day after day.

Why?

Why would he do this?

Matthew watched emotions play across Natalie's face. None of them were good ones. She looked stunned, betrayed.

He hadn't betrayed her. He'd gone after the position before he'd met her. He needed the relocation. Carrie needed to be with people who could take care of her.

Despite Dr. Luiz's assurances that Natalie would be on board with the unexpected change, Matthew had known better. Then again, he knew the whole story, knew about their weekend fling.

Weekend fling. The label repulsed him, but it was what they'd shared.

Why the label bothered him so, he couldn't quite define. He'd had flings before. Several of them. None had left him feeling raw. Then again, he'd never been in quite this situation, either.

Regardless, he had a little girl to think of.

Carrie's counselor had advised Matthew to be sure to nurture the child over the next few months as she adapted to her new environment.

Nurture her. How did one do that exactly?

"As head of the surgery team, you'll be working closely with Matthew, of course."

Natalie's golden eyes blinked. "*I'm* heading up surgery? Not Dr. Coleman?"

That she asked something Dr. Luiz had just explained in detail attested to how in shock she was.

"As head of the entire department, Dr. Coleman will oversee your work, of course, but I can think of no one better for him to have on his leadership team than a heart surgeon of your caliber." Dr. Luiz pushed his gold-rimmed glasses up the bridge of his nose. "You knew I planned to step down, Natalie, and that I was counting on you to take on further responsibilities. Surely, this doesn't come as a surprise?"

"I'm surprised," Natalie immediately assured, face flushed. "Rather blown away. I thought…"

Everyone in the room knew what she'd thought.

"Never mind," she murmured, seeming to pull herself together. She turned toward Matthew, stuck out her hand again. "Congratulations, Dr. Coleman."

Matthew barely clasped her hand when she pulled it away, stood, and faced her former boss. "If there's nothing else?"

Dr. Luiz regarded her through narrowed lids, then shook his head.

Before Matthew could speak, Natalie was out the door and Dr. Luiz was talking again, but this time it was Matthew not registering what he was saying.

"Excuse me," he interrupted, not waiting for an answer as he took off after Natalie.

"Don't touch me," Natalie hissed when Matthew grabbed hold of her upper arm. Didn't he know she'd left the room in a hurry to escape him, to be alone, not to have him follow her?

Of course he did, but it hadn't mattered.

"That's not what you were saying a few weeks ago."

Suffering major shock for the second time that day, she spun and practically hissed at him, "How dare you say that?"

"Because it's true." His voice was calm, and that irritated her all the more.

He didn't have to point that particular truth out, she thought, glaring with all her might, hoping that her evil thoughts about him were readily seen on her face.

"But inappropriate for our current situation, don't you think?" she accused. He grimaced and she further attacked, "I don't want you here."

"I didn't think you did."

Flustered and just wanting to escape to her office to regroup her thoughts without him there to witness, she asked, "Then why are you here?"

He took a long breath. "That, my dearest Natalie, is a long story."

"I'm not your dearest Natalie. I'm not your anything."

Matthew raked his fingers through his inky hair, then glanced down the busy hospital corridor. "Is there somewhere we can go to talk?"

"Are you asking as my new boss?" Okay, her tone had been a bit snarky, but at the moment she didn't care. "Because otherwise, my answer is that we have nothing to say to each other. Not ever."

"Natalie—"

"Don't Natalie me. From the moment we said goodbye at the airport, I've been Dr. Sterling to you. Nothing more. Your three days expired long ago."

His expression taking on the dark and dangerous one he'd worn so well at the airport and on the plane, he nodded, as if her response didn't surprise him. Then again, why should he be surprised? He'd known what he was doing: stealing her dream job.

"Fine. As your new boss, is there somewhere we can talk in private?"

Without a word, Natalie led him down the corridor of offices. When she came to the one with her name on the brass plate, she punched in a code, then twisted the handle.

Opening the door, she paused, facing him. "I'm only letting you in because you're my boss now. No other reason."

His expression just as terse as her insides felt, he nodded. "Understood."

She moved aside, let him into her office, then shut the door behind her, wondering if she could claim temporary insanity if she lashed out at him for invading and upsetting her well-planned life.

If Matthew had had the slightest doubt as to Natalie's intentions on inviting him into her office, she'd made it clear before letting him pass through her doorway, and immediately began reiterating her feelings the moment the door clicked closed.

"Is this some kind of sick joke to you?"

"A joke?"

"Taking a job in Memphis." As if she couldn't be still, she paced across the room. "Why in the world would you leave your research in Boston?"

"I didn't leave my research, just relocated the parts I'll remain involved with to Memphis," he explained, wishing she'd sit down and let him tell her about the events that had led him to this moment.

Interest piqued, she lifted her brows. "Your research with the Libertine robot? How can you do that?"

"The Libertine research will continue in Boston, but it has gotten approval for use and will soon be available to other areas. Expanding my work to a second location, bringing my experience, will be of benefit to the medical community as a whole."

"You just happened to choose Memphis for this expansion?" She shook her head. "I'm not buying it."

"Even if I didn't have personal reasons, with Memphis Children's Hospital and St Jude's located here, it's a great location for my research. You can't deny that."

"Personal reasons?" She glared at him with pure loathing. "If you think for one minute your being here changes anything between us, you're wrong."

His being here changed everything, including how he could think of Natalie. What had been a pleasant interlude from reality had turned into a nightmare for them both.

"I chose Memphis before I ever met you."

As what he said sank in, her eyes widened. "You knew about this when we were in Miami? That you were moving to Memphis?"

Matthew raked his fingers through his hair again and sought for the right place to begin, to make her understand how they'd ended up in this exact moment.

"How *could* you?" she accused before he got a word out. "How could you smile and laugh with me when you knew that we were going to have to see each other day after day, that you were going to be my boss. You had sex with me anyway?"

The vehemence in her voice had him internally flinching, but he stood his ground. "When I boarded that plane to Miami, I was under the impression my moving to Memphis was a no-go and Dr. Luiz's position would be filled by someone other than me."

"Right." She rolled her eyes. "You, the great Dr. Matthew Coleman, interviewed for my job and you thought they weren't going to hire you? Puh-*lease*."

"I was never told it was your job, Natalie." He wanted to be clear on that. "Dr. Luiz, nor the board, ever mentioned any intent to offer the position to you. Not once." She acted as if he'd intentionally taken something of hers. He hadn't done anything wrong. He'd needed this opportunity in Memphis and when it was offered he'd taken it. "Were you told they were going to offer you the position?"

The pain that flittered across her face stabbed into Matthew's chest. Never had he wanted to hurt Natalie. Far, far from it. But they needed to clear the record on what had happened, to establish some professional ground rules if they were to work together. Maybe it would even be easier on them both if she hated him.

"No, but I was given reason to believe it would happen." Her face full of accusation, she asked, "For the record, if you had been aware of the possibility that the job would otherwise be mine, would it have changed anything?"

Technically, he *had* known it was a possibility, but even if he'd been point-blank told the job was hers if he said no, his reasons for wanting to relocate to Memphis took precedence.

Carrie took precedence.

He shook his head. "No."

A steely resolve settled into her eyes. "I don't want you here."

"I think you've already established that." He moved toward her, stopped when she flinched and backed away as if she couldn't stand the thought of him being close enough to touch her.

He rammed his hands into his pockets to keep from doing something stupid. Like doing just that. The last thing he needed was to touch Natalie. They were work colleagues now. Nothing more.

"My reasons for relocating have nothing to do with you," he assured. "I met with the hospital board and Dr. Luiz the day prior to flying to Miami, but the hospital initially wasn't willing to meet my terms. I thought that was the end of it, until Dr. Luiz called to say the board had reconsidered."

She didn't look any less ticked, just more suspicious. "When was that?"

"A month ago."

A fresh wave of betrayal blanched her already pale face. "Dr. Luiz has known for a month that the job was yours? He…he never said anything." She winced, paced back across the room, turned and met Matthew's gaze with a world of hurt shining in her eyes.

A desire to take away her hurt hit him, to somehow undo what had been done. Impossible. He knew that. But he hated his indirect role in the pain she was suffering.

"He should have told me. I deserved to know before an announcement was made."

"He told you today. Before an announcement was made," Matthew pointed out. "He has great respect for you. He was adamant you have a prestigious place on my team."

"As your second-in-command," she bit out, not impressed. "Just as I'm *his* second-in-command."

"You're young, Natalie."

"What does that have to do with anything?" she huffed. "I have been with Dr. Luiz for years. Did my residency at Memphis Children's. I've worked my butt off to build our neonatal cardiology program. I'm more than qualified. What does my age have to do with anything?"

She was right. Had Matthew not intervened, she would have been named Head of Neonatal Cardiology with Dr. Luiz's semi-retirement.

"I don't know what to tell you, Natalie. I can't speak for Dr. Luiz or the hospital board. I interviewed for a position that I needed, and when my terms were met, I accepted."

"That you needed?" she scoffed. "You head up your team in Boston at one of the most prestigious hospitals in the world. Why come here?"

She was right. He'd never have chosen to leave Boston had it been just him involved.

"Relocating to Memphis makes Carrie's life better."

Taken aback, she stared at him, then asked in a voice he barely recognized, "Who is Carrie?"

Matthew took a deep breath. "My...daughter."

CHAPTER SEVEN

THE HOSPITAL WAS abuzz with news of the handsome new heart surgeon taking Dr. Luiz's place. How wonderful for the hospital that such a gifted surgeon had taken over their department. *Blah, blah, blah.* Natalie was sick of hearing about Matthew.

Sick. Of. It.

She simply could not escape him.

At work, everyone was talking about him.

At home, he invaded her sleep.

With her friends, well, she was seriously considering placing ads for their replacements if they didn't quit going on about how lucky she was that her fabulous holiday lover had shown back up in her life. Permanently.

"You're thinking hard on something," Dr. Luiz said, drawing Natalie's attention to where he had entered the break room just off the neonatal cardiac care unit where Natalie had made rounds. She'd stopped to get a cup of coffee because she'd been dragging.

She'd been dragging since she walked into Dr. Luiz's office expecting to celebrate the culmination of years of hard work and instead had come face to face with her vacation fling.

Stirring the one packet of sugar she'd added to her cup with a tiny red straw, Natalie cut her gaze to Dr. Luiz, but didn't meet his eyes. How could she, when she felt so betrayed?

"It's been a busy morning," she mumbled.

She'd had two new patient consults, plus had checked in on a five-day-old who she hoped to be able to transfer to a step-down unit soon.

Besides, what else could she say? She couldn't really scream and yell at Dr. Luiz, could she? If so, what would she say? That she felt as if a man she'd trusted, her mentor, had betrayed her by bringing in Matthew?

"The Harris case?" She *should* have been thinking about the Harris case rather than what, or more truthfully, who, she couldn't get off her brain. "The board approved the procedure," Dr. Luiz continued. "I thought you'd have scheduled the surgery the moment the board gave you a thumbs-up."

"I'm not sure Delaine Harris is the right first case."

She'd been over and over the woman's file. Delaine Harris was twenty-five years old and was pregnant with her first child. She'd already signed consent forms for the experimental procedure. They'd only been waiting on the board's approval, which had come through the day before. At just under five months pregnant, Delaine had known her baby's heart didn't work properly due to her vessels being transposed since her first ultrasound. If they were going to do the surgery in utero, precious time was ticking away.

Timing was everything.

Natalie wanted to make sure Delaine Harris's baby had every fighting chance and that doing the procedure in utero improved those odds, that nothing went wrong.

"Any particular reason why?"

None that she wanted to share.

Which was disconcerting, as she'd always discussed everything with Dr. Luiz. He'd mentored her from day one of her residency, when she'd been lucky enough to work with him.

Now, because of the situation with Matthew, she felt as if he'd let her down. Logically, she knew that wasn't what had happened, but it wasn't logic guiding her emotions.

"I've known you too long not to recognize that you're upset about Dr. Coleman."

Yeah, he'd also known her long enough to know she'd expected to be in Matthew's place. Still, what could she say? Dr. Luiz and the board had done what they believed was best for the hospital. She couldn't present a valid argument that said otherwise.

"He's an excellent pediatric heart surgeon," she said, for the sole reason that Dr. Luiz waited for a response.

"He's someone whose work you've admired for years."

"True." But only because he hadn't snatched her dream job. Which was unfair, but she didn't care. Fair quit being a priority when he'd slept with her knowing he'd interviewed for her job and he hadn't bothered telling her.

"It caught the board and myself off guard when he approached us about working at Memphis Children's."

"I can imagine." For all her gruff over Matthew being at her hospital, she did recognize his credentials.

"He's told you his reasons?"

Oh, he'd told her all right. He had a daughter.

She'd not let him tell her more. She hadn't wanted to know, because at this point, what had it mattered?

A daughter.

That seemed like a big something to have not mentioned while they'd been in Miami.

While they'd been in bed and…

She took a sip of her coffee, ignoring that the hot liquid scalded her tongue.

He hadn't lied to her. Not exactly. He'd said he wasn't married or involved with anyone, but he hadn't said he didn't have children. Not that she'd asked. Silly her. She'd add that to her list of things to know about a man before sleeping with him.

Ha. As if. Between Jonathan and Matthew, she was finished with men.

Not that she supposed Matthew's being a father mattered for their weekend purposes. Still, a woman should know something like that about a man she spent three days having sex with.

She should also know if he was vying for her job.

"I never met Dr. Fisk, but I think it's admirable what Matthew is doing to raise that little girl."

Dr. Fisk. So, the girl's mother had been a doctor. Why was Matthew raising the child on his own? Had something happened to "Dr. Fisk" or had the woman walked away?

The question of the girl's mother had haunted Natalie for the past week, but she'd refused to talk to him further about it. She just wanted to forget Miami, to forget him.

Pain throbbed at her temple and she resisted the urge to massage the ache.

What did it matter why he was raising the girl by himself? It was nothing to do with Natalie. He was nothing to her.

Other than that he had ousted her from her dream job and she'd once spent a weekend all wrapped up in him. No big deal.

Despite the fact she'd barely touched her coffee, she poured the remainder down the sink. "If you'll excuse me, I need to get back to clinic. I've a full day ahead."

Dr. Luiz nodded, but not before giving her a knowing look.

What he thought he knew, Natalie wasn't sure, but she made her escape before he asked about things she didn't want to think about, much less discuss.

In a private examination room off the Neonatal Intensive Cardiac Care Unit, Natalie ran the ultrasound wand over the tiny chest of Andrea Smith, studying the monitor as she did so.

"Shh, it's okay," the baby's mother cooed, holding the six-pound baby in her arms. "Is her heart any better?"

Wishing she could offer the new mother affirmation, Natalie continued to run the wand over the baby's chest and told her, "I'll go over the results when I've finished having a look."

The mother winced. "Sorry. I'm just so anxious to know how she is."

Natalie glanced away from the monitor long enough to offer the woman an empathetic smile. "It's okay. I understand. It's just better if I finish the test, so I can give you a more complete answer."

When done, Natalie didn't have good news. The child would have to have surgery sooner rather than later to repair the aortic arch hypoplasia and left ventricle size deformities the child had been born with. She called the operating room scheduler and set the wheels in motion to take the child to surgery for repair.

Imagine her surprise the following morning when, after scrubbing in, she joined the rest of her surgery team and had an unexpected member with the palest blue eyes she'd ever looked into.

"What are you doing here?" she asked, unable to stop herself. *Be professional, Natalie.* In front of the surgical crew wasn't the place to air her animosity.

"Scrubbing in as second."

"Shouldn't you have given me a heads-up you'd be taking Dr. Bingham's place?"

"No better way to learn how things work at Memphis Children's than to jump right in."

More than two hours later, while struggling to get the aortic valve leaflets to precisely lie as they should, Natalie became more and more frustrated that she was under

Matthew's watchful eye, blaming him rather than the difficult nature of the surgery.

"May I?" he asked at one point, causing Natalie's gaze to lift to his astute one.

Seriously? What was she supposed to say? Although Dr. Luiz's official partial retirement date hadn't yet arrived, Matthew was her boss.

She watched with reluctant fascination as he made a deeper cut in a modified Ross procedure and then meticulously worked to repair the uncooperative valve leaflets.

When he was done, the flaps fell into place perfectly between each beat.

Ecstatic for her patient and what should be a great surgical outcome, Natalie found her annoyance with Matthew slipping a little over her excitement at what she'd just witnessed.

How could she be annoyed with him when what he'd just done had been nothing short of genius?

If only she hadn't had sex with him.

When their tiny two-day-old patient was off to Recovery, Natalie was all too aware of Matthew beside her as she left the operating room and slipped off her protective gear.

"Tell me why that worked so well, what it's called, and if it's something you've been working on for a while or just came up with."

Stripping off his protective gear, Matthew regarded her. "You know the Ross procedure?"

"What you did was a modified version. I caught that. When you were finished, the valve leaflets fell perfectly."

"Only because you did a great job with the resection on the ventricle," he praised, leaning against a long sink used for scrubbing. "Otherwise, what I did wouldn't have worked."

"You've done this before, then?"

"A few times."

"Success rate?"

"So far we're at one hundred percent."

Natalie's eyes widened. "Seriously? What are the parameters?"

"I did my first one just over a year ago. About a year and a half ago, now," he amended. "Currently, she's had no further need of surgery."

"Valve is growing with the body? No issues with scar tissue causing stenosis?"

"Thus far, it's a success, but we won't know for sure until Kenzie gets older."

Kenzie. The name clicked.

"I read about her," Natalie admitted, wishing his work didn't fascinate her so much, wishing there wasn't a hint of a smile in his eyes. "You used the Libertine robot during that procedure."

"Yes."

"She had other heart issues." She thought back. "Something to do with her pulmonic valve."

He seemed surprised. "That's right. I did a repair of her pulmonic and aortic valves."

"I read the piece you published on the procedure, but I don't recall anything about what you just did on my patient."

"There wasn't anything in the article about what I just did. The article was about the Libertine, not the specifics of the valve repair. I've done that particular procedure a total of five times, including the one I just did. More research needs to be done prior to anything being published."

"Did you record Kenzie's surgery?"

His lips curved into a smile. "You want to watch my private stash?"

Natalie did.

But she didn't.

But she really, really did. If she was going to have to

put up with him being in Memphis, being at her hospital, she should have some perks, right?

"Would you let me?"

He didn't hesitate, just held her gaze. "I would."

"Because you want to further the knowledge of your staff?" Why she pushed, she wouldn't delve deeply to label, just that she wanted his clarification.

"Because you asked," he corrected, his gaze locked with hers. "Although, you're right. Part of my position is to further my staff's knowledge. The hospital is great, otherwise I wouldn't have considered the move. But I hope to bring positive changes. Dr. Luiz suggested I discuss those with you as he thought some of our ideas overlapped, and you could be key in the implementation process."

He was completely sincere, and Natalie found herself being sucked into the idea of working with someone who'd been operating on the cutting edge his entire career. He'd been at a hospital with the resources to make history, not follow in its footsteps. He wanted to bring that to her hospital.

"If we hadn't met in Miami and you hadn't stolen my dream job, I might like working with you," she admitted, somewhat reluctantly.

He studied her a moment, then asked, "Do you expect me to say I'm sorry, Natalie? I won't." He had that dark and dangerous look about him that had her glancing away. "I'm not."

For Miami or taking her dream job? *Or both?* Natalie wondered. Either way, her adrenaline rush from the successful procedure and watching his innovative surgical technique was wearing her down, leaving her restless and needing to get away.

"Are you going to the retirement party for Dr. Luiz?" he asked.

The party was almost two weeks away, sponsored by the hospital, and a big deal.

"What kind of question is that?" The man had been her mentor since residency. "Of course I'm going. Just because he sold me out to the board in favor of you doesn't mean I'd bail on his retirement party."

Matthew's expression tightened. "Is that really how you see what he did?"

Natalie closed her eyes, took a deep breath. "He did what was right for the cardiology department, for the hospital, and for Memphis. I don't fault him for that."

"Sure you do."

He was right. She did.

"I understand why he did what he did." She did understand why the board preferred Matthew. "What I don't understand is why you left an amazing hospital and research facility to come here."

A weary look crossed his face so briefly that Natalie wasn't sure she hadn't imagined it. Maybe she had, because he just shrugged and said, "I like a challenge."

"Ha. Getting this hospital anywhere close to what you left is going to be a challenge. An impossible one, because we don't have the funding you're used to."

He studied her a moment, then shrugged again. "Sometimes challenges can be a good thing."

"You should bring a date," Monica encouraged as Suzie nodded her agreement, and Natalie wished her friends would find a new topic of conversation.

Every time she saw them all they wanted to discuss was Matthew. When was the last time she saw him? What did he say? What did he do? It was getting old.

"Make him jealous."

Natalie rolled her eyes. "I don't want to make him jealous. I want…"

She wasn't sure what she wanted. Honestly, she understood the hospital hiring Matthew. He was brilliant. The man had been improving pediatric cardiac outcomes for over a decade and the entire hospital was ecstatic to have him join them.

If only Natalie could feel that same joy.

On a personal level, she knew it would have been better never to see him again.

On a professional level, he'd taken the job she wanted.

She resented that he'd invaded her life and turned everything topsy-turvy. Yet she couldn't stop thinking about him, even now as she gave all she had to the elliptical machine. Monica was to her right, Suzie to the left. All three of them had worked up a sweat.

"What is it you want, Natalie?" Suzie insisted when Natalie didn't finish her comment.

To forget Miami and her career goals so she could join the ranks of her coworkers, ecstatic that someone of Matthew's caliber had joined their team.

Wasn't going to happen, but it would help if she could.

Looking at him did wacky things to her insides. Like throw her heart rhythm and make her lungs forget how to diffuse oxygen. As much as she'd like to blame Miami, how her body reacted to Matthew was instinctive rather than a Pavlovian response.

Although memories of Matthew's kisses, his touch, his... *No, no, no.* She sped up the movement of her legs as fast she could go, faster, faster, faster. *Forget Miami.*

Obviously he had. Not once had he made one untoward move around her. Other than their first few encounters at the hospital, he'd been professional and, if anything, a bit aloof, as if he didn't want there to be any misunderstandings of his intentions.

"In case you've forgotten," she huffed out as she struggled to maintain her crazy pace, "I haven't been on a date since Jonathan and I broke things off. Not counting Miami—and Miami doesn't count."

"Speaking of the ex, did you hear that the bimbo he was messing around with is wearing an engagement ring?"

Monica's question curled Natalie's nose. "Better her than me. I don't want the man or the ring."

Monica smiled. "I'm so glad you're over him."

Sadly, she was over him before it was over. She'd cared about him, but she'd never needed him. Or craved him. Or thought about him all the time.

"What are you going to do about Matthew?"

Ignoring the sweat running down her brow, Natalie kept moving, pushing harder and harder against the elliptical. "Absolutely nothing. He was supposed to be just a pleasant memory, but I didn't get that lucky."

"Some would say him showing back up in your life makes you lucky," Suzie pointed out.

"Yeah, well, I'm not a girl who wants to be face to face with a man she thought she was only spending a weekend with."

"Maybe you need to rethink that."

"Rethink what?"

"Just spending that one weekend with him. Monica and I are going to dress you up for Friday night's party and you should go for it."

"For old times' sake," Suzie added.

"Uh-uh. Getting involved with Matthew, my boss, is the last thing I need to do."

"Why?"

"Shall I count the reasons?" At her friends' expectant looks, Natalie continued. "One, he took my dream job." Her friends didn't seem impressed at the gravity of just how devastated she was. "Two, he's my boss." Again, her friends didn't seem to understand what that implied. "Three, he has a kid."

"I'm not seeing a problem," Suzie said.

"The last thing I'd want is to get involved with a man who has kids."

"What's the deal with this kid, anyway? He never mentioned her in Miami?"

"No, and I don't know."

"You should ask him."

"Why would I do that?"

"Because you want to know."

"You mean *you* want to know," Natalie corrected, cycling as fast as she could on the elliptical.

"Protest all you want, Natalie, but this guy gets to you."

"Not in a good way."

Both her friends had the audacity to laugh.

CHAPTER EIGHT

NATALIE STARED AT the quiet little girl playing on a tablet computer in Matthew's office.

His daughter? Had to be.

Natalie wanted to turn and run, because she didn't want to be confronted with the child. She wasn't sure of all the reasons why, just that a self-defensive part of her warned to run. But the girl looked up from her game and met Natalie's gaze with big brown eyes, stopping any unnoticed retreat.

Although she was beautiful, Natalie couldn't help but think it was a shame the girl hadn't inherited Matthew's unusual pale blue eye color or his dark features. Still, with her sagging ponytail, dimpled cheeks and big eyes, the girl was undeniably adorable.

"Hi! Uncle Matthew isn't here."

Uncle Matthew? Why had the girl called him "Uncle", and what was Matthew doing leaving the girl unattended in his office? Natalie knew next to nothing about parenting, but she knew enough to know that one didn't leave a small child by herself.

"He's in an important meeting. Stephanie," the name came out with a cute hesitation of each syllable as the girl made sure she said the name correctly, "is watching me."

Only Stephanie was nowhere to be seen.

"Where is Stephanie?"

"The bathroom. She wasn't feeling good and keeps going to the bathroom." The child wrinkled her nose. "She has diarrhea." Again, she put emphasis on each syllable to make sure she properly enunciated.

"Poor Stephanie," Natalie commiserated, not sure whether to walk away or to stay. The kid was too young to be by herself. "I'm Natalie. What's your name?"

Why did this conversation feel so weird? She was a pediatric heart surgeon. She dealt with children on an almost daily basis. Why were her palms clammy?

"Carrie. I'm four. Do you want to see my game?"

No, Natalie didn't. She wanted far, far away from the evidence of Matthew's deceit—but the hopeful look on the child's face left her unable to do anything more than cross to where the little girl sat. She stooped down.

"What kind of game is it?"

"A fashion game." Carrie's eyes lit up as if it was the most fabulous game ever. "See all the pretty clothes?"

Natalie had never been a girly girl and fashion wasn't her forte, but she nodded her agreement as she studied each item the child clicked on.

Big brown eyes regarded her. "Which one is your favorite?"

"They're all great," she assured, studying the colored images. "Which makes it difficult to choose, but I like the blue dress best."

She nodded as if she'd expected Natalie to say as much. "That's Uncle Matthew's favorite, too. It's the color of his eyes and makes me think of a robin's egg."

There went the "Uncle Matthew" again. And there went Natalie's cheeks, bursting into flames. "That's not why I liked it best."

"It's the mermaid tail, isn't it?" Carrie said with a knowing tone.

"The what?"

The little girl pointed at the screen. "The skirt. It's why

you like that dress? My mommy's wedding dress had a mermaid tail. It's my favorite, too. I like clothes, especially mermaid tails."

Her mommy's wedding dress. Matthew had been married to the girl's mother once upon a time. Where was she now?

"Um, yes. The mermaid tail." Thinking her conversation with the child was getting more and more awkward, she stared at the computer screen. What she really wanted to do was get out of Dodge, but she couldn't bring herself to leave the girl alone, so she resolved to stick around until Stephanie got back from the bathroom. Still, a subject change was overdue. "How does your game work? You design the clothes and then fill in the colors?"

Carrie happily demonstrated how to select and manipulate an item on the screen with a stylus pen. "You want to try?"

"I'd rather watch you. I'm not much on clothes or fashion."

The girl studied her scrubs then nodded. "I can tell. Pretty boring."

In spite of how awkward she felt, Natalie laughed. "We should send a memo to my new boss to up the appeal of our hospital wardrobe, eh? Maybe add some mermaid tail scrubs."

Natalie's boss thought her appeal was just fine as was. More than fine. Of course, Matthew wasn't thinking of her hospital wardrobe, just the woman. Not that he should be allowing himself to think of her as anything except a fellow neonatal heart surgeon and colleague.

Why did he keep struggling with that? Of course, he knew. Miami. How was he supposed to relegate her to a mere coworker when he knew just how hot her fire burned?

When he'd finished with his meeting and returned to his office to collect Carrie, he'd expected to find the nursing assistant with her. Running the little girl to his mother's place on his day off for the hour or less the meeting would take seemed unnecessary, but yet again it seemed he'd made a bad parenting judgment call, because Stephanie was nowhere to be seen.

Still, finding Natalie stooped next to Carrie was a pleasant surprise, especially since much of the meeting he'd just attended had involved Natalie and her role in the department.

"Oh, Dr Coleman!" Stephanie gushed, hastening behind him. "Glad you're back."

"Speaking of being back..." he frowned at the nursing assistant he'd thought he could trust "...where have you been?"

The woman's face reddened. "Sorry, sir, but I've developed an awful case of what I think is food poisoning. Now that you're back, I'm checking in with my nurse manager, clocking out and heading home to the privacy of my own bathroom."

"She has diarrhea," Carrie piped up from where she sat at his desk, making the word four syllables.

The nursing assistant's flush brightened even more.

"Yeah, well, glad you're back," the young woman said, then to Carrie, "Maybe next time we meet I won't get sick. Dr. Sterling," she acknowledged Natalie, then disappeared.

"Thank you for staying with Carrie while Stephanie was otherwise occupied."

Looking uncomfortable, Natalie stood, smoothing her hands over her scrubs. "She was showing me her designs."

"Carrie plans to take the fashion world by storm someday, don't you, kiddo?"

Rather than answer his question, Carrie lifted big eyes to him and reminded him of something else he should have done prior to the meeting, but had run out of time when she'd not cooperated in his trying to get her dressed.

"Can we go eat now?"

Had he fed her breakfast? He thought so...

"Soon," he told her guiltily, wondering if he had a protein bar in his desk he could give her to tide her over for another thirty minutes or so. "I need to finish a few things here, then we'll go." Was it wrong of him to make her wait while he finished? He couldn't see leaving to eat and then having to drag her back by the hospital afterwards.

"Can Natalie go with us?"

Matthew watched Natalie's expression tighten and started to come up with a reason why that wasn't a good idea, because the last thing he needed was to spend time with her outside the hospital. But the color draining from her face and an onslaught of frustrated pride had him saying, "Of course she can go with us."

Natalie's eyes widened and she gave him a warning look. "Sorry, I've a dozen things to do before I leave for dinner."

"We could wait on you," Carrie offered, looking way too eager for Natalie to say yes, especially as Matthew knew she was hungry.

Natalie's cheeks flushed. "I'd hate for you to have to do that."

"We don't mind, do we?" Carrie looked up at him expectantly, making him feel a jerk for having let her think there was any hope of Natalie going with them. Why had he?

Because whether he wanted to or not, he *liked* the idea of Natalie going with them. She'd seemed comfortable with Carrie, as though she knew what she was doing while she'd been sitting next to her looking at her tablet.

"We want to make new friends, right?" the child continued. "I could show you more of my game. There are more dresses with mermaid tails!"

Natalie was looking downright panicked. Matthew toyed with the idea of letting her off the hook, but he was curious as to why Carrie was so eager for her to go with them. Other than with regard to his mother, sister and nieces, she'd not shown interest in making new friends or getting to know anyone. Until Natalie. Go figure.

"That's right," he agreed. "Plus, I owe you for sitting with my favorite fashionista."

"I was only here for, like, five minutes," Natalie rushed to clarify. "Ten at the most. You owe me nothing."

Her comment reminded him of her teasing in Miami. He'd liked owing Natalie because the paying up had been a lot of fun.

"Please?" Carrie pleaded in her most appealing voice, the one Matthew hadn't learned to say no to. "He'll take us to get really great food…" She named the restaurant they'd visited way too often over the past few weeks. Matthew didn't normally eat fast food, but apparently kids loved it.

Natalie's nose wrinkled and she frowned at him. "Not a very healthy choice for a four-year-old, is it?"

Probably not, but he'd just been so grateful when Carrie had started eating again that he'd fed her whatever she wanted. Still, as a cardiologist, he knew the dangers of too much high-fat, low-nutrition food and should have been making Carrie eat healthy. Another thing to feel guilty over.

Carrie turned pleading eyes toward Natalie. "Please say you'll go. *You* can pick the restaurant."

Still Natalie hesitated. If she could have thought of a way to get out of going, she would have. That was written all over her face.

Sensing Natalie was about to make a break for it, Carrie launched into a new plea. "I'll be extra-good and eat something healthy. I promise!"

"You're always extra-good." Matthew tugged on her lopsided ponytail, wondering how it had worked loose when he'd thought he'd finally gotten it right. Then again, she acted as if he were ripping her hair out every time he brushed it or went to pull it up. He wouldn't take back his comment, though. She'd dealt with so much that he figured a little acting out here and there was normal.

Carrie lifted her big eyes to Natalie again. "Please. Don't you want to be my friend?"

How had Natalie gotten manipulated into this? She still wasn't quite sure. The last two people on earth she wanted to be having dinner with were Matthew and his daughter.

She wasn't sure Matthew wanted her there any more than she wanted to be there.

Yet she sat at the organic food restaurant, eating kale chips and freshly made salsa one after another to give her hands something to do while observing Matthew with Carrie.

He obviously loved the girl. Which seemed an odd thing to think. Of course Matthew loved his daughter.

The girl obviously adored him as well.

But there was something about their relationship that didn't feel quite right, almost an awkwardness in how Matthew regarded her and how she regarded him. Still, Carrie truly had been well-behaved, had listened closely to her menu options but then let Natalie choose her meal for her, promising to eat every bite.

They'd been at the restaurant about fifteen minutes when the child dropped a bombshell that caused Natalie to almost choke on a chip.

"My mommy and daddy died in an airplane crash and I live with Uncle Matthew now." The child kept talking, very matter-of-fact, but Natalie didn't catch anything else she said.

Just that her mommy and daddy had died.

Which brought back some terrible memories of her own, and gave Natalie a whole new empathy for the girl. Eyes blurring, she took a drink of her water, wishing she'd ordered something a lot stiffer, then offered, "I'm sorry about your mom and dad. My parents died when I was young, too."

Why had she offered that last tidbit? Matthew didn't need to know about her sordid childhood. Nor did she need to form any connection with this child.

"Did they die in a plane crash?" Carrie asked at the same time as Matthew's leg brushed up against her from across the table and he said,

"I'm sorry."

She didn't want his sympathy. She didn't want anything from him. Or Carrie. Just…

"No," she managed, hating that her eyes watered. "But they were in an accident. A car wreck." She fought the sadness that threatened her when she recalled the horror of losing her parents. "It was a long time ago. I was around your age."

"It feels like forever since my mommy and daddy died." Carrie turned sad eyes on Matthew. "How long has it been?"

"Just over four months."

Four months. That wasn't long ago. Poor Carrie. How had Matthew ended up with the girl?

"Carrie's parents were my best friends," he said, seeming to have read her mind. "I was her godfather and now she's stuck with me."

In the way that children do, Carrie jumped to another topic. "Did you know that a baby giraffe is about to be born at the zoo?"

Natalie shook her head.

"It's so exciting!" Carrie continued, her eyes glowing. "You can watch the momma giraffe online and they have a special app for your phone. Do you have it?"

Again, Natalie shook her head.

"You should get it so you know when Zoie is about to be born."

"Zoie?"

"That's what they're going to call the baby giraffe. It's a girl. The zoo held a contest on naming her and Zoie won. You want the app?"

"Um, maybe."

"I can help you," Carrie offered, reaching for Natalie's phone.

Not sure whether she should trust a four-year-old with her phone or whether she wanted a zoo app to notify her about a giraffe, Natalie handed the device to Carrie.

She tapped several buttons, explaining to Natalie each step of the way, as if Natalie were the child and Carrie the adult.

"There," she said, handing the phone back. "Now you have the zoo app and you'll get Zoie updates."

"Thank you," Natalie said, sliding the phone into her scrubs pocket.

"Uncle Matthew says I can have a puppy soon as we get settled."

"A puppy?" Natalie had never owned a pet. Her foster parents had often said it was enough work raising her without adding an animal to the mix. A few of them had acted as if *Natalie* were an animal… To redirect her thoughts, she met Matthew's gaze. "Are you sure? I hear puppies are a lot of work."

"It's not as cool as a baby giraffe, and I'd rather have a big dog," Carrie interjected, "but Uncle Matthew says I have to pick a small one that can stay in the house because we're gone so much." Carrie wrinkled her nose. "But if we get a puppy we shouldn't be gone so much, especially if it's a little puppy."

Natalie lifted her gaze to Matthew.

"She makes sense, and," he bent to Carrie's level, "I'm working on being home more. That's why we're in Memphis, remember?"

"To be near Grandma and Aunt Elaine and Mandy and Liz. They are excited about the giraffe, too."

So much began to click.

"I guess it is easier living closer to your family," Natalie mused, then went hot-cheeked, straightened, and brushed her hands over her scrubs. "Not that it's any of my business."

"Oh, it is definitely better being close to my family. My mom's awesome. Since I couldn't convince her to move away from the rest of the family to come live with me in Boston, we came here."

Natalie traced her finger over the rim of her water glass. "Do you have a big family?"

"Big enough. A sister and several aunts, uncles and cousins. It's a few years since I've been to a family get-together, but they're unforgettable." He shook his head as if recalling past holidays. "They can get a little crazy."

Having little memory of any family other than what she could recall of her parents, Natalie struggled to imagine what it must be like at those holiday gatherings.

How many times over the years had she longed to belong to a family? To make memories like the ones Matthew was obviously recalling? How could he have missed family holiday gatherings? Didn't he realize how blessed he was?

She stuffed another kale chip in her mouth.

"Do you have kids I could play with, too, Natalie?"

Coughing to clear her throat of the chip that lodged there, Natalie shook her head. "No, I don't have any kids."

Carrie's brows veed together and she shook her head, making her ponytail sag further. "Well, that's just sad."

Yes, Natalie supposed it was, but bringing a child into the world just so she wouldn't be alone would be just as sad. She'd once thought she'd meet someone who would want to stick around, who wouldn't leave her, who'd want to have babies with her. But after Jonathan's betrayal she wasn't so sure. Maybe some people weren't meant to ever be a part of a real family. Certainly she never had been.

"Some people might think so, but I'm not sad. My life is very full," she defended, not wanting the child or Matthew to feel sorry for her. At Carrie's continued look of skepticism, Natalie continued, "I'm quite happy with my life, really."

Mostly, she told the truth. Except for the part where Matthew had taken her job and occupied her thoughts.

"Here, let me fix your ponytail before your hair gets in your food," Natalie offered, removing the loose band and using her fingers to comb Carrie's hair back into a ponytail.

Natalie could feel Matthew's hot scrutiny and finally she looked up, meeting his eyes.

"You make that look easy."

Natalie shrugged. "Not much to it."

"Maybe not, since she sat perfectly still for you." Matthew gave Carrie a pointed look.

"She didn't hurt me," the child defended, then gave Natalie an exasperated look. "He pulls my hair out when he does it!"

"I'm getting better," Matthew assured, his expression almost one of need for Carrie to reassure him that he truly was improving. Carrie gave Natalie a look that said she didn't agree with Matthew's assessment, then rattled on in her four-year-old chatter about how her mother had used to style her hair.

Finding herself wanting to give Matthew that reassurance, Natalie stopped herself. She shouldn't be here, shouldn't be seeing this side of Matthew. A side where a renowned heart surgeon who topped his field took on raising an orphaned child who had no one else, even when it meant giving up a job he loved and becoming a fish-out-of-water parent.

She stared at him, fighting a barrage of swirling emotions.

Oh, good grief. The last thing she needed was to soften

toward a man who was supposed to have only been a three-day vacation affair and had ended up turning her life topsy-turvy.

Natalie loved her patients. From the tiny babies to the teenagers she cared for, she never felt awkward or self-conscious. The only other children she'd been around had been other foster children. Kids who'd been down on their luck and as defensive as she was.

Then there'd been the birth children of the foster families. The loved children who'd often seen her as inferior and felt they had the right to lord it over her, to abuse her verbally and sometimes physically.

She hadn't gotten close to any of them, had more negative memories than positive ones about those encounters, and would forever be grateful for the final foster family who'd taken her in when she'd been fourteen. She'd stayed with the McCulloughs until she'd left for college. They'd never had children of their own, but had raised several foster kids. It was after she'd been taken in by that wonderful couple that she'd met Suzie and Monica and made her first real friends.

None of that had prepared her for Matthew's daughter and the bond she already felt with the orphaned little girl.

Dinner had been interesting. They'd eaten their healthy dinner while Carrie told Natalie about going to the park with her grandmother the day before.

"I was only supposed to be at the hospital for less than an hour or she'd have gone to Grandma's today," Matthew added.

"Uncle Matthew used to take me to the hospital a lot before we moved." Carrie didn't sound happy about the memory.

"Now that we're closer to Grandma, that shouldn't happen too much. Plus, Aunt Elaine can watch you some and has a list of sitters for me to interview. You shouldn't get stuck going too often once I get settled in at work." Matthew turned to Natalie. "She doesn't like going to the hospital."

"Because you take so long," Carrie reminded.

"Because I take so long," he agreed, then tried to lighten the mood. "And because the hospital isn't the place for high fashion. She'd much rather I take her to the mall."

Natalie found herself wanting to defend Matthew, to help Carrie see how difficult it must have been for him to have had a child thrust into his busy life.

"You could use your hospital trips as research to design us new scrubs with the mermaid tail like we talked about earlier," Natalie suggested, trying to ease the underlying tension between Matthew and the child.

The girl's nose wrinkled. "Scrubs are boring clothes."

Natalie glanced down at the blue ones she wore. "Completely boring."

Yet they were her preferred wardrobe and what she had on more often than not.

"Which is why doctors and nurses around the world need you to come up with something stylish for us. Help us be more fashionable."

Carrie seemed intrigued by that idea, and she and Natalie carried on a quite lengthy conversation about hospital fashion.

The conversation jumped from one topic to another and before Natalie knew it she was at Matthew's house. How had that happened? She'd had no intention of going to his house. Or spending one second more with him and his daughter than was absolutely necessary.

Only Carrie had wanted to show off her new bedroom, something she was excited about and super-proud of. Natalie hadn't had the heart to say no, and when she'd looked at Matthew for guidance he'd just shrugged as if to say he didn't care one way or the other.

She supposed he didn't.

Since his Memphis arrival, he'd been professional and nothing more. He'd probably forgotten all about Miami. It was what she needed to do. What she wanted to do.

For most of dinner, he'd listened to her and Carrie's conversation, throwing in a comment here and there, but almost seeming as if he was studying their interactions.

His house was in an upscale neighborhood on Mud Island not too far from where she lived, and just ten minutes from the hospital. A modern brick monstrosity within a gated community with a circle drive and a fenced back yard. It was a house for a family, not two people.

"Excuse the lack of furniture. I sold most of what I had in Boston, rather than move it. Carrie and I are working on buying furniture as time allows. It's our weekend project to put our home together piece by piece."

"Let me show you my room!" Carrie grabbed Natalie's hand and led her through the mostly empty house.

When she pushed open a door, Natalie expected little more than a bare room with a bed, or perhaps a cot. Instead, it was as if she'd stepped into a fantasy.

The opposite wall from the door housed a painted wooden floor-to-ceiling castle with a stairwell leading up to a tower with only a small peek hole. The walls were painted in a fairyland motif, complete with another far, far away castle, unicorns and other friendly-looking animals, puffy white clouds, blue skies and rainbows, and even a waterfall.

"Wow," Natalie breathed, taking in the room. "Just wow."

"I know," Carrie agreed, sounding a bit breathless herself.

Natalie walked over to the bed, with its pink comforter and sheer white drapes that gave it a mystical tent appearance.

"Don't you just love it?" Carrie whispered, clasping her hands together.

"I want to move in here." She turned to Matthew. "You did this?"

"Carrie found photos of what she wanted. We picked out the key pieces of furniture and I hired a decorating firm to make it happen. My mother oversaw the work while Carrie and I were wrapping up in Boston."

"Is the decorator doing the rest of the house?"

"We may enlist her help again," he admitted, "but for now I had her to do my room, Carrie's room and the kitchen."

"You have castles in your bedroom, too?"

He shook his head. "No castles or unicorns. Not even a princess."

"You have me," Carrie reminded. "I'm a princess."

"That I do," Matthew agreed, touching the top of the girl's head. "And that you are."

"And you'd have a dog if you'd just get one." Carrie's eyes were huge and fairly puppy-like as she regarded him.

Natalie suspected Matthew's big house would be filled with the sound of barking before long. Carrie seemed to have a way of getting people to do what she wanted with a flash of her big brown eyes and precious smile.

After all, Natalie was at Matthew's house, and who would have ever thought that possible?

CHAPTER NINE

"How's our girl this morning?"

Natalie jumped at the sound of Matthew's voice behind her. Straightening from where she'd been examining the tiny baby in the special ICU bassinette, she faced him.

"So far, so good."

"Her color is good."

It was. The baby's skin was a nice pink. If everything held course, they'd start removing some of the lines later today, and continue to monitor the baby's progress closely over the next several days.

"Thank you for your help with her."

He gave a half-smile. "You'd have gotten the valves to work if I hadn't been there."

He was right. She wouldn't have stopped until she'd done all she could for the baby. He'd just made it easier.

And taught her a new technique.

Had they not had an affair, she might have liked him.

He smiled at her and her heart fluttered.

Ha. Part of her still liked him.

A lot.

Good thing there was that part of her that didn't like him, else she might be in trouble for having inappropriate thoughts about her boss. Her boss whom she'd slept with before he was her boss, and before she'd known what he was doing for a little girl who could have easily ended up in foster care, as Natalie had.

Not wanting to have empathetic thoughts about him, she turned back to the baby, taking another listen to her tiny heart.

"Thank you for going with Carrie and me last night."

"I shouldn't have." Her response was automatic, the truth, but a part of her didn't regret having gone, having seen that uncertain part of him that wanted to do right by Carrie so desperately, yet didn't seem to know quite how.

"I didn't expect you to," he admitted from where he stood next to the bassinette.

"She's hard to say no to."

He gave a low laugh. "Tell me about it. I'm going to have to learn, though, or I'll have her spoiled rotten. It's so difficult not to give her everything she wants to try to make up for all she's dealing with."

Natalie could only imagine. She barely knew the child and she'd found herself drifting off to sleep thinking about puppies.

"Including getting stuck with me."

"She seems to be a good kid, overall," Natalie mused.

"She is. The best. She's..." His voice trailed off. "Sorry, I know you don't want to hear about Carrie. Or anything to do with my personal life. Sorry she roped you into last night, but I do appreciate your going with us."

Natalie swallowed the lump in her throat. Yeah, she shouldn't want to hear anything about Carrie or his personal life, but part of her was sorely disappointed he'd stopped talking, that he'd felt the need to.

Which was ridiculous. She understood and embraced that need to halt anything even slightly personal between them. It was how it needed to be.

Just as she needed to put some distance between them because last night had her all mixed up.

"Have you made a decision about the Harris case?"

His question jolted her back to reality. Focusing on the baby rather than looking up at him, Natalie nodded. "I'm going to operate."

"I'd like to be in surgery with you."

She'd thought he might. Perhaps that had been part of her hesitation in making the decision, but her window of opportunity was quickly passing. If the Harris baby was going to have her vessels repaired in utero and have time to heal prior to entering this world, the operation had to take place soon.

"You planning to take over again?"

His gaze narrowed. "Is that how you saw what happened?"

No, it wasn't. Her comment had been unfair and unwarranted. Matthew had been nothing but kind since his arrival in Memphis. So why had she snapped at him?

She knew why. The same reason her insides were twisted into knots. Last night—seeing him vulnerable when she'd thought him invincible, seeing him giving up so much to try to take care of his best friend's daughter.

And then there was Miami.

She couldn't look at him and not remember how his lips had felt against her body, how his body had felt against hers, how they'd laughed together, played together, how she'd let loose and relaxed with him because she'd thought she'd never see him again.

That was the reason she'd been so relaxed with him, wasn't it?

Yet here he was in Memphis.

Driving her crazy. Mentally, emotionally, physically.

"You can do as you please," she assured, trying not to let too much of her unease come through. "It's not as if I have the authority to say no."

She made the mistake of looking up, catching his light blue gaze darkening as he studied her.

"Is there someone you'd rather have in this particular

surgery with you than the surgeon on staff who has the most in-utero surgical experience?"

She took a deep breath, then glanced beyond him to make sure no one was near enough to overhear their conversation.

"Of course I don't want you in surgery with me." Only, she did. Which annoyed her all the more. Then again, she'd admired his skills long before she knew just how far they extended.

"Explain."

"We had sex," she whispered.

"So what?" He kept his voice low. "That has nothing to do with this."

"It has everything to do with this," she assured. "If I'd known there was even the slightest possibility that I'd someday work with you, we never would have."

With one last look at the baby, she walked away, ducked into a dictation room for a moment's privacy to calm her racing heart. She should have known Matthew would follow her.

"Our having sex is in the past," he said matter-of-factly, filling the doorway to the small closet-like room. "We can't change the past. But how we proceed in the future is something we do have control over. I let you dictate the animosity between us from the moment I arrived on the Memphis scene because I agreed that keeping our distance was for the best. But I was wrong. The reality is, we can't keep enough distance to avoid the truth."

"What truth?"

He raked his fingers through his dark hair. "You want me."

Three simple words spoken softly but they echoed around the tiny room.

"You're mistaken," she denied.

"You want me as much as I want you," he clarified, causing her breath to lodge in her throat. "You want to know if we made love again if it would be as intense as in Miami."

"You're crazy." Natalie shook her head. She didn't want to know that. If it was she'd never be able to maintain a professional relationship with him.

She had to maintain a professional relationship with him.

"But my working here complicates things. My being your boss complicates things. I get that. Especially as making this cardiology program everything it can be is important to me." He took a long breath, raked his fingers through his hair again. "I won't let you or anyone keep that from happening. I need this position to work. For my sake and for Carrie's."

Natalie winced.

"If you think it's impossible to work with me because of our physical attraction then we need to figure this out before it compromises the program."

"I'd never do anything to compromise the program or any patient," she adamantly denied, ignoring the rest of what he said. She'd devoted her professional life to Memphis Children's Hospital. How could he question her loyalty?

"Great," he said as if he'd just won a major argument, his entire demeanor relaxing and an easy smile flashing across his handsome face. "Then you'll be fine with the fact that I'm assisting on your surgery this afternoon on the Givens baby, who's being flown in right now." His expression grew a little more serious. "I will also be in on the Harris case."

Natalie could almost forget that Matthew stood across the operating table from her. Almost.

Okay, so not really.

Thus far, he had assisted, but otherwise hadn't pushed for a more controlling role in the Givens baby's surgery.

Andy Givens had been born in an outlying community hospital that morning and had quickly gotten into distress and been transported via helicopter to Memphis Children's.

Being the surgeon on call that day, Natalie had been assigned the case and had shifted her clinic schedule to perform the repair of the baby's tiny valve and vessels.

With Matthew working right along beside her.

It would be easy to get distracted by the efficient movements of his hands, of the skill with which he worked, but she kept her focus on the repairs rather than where Matthew worked on the baby's tiny heart simultaneously via the robotic device that allowed such fine manipulation.

When they'd finished, Natalie scrubbed her hands, ignoring that Matthew joined her. He made a few comments, but she brushed them off.

Surgery with him was getting to her. Spending time with him was getting to her. His earlier claims were getting to her.

She didn't want anything about him to get to her.

Her insides felt raw, her mind raced, her heart ached. She needed to be alone, to assimilate the evening's events. The last thing she wanted was to get caught in conversation with him, but he seemed to have other ideas as he fell into step beside her. "You okay?"

"Ecstatic."

"No regrets?"

Without slowing her pace, she cut her gaze toward him. "Regarding?"

"My being in there with you."

"It's not what I would have chosen, but everything seems to have gone well, so..." She let her voice trail off as she punched the elevator call button.

"Is my being in surgery with you that big of a problem, Natalie?" he asked as they stepped into the empty elevator.

She pressed the button for the floor where her office

was located and wished he'd push another button indicating he was headed to another floor. Any floor but hers. Which wouldn't make sense since his office was located down the hallway from hers.

Staring at the elevator floor indicator and wishing it would hurry up, Natalie said, "The surgery went well. That's what's important."

The elevator dinged then the door slid open. Matthew stood back, letting Natalie exit first. Not that he had a long wait—she practically leapt out. They headed down a long hallway and entered the cardiology center, where an office complex was located. It being late in the evening, the corridor to their offices was eerily silent, and to get to his office they had to walk past hers first.

Sensing Matthew standing behind her, she punched in the security code that would unlock her office, and when the door clicked open she drew in a deep breath.

"You planning to stay here tonight?"

Without turning to face him, she nodded. "I'm on call, so I planned on going to the computer lab to work on the Harris case. Plus, I want to be close if there are any changes on the Givens baby."

"Call if you need me."

A million thoughts ran through her mind. None of which had anything to do with her cases. Heat flooded her and she was glad he couldn't see her face. But he must have sensed what was on her mind, because when he spoke his voice was low.

"It's moments like these where I have to remind myself that I promised to leave you alone on a personal level, because right then I almost turned you to face me, Natalie."

Her breath caught and she squeezed her eyes shut as if that would somehow stop the onslaught of emotions hitting her.

"For the record, I don't find not touching you easy."

Neither did she, which was why it was so important they keep a distance.

His words from before struck her. Was he right? Was there no distance great enough to stop her from wanting him?

She *did* want him, hadn't stopped wanting him. He was here, right behind her, alone in this private section of the hospital office complex. All she had to do was turn, reach out and touch him, and…and then what?

Her heart pounded in her chest. Her hand fell from the code pad and she turned, met his pale eyes.

He stared at her, seeing what she wasn't sure because she couldn't label the confusion swirling within her. She wanted him to disappear, to have never met him, for him to be back in Boston performing his miraculous surgeries.

But even more she wanted him to touch her, to take charge and take what he wanted—what she wanted.

So why wasn't she reaching out to touch him?

Because if she touched him she had to acknowledge that everything he said was true, that maybe she couldn't work with him day after day and ignore what was between them. Because pretending she didn't want him, that Miami had been one big mistake, was a lot easier than acknowledging he was a part of her daily life, and that scared her.

Her lips parted. To say what, she wasn't sure, just that so much emotion churned within her she needed to let it out somehow. Or maybe she'd been offering a subconscious invitation.

Regardless, Matthew's gaze didn't soften—instead it took on that dark and dangerous look that made her wonder how she'd ever thought him vulnerable the night before.

"Goodnight, Natalie," he said. "Great job in surgery today. If there are any unexpected changes, let me know."

With that, he opened her office door, practically pushed her inside and walked away without a backward glance.

* * *

Dr Luiz's retirement party was a huge success. The hospital's CEO had given quite the toast to the man early on in the evening. Hospital staff, along with VIP members of the medical community and from Memphis's social and political scene, had been slapping the retiring doctor on the back all evening, and still came up to do so every so often.

At the moment, a couple had interrupted Matthew's conversation with the older surgeon to tell him how missed he would be at the hospital. Matthew let Dr. Luiz explain that he was only semi-retiring and would still be around the hospital, just significantly scaling back on his duties and no longer overseeing the department.

His semi-retirement was one of the things that made the position work for Matthew. With Dr. Luiz still there part-time and with a second-in-command of Natalie's caliber, Matthew's workload wasn't near as heavy as in Boston. Which gave him more time to spend with Carrie, for them to figure out this new life of theirs.

Maybe he'd get used to the idea of working less and parenting more. Maybe he'd get better at it. Hopefully. His sister had Carrie tonight, and the little girl would have a good time with her cousins. Would be in a home where the adult in the household knew what she was doing.

Something Matthew wondered if he'd ever figure out.

The couple were still chatting with Dr Luiz, and Matthew spent the time glancing around the crowd, wondering if Natalie was there yet. Sweet and sassy Natalie, who was determined to keep him at arms' length. Which he should be grateful for. He didn't need to risk anything—anyone—messing up his new life in Memphis.

He'd gotten a whole lot wrong over the past few months, but moving to Memphis had been right—the best decision he'd made in a long time.

There had only been one negative: Natalie and their strained working relationship.

If he'd known there was even the slightest possibility Memphis Children's would come through, he'd never have given in to his desire for her.

At least, he'd like to think he wouldn't have.

There was something about her that messed with his head, so who knew if in sunny Miami, away from all the stresses of his life, he'd have been able to resist the temptation she'd presented with her quick smile and desire-filled eyes?

He missed that Natalie. The one who had looked at him with delight, touched him with longing, carried on long, flirty conversations with him and shared nights that had passed much too quickly.

Maybe that was part of him missing his old life, the life where he'd been free to have as many affairs as he wanted, where he'd been free to focus on his work. Where he hadn't had to second-guess every decision he made and how it would impact a child.

Or maybe it was just Natalie.

Searching the crowded ballroom, he had no difficulty spotting her. She stood out in any room, but looked particularly lovely tonight. She wore a figure-hugging black dress that accentuated her rocking body. Her hair was down—something he hadn't seen since Florida, as she always kept it pulled up at the hospital. Memories of running his fingers through those locks haunted him, making him long to cross the room and touch the silky strands.

To think his fascination was anything other than unique to her was foolish. No woman from his past had monopolized his thoughts, his desires, the way Natalie did.

"Ah, Dr. Sterling is here."

Apparently the couple had moved on without Matthew noticing and the guest of honor's gaze had followed his.

He didn't turn to meet Dr. Luiz's eyes. No need. The man wasn't stupid and had made several comments over the past few weeks that let Matthew know he might not know details, but he knew something was up.

"She is," Matthew agreed. In her scrubs, hair pulled up and no make-up, Natalie was gorgeous. Tonight, dressed to shine, she should have been featured in one of the fashion magazines Carrie loved to look at.

"I have to admit," the older man said from beside Matthew, "I thought she'd have warmed to you by now."

"She may never warm to me. I took what she saw as hers."

"That's not it and we both know it."

His confident tone had Matthew's gaze dragging off Natalie and glancing toward the astute older man.

"I've known her for a decade and have never seen Natalie react to anyone the way she does to you. You agitate her."

"Agitation's not a good thing."

"Matter of opinion, but I'd say it's not a bad thing."

Matthew's gaze narrowed on the man he greatly respected. "Our opinions differ on that. She resents me, and you, too, for what she sees as a direct betrayal and slap in her face career-wise in that she didn't get to take over the department."

"I'd put money on the fact that her agitation with you has nothing to do with anything that's happened in Memphis."

Which implied the man suspected something had happened *before* his arrival in Memphis.

"I didn't do anything in Miami to make Natalie dislike me, if that's what you're implying."

"I didn't say she disliked you." The man's brow furrowed. "Unlike the idiot who is falling all over himself in front of her in hopes she'll beg him back."

Matthew's gaze returned to Natalie to see a tall, slim, suited man fawning over her. Natalie's expression wasn't pleasant, but it also held enough emotion to give away that the man wasn't a casual acquaintance. Even without Dr. Luiz's comment, Matthew would have known the guy had to be her ex.

The one whom she'd lived with for a couple of years.

A man who'd shared her life, her bed, her body.

A man who was reaching for her hand even as Matthew watched.

Green acid gurgled within him, and it had nothing to do with anything he'd eaten and everything to do with the man touching Natalie.

The man—*what had his name been?*—lifted her hand and pressed a kiss there. The acid in Matthew's belly erupted into full-blown volcanic burn.

His vision blurred.

Did the fool think he could have her back?

Not that Matthew had any say in the matter, but Natalie was smarter than to take back a man who'd cheated.

Only, she wasn't telling the guy who still held her hand to get lost, and Matthew knew first-hand that she had no problems whatsoever with saying those words.

CHAPTER TEN

"YOU'RE LOOKING ESPECIALLY beautiful tonight, Nat."

Before Natalie realized what Jonathan was doing, he'd grabbed her hand and kissed it in what he clearly hoped would appear as charming.

Natalie was not charmed.

Shock reverberated through her. Wasn't he engaged to the woman he'd been cheating with, or had her friends been mistaken?

Either way, Natalie wanted nothing to do with him, and attempted to jerk her hand free, but his hold tightened. "I can't say it's nice to see you," she said.

His smooth smile didn't waver and neither did his hold. "Nat, Nat, Nat. You aren't still bitter about what happened?"

"No." She wasn't bitter. "Bitterness would imply I care. We both know that you screwing around on me did me a big favor. Let my hand go."

"Ouch!" he exclaimed, but didn't look as if Natalie's words fazed him. Instead of letting go of her hand, he brought it to his lips again and pressed another kiss to her fingertips. "I miss you and that sharp wit of yours."

Stunned by his public show of affection when they really hadn't been into a lot of PDA when they were together, she stared at him in confusion, and more than a little irritation.

"You have to be kidding me. Aren't you and what's-her-name engaged? I know I saw her with you earlier. Why are you even over here talking to me? You should be with her."

He tsked. "You shouldn't believe everything you hear."

"You aren't engaged?"

His gaze didn't quite meet hers; instead he studied where he held her hand. "I didn't say that."

Natalie rolled her eyes and managed to pull her hand free.

"Tell me you don't miss me." He took a step toward her and Natalie automatically took a step back.

"That you don't come home," he continued, stepping closer yet again, "and wish I was there in our bed."

"Ask me to do something difficult because this one is way too easy." She lifted her chin a little, looked him square in the eyes, and said, "I don't miss you, and I'm glad you're not in my bed."

"I don't believe you." His utter arrogance amazed Natalie. How had she not realized what a smug idiot he was?

"I don't care what you believe. Not anymore." She wasn't sure she ever had. Which was sad. She'd lived with him, had sex with him, hoped he'd be the one to love her and never leave her. She had cared about him once upon a time.

"You don't miss our nights together?" He loomed, his expression sneering, suggestive, as if he really believed her to be pining for him to return. "Aren't you lonely, Natalie? Missing a man's touch?"

When had he backed her into a corner? And how had he done so without her realizing? She opened her mouth to tell him what a fool he was and to push past him, but before she could someone answered for her.

"Not in the slightest."

Natalie jumped at the male voice, at the strong hand that slid around her waist and settled possessively on her low back as Matthew's body inserted itself between her and Jonathan.

"I assure you she's not lonely," he continued, donning a smug look of his own. "But then, only a fool would believe a woman as beautiful and passionate as Natalie would be lonely."

Natalie didn't know whether to slap Matthew or to hug him. Hug him because Jonathan's smugness had completely vanished. Slap him because they were in a room full of their peers and she'd just as soon no one wondered what was up with her and her sexy new heart surgeon boss.

Glancing around the room, she thought it didn't seem anyone was paying the slightest attention. Plus, Jonathan had backed them to where they were semi-blocked from most of the other guests.

She should be grateful Matthew hadn't added "or missing a man's touch".

Then again, that wouldn't have been true because she *had* been missing a man's touch. Just not Jonathan's. She missed Matthew. His smile. His conversations. His kisses. His touch.

Even now his fingers burned through the thin material of her dress and scorched her back, making her want to arch into him, making her want to forget all the reasons why anything other than a purely professional relationship between them was a very bad idea.

"And you are?" Jonathan's expression was snide as he visually measured Natalie's rescuer.

Resisting the urge to pull away from Matthew, Natalie smiled instead and introduced the only two men she'd ever been intimate with. *How weird was that?*

"You're Natalie's new boss?" Jonathan's gaze bounced back and forth between them. His grin was vicious. "Having to resort to sleeping your way to the top now? First passed over for another woman, and just a few months later passed over for another heart surgeon." He gave a low laugh. "Not being quite good enough yet again has to sting, Natalie. Especially when you worked so hard for this."

His words were meant to hurt. Natalie knew that. She tried not to let them, but they reached their mark. Why had she ever shared her past hurts, her future aspirations with this buffoon?

"Dr Coleman deserved the position." Oh, how it hurt to say that out loud. "His credentials are excellent." They were. "Memphis Children's is lucky to have a doctor of his caliber join our staff."

Jonathan laughed. "You forget I lived with you for over two years and know you better than anyone," he reminded. "All your long hours being for nothing must kill you."

It did.

"My work wasn't for nothing. I saved lives, Jonathan. Something you have no concept of."

"You sound so altruistic," he sneered.

Matthew's body tensed and Natalie continued, trying to diffuse the situation. The last thing she wanted was a scene at Dr. Luiz's party. "You must not have been paying attention all those years you claim to have gotten to know me." She cast what she hoped was a look of appreciation toward Matthew. "I've always admired Matthew's work and look forward to learning all I can from working with someone of his talent."

"Right. This guy comes along and you're suddenly okay with not getting the position you've been busting your butt for since the beginning?" He turned to Matthew. "Better watch out, buddy. Her career means everything to her and you got in the way. You know that old saying about keeping your friends close and your enemies closer? You might be enjoying being in my old bed, but I'd watch my back if I were you."

Matthew, who'd been watching their exchange, had

that dark and dangerous expression he wore so well. "I'm not worried."

His look said Jonathan would be wise to be worried, though.

"Pity," Jonathan mocked, getting in his parting shot. "You should be."

Natalie stared at the retreating back of her ex and shook her head. How could she have ever had a relationship with such a sleazeball? And she was *so* replacing her bedroom furniture ASAP.

"Real winner there, Natalie."

Like she needed him to tell her that.

"Yeah, I can really pick them, can't I?" She gave him a pointed look. "Why did you interrupt?"

"I didn't like how he was crowding you into a corner."

Neither had she, but she lifted her chin and glared at Matthew. "I can take care of myself."

"Apparently. I'll be sure to wear chain mail beneath my scrubs."

"You're too funny." Her heart pounded. "It was none of your business."

"I felt as if it was. I really didn't like how he was looking at you." Matthew's eyes searched hers. "How he kissed your hand and wouldn't let go."

"It wasn't anything to do with you," she reminded, feeling way more crowded than she previously had. But in a different way. Matthew made her feel...breathless.

Watching her for a few long moments, his pale blue eyes softened and he said, "Dance with me, Natalie."

Where had his invitation come from?

"I thought you agreed that we needed to keep things professional between us?"

"Dr Luiz thinks you don't like me, that there is animosity between us. If he's picked up on it, then others may have. We need to put on a united front. For the department," he added when she readied to argue. "Besides, we danced together in Miami, so this really isn't that big of a deal."

Touching Matthew, dancing with him, would be a very big deal.

"Dancing in Miami was different."

"Everything in Miami was different."

She nodded, forced herself to look away. Everything *had* been different. He'd been a stranger, someone she was free to be silly with, someone she was never supposed to see again, someone who wouldn't interfere with her life or her career goals.

Now he was her boss, had a child, and was someone she saw almost daily.

"Dr Luiz suspects something happened between us."

She thought so, too. "Probably."

"You don't sound upset. Did you say something to him?"

She gave a horrified look. "Why would I do that? Besides, why does it have to be me who said something? Maybe it was something you said."

"Maybe," he admitted, his gaze going off to where Jonathan had rejoined the woman he'd come with.

Poor girl.

"I wanted to punch him when he kissed your hand."

Shocked, Natalie shot her gaze to Matthew. "You're too talented a surgeon to risk anything that stupid. He's not worth messing up your hands. It'd be a shame if you couldn't operate."

The dark color to Matthew's face morphed into a full-blown smile. "Always thinking work, Natalie?"

She didn't respond.

"I was saying I wanted to defend your honor, admitting to being jealous, and your response is that I should protect my surgeon hands at all cost?"

Warmth at his admission spread through Natalie and she fought melting against him.

Monica's and Suzie's comments about making him jealous popped into her mind. She hadn't been trying to do that, especially not with Jonathan. They'd have a field day with that one.

Still, she needed to keep focused on what was important, on what her real goals were.

"Admitting to jealousy is personal, Matthew. We only have a professional relationship, remember?"

"I keep forgetting."

Needing to put a sharp halt to that line of thinking, Natalie asked, "Where's Carrie?"

"Spending the night at my sister's. I'm a single man tonight. Home alone. You could come over, keep me from getting lonely."

Natalie ignored the single man part, the being home alone part, the coming over part, the keeping him from getting lonely part, because she couldn't let herself think about why he'd tell her those things. She just couldn't.

Even not allowing herself to think on those things had her heart-rate kicking up several notches.

"You have a sister?" He'd mentioned her before, but focusing in on that comment seemed the safest route.

He laughed. "You make it sound as if I must have come from a test tube. You mentioned your parents were killed in an automobile accident, but don't *you* have other family?"

She so wasn't going to go there. Not with Matthew. Not with anyone. She didn't talk about her sordid foster life prior to the McCulloughs taking her in.

"Does your sister live close?"

Letting it slide that she had answered his question with one of her own, he nodded. "About a twenty-minute drive from the hospital. She's just down the street from my mother. It's great being near them."

"Why have I never read that you were from Memphis?"

"If you read anything about my background, which is

unlikely, it would have said I was from Arkansas. I grew up in a small town just over the state line. Until the past month, I've never technically lived in Memphis or Tennessee."

"I see."

"I'm not sure you do."

Her gaze met his and she saw things that would be better not seen.

Because she saw what he'd admitted to—jealousy, possessiveness, desire, longing.

She'd told him he had no right to feel those things, yet she'd never stopped feeling desire for him. Longing for him.

Lord help her if he ever showed up with another woman; she'd feel possessive, jealous.

Which was ridiculous. She should not want Matthew.

He'd been a fling.

He'd taken her job.

She was pretty sure spending time with him would destroy everything she held dear.

Yet she wanted him anyway.

"You were right to say no to dancing with me, Natalie." He looked at her as if he were going to gobble her up.

She was probably looking at him as if she wanted him to.

"Why's that?"

"Because the moment your body was next to mine everyone in the room would have known how much I want you. I've never been good at pretense or games, and denying whatever this is between us is getting more and more difficult."

She glanced away, not sure what to say. She wanted him, too, but admitting that sure wasn't on the tip of her tongue.

"This whole thing is impossible."

"What thing?" he asked.

"You being here. You working at my hospital. You. Just everything about you."

He studied her, then, grinning, asked, "Do I agitate you?"

Why was he grinning? What was up with his question? "What?"

"You sound agitated."

She frowned. Had he lost his mind? "I am beyond agitated. You annoy me no end. Go away."

But rather than him looking hurt or offended, Matthew's grin widened. "You want to get out of here with me?"

Had he not heard a word of what she'd said?

"No."

"That's not what I meant. Well, that always seems to be in the background of what I'm feeling where you're concerned, but I was thinking more along the lines of going somewhere to get a cup of coffee and talk. This," he gestured around the party in full swing, "isn't really my scene."

Hers neither. She'd talked with the board members and their significant others, had put in an appearance because she respected and adored Dr. Luiz, even if she hadn't quite forgiven him. She was ready to leave. But with Matthew?

Get a cup of coffee and talk. It sounded so innocent.

So tempting.

"Fine. Coffee. Talk. Nothing else."

But if it really was innocent, if she really believed she was just going for coffee and talk, why did every warning bell in Natalie's head sound?

CHAPTER ELEVEN

MATTHEW LET NATALIE make the rounds saying her fare-wells to several of their colleagues, to Dr. Luiz and his wife. He waited for her to leave, alone, kept an eye on her bozo ex to make sure the idiot didn't follow, and within fifteen minutes made his own farewell rounds and left the party still in full swing.

He half expected Natalie to have changed her mind, for her to not be sitting in the coffee shop where they'd agreed to meet. It didn't take a genius to see how torn she was about him.

That he understood.

There was a lot about her that had his insides torn as well. But having seen her ex pawing at her seemed to have tossed out his common sense and good intentions.

When he arrived at the coffee shop, she was sipping on a cup of something hot and reading on her phone. To the casual observer, she looked calm. Matthew wasn't a casual observer. He noticed the little tremor in the hand that held her phone, the way she moistened her lips several times, the way her eyes closed and she appeared to be praying.

For what? For strength to tell him to get lost? For him not to stand her up? Or maybe the opposite; maybe it would be easier if he just turned and left, giving her something else to hold against him?

Something shifted inside his chest. Something monumental.

All because of this woman.

He wanted her.

At the moment, fighting the way she made him feel seemed ridiculous.

Which was, itself, crazy. Even if he could convince Natalie they weren't toying with insanity and risking their careers to spend the night together, even if he could convince her to say yes, how would they react to each other on Monday?

Was it possible that if they had sex again it would dampen the fire burning between them? That maybe they could move on and have a truly professional relationship?

Could he risk everything to find out?

Carrie was adjusting to Memphis so well, loved being near Matthew's family. No wonder, when he was such a screw-up stand-in parent and his family had stepped in and pulled the child into their fold. His sister had wanted Carrie to spend the night with her two girls. They'd been headed to a movie then having a girls' slumber party. Carrie was no doubt having a blast with five-year-old Mandy and three-year-old Liz.

Matthew wanted to have the time of *his* life.

With Natalie.

What would one night hurt?

Perhaps sensing him watching her, she glanced up from her phone and spotted him, looking a little leery, like she wasn't sure if she was glad he was there or not. Still, she managed a soft smile, and Matthew knew he was a goner.

Perhaps he'd been a goner from the moment he'd noticed her in the airport and not been able to get her out of his brain since.

Either way, he wanted her, knew she wanted him.

He intended to have her.

* * *

Natalie resisted the urge to squirm. Matthew was looking at her oddly. Like he wanted to gobble her up in one swift bite and slay dragons for her all at the same time.

It was a heady, very confusing expression, and her head spun as she watched him approach her table.

Not bothering with ordering a coffee of his own, he came over, sat down and smiled a smile that didn't ease the nervous tension running through her.

If anything, more tension thrummed to life.

"What?" she asked, setting her phone on the table. She'd read the same first line of the article she'd been trying to read a dozen times and still couldn't tell what it said.

Why was she staring into his smiling face, thinking he was too handsome to be real, and recalling that she'd held that face, kissed that face, woken up to that face just a couple of months before?

"Thinking how lucky I am that you're really here. I wasn't sure you would be."

Her nervousness mounting, Natalie rolled her eyes. "Cut it with the corny comments."

"Nothing corny about telling a beautiful woman you appreciate being with her."

Heat flooded her cheeks. They shouldn't be here. Shouldn't be having this conversation. "What are we doing, Matthew?"

His pale blue eyes twinkled. "Having coffee?"

"You don't have coffee."

He glanced down in front of him at the empty table as if her announcement was news to him. "Would it make you feel better if I ordered a drink?"

Her heart beat wildly in her chest, pounding against her ribcage, beating her logic into submission. "This is crazy."

He leaned across the table, his gaze holding hers with an intensity that made breathing difficult. "Wasting time is always crazy. A very wise woman pointed that out to me in Miami not so long ago."

Her gaze dropped to his lips. To his magical, glorious lips that felt so good against hers. Lips that had just implied they were wasting precious time when they could be… Natalie lifted her gaze back to his, but realized that didn't help.

She knew what he was saying, what he wanted.

The same thing she wanted.

The same reason those warning bells had gone off when she'd agreed to meet him for coffee. Because she wanted him.

Felt as if she'd always wanted him.

He wanted her, too. He was using those hypnotic eyes to will her to cut to the chase and admit what she was feeling.

Why not? a little voice asked. Why not give in to his temptation and let him do marvelous things to her body? Nothing would be different. They'd had sex in the past. What would one more night hurt?

Maybe another night would even help. Maybe having sex with Matthew in Memphis wouldn't be nearly as good as she thought having sex with him in Florida had been.

"I want to take you home, Natalie."

Her insides melted.

"To spend the entire night making love to you. In *my* bed."

Visions of his bedroom, of his big bed, flashed into her mind. Visions of her, of him, naked, their bodies locked together in his massive bed.

Her memories were playing tricks on her, right? Miami hadn't really been as magical as her mind made it out to be. He hadn't really made her body sing song after glorious song.

"Let me make love to you, Natalie."

Who was she to deny him?

After all, she was merely mortal, not some super-heroic woman. Who could resist his out-of-this-world allure?

Yeah, logic had been pulverized, because, rather than reminding him of all the reasons they shouldn't, she stood and tossed the remainder of her drink into the closest trash bin.

"Time's wasting," she reminded when Matthew still sat at the table, watching her every move. "You coming?"

Natalie woke with a start, realized she wasn't in her bed and pulled the covers up higher over her bare breasts.

Her bare everything.

Because she was naked and in Matthew's bed. In Matthew's house.

In Memphis.

She turned her head, stared at the sleeping man next to her and fought a million emotions.

He was so darn good-looking and so sexually gifted that it was no wonder she'd ended up back in bed with him.

It was more than that.

He was more than that.

Her mind hadn't been playing tricks on her. If anything, Matthew had been better than she recalled. Had developed even more superpowers to reach inside her body and melt every single cell into ooey, gooey, orgasmic, floating nothingness.

Who knew sex could be like that? That a woman could be so in tune with a man that his every move felt an extension of her own being?

Unable to resist, she touched him, tracing over the strong lines of his face.

Immediately his eyes opened, their pale depths focusing on her, and he smiled. "You really here or am I dreaming?"

She knew what he meant. None of this seemed real.

The night before had seemed as something from a fantasy, not real life.

Because when Matthew had made love to her the first time last night there had been an intensity, a fervor, that surpassed anything they'd experienced in Florida.

It had been as if he'd been claiming her as his own, his body telling her she was his, and no time, distance or anything else would change that.

The second time there had been a sweetness, a tenderness mixed in with his urgency and passion. Every touch had been all about her, about giving pleasure, and pulling every single nerve ending to maximum sensory overload.

He had.

Dear, sweet heaven, what this man had done to her body.

He captured her fingers within his, brought them to his lips and pressed a kiss to their tips. "Real."

She bit the inside of her lower lip. This was real.

She was in bed with Matthew. Her boss.

She knew better, knew how risky doing something so stupid was. Yet with Matthew, she seemed unable to heed logic.

"You're thinking too much, Natalie. You have a nasty habit of doing that."

"Sorry," she said, shrugging her shoulders and realizing she'd caused the covers to slip and expose the upper swell of her breasts. "Sorry," she repeated, tugging on the covers.

"Don't be. Embrace this the way you did in Miami."

"This was supposed to have ended in Miami," she reminded him.

"But it didn't."

"No," she admitted. Nothing had ended in Miami. Even before he'd arrived in Memphis, she'd not been able to stop thinking about him, wondering what would have happened if she'd told him she wanted to see him again. "It's not good that we didn't end it."

He was silent a moment, then asked, "Because of work?"

"You're my boss," she reminded. "We both know if it came down to having to let one of us go that I'd be the one ousted."

"I'd never use our relationship against you."

"I didn't say you would. If things didn't work and got nasty between us, you wouldn't have to say anything. The hospital board could opt to take matters into their own hands."

"There's no policy against our being together, Natalie."

"I don't think they'd encourage us to be in your bed, risking possible drama down the road."

"Maybe not, but we're good together. Unlike anything I've ever known. You feel it, too." In some ways what he was saying was magic to her ears. In others, he scared her. "Neither of us is into drama," he pointed out. "I don't see either of us letting our physical relationship interfere with our work."

She wanted to believe what he was saying.

"I'd like to do this again," he admitted, lacing his fingers with hers.

"As in?"

"I want to keep having sex with you."

Keep having sex with Matthew. It sounded so simple, so tempting. Yet, what was he really saying?

"Do you mean as in us dating?" she asked.

"I'm not looking for anything long-term, but yes, I'd like to date you."

He sounded as surprised at his admission as Natalie felt.

"I'm not good at dating." Just look at how her relationship with Jonathan had ended.

"Because you haven't dated *me*."

Part of her wanted to snort at his arrogance, but how could she scoff when he was right?

"I wasn't the only one who only wanted three days in Miami and said there couldn't be anything beyond that," she reminded him. "I assume your reasons had to do with Carrie."

That had him pausing, raking his fingers through his hair, then pulling her to him. Inches separated their faces as he held her close. "Carrie thinks you're cool."

Carrie had thought she was cool?

"She's a great kid," he continued, as if he needed to sell her on the little girl.

"She is, but…" Natalie took a deep breath. "What if our being involved is a problem? What then?"

"Do you overanalyze everything?"

"Yes. It's what a good heart surgeon and researcher does."

"True, but there are times when you have to just trust your gut instinct."

"If I trusted my gut instinct I wouldn't be in your bed," she admitted rather bluntly.

"Fine, don't trust your gut instinct," he quickly corrected, not looking in the slightest deterred. He rolled, pinning her beneath him, but keeping his weight to where if she wanted to get free she could easily do so. He brushed the tip of his nose against hers. "Trust in me, Natalie."

His plea sounded so simple, yet nothing could be less true. Everything about her spending time with Matthew was complicated, and trusting him? Ha! How could she when not only would her personal life be on the line, but also her professional one?

"Trust in this." He kissed her. Softly, slowly, tenderly.

His lips felt so good on hers, so perfect.

She should tell him to stop, to not further muddy her mind with lust. But she didn't want him to stop. She just wanted to feel, to squeeze every precious memory from the moment.

To give in to the lust.

It *was* just lust she was feeling, right?

"Promise you'll give us a chance," he whispered against her lips, pausing to drop another lingering kiss against her mouth.

She blinked up at him. "Are you using sex to seduce me into agreeing to continue to have sex with you?"

He chuckled. "I want you, Natalie. I'll use whatever means necessary to convince you to agree with me."

He set about doing just that, loving her so intently that Natalie was left gasping for air and wondering how she'd ever thought she could deny him anything.

Once they got out of bed, Matthew made Natalie breakfast, then drove her to her apartment to let her shower and change prior to their both going to the hospital, where they rounded on their patients and took care of paperwork. When done, Natalie headed to the cardiac computer lab to review the Harris case yet again.

Which was where Matthew found her.

"Tuesday morning would be a great day to schedule this."

Glancing up from the computer screen, Natalie caught her breath at the vision of him leaning against the door jamb.

Her body had been all tangled up with his just hours before.

Lucky her. Only… No, she wasn't going to think about that. Not right now. No doubt later logic would regain its strength and take the reins back, but for now she was going to pretend logic didn't exist, had never existed.

She arched a brow. "You're available that morning?"

Surprise at her comment lit in his eyes. Pleased surprise. "The first surgery of its kind performed at this hospital? I'd clear my schedule."

She nodded. "The possibilities of where this could take treatments for transposed vessels is exciting, isn't it?"

"Very. Walk me through the case."

Natalie ran through the computer simulation, just as she'd done dozens of times before. Only this time Matthew was with her, offering praise, making suggestions, discussing possible scenarios that could come up and how they'd respond.

Natalie made mental notes, knew she'd be writing them down later, would be going back through the simulation at least a dozen times more prior to putting Delaine Harris on the operating table to repair her baby's heart.

So many things could go wrong.

So many things could go right.

If she failed, Delaine's baby would face even greater health issues than she would have had they waited until she was born. There was a risk the procedure could force her baby to be born much too soon.

If she succeeded, Delaine's baby would never be a "blue baby", would be able to go home with her parents much sooner, would have a much stronger heart due to the healing that would take place while she was still growing inside her mother, would have less complications later in life.

If what Natalie and several of her colleagues believed was true, the overall benefits of doing the repairs while the baby was still in utero rather than waiting until after birth far outweighed the risks.

But there were always things that came up that one wasn't expecting. Which was why she kept running through the computer simulations, trying to plan for anything unexpected.

Matthew had been pioneering new pediatric heart surgery techniques for years. She'd draw on his experience, and would welcome his assistance. Because of Delaine and her baby, not because she'd had sex with him again.

Phenomenal, out-of-this-world sex.

Last night and again that morning.

Everything seemed wonderful, but Natalie knew it was only a ruse, that this euphoria wouldn't last, and that when it came to an end she'd be the one hurt.

Still, it would take a stronger woman than she was to withstand the power in his blue gaze.

As head of the department, Matthew had already familiarized himself with the Harris case and Natalie's innovative treatment plan. He let her walk him through the simulation step by step, how she'd prepared for the surgery, what precautions she'd taken for anything unexpected, and marveled at this amazing, intelligent, gifted woman he was working with, and that Delaine Harris's baby's heart was in good hands.

He'd known. In Miami and since moving to Memphis. But watching her, listening to her explanations, beat him over the head with the fact that he'd never met anyone like her.

"You aren't listening to me."

He smiled. "I've listened to every word you've said."

"You were a million miles away," she accused, her gaze narrowed.

"I was listening. There's nowhere else I'd rather be than right here with you."

Her forehead creased as she frowned. "So what were you thinking about?"

"Delaine Harris."

Natalie's brow arched. "Really?"

He leaned forward, dropped a kiss to the tip of her nose. "No worries. All my thoughts were professional."

"That's not what I— Oh, you." Natalie rolled her eyes. "I wasn't worried. Not about that."

"No worries on the surgery, either. The Harris baby is the perfect candidate. In your heart, you know that."

Her gaze met his. "I just don't want anything to go wrong. Not ever, but especially not on this first procedure."

"No matter how much you prepare, or worry, when dealing with human lives something can always go wrong."

She nodded. "I'd thought Dr. Luiz would be in surgery with me when I did this live for the first time."

"I'm sure he'd step in if you prefer?"

She shook her head. "No, I want you."

Magic words that had him grinning.

Natalie rolled her eyes again. "Again, not what I meant."

"But true," he teased, knowing his words to be so.

It wasn't a question. He didn't need her to tell him.

She'd shown him.

What was taking Matthew so long? Natalie leaned against the pillow she'd propped against the headboard. He'd disappeared while she'd been in the bathroom.

How did one get ready for bed with the great Matthew Coleman?

She'd done all her usual routine—washed her face, brushed her teeth and hair, flossed, moisturized. She'd even taken a few extra steps of freshening up all over, because she knew what the night was likely to bring.

Perhaps she should have searched for something more glamorous than the cotton pajama shorts and tank top she'd packed at her house when they'd swung by after leaving the hospital. He'd spoken with his sister and she'd asked to keep Carrie another night. But truthfully, Natalie figured no matter what she started off wearing, she'd likely end up naked before long.

She adjusted the strap of the tank, letting it fall off her shoulder, then, feeling stupid, straightened it.

"Matthew?" she called, wondering if he'd fallen asleep on the sofa or something.

"On my way," he answered, and he must really have been because he almost immediately walked into the room, bare-chested, in a pair of to-the-knee gym shorts.

He was carrying a bowl of popcorn and a large water bottle.

"What's that for?" She'd thought he'd dive straight into bed and make haste to remove her pajamas, not bring a snack.

"Us." He put the bowl and drink on the night stand. The buttery scent of popcorn filled her nostrils, making her want some even though they'd grabbed dinner on the way home from the hospital.

"We'll get popcorn in the bed," she warned, reaching out and tossing a few warm kernels in her mouth.

Not looking as if he cared if they covered the bed in popcorn, he grinned.

"Mmm, that's good." She grabbed a few more.

He picked up a remote control, pushed a button that dropped a big screen down out of the ceiling.

"Wow."

"You haven't seen anything yet," he teased, climbing into bed beside her and holding the remote out toward the screen.

"You're wrong about that."

Glancing at her, he laughed. "What's your favorite genre of movies?"

Natalie stared blankly at him.

"Come on, you have to have a favorite."

"Not really. I don't watch much television and haven't been to the movie theater in years."

"Seriously?"

Feeling self-conscious, she shrugged. "It's really not a big deal."

"Sure it is. You were in a relationship for a couple of years. Didn't he take you out?"

Touchy subject, Natalie thought. "We went for dinner."

"That's it?"

"He went with me to hospital functions. I went to his

work functions. It worked for me. Obviously, it wasn't working quite so well for him."

"His law firm represents the hospital? That's why he was at Dr. Luiz's semi-retirement party?"

She nodded. "His family has a lot of connections to the hospital. It's how we met."

"I've said it before and I'll say it again: he's an idiot."

Not wanting to talk about her ex any more, she scooted closer to him and traced her fingers down the indentation in the center of his abs. "That's two of us who think so, but let's not waste time talking about him. He doesn't matter."

His skin prickled with goosebumps beneath her fingertips.

"I'm taking you to the movies, Natalie," he surprised her by saying. "You, me and Carrie. We're going next weekend."

She just stared.

"That work for you?"

Still wondering what she had gotten herself into, but knowing she was on this roller-coaster ride, Natalie nodded.

Matthew's smile was brighter than the screen he'd just clicked on when he said, "It's a date."

CHAPTER TWELVE

MOISTURE TRICKLED DOWN the back of Natalie's neck and beneath her scrubs. A surgical nurse kept the sweat from her face by dabbing gauze over it every so often. Delaine Harris's abdomen had been opened and the sweet little girl inside was being operated on while still attached by the umbilical cord. They'd been carefully making incisions into her tiny body as they threaded the smallest possible arterial catheter into her heart.

Via the catheter, Natalie and Matthew had repaired the blockage in the pulmonary artery that, once the baby was born and having to breathe on her own, would have prevented her body from getting oxygenated blood.

Everything connected with repairing the blockage had gone smoothly and they'd made the decision to repair the large ventricular defect with a patch. Using the computer for guidance and just as she'd practiced dozens of times, Natalie placed the patch, closing the abnormal defect one painstaking suture at a time. Matthew stood on the opposite side of her, working to suture the patch as well.

As much as she wanted to glance away from the screen to meet his eyes, to see his wink of encouragement, she didn't dare look away from the image of Delaine's baby's tiny heart.

No matter. She could feel Matthew's presence, feel his encouragement as surely as if he were speaking the words.

Along with the obstetrician, a neonatologist, an anesthesiologist and a slew of nurses and surgical techs, Matthew was a valued member of the surgical team.

Having him there meant everything.

Which was a little scary.

She didn't want to get too dependent upon him. She didn't want to depend on anyone. Hadn't she learned her lesson over and over—that to depend on someone was to set oneself up for disappointment?

Natalie worked on reattaching one set of vessels while he worked on another. Considering their tiny workspace, how well they worked together was quite impressive.

Not once did he attempt to take over—he just followed her lead, perfectly performing his repair while she made hers.

An alarm sounded, indicating that Mom's heart rate was dipping.

"Got this," the anesthesiologist assured, as he and the obstetrician made medication and fluid adjustments.

Natalie hoped they were right. Everything was proceeding according to plan, but it would be another few hours before they were done.

When they'd finally finished the baby's heart surgery and stepped back to let the obstetrician take over safely closing the baby inside her mother's uterus, Natalie felt like her insides might explode with excitement.

She'd done it.

Something she'd dreamed of doing for years, since being in residency and proposing the idea. She'd performed her first in-utero vessel transposition repair. She'd written papers on the procedure, done hundreds of computer simulations, believed it would improve the long-term outcomes of her patients.

Emotions rushed through her as she realized she'd just performed what could be the most important surgery of her career. If it worked—it had to work—it could change the entire way "blue baby" care was approached.

Now, for the next few months, they'd wait and see if she'd been correct. Wait, and do a whole lot of praying.

Which was okay. Natalie did a lot of praying with each surgery she performed because that was someone's precious child.

Because some children were wanted and loved.

Not all kids ended up in the foster program as she had.

Just look at Carrie.

Natalie slipped off her surgical mask, slumped against the wall of the room she'd just entered, and prayed that Delaine and her baby continued to do well—better even.

"You did an amazing job, Dr. Sterling," Ben Robards, the obstetrician who'd been in on the surgery, praised when he entered the room, along with Matthew. Both removed their surgical masks. "Thanks for letting me be a part of this."

It was Ben who'd initially come to her with his patient, discussed with her the possibility of Delaine's baby being the first at Memphis Children's to have her heart deformity repaired while still in utero.

"Without the long hours you put in, today wouldn't have been possible," she assured him. "You did a fabulous job with Delaine. The whole team did."

"Agreed," Matthew said. "Now we wait to see."

"When you think mom and baby are stable enough to consider sending home with fetal monitoring," Dr. Robards said, "I'll give you a call to be sure we cover all our bases."

"Sounds perfect."

"Nice man," Matthew commented after the obstetrician had removed his protective outer coverings from his scrubs, thoroughly cleaned his hands and left the room. "I met him briefly at Dr. Luiz's retirement party, but hadn't talked with him much until today."

Natalie still leaned against the wall and stared at him. "Exhausted?"

"In some ways. In others, I feel exhilarated."

He grinned. "I know what you mean." First glancing through the window on the door going into the operating room to make sure no one was close to coming into the room, he reached out and cupped her face. "You were amazing in there, Dr. Sterling. Deserving of every praise Dr. Luiz ever uttered."

Casting her own nervous glance toward the doorway, Natalie smiled. "He's a smart man, that Dr. Luiz."

Matthew studied her. "Even though he played a key role in my being hired?"

Natalie hesitated only a second. "Especially because of that."

"Natalie," he groaned, leaning in to kiss her, but, wide-eyed, she pushed off the wall and shook her head.

"Uh-uh. Not at the hospital."

"Won't Carrie find it odd if I go to dinner with you unexpectedly?"

Matthew stared at the woman he'd missed in his bed the past three nights. Two nights of holding her, of waking with her next to him, and then being by himself in that big bed had just felt wrong. Not that he hadn't understood why she wanted to stay at the hospital to keep close tabs on the Harris baby.

That had been last night. Tonight, she could go home.

He'd come to her office on his way out so he could convince her to go to dinner. Stubborn woman had refused earlier when he'd asked, just as she had the previous two evenings, and it seemed she was sticking to that trend.

"Why would she find it odd?" he asked, not understanding her line of thought. Carrie liked Natalie.

"Maybe she'd prefer to spend time with just you after being away from you all weekend."

Elaine hadn't brought Carrie home until late Sunday. Natalie had been gone for just over an hour when his sister had pulled into the drive. He hadn't wanted her to go, but from the point his sister called to say she'd be headed that way in an hour or so, Natalie had become guarded and had quickly left.

"Over spending time with us?" he clarified, trying to make sense of her reticence. "Spending time with you wouldn't bother her. She'd like it."

Natalie didn't look convinced. "Before was different because I wasn't having sex with you. It didn't matter if she didn't like me. Unless you are hoping she *doesn't* like me so you have a reason to end this now?"

She was right. What Carrie thought did matter. A lot.

"You know I don't want to end this, and Carrie already likes you," he reminded her. "Do you not want to have dinner with me, Natalie?"

"I do want to have dinner with you. It's just…"

"I have Carrie," he guessed. She wasn't saying no because of him, but because of his little girl. They'd had such a great time over the weekend, had worked together at the hospital in complete harmony. Why would she hesitate to spend time with him because of Carrie?

Looking guilty, she said, "I'm sorry. I'm just not much of a 'being around kids' person."

"You're a pediatric cardiologist," he reminded her, not bothering to hide his annoyance.

"So?" she challenged, crossing her arms over her chest as her chin lifted several notches.

"So, you make your living by spending time with kids. Carrie doesn't bite."

"I could point out that I specialize in neonatology. Most of my patients aren't even a year old." Natalie's expression didn't waver. "So don't make fun of my concerns, Matthew. This is serious."

"You think I don't know it's serious? I want to spend

time with you, want you to go to dinner with me, and you won't because Carrie is going to be there." He made it sound a crime, as if she should be ashamed for saying no.

"I should stay here and work."

"Nice try, but there's nothing you have to do until bright and early in the morning."

"Have to and need to are two different things. Besides, being close in case Delaine has issues isn't a bad idea."

"You can be close without spending the night at the hospital. I live ten minutes from here," he pointed out. When she started to argue, he added, "I want to celebrate the fantastic job you did yesterday, Natalie. Away from work. This is a big deal. Let me share it with you."

For a brief second she looked as if she might relent, might go to dinner with him and Carrie, but she shook her head.

"I'm sorry to disappoint you, but I'd rather not tonight, Matthew." Her expression remained conflicted. "Please understand."

His sigh was full of frustration. "I want to talk you into changing your mind, but I'm not going to be that guy, Natalie. The one who keeps on every time he doesn't get his way. If you want to go home rather than go to dinner with me and Carrie, then you should go home."

"Thank you." A great deal of her tension visibly eased.

"But don't expect me to understand, because I don't. I really think—"

"Matthew?" she interrupted.

"Right," he said, not finishing the argument he'd been about to present. Glancing at his watch, he cursed at the time, knowing he had to get Carrie from her extended preschool program. "Am I allowed to call you once I've put her to bed?"

"I'll be here until late."

"Your boss must be a horrible slave-driver."

A smile toyed at her lips. "He's not so bad."

"Good to know." He crossed the room, wrapped his arms around her waist and pulled her in for a goodbye kiss. "I was beginning to think you didn't like him."

"I like him well enough," she admitted, staring into his eyes.

"Just well enough?" he asked, his lips hovering above hers.

"A little more." She stood on her tiptoes and kissed him.

That she initiated the kiss, that her hands wrapped around his neck and held on to him tight, just about undid every good intention Matthew had.

"No, we are not doing anything on my desk," she said, reading his mind. "You've got to pick up Carrie."

"I do."

"So go."

"I don't want to leave you."

"I'll be here tomorrow."

"Tomorrow seems like a long time from now."

Smiling, Natalie pushed him toward her office door. "Goodnight, Matthew."

"I'll call later," he promised, leaning in for a last kiss.

"I'd like that."

Matthew didn't try to talk her into dinner when Natalie said no on Thursday, but that night when he called their conversation quickly morphed into conveying his frustration.

"I want to see you outside the hospital."

"I'm on my way home now," she told him, truly being in her car driving toward her condo.

"Carrie's down for the night. What am I supposed to do? Wake her and drag her to your place so I can hold you?"

"You know I don't want you to do that."

"I miss you in my bed, Natalie."

"I miss being there," she admitted, keeping her eyes

glued on the road as she drove. It had only been a few nights since she'd been there, but oh, how she missed his body pressed up against hers. How had she gone all those weeks without him?

"Come to me, Natalie." His voice was low, full of temptation.

"Now?"

"Yes."

A million responses formed in her head but none of them came out of her mouth.

"You're silent because you're rerouting your GPS to take you to my house, right?"

She couldn't go to his house. She just couldn't.

"I remember how to get to your house," she admitted. After all, she had spent most of the weekend there.

"Then you have no excuse. How soon will you be here? I'll put the popcorn on."

Natalie's cheeks heated. "No popcorn."

"You prefer something stickier?"

"I haven't eaten, but…"

"It's after nine, Natalie. You're just now leaving work and haven't had any dinner?"

She didn't deny his claim because, in her excitement over how well Delaine and her baby had been doing when she'd checked in on the pregnant woman and getting caught up in documenting her findings, Natalie had forgotten to eat.

"Your boss really is a jerk."

He sounded so outraged, she laughed. "I'll let him know you said so."

"How soon will you be here?"

"I'm not coming, Matthew. It's late. I'm going home, showering, eating, reading for a while, then going to bed."

"You can do all those things at my house."

Natalie blinked. Without even realizing it, she'd already

turned onto a street that took her toward him and away from her apartment.

Natalie didn't make it home that night. Sneaking out of Matthew's bed at just before dawn to go home and grab a shower and clean clothes didn't count.

She must have had a guilty expression on her face because when she walked into the gym the next day Monica and Suzie both gave her a knowing look.

"What?"

"You saw him last night."

"I see him every day at work," she said flippantly, sliding onto the vacant elliptical next to Monica's and wondering why she was bothering working out that morning. She'd gotten more than enough exercise during the night.

"You're glowing."

"Don't be ridiculous."

"Don't bother denying that he makes you happy."

Natalie punched in her settings, then began churning away at the elliptical. All the while her mind churned with Suzie's comment.

Matthew did make her happy.

Happy in a way she didn't recall being. Which seemed a strange admission, because she hadn't been *un*happy.

Not that she'd been pleased to learn Jonathan had been cheating on her, but even then, she wouldn't have called herself unhappy. Maybe part of her had always expected him to leave.

Then along had come Matthew.

Who would also eventually leave, and then what a mess there would be in his wake.

"Are you officially dating now?"

"Our relationship is complicated," she admitted, not wanting to lie to her friends, but not wanting to dish out details either.

"Because you work together?" Monica asked.

"You like him, Nat. A lot. From the sound of things, he likes you, too," Suzie added.

Natalie nodded. Matthew did like her. It seemed unbelievable that he wanted her so much, but he did.

"I really think this guy is the one, Nat."

Natalie sighed. Her friends just didn't understand. Not really, because it wasn't them involved. No matter. She loved them anyway, as they did her. Thank goodness they'd come into her life and welcomed a lost young girl into their hearts.

Maybe, just maybe, she should thank goodness Matthew had come into her life and welcomed her into his heart, too.

If only he wouldn't eventually leave.

The popcorn wasn't as good as what Matthew had made for their in-bed movie, but Natalie wasn't complaining.

She glanced over at him. Matthew's eyes were glued on the theater's big screen playing the latest animated children's feature, but he must have sensed her gaze because he looked her way and winked.

Carrie had seemed excited to see her again, had chatted away about her school and her new friends and having gone to the zoo over the past weekend with her cousins to check up on baby giraffe Zoie's progress to making her grand entrance into the world.

Natalie felt such an affinity for the child. Probably because of the bond they shared over having both lost their parents at such a young age. Recalling the loss Carrie was dealing with made her want to wrap the girl in a hug and protect her from everything the world might throw at her.

Which was also part of why she felt the need to keep Carrie from getting too attached to her.

Natalie's gaze dropped to her hand. Her hand that was encased in a small, warm one. The girl's other hand was clasped with Matthew's. To anyone looking their way, they probably looked like a happy little family.

The reality was, her and Matthew's relationship was temporary. It was why she was so reluctant to spend time with the girl. How could she let Carrie get attached when she knew eventually she'd no longer be in her life? That she'd have to leave the child, the way so many had come in and out of her own childhood?

But the little girl taking her hand and clasping it tightly had given Natalie a warm, fuzzy feel inside, making her wish she was truly part of a family, *this* family, making her wish this were real and not temporary.

She glanced up, realized Matthew was still watching her and blushed a little that he'd caught her staring at her hand laced with Carrie's.

Could he see how torn she was? How part of her thrilled at the child's affection? How part of her wanted to shield herself and Carrie from future pain?

Although she'd not explained her feelings to him, no doubt he'd realized her current biggest hang-up centered around Carrie and not the hospital. When things went south with their relationship, work could, and likely would, be problematic. If things went sour that would prompt her to look for a department head position over her own pediatric cardiology unit. As long as things were good with Matthew, she didn't see herself stepping outside the comfortable box she currently found herself in.

Comfortable? That might be stretching it.

She wasn't comfortable with her relationship with Matthew.

Eventually, his desire for her would change. Just as Jonathan's had.

And then he'd leave.

Definitely better not to get too attached to Carrie, and not to let the innocent girl get too attached to her, when

Natalie knew how that ripping away of relationships felt in the wake of tragedy.

Better for her not to get too attached to Matthew, either. She feared she might be too late on that one.

CHAPTER THIRTEEN

Natalie couldn't recall ever having been this nervous.

Carrie had gone to a sleepover birthday party for Matthew's youngest niece, and so he had invited Natalie over for a sleepover party at his place. She'd packed a bag and spent the night. Somehow, that morning over breakfast, he'd talked her into going with him to have a birthday lunch for his niece at his mother's. Probably because she'd caught that vulnerable look in his eyes that parental tasks to do with Carrie so often brought out in him—that look that was so at odds with everything else about him.

Still, she shouldn't have agreed.

"This is a bad idea."

Matthew glanced over at her from the driver's seat. "Why's that?"

"I shouldn't be here."

"Of course you should. I want you here."

"What about your family? What are they going to think when I'm with you? What about your sister? She's going to know we spent the night together. Your mom, too."

"That bothers you?"

Apparently, it did.

"Don't worry. All my family will love you."

Amazingly, they seemed to do just that.

Natalie had been hugged and had her cheeks kissed a dozen times. She'd been introduced to aunts, uncles, cousins, neighbors, and hoped there wasn't a pop quiz because no way would she ever remember all their names.

Elaine shared her brother's pale blue eyes and dark hair and was a beautiful woman, as were her two daughters. Her husband was a boisterous Italian who worked in the restaurant business, but Natalie didn't catch any more details than that.

Matthew's mother was a feisty, petite woman who ran her household with a drill sergeant's efficiency yet with hugs and kisses. She had dark eyes that seemed to constantly smile. Obviously the siblings had gotten their eye color from their father, who'd passed many years before.

His mother had invited several friends and neighbors. The house was crowded, loud, warm, exactly what Natalie thought a family gathering should be. How had Matthew moved away and missed out on so much love for so many years? Nothing in Boston could have lured her away from this lovely family.

Glancing his way, she noted Matthew wore a slight scowl as he surveyed the crowded setting. Maybe he'd hoped for a small family gathering to spend quality time with his mother and sister rather than all the friends and extended family his mother had welcomed into her home. Or maybe he was worried she'd be overwhelmed by the crowd.

"You have a beautiful family, Matthew. I envy you that."

He raked his fingers through his hair, glancing around the room. "Don't envy me this."

"Your family?" she asked, confused.

"Being forced back here, giving up Boston, my life? This chaos isn't what I would have chosen."

"This?"

He gestured around the noisy room. Children ran around with parents yelling orders for them to "Be careful". And "Don't do that". Several family members cleaned the kitchen after the birthday festivities. A handful sat in the living room, watching a sports game, except for one young father who had a sleeping baby on his chest and he was catching a cat nap, as well. Others had gone out to sit on the front porch, possibly to escape some of the noise.

"I shouldn't have insisted you come here."

She was having a good time, enjoying his family and the warmth with which she'd been welcomed. Natalie arched her brow. "You don't want me here?"

"*I* don't even really want to be here." He looked around. His gaze landing on the dad with the sleeping baby on his chest. The skin pulled tight over his face, then he seemed to shake off his mood as he turned back to her. "You have to admit last night was a lot more fun."

Natalie eyed him curiously. Last night had been fun, but so was this, just in a different way. Surely he understood that? Did he feel uncomfortable around his family? Or maybe he was nervous since he knew she'd grown up without any real family life.

"I'm good and enjoying meeting your family," she assured him. "Besides, Carrie is having a great time with her cousins."

Raking his fingers through his hair, he nodded. "You're right, only…"

"Only?" she prompted.

At her frown, he tried to explain. "Don't get me wrong. I love my family. My mom and sister are the best. Just, this makes me feel…" His gaze landed on where Carrie played a board game with her cousins and some new friends, then his gaze made its way back to the dad holding his baby. "All of this makes me feel inadequate in regard to Carrie and wonder what I was thinking to ever agree to any of this. Almost to the point of claustrophobia."

Matthew knew he had revealed too much. He could see it in Natalie's surprised eyes. But watching the women, the men, interact with their kids at this party had left him daunted at the reality that he alone was responsible for Carrie. For her mental, physical and emotional well-being. If he screwed up too often, it was that innocent little girl who would pay the price.

Maybe if he'd started at the beginning preparing himself for a father role he'd be better at it, feel semi-competent. As it was, more and more he found himself wondering if Carrie would be better off living with his sister. She'd talked about the option to adopt Carrie into her own family not long after Robert and Carolyn's death, but Matthew had been reeling at the loss of his friends and hadn't been able to bear the thought of letting Carrie go. That had been selfish of him. If he'd truly had Carrie's best interests at heart, he'd have given her to Elaine, where she'd have had a nurturing environment.

"What makes you claustrophobic makes me nostalgic for something I never had," Natalie said softly, disappointment in her eyes.

"You like this?"

She nodded. "You're lucky to have such a great family. To belong and be loved just because you were born into this family. It's something a lot of people never have."

Something *she'd* never had.

At that moment his Uncle Kenny belched, a cousin high-fived the balding man and a couple of the kids yelled out, *"Eww!"* amidst giggles.

"Yep, lucky," he mused, although none of his family's antics had ever bothered him in the past. Today felt different.

"I always got the impression you were close to your family."

"I am." He was. "Now I'm the one overthinking." He gave a low laugh, although he felt no humor. "Ignore me."

Why the day had gotten to him so completely, he wasn't sure. Just that more and more he felt inadequate in his thrust-upon role as Carrie's parent, and being here among all these other real parents made him feel like the odd man out.

"Come on, Natalie," he prompted, hoping to rid her eyes of the disillusionment. "Let's take the kids out back to play."

She looked uncertain. "Are you sure?"

Determined not to let his insecurities about Carrie put a complete damper on what had otherwise been a good day, he nodded. "Positive. Come on. Let's have some fun." The fun stuff was something he knew he could cope with, at least.

His mother's back yard was a fenced-in area that was approximately two hundred by two hundred feet. A sandbox and a swing set were off to the left corner.

"Swings or sand?"

Natalie's eyes widened. "Aren't we just watching the kids?"

"What's the fun in that?" He took her hand and walked her over to the swing set. "Have a seat, Natalie."

"I…"

"Are you afraid of heights or get motion sickness?"

She shook her head.

"Then sit."

She sat.

Expecting him to take the swing next to hers, she'd barely gotten her grip when he warned, "Hold on tight." Then gave her a hefty push.

Natalie had been on a swing before. At some point during her childhood, she was sure she had. Probably during grammar school. But she had no recall of having had someone push her. She smiled.

"Me, too!" Carrie pleaded as she climbed up on the swing next to Natalie's. "Push me, too!"

Matthew immediately gave the child a big push, setting her swing in motion and triggering a trail of pleased squeals.

Matthew's eldest niece joined in, adding her pleas to be pushed.

The moment his niece was settled in the next swing Matthew added her to his routine, giving her a couple of pushes to get her moving, too. He moved back and forth between the three swings, keeping them all going higher and higher. Carrie was squealing with delight, as was Liz.

Way back in the recesses of her mind, a memory tugged at Natalie. Or maybe more of an emotion than memory. One that had a lot to do with being tossed from one foster home to another. To never having *had* anyone like Matthew to push her on a swing.

"Higher, Uncle Matthew! Higher!" Carrie cried.

Carrie had lost both of her parents, had no other family, just as Natalie hadn't. She could easily have ended up in the same situation as Natalie had.

"To the moon and back?" he asked, getting a resounding "Yes!" as his answer.

Thank goodness she had Matthew.

He thought he was inadequate in his parent-figure role. From time to time those insecurities bled forth, such as today. Natalie wished he could see what she saw when she watched him with Carrie, when he spoke of the child, the love that shone in his eyes.

Natalie smiled at the happiness of the moment.

"Me, too, Uncle Matthew. Me, too," Liz cried.

If Natalie had thought Matthew was going to let her swing slow as he kept the other two girls going, she'd been wrong. He gave a hard push any time her swing appeared to be slowing. His youngest niece climbed to the top of the slide for a bird's-eye view and cheered them onward.

"Do you want my swing?" Natalie called to the girl.

The just-turned-four birthday girl shook her head.

"If you decide you do, let me know," she offered.

Giggles abounded from Matthew's other two swingers.

He seemed to have relaxed and let out a few laughs. The happy sounds made Natalie warm inside.

This, she thought. This was what she wanted.

The crazy, loud chaos from indoors. The preciousness of this moment with Matthew and the kids. Only she wanted it to be real. For her and Matthew to be a couple, for Carrie to be theirs.

She wanted a family. Matthew's family.

Which scared her.

To want those things was foolish and a waste of energy. Maybe someday she'd have this, a family of her own, but it wouldn't be with Matthew. He'd made that plain in Florida and again in Memphis. He wasn't looking for anything long-term, wasn't that what he'd said?

She closed her eyes, gave in to the rhythm of the moving swing, pushing off each time her feet came near the ground, welcoming the momentum each time Matthew's hands made contact and gave a hardy push.

Higher and higher she went, her mind clearing and a sense of flying taking hold, making her want to stretch her arms out and go soaring through the air.

Lightness came over her and before she thought better of it she leapt out of the swing, laughing as she landed on her feet with her arms outstretched. "Ta-da!"

"What was that?" Matthew laughed from where he stood behind the swings, giving the girls another push.

"Me reliving my youth," she blurted out, although it wasn't exactly true. She couldn't recall having ever jumped out of a swing in the past, just had memories of watching other kids do so while playing with each other as she watched from the sidelines.

"Looks good on you."

Her eyes met his. Her breath hiccupped in her throat. No wonder she wanted this. Wanted him. Despite his struggles over his thrust-upon parenting role, he was a

good man, was an excellent heart surgeon, was a fantabu-
lous lover and was beautiful to look upon, inside and out.

"Thank you," she told him as she made her way back
over to her swing and set it in motion again, aided by the
feel of Matthew's hands against her bottom for a brief
moment.

She definitely should have played more on swings as
a child. And more taking chances in her life after that,
instead of always playing it safe.

Or was this her brain's way of trying to convince her
that taking a chance with Matthew was okay? That she
wasn't making the biggest mistake of her life by being
here with him today? That she wasn't setting herself up
for horrific pain? That she wasn't setting sweet little Carrie up for pain, too?

Leaning back into the swing, Natalie closed her eyes
and gave in to the swinging motion again.

"I want to jump, too," Carrie called out.

"Go for it," he encouraged. "You got this."

Natalie opened her eyes just in time to see Carrie let
go of the swing's chains and do exactly what Natalie had
done minutes before.

Only Carrie's flight wasn't a liberating soar. Instead,
she flailed through the air.

"Carrie! No!" Natalie warned, planting her feet on the
ground to slow her swing the moment the child let go and
practically flipped out of the swing seat.

She reached Carrie milliseconds after the little girl hit
the ground.

Carrie's leap from her swing and into the air played in
slow motion in Matthew's head. Even before she hit the
ground, he knew her landing wasn't going to be pretty.
She'd come off the swing too high and at the wrong angle,
almost as if she had just let go and fallen forward out of
the swing rather than leaping.

If only the jump really had been in slow motion and he could have gotten to her in time to catch her.

If only he could move at all.

Carrie's returning swing slapped against his chest in his frozen state as she landed on the ground hard, and all wrong.

"Carrie!" Natalie knelt next to the unmoving child.

Fear slammed Matthew, paralyzing him. Fear that he'd let something happen to Robert's child. Fear that she might be seriously hurt. Fear that he'd failed so quickly, so *horribly* at this parenting thing.

His heart wrenched as Carrie's cries filled the air, but so did a sense of relief. Cries required life.

He'd had horrors of her landing on her neck.

As Natalie knelt beside her she sat up, tears streaming down her face and sobs escaping from her lips.

Seeing her moving had Matthew wanting to sob, too.

He should go to her. It was what a parent would do. He should take her in his arms and comfort her.

It was what *Natalie* was doing.

"What hurts, sweetie?" she asked quickly, her gaze raking over Carrie, searching for injury, connecting with how Carrie held her left arm at an awkward angle.

Eyes wide, she gasped between tears, "My arm."

Carrie was hurt and he was frozen in place like a blazing idiot.

"Try to hold still, sweetie," Natalie encouraged. "I'm going to check you over."

But Carrie was panicking, guarding against Natalie's attempts to do so. Other than scraped knees Matthew didn't recall any injury in the child's short four years with her parents, so the fall had to have her frightened.

Why wasn't he moving toward her? Why wasn't he checking her? What was wrong with him? He should be the one checking Carrie. She was his *responsibility.*

"Am I going to die like Daddy and Momma?" she sobbed, her big brown eyes glassy from her tears.

Failure sucker-punched Matthew in the gut. He hadn't even considered that she might associate her pain to her parents' death.

Natalie kissed Carrie's forehead. "No, sweetie, of course not. But you are hurt and I need to check you."

She gently examined Carrie's arm. It didn't take a degree to see the odd angle of her forearm. Matthew's stomach threatened to spill the birthday cake he'd eaten earlier. How could he have let this happen?

"Is Carrie okay, Uncle Matthew?" Liz asked, tugging on his shirt and drawing Natalie's gaze to him momentarily.

Her expression was one of confusion—as in, why wasn't he by her side helping check Carrie, helping reassure her that she was going to be okay?

Good question, with the only answer being that he was a total failure of a parent.

His other niece squatted down next to Carrie. Mandy patted her right shoulder, telling her it was going to be okay.

"She's hurt, Uncle Matthew," Liz said, sounding a little panicked. "Carrie is hurt."

He glanced down at the little girl staring up at him with big eyes that begged him to do something.

Do something, he ordered himself. He was a renowned heart surgeon, had never frozen like this no matter what the circumstances. What was wrong with him?

"Matthew?" Natalie's voice broke into his self-recriminations.

Snapping out of his frozen state, he scooped Liz into his arms and moved toward what was difficult for him to look at because Carrie's broken limb was the culmination of all he was lacking as a parent.

"She will be okay." He wasn't sure if he was talking

to himself or to his niece. "But we're going to have to get her to the emergency room to get a special picture taken of her arm."

He looked directly at Carrie, hating that the child was having to deal with anything negative so soon on the heels of losing her parents.

"You've broken your arm," Natalie told her in a calm voice. Much calmer than Matthew felt. "You're going to need the bone reset, okay? We're going to have to take you to the hospital," she continued.

Hopefully, that was all Carrie would need done. She looked so tiny, so helpless sitting there crying, tears staining her shirt, so much of his two best friends blended in her features.

How could he have allowed anything to happen to her?

"I don't want to go to the hospital," Carrie cried, looking at Matthew as if he were responsible and clinging to Natalie as if she was a lifeline.

He didn't blame her. If he'd known what he was doing, he wouldn't have allowed this to happen.

"Can we come?" both nieces asked in unison.

Setting Liz down, Matthew knelt beside Carrie. "Go in with the girls and tell the others what happened," he told Natalie. "I'm going to load Carrie into the car. Meet me around front."

"I want Natalie!" Carrie cried, clenching her fingers into Natalie's shirt. "Please don't leave me."

"And could you grab a clean button-up shirt and shorts from one of the girls for Carrie to put on when we're through at the hospital?" Matthew continued, ignoring Carrie's pleas.

Natalie looked hesitant, but then pried Carrie's hands free of her shirt, took Liz's and Mandy's hands into hers and headed into the house with the girls in tow.

Taking care not to bump Carrie's left arm, Matthew scooped her into his arms and stood with her.

She felt so little in his arms, so helpless. Shame that he'd let this happen to her filled him. Shame that he hadn't done better by her. He'd known he wasn't cut out for parenthood yet he'd played around at it for the past five months, pretending he could do this.

Obviously he couldn't, and needed to do what was right for Carrie.

Natalie and Matthew's family rushed out of the house, requested items in hand, just as Matthew was buckling Carrie into her car seat. He shut her door and motioned for Natalie to get in the driver's seat.

"Could you drive so I can sit back here with her? I didn't want to put her into her car seat, but two wrongs don't equal a right and it's my job to keep her safe."

His tone implied that he thought the little girl's fall was his fault.

Natalie reached out to touch him, to reassure him that Carrie's injuries were an accident, but he shrugged away her touch.

"Oh, honey." Matthew's mother winced, taking a peep into the car at the child. "Grandma will be there with you in a few."

"It's okay, Mom," Matthew immediately corrected. "Stay here with your company. I'll call when I know something."

His sister and a few of the other guests said things, too, but they blurred in Natalie's head. Everything was blurring in her head.

Why had Matthew shrugged away her touch? For that matter, why had he stood at the swing for so long after Carrie's fall?

Wanting to ask him about his odd behavior, but knowing now wasn't the time, Natalie climbed in, pushed the button to start the car and had them on their way.

Her mind racing, she drove on autopilot.

Carrie went back and forth between whimpering and

crying on the drive to the hospital, saying she didn't want to go to the emergency room, that she didn't want Matthew, that she wanted her mommy and daddy.

As she glanced in the rear-view mirror Matthew's pale, gaunt expression tore at Natalie.

"You're going to be okay, Carrie," he soothed from the back seat. "This is going to be okay."

He didn't address her request for her parents, but then, what could he say?

The emergency room doctor consulted a pediatric orthopedic surgeon who'd taken Carrie to surgery to reset the bones, leaving Natalie and Matthew in the waiting room.

Carrie was wheeled away while Matthew looked as if he might pull rank and stay at her side during surgery.

Natalie understood. Part of her wanted to be at the child's side to make sure nothing went wrong, too. Logically, she knew that Matthew or herself would just be in the way, a distraction that might cause a problem. They needed to let the surgeon do what he'd been trained to do.

She tried to comfort Matthew, but again, he wasn't receptive to her touch. Natalie sank into one of the waiting room chairs and watched him pace back and forth.

His mother, sister and a slew of other family members arrived minutes behind them, despite Matthew's request that they stay home. His family hugged him and comforted him and he semi-let them. Natalie watched, feeling more and more like an outsider.

They'd been waiting for what seemed like hours before Matthew got a call Carrie was in Recovery, that everything had gone fine and they'd allow him to come to see her very soon.

"I can't believe I let this happen," he berated himself, pacing across the lobby while he waited on the okay to head to the recovery room.

"These things happen." Matthew's mother wrapped

him in a hug again and plopped several big kisses on his cheeks. "Don't you recall how many broken bones you and Robert had between the two of you? His mother and I knew the emergency staff by name."

"That was different."

"How?"

"We were boys, and Carrie has already suffered so much."

"Being boys makes it okay how?" his sister piped up. "Just because you and Robert were guys didn't make it okay. You scared us all several times. Remember that time you...?"

While his family continued to go on and on about the past, about how accidents happened and how a parent couldn't bubble-wrap their child, more and more unease took hold inside Natalie.

Matthew hadn't wanted her touch, her comfort.

Of course he hadn't. She was nothing more than a temporary lover.

As she recalled her thoughts when they'd been playing on the swings, her longings for their relationship to be real, nausea churned.

She was getting too involved in his life, in Carrie's.

Seeing the child hurt had torn at her heart, had filled her with a protectiveness for the girl that surprised her. She'd have willingly taken Carrie's place, taken the pain so she wouldn't have to experience it.

Natalie wasn't supposed to get attached, nor was she supposed to let the child get attached to her.

Carrie's pleas for her to stay echoed through her mind, reminding her of her own silent cries over the years not to be left behind yet again by one foster parent after another.

Yet she'd always been left.

Just as she'd be left behind this time, too, if she didn't make a preemptive move.

Matthew's mother had her arm wrapped around him

and was telling another childhood story. Part of Natalie would have liked to hear it—and all of her would have liked to know what it felt like to have a mother's arm wrapped around her. It had been so long since she'd been held with love. None of her foster parents had really shown her love. The McCulloughs had been wonderful, encouraging, but they'd not been warm and fuzzy kind of people. Jonathan sure hadn't loved her. Matthew's touch gave a glimpse of what it could be like, but she didn't want to fool herself. He didn't love her.

She needed to get away, to escape childhood memories and personal demons, to go somewhere to decompress, to get her head on straight and put an end to this fiasco she was caught up in with Matthew.

It was time to leave.

CHAPTER FOURTEEN

"WHERE DID YOU GO? Do you have any idea how embarrassed I was when I came back from seeing Carrie, expecting you to be waiting, and my family said they hadn't seen you since prior to my going to Recovery?" Matthew demanded, storming into Natalie's office and closing the door behind him with a loud thud.

Looking up from her desk, Natalie cringed, but didn't defend her actions. Then again, what could she say? She'd bailed when he'd needed her, when Carrie had been hurt.

How could she have just left without a word?

At first, he'd thought she'd slipped out to go to the restroom. When he'd finally gotten to see Carrie in Recovery and had reassured himself she was going to be okay despite his poor care, Natalie was nowhere to be found.

He waited for her to say something, pacing across her office, then turning toward her. "Why?"

She didn't quite meet his eyes. "I didn't belong."

"I invited you. Of course you belonged. Probably more so than I did."

Visibly rattled, she shook her head. "I was just a temporary lover, Matthew. Taking me to your family function was inappropriate."

"A temporary lover?" He frowned. "We're dating, Natalie."

"We were," she said quietly.

He stared at her. "We could have had something really great while it lasted."

"You think that's fair to Carrie? To bring someone into her life, let her get close to them, and then when you get bored and say adios, then what? You think Carrie isn't going to suffer?" She stood, leaned toward him. "I assure you, Carrie will be hurt by the women you have come and go in your life."

"What women I have come and go? There's only been you for months, Natalie. There are no other women."

She looked taken aback at his admission. What had she thought? That he'd been dating woman after woman since Miami, before moving to Memphis?

"But you're probably right. That's just one more in a long line of things I'll do wrong where Carrie is concerned."

He'd always thought of himself as a great uncle. Being Carrie's uncle had been fun. He could sweep in, have a good time with her without any responsibilities. But he had never been meant to be her father. That had been Robert's place.

Only Robert wasn't here, and Matthew was doing a crappy job of trying to fill his friend's shoes.

He'd liked his life. He had liked being a bachelor, being devoted to his career, being a best friend, being an uncle. He wasn't sure he liked anything about his current situation—especially his failing relationship with the woman across from him.

"Our ending whatever this is between us now, before anyone gets hurt, is for the best."

Matthew narrowed his gaze. "The best for whom?"

"Everyone."

Ending things with Natalie didn't feel like the best thing. But maybe she was right and he needed to think of Carrie, of doing what was best for her.

Which didn't include being raised by someone who had no clue what he was doing.

Two weeks had passed since Carrie's accident. Two weeks in which Natalie had avoided Matthew as much as possible, as she was doing now by hiding out in her office working on charts.

She'd assisted during two surgeries with him, but had otherwise not spent more than a few awkward minutes with him here and there when their paths crossed in the neonatal unit or in the cardiac lab.

Her heart ached with missing him, but it was better things had ended sooner rather than later. The longer their dalliance had gone on the more difficult their demise would have been. The harder on Carrie.

The harder on Natalie.

She didn't think she could handle much more than her current devastation. She missed him so much. Missed Carrie so much, too. Not that she was admitting it to anyone. Not to Monica, Suzie or Dr. Luiz, who'd stopped by to question her about what had happened between her and Matthew.

Nothing. Nothing had happened.

Nothing ever would happen.

The University of Florida had contacted her about a research opportunity for a new surgical device they hoped to bring to the market and needed someone to head up the project. They'd requested she come for an interview.

An interview she was considering.

She wouldn't have to see Matthew anymore. Wouldn't have to think of him anymore. Would be able to forget he'd ever existed.

Nor would she have to wonder about Carrie. Wonder how the little girl was healing, how she was coping with having her arm in a sling.

She didn't want to think about Matthew, or Carrie.

She'd go to the interview. What would it hurt to find out more?

"Have you seen Carrie?"

At Matthew's barging into her office, Natalie jumped, startled at his interruption and frantic appearance. "What? No, why would I have seen her?"

The hopeful expression on his face fell, replaced by one of pure wreckage. "She's gone. She was in the yard at preschool, there one minute and gone the next. Video surveillance shows her on a computer, then sneaking out. They've already got the police out looking for her."

Panic filled Natalie. The girl was only four. So many things could have happened.

He glanced around her office as if still hoping to spot the child. "I think she overheard me talking to Elaine about arranging for her to go and live with them."

Shock reverberated through Natalie. "What? Why would you do that?"

"Because I thought she'd be better off without me." He sighed, raked his fingers through his hair, turning quickly to leave. "If you hear from her, call me."

Standing, Natalie nodded. "Can I help look for her?"

He paused, his shoulders sagging, and nodded. "There are officers on their way to talk to me, get photos of her, et cetera." His pale eyes lifted, full of pain. "Liz told Elaine that Carrie had been talking about taking a trip. I think she's run away because she thinks I don't want her anymore." His voice broke, then he sucked in a deep breath. "The police are checking the airport and bus stations in case she made it that far." His eyes bereft blue pools, he met her gaze. "What am I going to do if I don't find her?"

Despite everything wrong between them, Natalie couldn't help herself. She walked to the other side of her desk and wrapped her arms around him tight. "I'm so sorry, Matthew. I know they'll find her soon and you can tell her how much you love and need her."

He nodded, then seemed to realize he was standing still instead of looking for Carrie, and extricated himself from her hold. "I'd better go. The police are coming to the house."

Natalie would have offered to go with him, but he left her office as quickly as he'd burst into it.

Carrie was gone. She had possibly run away. Had possibly overheard Matthew talking to his sister about letting Carrie live with her family. Had she felt the same abandonment Natalie had when she'd been shuffled from one foster home to another?

Walking around to her desk, Natalie closed out her computer program. Her brain was shot. She wasn't going to accomplish anything until Carrie was found. The sheer terror she felt at the thought of the girl being on her own couldn't begin to compare to what Matthew must be feeling.

Especially as he was blaming himself.

She wanted to be with him. To comfort him. To help him look for Carrie. But she had no right. He'd only come to her, asked if she'd seen the child because he'd been desperate and had thought Carrie might have reached out to her. If only.

Natalie pulled her phone from her scrubs pocket and checked it, hoping it would magically ring and Carrie be on the other end. Nothing happened, of course.

Restless, she flipped through her messages. One in particular caught her eye.

An alert from Memphis Zoo.

Heart pounding, Natalie grabbed her keys and purse.

Natalie searched the crowd in front of the giraffe exhibit at the zoo. Not an easy feat as the pending birth of Zoie had captured more than just Carrie's heart and people were everywhere, waiting to catch their first glimpse of the giraffe. The weather was just windy enough to have folks bundled up in light jackets and hats.

Please be here, Natalie prayed. *Please. Please. Please.*

Continuing to make her way through the big-screen spectators, Natalie was just about to decide she'd been ridiculous to think she'd known where the girl was when a familiar voice called out.

"Natalie! I knew you'd come!" Carrie beamed, jumping up and down in her excitement. "Isn't it wonderful?"

Finding her was the most wonderful thing ever.

Natalie collapsed to her knees and pulled the girl into her arms, being careful not to jar Carrie's left arm, safely tucked into its sling.

"Carrie," she breathed against the child's head. "Never run off like that again! Thank God you're okay."

When she pulled back, the girl was eyeing her curiously and giggled. "I'm not the one having a baby giraffe."

If not for the seriousness of the moment, Natalie would have smiled at the child's logic. "Everyone is looking for you. We were scared something had happened. Your Uncle Matthew is beside himself."

A sheepish look came over Carrie's face. "I'm in trouble, aren't I?"

Still not quite believing she'd found her, Natalie nodded. "You really scared him, your family, me," she added, pulling her phone out to call Matthew. "You shouldn't have left without telling anyone where you were going."

"But I wanted to see Zoie be born and I was going to go back to school before time to be picked up!"

Natalie's heart pounded as Matthew picked up on the first ring.

"I'm with Carrie," she rushed out, wanting to ease his worry as quickly as possible. "We're at the zoo."

Matthew's breath whooshed out over the phone. "The zoo? She's okay?"

"She's fine. I found her at the giraffe exhibit. They

have a big screen set up as Zoie is about to be born. She wanted to be here."

"Thank God." He disconnected the call to notify his family that he'd found Carrie.

"Is he mad?"

Staring at the child, Natalie nodded. "You gave him a bad fright. He loves you very, very much."

Carrie nodded, then looked uncertain. "I make his life," she paused, sounding out the word, "complicated."

Which must be part of what she'd overheard with his conversation with his sister.

"Don't worry about that now, okay? Your Uncle Matthew would do anything for you, Carrie. He wants you to have the very best in life." Carrie nodded as if she understood what Natalie was saying, but Natalie wasn't sure the child did, or even could at her young age. "Why didn't you just wait and ask him bring you to the zoo after preschool?"

"It might have been too late. I might have missed Zoie being born!"

Unsure what to say, Natalie hugged the little girl, then sat down on the pavement next to her to watch the screen along with the dozens of others who were there. When Carrie scooted next to her, Natalie automatically pulled her into her lap and wrapped her arms around her. Carrie laced their fingers and leaned back against her as if it was the most natural thing in the world.

This, Natalie found herself thinking again. She wanted this.

Was that why she'd run from the hospital? Because of how much she wanted Matthew and Carrie as her own? Because of how it had hit her, scared her?

On the big screen, they watched as little Zoie came into the world, and cheers sounded from all around. Natalie and Carrie cheered right along with the others.

Carrie cocked her head, grinning up at Natalie with a look of pure awe. "That was amazing."

It was.

Sharing the moment with Carrie had been amazing, too.

She might have said more, but her phone rang.

"Where are you? I can't spot you in this crowd."

Helping Carrie to her feet first, Natalie stood, spotted Matthew and waved.

"There. I see you."

He disconnected the call.

Carrie's hand slipped into hers. "I don't want to leave until Zoie takes her first step! Make Uncle Matthew promise!"

"I'm not sure I can stop him."

Carrie looked up at her with big, trusting eyes. "Just ask him to stay and he will. He'd do anything for you."

Natalie wasn't so sure.

"Carrie." Matthew scooped the child into his arms, hugged her close, kissed the top of her head. "I have never been so scared in my whole life."

"Sorry," came the muffled reply.

He set her down, knelt to her level. "What you did isn't okay, but we'll talk about it when we get home." Holding on to Carrie's hand, he stood. "Thank you so much for finding her, Natalie."

Carrie gave Natalie a pleading look.

"You're welcome. Can Carrie watch with me a few more minutes?" At Matthew's look of complete confusion, Natalie added, "Please. It would mean a lot if Carrie could watch Zoie's first steps with me."

"Please, Uncle Matthew?" Carrie said, giving him a big-eyed look. "It would mean a lot to me, too."

He glanced down at the girl, tugged at the hair that poked out from beneath her cap. "I'm not sure you get a say at the moment. I still can't believe you did this.

You're not going to be playing with that tablet computer for a long time."

Carrie hesitated at that, then cranked up the volume of her big brown eyes. Matthew sighed.

"But, since we're here, it would be a shame to miss Zoie's first steps."

After Matthew had reassured his family that Carrie was okay yet again, bathed the child and put her to bed, he turned to the woman who'd been with him all evening. He'd expected Natalie to leave right after his arrival at the zoo, but she hadn't.

Probably because smart little Carrie had used her as a shield from how upset he was at what she'd done. They'd had a long talk and the child had promised never to pull a similar stunt again.

"I've been meaning to ask—how *did* you know she'd be at the zoo?" he asked when he went back into his living room.

Natalie shrugged. "After you left my office, I pulled my phone out and saw the alert that Zoie was about to be born."

"Thank God you did. Anything could have happened to her."

"You have to admit, what she did was quite impressive for a child that's not quite five. You're going to have your hands full when she hits her teenaged years." Natalie averted her gaze, then asked a question so soft he barely heard. "I heard you talking to her in her room. Did you mean what you told her?"

"About how foolish I was to think I could ever let her go live with anyone other than myself?"

Natalie nodded.

"Every word. She's mine. For better or worse, she's stuck with me for the rest of her life. I was a fool to think I could let her go, that she'd be better off elsewhere."

"Good. She loves you. Not that that doesn't mean she's not going to give you a run for your money at times."

"That she will," he agreed, sinking onto the sofa next to her. "You going to help me keep her in line when she does?"

A look of guilt passed over her face. "Who knows where either of us will be when Carrie's older?"

Then he knew. Natalie planned to leave Memphis.

A new wave of panic swept over him. Different from the one that had hit him when he'd learned Carrie was missing, but one that ripped at his insides all the same.

"When?"

"When what?"

"When are you leaving?"

"I'm sorry." She went to stand. "I didn't mean to stay beyond my welcome."

He grabbed her wrist, pulled her back down beside him. "That isn't what I mean and you know it."

"I can't give you an answer on where I'll be in ten years."

"Or even in six months?"

Another flash of guilt contorted her face. "I'd rather not discuss it."

"Because you're leaving Memphis Children's?"

"I didn't say that."

"You didn't say you weren't."

She dropped her head back against the sofa, closed her eyes. "It would be better for both of us if I left."

Matthew was suddenly struck by the memory that Robert had always said someday he'd meet someone and know exactly how Robert had felt about Carolyn. Matthew hadn't really believed his friend. What Robert and Carolyn had had wasn't what most people had. It wasn't what anyone else Matthew had ever known had had. They'd been best friends and colleagues as well as lovers.

He finally understood what his friend had been telling him.

Understood and wanted all it had to offer.

He took her hand into his. "I want you, Natalie. In my life. In Carrie's life, helping me with her. Because I'm falling for you."

CHAPTER FIFTEEN

NATALIE WAS SURE she'd misheard. Matthew couldn't have just said he was falling for her. Why would he say that? Why now?

But she knew. The scare with Carrie had him overly emotional tonight.

"I think you're just grateful I helped you find Carrie and that's why you think you want me."

He laughed. "You think how I feel toward you is gratitude?"

"That and that your friends died and you have a void in your life, Matthew. A void you're trying to fill and I just happened to come along at the right time."

"Robert dying gutted me. He was my best friend from my earliest memories. But you and I have nothing to do with any of that." He stood, paced across his living room. "But if that's what your thoughts are when I tell you I'm falling for you, then I guess that says everything, doesn't it?"

"I suppose so." She stood, knowing it was past time she left. She should have gone long ago. Or not have given in to Carrie's request that she come home with them in the first place.

She might not have, except she'd been so worried about the girl, felt so connected to her, and wanted to make sure Matthew reassured her that he wasn't ever going to leave her.

He wasn't. Natalie knew that in her heart. Carrie would always be loved and cared for.

"Thanks for coming, Dr. Sterling. I'd thought you'd want to be here."

"You thought right." At the call from Dr. Robards, Natalie had dropped what she was doing and scrubbed in for surgery. Cesarean sections weren't her thing, but she did want to be there for this particular one.

"I wish we'd had longer before Delaine went into labor."

"Me too, but I couldn't get the labor stopped and can't delay any longer without worrying the baby is going to get into distress."

"A month is a blessing," Natalie assured, following him into the surgical suite where Delaine's baby would soon be born. "I just hoped for longer healing time prior to birth."

"As did we all."

Natalie glanced at Matthew. She should have known that Dr. Robards would have called him, too. Actually, the room was filled with neonatologists and specialists, all ready to jump into action when Delaine's baby entered the world.

Natalie avoided meeting Matthew's gaze. What was the point?

They'd said what needed to be said.

Two weeks had passed since Carrie's zoo trip. Two weeks in which Natalie had missed Matthew and the little girl, but knew she was doing the right thing in staying away.

She'd flown to Florida the previous Friday, met with the execs who had the power to extend the generous package she'd been offered. It was a wonderful opportunity, but she'd yet to make her final commitment.

"Witnessed many births?" Dr. Robards asked.

Natalie wasn't sure whether he spoke to Matthew or to her, but Matthew was who answered.

"I delivered a few babies during med school, but the only one I've been in on for the past ten years is my god-daughter's."

Dr. Robards made a cut along Delaine's bikini line close to where she'd been cut for last month's surgery on the baby's heart. "Nothing like witnessing the miracle of life. Been in on thousands, but each one never fails to humble me."

Within seconds, he was pulling Delaine's baby from her womb, handing her over to the nurse, who brought her to the waiting incubator and neonatologist.

The neonatologist worked rapidly on the premature baby, doing a quick assessment, clearing the airway and inserting a breathing tube.

While monitors and lines were attached, Natalie and Matthew performed an ultrasound on the baby's tiny heart.

"We have good flow," Natalie said, relief filling her. Delaine's baby was early, but, at thirty weeks, had a fighting chance. "Just look. Her little heart is working."

Matthew tried not to let Natalie's joy get to him, but was happy with what he was seeing, too. The baby's chest, although scarred, looked great for a month out from surgery. As they'd predicted, healing had been accelerated in utero.

"She's not out of the woods yet, but, I admit, what I'm seeing is encouraging."

Natalie nodded, stepping back so the neonatologist could check a line.

At this point, taking care of the baby's prematurity needs took precedence over her heart surgery, which thus far seemed a success. Hopefully, nothing would happen to change that status.

Natalie and Matthew left the unit together, stripped out of their surgical gear and trashed the protective equipment.

"Carrie okay?"

Surprised by Natalie's question, he paused. "She's good. We've started counseling to help us, mostly me, deal with our grief and our new family dynamics."

"That's good. Carrie is so resilient. She's going to be fine."

"Resilient and brilliant."

Natalie nodded. "Have you taken her back to see Zoie?"

"We've practically taken up residence at the zoo."

Recalling her own zoo adventure with the girl as they'd watched Zoie's birth, Natalie smiled. "I'm sure that makes her happy."

Matthew wanted to ask what made Natalie happy, but what was the point? Obviously, he wasn't the answer.

"You want to talk about this?"

Natalie glanced up to see her former boss standing in her office doorway, her resignation letter in hand, then glanced back at her computer screen to save the work she'd been charting. She motioned for him to come into her office.

"There's really not anything to say. It's a great opportunity."

"That's not why you typed this letter," Dr. Luiz corrected, causing Natalie to look up from where she'd been studying her computer screen to keep from having to meet his gaze.

"If you're talking about Dr. Coleman, I accepted the fact that he was given the position I'd hoped I'd fill weeks ago."

The man she'd admired above all others stared at her so intently she could avoid his gaze no longer. Still, she owed him nothing beyond that she'd given him a copy of her resignation first. She had two others ready to be delivered—one to the board and one to Matthew.

Dr. Luiz walked over, sat down in the chair opposite

Natalie's desk, and regarded her for long, silent moments. "From the time I met you as a bright-eyed resident, I've felt a special bond with you, Natalie. Treated you almost as if you were my daughter. I want good things for you."

Feeling a wave of emotion wash over her, Natalie waited for him to continue. He didn't disappoint.

"When I first announced my intent to semi-retire, I never questioned that you could step up to fill the vacancy. I've no doubt you'd have done so successfully if the circumstances were different, because you'd have put your whole heart, your whole being into this hospital."

He was right. She would have.

"If relocating is what you believe in your heart is right for you, then I support your decision."

Natalie closed her eyes. Accepting the offer was the right decision.

"But I don't agree that it is in your best interests to relocate. I want more for you than that, but I'm not convinced you want more for yourself."

She arched her brow.

"Something changed for you in Miami. I couldn't put my finger on it until I saw you with Matthew. Hiring him was the right thing for Memphis Children's, but it was also the right thing for you."

"You're wrong." It would have been better if Matthew had stayed a fantasy fling.

Wouldn't it?

Dr Luiz leaned forward. "I don't know everything that happened between you two, but I do know you need to figure it out before anyone else sees this."

He crumpled up her resignation letter and tossed it onto her desk.

His words making her question conclusions she'd already come to, she shook her head. "There are a lot of things you don't know. Just take my word for it when I say that taking this job is the right thing."

"Lucky for them that you think so. Pity for you."

Dr. Luiz was wrong. The position in Florida opened a whole new world of opportunities. She'd be a fool to stay. Staying meant seeing Matthew regularly. She needed to forget him. To forget the things he made her long for.

Natalie winced. She wasn't longing for anything.

She wasn't.

If she was, she'd have reacted differently when Matthew had confessed he was falling for her, right?

She wouldn't have questioned his motives in what he'd said. Wouldn't have assumed that he was only saying he wanted her because she'd found Carrie and he'd been overcome with emotion.

At his words, she'd locked up inside, felt panicked. She'd felt the need to run, been scared to believe him.

Most of the people who'd come into her life had been temporary, had come and gone, and she was the one left behind.

Why should she expect him to be any different?

Emotions were messy, set a person up to get hurt. She'd been hurt enough during her lifetime. More than enough.

She hurt now.

Shocked by her admission, Natalie dropped her head onto her desk, the wadded-up letter crunching beneath her forehead.

Ugh. What was she doing?

Leaving for Florida. Was that nothing more than running away because she was afraid of Matthew, of what he made her want? Afraid of caring for Carrie?

Afraid or not, she did care. And she did want.

Straightening, Natalie sucked in a deep breath, fought back the moisture accumulating in her eyes, and rubbed her temples.

She'd pushed Matthew away, had shut him out, because she'd been afraid of his leaving her someday.

Only, what if he didn't ever leave? What if he could love her, really love her, and she could be a real part of their family?

Matthew wasn't nearly as enthralled with Zoie as Carrie, but the baby giraffe was growing on him. Which was just as well, since Carrie would have them visiting daily if he'd agree.

Fortunately, some days she was satisfied with online viewing via the Zoie cam—but not today.

"Uncle Matthew, can we get ice cream when we finish visiting Zoie?" Liz asked, tugging on his hand. "Momma says we can if you're okay with it."

Matthew shot his sister a *Gee, thanks* look, then grinned at his niece. "Sure thing, kiddo. If the three of you are good, then ice cream it is. Two scoops, even."

"We're always good," Mandy pointed out matter-of-factly.

Matthew laughed. "Most of the time."

"Natalie?" Carrie's surprised question had Matthew turning toward where the child was looking.

Sure enough, Natalie stood a few feet from them, holding a stuffed giraffe and looking uncertain about whether to approach.

"I've missed you." Carrie had no qualms in running over and wrapping her good arm around Natalie. "Did you see Zoie? Isn't she just the cutest?"

Natalie lowered her gaze to look at Carrie. "She is, and I've missed you, too. I bought this for you." She held out the stuffed giraffe. "I thought you might like to hold her when you're watching Zoie on your computer tablet—if you're allowed to use it now," she added with a smile.

"Thank you. I love her." Carrie took the gift and gave the giraffe a big squeeze. "I'm naming her Chloe because that rhymes with Zoie." She made her declaration in a sing-song fashion, then grinned up at Natalie. "We've been studying rhymes at school and I like rhymes. All the time," she added, then giggled.

"I see that."

"Why are you here?" Matthew asked, since she'd made such a point to avoid him.

"To see Zoie," Carrie answered for her with a "duh" expression.

"I…" Natalie paused, then met his gaze. "I needed to talk to you about what you said to me, and when I went to your house and you weren't home I went to your mom's and she said you were here." Her face pinched nervously. "So, here I am."

"You went to my mom's?"

She nodded. "Did you mean it when you said you were falling for me?"

Matthew sent a look to his sister, who was watching the exchange curiously, as were three little pairs of eyes.

"Girls, let's go get that ice cream." A round of cheers went up at Elaine's suggestion. "I'll take your little rhymer home with me afterward." She leaned over and gave Natalie a little hug. "Good to see you again."

Before Matthew could say a word, Elaine had all three girls rushing off.

"Sorry," Natalie apologized, looking hesitant as she met his gaze. "I probably shouldn't have blurted that out."

Looking around at the semi-crowded zoo exhibit, Matthew raked his hands through his hair and nodded. "Probably not, since it no longer matters. Dr. Luiz called. I know you're leaving."

Natalie would be okay with the ground opening up and swallowing her. Surely that would be preferable to Matthew staring at her as if he *wished* she'd disappear?

"Can we go somewhere and talk?" She needed to speak to him, to explain everything swirling in her head.

Her head?

Ha. More like that wildly thumping organ beating against her ribcage.

"What's the point?" His eyes had that dark and dangerous quality to them. The one she'd first seen at the airport. Now she knew the look had been related to flying for the first time since his friends' death.

This was her fault, she reminded herself. Her fear had done this. Easily her fear could have her turning, leaving, and never risking his further rejection.

But fear couldn't win this time. She wouldn't let it.

"If we go talk," she said as calmly as she could, "I'll explain what my point is."

He looked ready to refuse, then shrugged. "Fine. Let's go."

Natalie's hands shook as she unlocked her car doors, as she climbed inside, Matthew getting in on the passenger side.

Without a word she started the car, took off down the road, not sure where she was going until she pulled into his driveway.

He hadn't said a word during the drive and didn't speak as he climbed out of the car and went to open his front door.

Natalie followed. Closing the door behind her, she went into his living room. He stood at the window, staring out.

"What did Dr. Luiz say to you?"

He didn't turn toward her, just continued to look out the window. "That you'd been offered a job out of state and had turned in your notice."

"He didn't tell me he was going to tell you."

"*You* should have told me." His tone dripped with accusation.

"I was going to, but I needed to tell Dr. Luiz first."

At that Matthew turned, met her gaze with hurt blue ones. "Seriously? You needed to tell him first?"

"For whatever it's worth, I didn't put in for another job. The university contacted me."

"It was only a matter of time before you left." He turned back to the window. "He also told me to fix whatever was between us and convince you to stay."

"Well, you're doing a bang-up job," she said sarcastically.

His gaze narrowed. "You want me to grovel?"

"No." She didn't. She wanted… "I want you to love me."

"So you can break my heart? No, thanks."

"I don't want to break your heart, Matthew. I want to claim it as my own."

"Right. You suddenly realize you can't live without me but have agreed to move to another state." He gave a sarcastic laugh. "You expect me to rip Carrie up and go with you? Is that it?"

No, she didn't expect that, didn't want that, but heard herself asking, "Would you go with me if I asked?"

His expression was gaunt. "Are you asking?"

Natalie's heart pounded in her chest. "I am."

He raked his fingers through his hair. "Moving away from Memphis would throw my life, Carrie's life, into complete chaos. You know that?"

She nodded. She knew exactly what she was asking, what the implications of whatever answer he gave were.

Regarding her, his expression unreadable, he crossed his arms. "Tell me why I should agree to go."

Because she needed to know that he would. That he'd throw his life into utter chaos again just to be with her.

"Because of whatever this is between us, because of the way you feel about me." She took a deep breath. "Because of the way I feel about you. I love you."

There—she'd said the words out loud. No beating about the bush. She'd told him the truth. She loved him.

"I want everything you're willing to give me," she continued.

"Then my answer is yes."

She couldn't have heard him right. "Yes?"

"I'll go with you, but hell, Natalie, this isn't going to be easy on Carrie. Or me." He raked his fingers through his hair. "Plus, I'll have to figure a way out of my contract with Memphis Children's and—"

Not quite believing what he'd said, what it meant, about to burst with giddy happiness, she walked over and put her fingers over his mouth, silencing him. "You don't need to do any of those things. I shouldn't have said you did."

His eyes narrowed.

"There's no need for you to go with me because I'm not going anywhere."

He studied her. "You're not taking the job?"

She shook her head. "Why would I do that when everything I want is in Memphis?" To emphasize her point, she stood on her tiptoes and pressed a kiss to his lips. "When you and Carrie are in Memphis."

"You're sure?"

"Positive. I love you, Matthew."

"I love you, too." He pulled her to him. "Is this really happening?"

"I think so." She smiled. "I may just be the happiest woman who ever lived."

He grinned. "That happy, eh?"

"Happier."

"Good, because I want to make you happy."

"I want to be a part of your and Carrie's life, Matthew. I want to do right by her."

"Then that'll be two of us trying to do right by her, Natalie, because I'm learning as I go with this whole parenting thing."

"You're wonderful, Matthew. I watch you with her and

think how lucky she is to have you, how I wish I'd had someone like you in my life."

"I'm sorry about your parents, Natalie. I wish you'd had me in your life, too. Carrie is lucky because she gets both of us to love her and make sure she always feels wanted."

"I have you now and for that, for you, I am grateful." She laid her head against her chest, listening to his heart beat, peace coming over her that, whatever life threw at them, they would handle it. Together.

"I know something that would make me very happy this very moment."

"What's that?"

"You kissing me."

Matthew was happy to oblige—then, and every day for the rest of their lives.

* * * * *

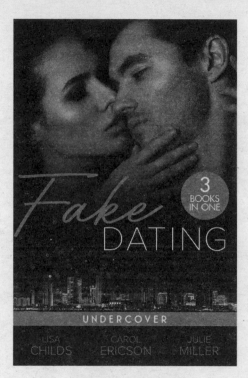

MILLS & BOON

MEDICAL

Pulse-Racing Passion

Set your pulse racing with dedicated, delectable doctors in the high-pressure world of medicine, where emotions run high and passion, comfort and love are the best medicine.

Becky Wicks
The Vet's Escape to
PARADISE

Luana DaRosa
Her Secret
RIO BABY

Amy Andrews
Nurse's Outback
TEMPTATION

Alison Roberts
One Weekend in
PRAGUE

Luana DaRosa
Falling Again for the
BRAZILIAN DOC

Janice Lynn
The Single Mum
HE CAN'T RESIST

Six Medical stories published every month, find them all at:

millsandboon.co.uk

LET'S TALK
Romance

For exclusive extracts, competitions and special offers, find us online:

 MillsandBoon

 @MillsandBoon

@MillsandBoonUK

@MillsandBoonUK

Get in touch on 01413 063 232

MILLS & BOON

THE HEART OF ROMANCE

A ROMANCE FOR EVERY READER

MODERN
Prepare to be swept off your feet by sophisticated, sexy and seductive heroes, in some of the world's most glamourous and romantic locations, where power and passion collide.

HISTORICAL
Escape with historical heroes from time gone by. Whether your passion is for wicked Regency Rakes, muscled Vikings or rugged Highlanders, awaken the romance of the past.

MEDICAL
Set your pulse racing with dedicated, delectable doctors in the high-pressure world of medicine, where emotions run high and passion, comfort and love are the best medicine.

True Love
Celebrate true love with tender stories of heartfelt romance, from the rush of falling in love to the joy a new baby can bring, and a focus on the emotional heart of a relationship.

Desire
Indulge in secrets and scandal, intense drama and sizzling hot action with heroes who have it all: wealth, status, good looks…everything but the right woman.

HEROES
The excitement of a gripping thriller, with intense romance at its heart. Resourceful, true-to-life women and strong, fearless men face danger and desire - a killer combination!

To see which titles are coming soon, please visit

millsandboon.co.uk/nextmonth